PRAISE

MICHEL BUTOR

"A gifted disciple of French antinovelist Alain Robbe-Grillet, Butor is notable because he uses a different technique with every book and turns out intense and interesting fiction just the same."

—*Time*

"*Degrees* is the most solid of Butor's novels, densely packed with hard objects and ascertainable facts. . . . By rejecting metaphor, emotion, most of the visceral, human content of the older novel, it looks comparatively empty; but it's also obvious that this emptying-out was necessary for it to achieve—rather like an abstract painting—its own special density."

—Robert Taubman, *New Statesman*

"Michel Butor is a major French novelist who has written several intricate and beautiful books which are just now getting proper attention in this country."

—*Virginia Quarterly Review*

"The interwoven strands of the book provide a brilliant picture of the perennial schoolboy—and the perennial teacher."

—*Library Journal*

"Emulating the great innovators of modern fiction—Dostoyevsky, Proust, Joyce, and Faulkner—Butor has sought new forms through which to express the problems of his time. . . . *Degrees* is an extraordinary book—one of the most unusual and the most challenging pieces of writing to have come from France since World War II. . . . His remarkable integration of message, symbolism, style and individual human experience into a unified, disturbing poem of consciousness and reality stamps Butor as a first-rate novelist."

—Leon Roudiez, *New York Times*

OTHER BOOKS BY MICHEL BUTOR
IN ENGLISH TRANSLATION

A Change of Heart
Description of San Marco
Frontiers
Improvisations on Butor
Inventory
Letters from the Antipodes
Mobile
Niagara
Passing Time
Portrait of the Artist as a Young Ape
The Spirit of Mediterranean Places

DEGREES

MICHEL BUTOR

TRANSLATION BY
RICHARD HOWARD

DALKEY ARCHIVE PRESS
NORMAL · LONDON

Originally published in French as *Degrés* by Editions Gallimard, 1960
Originally published in English by Simon and Schuster, 1961

Copyright © 1960 by Michel Butor
English translation copyright © 1961 by Richard Howard

Library of Congress Cataloging-in-Publication Data

Butor, Michel, 1926–
  [Degrés. English]
  Degrees / by Michel Butor ; translated by Richard Howard.
      p. cm — (French literature series)
  Previously published: New York : Simon and Schuster, 1961.
  ISBN 1-56478-340-5 (alk. paper)
    I. Howard, Richard, 1929– II. Title. III. French literature series (Normal, Ill.)

PQ2603.U73D4413 2004
843'.914—dc22

                                                         2004052735

      Partially funded by a grant from the Illinois Arts Council, a state agency.

      Dalkey Archive Press is a nonprofit organization located at Milner Library
          (Illinois State University) and distributed in the UK by
               Turnaround Publisher Services Ltd. (London).

                    www.centerforbookculture.org

      Printed on permanent/durable acid-free paper and bound in the
                      United States of America.

I

I WALK INTO the classroom, and I step up onto the platform.

When the bell stops ringing, I take out of the briefcase I have just laid on the desk the alphabetical list of the students and that other sheet of white paper, on which they themselves have indicated their seats in this classroom.

Then I sit down, and when all the talking has stopped, I begin to call the roll:

"Abel, Armelli, Baron . . . ",

trying to fix their faces in my memory, for I don't know how to recognize them yet, except the ones who were with me last year, you in particular, Pierre,

who raise your brown eyes when I come to your name,

after " . . . Daval, de Joigny, de Loups",

before going on to "Estier, Fage Jean-Claude, Fage Henri . . . ",

giving me a smile I don't want to answer, because it's obviously better if as many of your classmates as possible are unaware for as long as possible that we're related, so that in their eyes you're the same to me as any of them.

Your uncle Henri Jouret, on the other side of the wall behind me, is coping with his senior French students, calling the roll, trying to get their seats and faces straight before going on to the questions and the analysis of a page of Saint-Simon.

║▌█▌║█▌║█▌║█▌║█▌║█▌║ I HAVE ALREADY been in this classroom with you. It was our second geography lesson.

"Zola, what can you tell me about the atmosphere?"

"Wolf, what do you know about the internal structure of this planet?"

"And now, Voss, go to the blackboard and tell me about the history of the earth and its principal geological ages."

While he was standing there thinking up his answers, his hands behind his back, I was watching you out of one eye. The sun fell on your black hair, and on your hands with their bitten nails; your shadow spread over the book you were looking at, you spent a long time over a rather blurred photograph of the Grand Canyon that had a black spot in the middle, so heavy and irregular it looked as if you had made it yourself;

and your Uncle Henri was already on the other side of the wall behind me, with his senior French students, asking one of his pupils to begin with the death of Monseigneur, Dauphin of France:

"I found all Versailles gathered there . . . ",

frowning when he corrected mistakes, tapping his pencil point on the yellow wood of the desk that like my own was already pitted with little dents,

the same way he corrected your mistakes last hour, after collecting your first French compositions on this ultraclassical subject:

"Describe the one day of your vacation that has left the strongest impression in your memory; try to explain why it was this day that seems most memorable."

He questioned some of you about Rabelais' life and works, asked for a volunteer to explain Gargantua's letter to Pantagruel, and selected you from among those who raised their hands, saying in a tone of voice he wanted to sound particularly severe, without looking at you:

"All right, Eller, show us what you know."

You wondered if you were supposed to read the paragraph in small type, where the editor provided some information about the nature and content of the selection:

8

asterisk, "Having become a student, Pantagruel attends the various French universities . . . ",
   or else:
triangle, "Most of the chapters devoted to Pantagruel's studies . . . ",
   or else:
circle, "A more elaborate program will be found in *Gargantua;* here it is the wit itself . . . ",
   but suddenly, just as you were going to ask your question, you found yourself facing this uncle, and you stopped, disturbed, no longer sure how to address him, realizing you would have to say "Monsieur" and not able to, blushing, looking down, rushing through your reading almost wildly, pronouncing the words indistinctly, disregarding the punctuation:

"Now it is the minds of men are qualified with all manner of discipline, and the old sciences revised, which for many ages were extinct: now it is that the learned languages are to their Sistine purity restored . . . "

"Eller, please pay attention to the text; start that sentence over again."

"Now it is that the minds of men . . . "

"That's better."

"Are qualified with all manner of discipline, and the old sciences revived, which for many ages were extinct: now it is that the learned languages are to their pristine purity restored . . . "

"Go on."

"Viz., Greek, without which a man may be ashamed to fall . . . "

"To what?"

"To call himself a scholar, Hebrew, Arabic, Chaldean and Latin. Printing likewise is now abused . . . "

"Careful!"

"Is now in use, so elegant, and so correct . . . "

In the classroom directly underneath, I was explaining to your seventh-grade schoolmates, in front of the map of ancient Egypt that one of them had brought in from the superintendent's office,

that we knew the ancient civilization of this country from the monuments it had left, pyramids, hypogea, mastabas, obelisks like the one in the Place de la Concorde,

how Champollion had managed to decipher the hieroglyphics thanks to the Rosetta Stone (Rosetta was a city), now in the British

Museum in London, immediately extending our history several thousand years back into time,

how the first pharaoh of the first dynasty, Menes, had combined the crowns of Upper and Lower Egypt, of the valley and the delta, the red and the white, the vulture and the kite,

how this long series of kings and conversions was divided into three chief periods, the Old, the Middle and the New Kingdom,

before coming upstairs to meet your class here,

where I continue calling the roll:

". . . Jourdan? Absent too? Oh, no, there you are. Speak up! What were you dreaming about? Knorr?"

(he was absent yesterday too),

"He hasn't come back? All right. Limours?"

"Here."

"Mouron?"

Sitting in front of you in the first row, Limours casually arranges on his desk his spiral-bound notebook and his secondhand history book, on the first page of which he carefully crosses out the former owner's name with his ballpoint pen, in order to write in his own,

he too a pupil, this year, of one of his uncles, Monsieur Bailly, who at this moment is making his seniors on the floor above read Keats's sonnet "On First Looking into Chapman's Homer"

(Chapman: 1559–1634):

> ". . . Then felt I like some watcher of the skies
> When a new planet swims into his ken;
> Or like stout Cortez"

(Cortez, or Cortès: 1485–1547),

> "when with eagle eyes
> he star'd at the Pacific—and all his men
> Look'd at each other with a wild surmise—
> Silent, upon a peak in Darien."

(Darien: southernmost part of the isthmus of Panama),

a first cousin of both Monsieur Mouron, father of Alain Mouron who is in this class, and of Madame Daval, mother of Michel Daval sitting to your right, who is leaning over to ask you for a blotter, because his ink bottle, badly corked, has begun to leak all over his hands.

10

"You have the Seventeenth and Eighteenth Centuries on your curriculum. Last year, in tenth grade, you studied what happened from the beginning of the French Revolution to the end of the First World War; consequently, instead of proceeding chronologically, as you have done since the seventh grade, you're going to turn back and start two centuries earlier. It is therefore necessary to review briefly what you learned over two years ago, the great upheavals Europe had just witnessed . . ."

The single tree in the little courtyard, which you could see out the window to your left, still had many green leaves on it; the wind fluttered them gently, and shifted the patches of weak sunlight that caressed the first page of your graph-paper notebook, in which you had just written:

"History, first lesson",

waiting to find, in what I would say, some expression that could serve as a title.

The deep shadow of the plane tree moved from your desk to the one in the next row, coming closer to my own desk, passing it, hugging the wall behind me, sliding over the shiny blackboard, shifting to the classroom behind me, in which your Uncle Henri:

"Since we have no time to lose—finals will be here before you know it—you will hand in on Tuesday the nineteenth a composition on one of the following three subjects, all of which, of course, refer to your last year's curriculum, and will consequently allow you to do some useful review work. No extensions will be granted. Those who do not hand in their work when it is due will receive an F, with no exceptions; I want you all to understand that . . ."

He was talking to me about you on Sunday, in his apartment in the Rue du Pré-aux-Clercs

(your Aunt Rose was just getting ready to go out; it was a melancholy day with a penetrating drizzle that proved autumn was really here;

he couldn't make up his mind to extinguish the cigar he had been smoking too long; sitting behind his desk, a little the way he did in class, but instead of a blackboard behind him, there were a few

11

shelves of his bookcase, with the ochre, red and yellow backs of the Universités de France series, called the Guillaume Budé editions, and above them the motley colors of Erle Stanley Gardner detective stories, of which he is an avid reader, in the Presses de la Cité edition),

smiling over your singular situation among your schoolmates, with your two schoolteacher uncles, himself and me,

reminding me that you were not the only one in this position,

"There's that boy who's repeating, Denis Régnier, we noticed last year that he was a nephew—oh, a distant one, it's not the same thing at all—of two of our colleagues"

(along the soaking paths of the Verrières woods, wearing shorts and a navy-blue waterproof jacket mended in several places, your thumbs under the too narrow straps of your almost empty knapsack where the dirty mess kits rattled, hiking with your friends on the Bison Patrol, the youngest of whom was shivering, clenching his teeth to keep them from chattering, you tried to calculate from the map you had been given where you were and what direction you should take to reach the meeting place the leader had assigned);

and I answered him, staring out at the gray sky, and thinking that you were out of luck, that it was a bad day for this first hike of the Saint-Hilaire troop,

that it was quite possible there were even more groups of relatives within this eleventh-grade class, since two of our students had the same surname, Jean-Claude and Henri Fage, who weren't brothers, as we already knew, but who might be first cousins, and since another boy was named Hutter, which was also the name of our new German instructor,

adding that this unusual abundance of family ties, the fact that I knew you well, that I could obtain through certain other professors a good deal of information about a number of students and about their home life, had determined me to undertake a project I had been toying with for a long time, in fact: the description of a class.

Back at the lycée, in that dark classroom overlooking a back alley so narrow the lights have to be on almost all the time, I told my ninth-graders about the conquest of America, the frauds Cortez practiced against Montezuma, Pizarro's betrayal at Cuzco, the use of forced labor in the mines, the beginning of the slave trade, the flow of gold into Spain, the development of banks throughout Europe.

Under the skylight warmed by the pale sun that had come out again, dry now, wearing long trousers and shiny black shoes, you were drawing with charcoal, making thick, clumsy lines on a sheet of white Ingres paper fastened to the board with two clips, reproducing the main outlines of a head of Julius Caesar, and in your right hand you were squeezing an already gray chunk of kneaded eraser.

In the apartment in the Rue du Pré-aux-Clercs, your Uncle Henri emptied his pipe into the glass brick he uses as an ash tray, put it back in his pocket with his nail file and key ring, picked up his black brief-case, stuffed into it two notebooks lying on his desk, and bent down to pull *Eighteenth Century French Authors* out of one of the low shelves of his bookcase; he put on his raincoat, buckled the belt, walked to the kitchen down the hall lined with shelves full of dusty cartons, all neatly tied up and labeled, to say goodbye to your Aunt Rose, who was drying the dishes beside the sink.

He went down the stairs four at a time, like his sons when he isn't there, holding on to the banister, his arm stiff, slowing down the moment he heard the street door open, then lingering in front of book-store windows, going out of his way to cross streets between the white lines, but frequently glancing at his wristwatch, until he reached the lycée where he greeted the concierge, walked up the stairs while the bell was ringing, passed in front of your still empty classroom,

where, a few minutes later, after I had finished my questions, with of course some sarcastic comments on the poor quality of the answers, and threats of dire punishments if there was no improvement next time,

"Now, open your notebooks and write: second lesson, the earth in space",

as I was describing the solar system,

I saw your neighbor, Michel Daval, take a piece of eraser out of his pocket and while he was kneading it with three fingers whisper to you, keeping his head down, trying to hide behind blond, German-looking Francis Hutter, who, though one of the youngest, is nevertheless one of the tallest boys in the class:

"Is he really your uncle?"

indicating me with a movement of his left eye, and since you didn't reply because you were watching me, trying to make me think you were applying yourself, but writing in your notebook the word merid-ian instead of the word parallel,

"You know, I have an uncle who's a teacher too—Monsieur Bailly; he's my mother's first cousin; he came for dinner last Sunday."

(Monsieur Bailly, at the other end of the floor, was writing a passage from the *Jungle Book* on the blackboard, in front of his ninth-graders.)

Alain Mouron turned around toward you two to follow this conversation, his movement knocking over his briefcase which he had put down beside his foot, and this accident immediately made him face the front of the class again without my having to interfere. He bent down to pick it up, put back in his *Anthology of English Literature*, which he would be needing during the next hour, then he continued writing from my dictation:

"The time it takes the earth to revolve once on its own axis is called a day, it is the unit of measurement of time . . . "

Your Uncle Henri probably impresses him less than I do, for during the French class, while you were reading:

" . . . wherefore, my son, I admonish thee . . . ",

he was looking at his physics book on his lap, though he was in the first row, and of course your uncle noticed, glancing at the seating chart he too had made you fill out, and rapped with his fist on the desk:

"Tell me, Mouron, aren't you interested in what the rest of us are reading?"

He blushed, didn't answer.

"All right, Eller. Go on, Mouron. Oh, you don't know where we are. You'd better show me that volume you're trying so clumsily to conceal, since it seems to interest you so passionately. Physics, imagine. Of course I can only encourage such enthusiasm for the sciences, but it shouldn't divert you from the study of French literature. You're starting your year badly, my boy. Have you done your homework, at least? Show me your notebook. We'll see about that. Read, now. At the top of page twenty-six."

And as he began, slowly at first, stammering, then his voice growing surer, for he is intelligent and the text from Rabelais actually interested him a good deal:

" . . . Thou art at Paris, where the laudable example of many brave men may stir up thy mind to many gallant actions; and hast likewise for thy tutor the learned Epistemon . . . "

(Monsieur Bailly was having his ninth-graders recite irregular verbs),

your neighbor, Michel Daval, who had not done his homework, was trying to copy what little there was in your notebook: a three-line map, a list of a dozen words, so that if the magisterial thunderbolt ever fell on him, he would have something to show.

If I now consider that other group we were talking about on Sunday with your Uncle Henri: Monsieur Bonnini, Denis Régnier, Monsieur Hubert,

I know that the latter, your physics and chemistry instructor, in the amphitheater on the fourth floor, is demonstrating to them the first law of dynamics with the help of an Atwood machine,

that Denis Régnier, a pale, sickly boy repeating the course this year, sitting in front of me at the third desk in the second row, is waiting for his name to come after Nathan, Orland, Pelletier, before Spencer, Tangala, Tannier, to answer "here" in a low, bored voice, as if he were going to fall sick again, almost closing his eyes,

I know that Monsieur Bonnini, who has exactly the same schedule as our colleague Bailly, is having his seniors read and translate:

"L'alba vinceva l'ora mattutina . . . "
(The dawn was prevailing over the morning hour . . .).

That was yesterday, Tuesday,
in this classroom where I took his place after leaving you, where I hung over the blackboard a map of the United States,

in order to talk about New England and New York, the Great Lakes and Chicago, the South, Faulkner's country, Florida, the TVA, the Mississippi delta, New Orleans, Texas and its oil wells,

while you, with all your classmates, had climbed to the floor above, passing the physics students coming down, on your way to the amphitheater where Monsieur Hubert, in a white lab coat, was waiting for you behind his long, tiled counter, and you sat down in the third row, next to a window overlooking the roofs, under the big chart of Mendeleev's periodic classification:

"Hydrogen, helium, lithium, bore . . . ",
while your Uncle Henri, who had finished his day at the lycée, waved to the concierge, crossed the boulevard in long strides without waiting for the light to turn red, his raincoat flapping in the wake of a long Cadillac he had grazed, swaying his black briefcase,

had stopped for a moment, looked at the trees, the house fronts, the line of the roofs and chimneys, the clouds passing, the shifting patches of blue, the places where the sun glittered here and there,

and had taken the Rue du Marché-Saint-Hilaire, crossed the little Place d'Espagne to the terrace of the old Café Saint-André-des-Arts, taking his pipe out of one pocket, a book out of another, sitting over a glass of beer for almost an hour.

That was yesterday, and now he is once again on the other side of the wall behind me, with his seniors who are doing neither Latin nor Greek, trying to help them understand and enjoy the first scene of Racine's *Iphigénie*:

"Yes, it is Agamemnon, your king, who wakens you . . . "

The weather is almost as beautiful as it was eight days ago, and the sun, shining through the tree whose leaves have already turned yellow, some of which have fallen in this narrow courtyard littered with heaps of coal (the iron door is open; a truck is pouring out its black load; we all hear it, but none of us can see it),

falls gently on your hands and the page of your book open to the beginning of Chapter III: the representation of the earth;

I close the rollbook, in which I noted today's two absentees (Guillaume is back, but Francis Hutter is missing in the first row), and I ask Bruno Verger:

"Where is the earth located?",

then I ask Maurice Tangala (a Negro):

"Can you tell me what a day is?"

"And you, Georges Tannier, explain to the class what an hour is."

||||||||||||||||||||||||||||||||||||| I WAS ON THE deck of the boat, leaning on the wooden rail, watching Marseille come closer, Micheline Pavin beside me, a scarf around her hair to protect it from the wind, telling me:

"What a shame we didn't meet a little sooner in Athens . . . ";

You, at Les Étangs, with your brothers and your cousins, not in the house, of course, at this hour, since the weather was beautiful that day, but in the cabin you were building deep in the Herrecourt woods,

your Uncle Henri sitting at his black desk in front of the open window overlooking the garden with its fruit trees and beyond, over the little wall, the already harvested fields, the woods and hills of Bresles;

but it wasn't that he was looking at, while he was shifting his pipe between his teeth, inhaling the odor of the leaves that came in with the air that swayed the curtains,

it was the presents that had been given him for his thirty-ninth birthday, at lunch: a can of English tobacco, a blue-and-black tie, and a book about Italian painting,

which he put away a few weeks later, fifteen days ago, the window closed this time, beaten by the torrential rain of a storm that had been expected for two days,

in the big leather suitcase lying on this black desk, among the ash trays and the magazines he was leaving here, already full, and that he managed to close only with your help.

Your Aunt Rose:

"Henri, Denis, Pierre, hurry up! The car's here!"

I had been back in Paris long since, that Tuesday; I was in my room with Micheline Pavin; I was showing her some books, the articles I had already published in various magazines . . . ;

and the following Monday school started again; we met, you and I, in this classroom, no longer as uncle and nephew, but as student and teacher; that was the first time I had seen a good many of your classmates, and that is why, before beginning our geography course, I passed around a sheet of white paper, on which I asked you all to write your name, your address, your date of birth, and your father's profession in the rectangle corresponding to the seat you were occupying;

17

your Uncle Henri was doing the same thing with his seniors; then he discussed the curriculum they would be following:

"Monday and Tuesday: Eighteenth and Nineteenth Century literature; Wednesday: drama, first Racine's *Iphigénie*, then *Tartuffe*, finally Corneille's *Cinna*; Friday: Greek and Latin authors in translation, compositions once a month, due on Tuesday, returned the following Tuesday",

and tried to inspire them with a healthy fear of final exams, a healthy awareness of the swiftness of the time passing, of the small number of weeks that separated them from this ordeal,

a speech identical with the one he made to your class the next day,

for if you had already had several class hours together, two in Latin and two in Greek (so that it was no longer necessary for him to pass the seating chart-questionnaire),

as the result of one of those mistakes inevitable in the confusion of the first day of school, your hour of French with him on Monday from eleven to twelve had not yet been indicated in that square of his schedule and, unaware of his obligation, he hadn't been able to fulfill it,

so that your first French class was on this Tuesday, October 5, at two in the afternoon:

"Sixteenth and Seventeenth Century literature Monday, Tuesday and Friday; classical drama Wednesday, *Britannicus* first, then *l'École des Femmes* and Corneille's *Polyeucte*; French homework also due Tuesday; one week French, one week Latin, one week Greek, it's not difficult, returned the following Tuesday, no exceptions; those who fail to hand in their work when it is due will receive an *F*. Now let's get started right away: open your notebooks and write down this composition subject for next week:

"Describe the one day of your vacation that has left the strongest impression in your memory; try to explain why it was this day that seems most memorable",

with the usual admonitions:

"We must understand each other; if everyone obeys the rules, we'll have no difficulties",

and of course the scarecrow of graduation:

"Don't forget that you cannot do well in your senior year if you do badly on your eleventh-grade finals."

You were amazed by this tremendous metamorphosis taking place under your eyes; this man who was so gentle, so whimsical, so playful, and whom you knew so well, since he was your Uncle Henri and you had just spent a month of your vacation in his house at Les Étangs, eating every meal with him,

was suddenly someone else, hard, abrupt, rather sarcastic, his eyes never resting on you, as if he were trying to avoid seeing you, as if you embarrassed him,

and you felt that he was somewhat afraid of you all, and particularly of you;

you felt that it was in your power to make life extremely difficult for him,

that there was a way for you to take advantage of this unaccustomed situation, to acquire a certain prestige in your classmates' eyes by subtly ragging this relative, and that though there would be disagreeable consequences within your family, of course (your Uncle Henri might complain about you to your father or to your mother, and make all kinds of problems in that direction), in the class itself he would be virtually defenseless;

then you began to feel toward him a sentiment quite new to you, contrary, somehow, to all your earlier relations with him, particularly to those of the preceding month at Les Étangs,

you began to feel a little pity, and that seemed so strange to you that you blushed violently and rubbed your hands over your face with a shudder.

He saw that you were disturbed and, for a second, a little of his old smile from the summer vacation came back.

I was getting to know my seventh-graders: they would have to keep a notebook now, take notes; that wouldn't be difficult at the beginning, because I would dictate everything they needed to write, but soon I would be dictating only the titles of chapters and their main divisions; they themselves would have to make a choice from what I would say; and I would frequently check their notebooks; each time I would question them, they would be graded on these notebooks, and these marks would be as important as those given for their answers, they would have to prepare them neatly, with illustrations from old books or postcards they would find somewhere;

after giving them their first lesson: history and prehistory, I climbed the stairs in the corner of the courtyard and, walking past the tenth- and eleventh-grade classrooms, whose doors were opening, whose students were coming out to relax and stretch a little, greeting my old or new colleagues who were changing classrooms and audiences, I came into your class.

"Who can tell me what the Middle Ages are?"

Silence, of course, then three hands rose, with a slight hesitation. I chose the one closest to me, just in front of you, near the window, in the first row. I didn't know his name yet: he wasn't sure if he should stand up or remain in his seat.

"Well, what are you waiting for?"

He interpreted the gesture I made to encourage him to speak as an order to stand up.

"What's your name?"

"Alain Mouron."

"Where were you last year?"

"In Bourges."

"Now there's a city where you should know what the Middle Ages are. Well?"

"The period between the fall of the Roman Empire and the Renaissance."

(His Uncle Bailly was trying to speak to his seniors in English for the first time, to make them answer in English, knowing perfectly well that it wouldn't work, that a few weeks from now he wouldn't be able to make them speak any other English words than the ones they read.)

"Good. Sit down."

Michel Daval leaned toward you and murmured:

"That's my cousin."

Reluctant, particularly these first days, to bring down upon yourself a reprimand from me, but terribly eager to continue that initial conversation, that first contact, you began looking at your pen as if you had suddenly noticed it wasn't working properly, you thrust your arm into your briefcase to take out the list of textbooks recommended by the teachers, on which you hurriedly scribbled, as though to test your rebellious pen:

"A first cousin?",

then, as if this experiment had reassured you as to your pen's good condition, you quickly crumpled up this paper, which you left, a tiny, pale rock, on the window sill,

while your neighbor, his head straight, his shoulders pressed against the back of your chair, kept his eyes fixed on me

(standing in front of the blackboard, I was asking:

"And who can tell me why we call this period the Middle Ages?"),
signaling no to you with his left index finger.

It was only on Saturday that we met again in this classroom, for
the next history class, since the Wednesday geography class doesn't
meet every week, only every other week, alternating with an hour of
mathematics taught by Monsieur du Marnet,

(your Uncle Henri took advantage of his day off to finish, in his
low-ceilinged study in the Rue du Pré-aux-Clercs, the preparation of
the passage of the Odyssey with which you were to start reading
Homer: Ulysses' landing on the island of the Phaeacians; in front of
him, the selected passages you would be using, Bailly's dictionary to
his left, the mauve cloth of its binding mottled with ink spots of
various colors, some of which dated back to the time when he himself
was an eleventh-grade student in a lycée, fraying at the corners and revealing the gray, flaking cardboard,

the Bérard translation to his right, resting on the glass brick in
which he had forgotten his pipe whose tiny embers had gone out,

because these lines he started with every year at the same time had
enchanted him all over again, a swarm of ideas stirring as they did each
time, projects lying fallow in the boredom of school routine; and abandoning the strict curriculum, he read through the whole fifth book);

you were looking in your textbook at the double page of maps showing the great geographical discoveries of the Renaissance, with Vasco da
Gama's route to Calicut which you confused with Calcutta, the voyages of Columbus to the West Indies, and on the opposite page the
round-the-world voyage of Magellan's crew, on a circular and no longer
rectangular diagram of the planet, the north pole almost in the center, the continents spread around it as though girdled by this first
periplus, as though to mark the new importance, the new concrete as-
pect which the sphericity of the earth, hitherto a question of pure
speculation, would henceforth gradually assume;

then your eyes shifted toward the dusty globe abandoned on top of
the empty cabinet near the door, and you tried to imagine the waves,
and the ships with their sails, the night falling on the shores of the
Philippines that you people with palm trees,

vaguely hearing through the surge of the Pacific, the moaning backwash among the islands, some of your classmates reciting one after
the other in front of the blackboard I was making them cover with
crude and hesitant maps representing the Mediterranean or America,

my questions about the taking of Constantinople by the Turks

21

(that was our first question), of Granada by Isabella, the distribution of the newly discovered lands by the decision of Pope Alexander VI,

before the beginning of today's lesson, the Renaissance and the Reformation.

The next day, in your Uncle Henri's study, sitting back in the leather armchair, my eyes on a level with the table on which your Aunt Rose was setting the coffee tray beside the *Odyssey*, text and translation, open at the beginning of Book VII, the arrival at Alcinous' palace,

I notice through the half-open door on the other side of the hall your cousin Lucie, sitting on a little chair in her bedroom, knitting a blue sweater for her doll.

A gust of rain lashed at the windows.

In the Verrières woods, with the Bisons, sheltered in a tunnel, sitting on the ground with your back against the wall, watching the muddy stream that was swelling between you,

at war, assigned an important mission: to take to headquarters certain top-secret documents, plans for an atomic submarine which the far-flung enemy, the three other patrols, Chamois, Tigers and Squirrels, were obviously trying to get away from you,

still unaware of just where you were supposed to go, knowing only that an emissary who would give you an agreed-upon countersign would be expecting you at the foot of a certain big red beech five hundred yards south-southwest of the point you had started from, and that he would give you an envelope containing instructions in code and a topographical map,

you began to feel cold; the ground got wetter and wetter, and besides time was passing, it was already quarter to three by your watch; you decided to start; that red beech couldn't be much farther now; one of you ahead as a scout, then the others following, silent, peering into the thickets on either side of the path, wearing tied around your belts those scarves whose loss indicated death according to the rules of the game, you last, your thumbs under the straps of your knapsack, softly whistling the tune of a scout song, beginning to feel it was all nonsense.

Michel Daval was with his parents visiting our colleague Bailly in his Rue Pierre-Leroux apartment. They had sent Michel to the back bedroom with the children, who had been allowed, this once, to take out the electric train the Bailly grandparents had given them. (Lunacy, their mother had said, to spend so much money! And at

22

their age they can't play with it without breaking everything!); Michel had put it together for them, had made, with René's Meccano set, bridges and signals completely out of scale, with which he was letting them play by themselves now while he sprawled on one of the beds, looking through the pile of magazines he had discovered on a stand in the hall.

The room was so dark, with its window overlooking the tiny triangular courtyard on the second floor of a six-story building, that he had to turn on the light.

At the other end of the apartment, in the study-living room with its two windows overlooking the street, with the two desks of René and Elizabeth Bailly, with their two bookcases, Monsieur and Madame Daval, sitting on Louis XVI armchairs covered in faded cretonne, finally asked the question they had preferred not to discuss in front of the children:

"What about Elizabeth?"

Bailly stood up nervously, lit a cigarette and forgot to offer any, glanced through one of the windows for a moment as though in hopes of seeing a car drive up, then turned around abruptly.

"Yes, well, she drove down to Orléans to visit her family last night, and she won't be back until tomorrow night, it's Monday, you know, she has the day off. She's overtired; when she came home last Tuesday, after her first day at the Aulnoy lycée, she almost burst into tears, and when I asked her "Why not request a leave of absence", she got furious; anything I say exasperates her now. So I hope this weekend will do her some good."

In the Verrières woods, under the fine rain, in shorts and waterproof jacket, Alain Mouron, son of Henri Mouron who was Monsieur Bailly's cousin and also Madame Daval's, Alain Mouron of the Chamois Patrol, crouching in the bushes with his classmates, was spying on you and your Bisons, hoping to get the secret plans away from you; he kept still, careful not to move any branches; there were six or seven Scouts approaching, chattering, making no effort to conceal their presence, they passed quite close to him, but they belonged to another troop, there was no need to fight them.

The next day, Monday, he had sat down beside you during the drawing class and questioned you in whispers about that troop and its leaders, asking you if you had been in it long, where you had camped the summer before. The approaching footsteps of Monsieur Martin had made him stop talking; he drew away, winked, and in the middle of the oval of the face drew a line to indicate the position of the eyebrows.

The glints of sunshine on the plaster head of Julius Caesar had just disappeared, a whitish cloud passed over the skylight.

Monsieur René Bailly was saying to his seniors:

"Today, we will go on with scene three of Act One of *Macbeth*; you have it in your *English Literature* on page one hundred and seventy-six; but it is absolutely essential that you obtain the complete work, in any edition provided there is no French translation along with it, of course. Those who don't have it by next Monday will be penalized."

He rapped his fist on the desk. His pale lashes wavered in a tiny fit of rage; he sat down, calmer, opened his hand one finger at a time, laid it down flat beside the open book he leafed through, going back several pages, stopping at the picture of the three witches, after Fuseli, looked up.

"We're at Banquo's question:

'What, can the devil speak true?' "

It was your brother Denis he was speaking to.

"Why does Banquo say this? Can you tell us what has happened?"

The son of his cousin Germaine Daval, nee Mouron, saw the head of Julius Caesar almost in three-quarters. His sheet of Ingres paper was still untouched. He was carefully sharpening his pencil when Monsieur Martin came over to him:

"Haven't you even started yet?"

He looked at the pencil, took it, tried it.

"Look here, my boy, this lead is much too hard! Haven't you any charcoal? I'll give you a piece of mine this time, but you have to get into the habit of coming with your own supplies; the boy next to you will let you have a little of his eraser if you want to rub something out."

Michel Daval took the charcoal, began to draw Caesar's ear, his cheek, the tip of his nose, the laurel wreath, quite surprised by the result, the total absence of resemblance between this grimacing face that grew increasingly horrible and sarcastic, and the emperor's plaster face he was looking at, stopped, not knowing what to do next, waiting until the teacher came to correct his mistakes, then, since the latter was nowhere near, asked for the eraser from his neighbor Denis Régnier, repeating the year,

who during the next hour, while Monsieur Hubert, in the amphitheater, was showing his seniors how General Morin's machine verified the law of falling bodies,

in this eleventh-grade classroom, instead of writing the heading "Time" in his notebook and listening to what I was telling you, simply confirmed that this was what he had written there a year ago, and with his pencil point began to decorate his own name that he had cut into the wood of his desk before falling ill six months before.

Monsieur Bonnini was starting to read a passage of Silvio Pellico in the tenth-grade classroom where I went after having left you; some of the students who had just been listening to Monsieur Bailly were coming in, jostling some of the students who had just been listening to Monsieur Bonnini and who were now leaving to return to their usual classroom next door,

taking their seats again, opening their briefcases to get out their history books and notebooks.

When all the talking stopped, after questioning some of them about the Old Regime and its problems, I told them about the beginnings of the French Revolution, the fall of the Bastille, the Declaration of the Rights of Man, the flight of the king and his arrest at Varennes.

Without leaving your seat, you had put your geography book and notebook back in your briefcase, had taken out your *Anthology of English Literature,* which you had opened to page 120, knowing that you were supposed to begin *Julius Caesar*

(there was a picture of the dictator, and you were wondering how this could be the same man as the one whose features you had tried to draw, under Monsieur Martin's supervision, two floors above, just a few minutes ago; the two faces had so little in common),

after half your classmates had left, some to go to the classroom next door where Monsieur Bonnini had just come in, the others who were doing German or Spanish to go home,

and after they were replaced by other eleventh-grade students, followed by Monsieur Bailly, tall and nervous in his pale tweed suit, with his perpetually irritated look, who slammed the door shut behind him and threw his pigskin briefcase on the desk, immediately producing silence.

Your Uncle Henri was coming down the stairs. He greeted the concierge, walked along the wall of the lycée, turning left at the elementary-school door where, as every day at the same time, save when it was your Aunt Rose who called for them to take them shopping, his youngest children, Claude and François, were waiting for him.

He took them by the hand, walked past the handsome, high-Gothic porch of Saint-Hilaire, whose tympanum, which represents the resurrection of the dead, unfortunately dates from around 1890, the original, certain fragments of which are exhibited in the nearby Cluny Museum, having been disfigured during the Reign of Terror,

coming out onto the Boulevard Saint-Germain where he had to wait, in order to cross, for several minutes before the flood of cars stopped at the red light, walked past the little garden bordering the famous abbatial church, the terraces of the Deux Magots and the Flore, the little garden bordering the Ukrainian church, turned into the Rue du Pré-aux-Clercs, walked up the six floors (no elevator in this old building); on one of the doors, on the fourth floor, a visiting card with Henri Mouron's name on it, but he didn't notice it.

The two children had run up the stairs at first, chasing each other, but quickly lost their breath; the youngest one had taken his father's hand again when they found your Aunt Rose in the kitchen, ironing.

On the table with its red-and-yellow checked oilcloth, there were two bowls of hot milk, slices of bread and chocolate.

The next day, Tuesday—yesterday—after lunch, his coffee drunk, his pipe smoked, when your Uncle Henri had already put on his raincoat and taken François' hand, your Aunt Rose, buttoning up Claude's coat, exclaimed:

"Good God! I think today's Pierre's birthday."

"Pierre Vernier?"

"No, your nephew's, you know!"

"You must be right; he looked at me in a funny way this morning."

"You're his teacher, you see him almost every day, you can't forget a thing like that; he must have been very disappointed . . . "

"But I couldn't say anything to him in front of all the other boys . . . "

"All you have to do is ask him back here after school, I'll try to find something for him this afternoon when I take the children to the store. What kind of things does he like?"

"The best thing would be to telephone him right away, but he's probably left already."

"Oh no, the Rue du Canivet is closer to the lycée than we are. He was born in thirty-nine, I think, he must be fifteen."

26

You hadn't left yet; you were entitled, on the occasion, to a glass of brandy which you savored down to the last drops. Your father went to answer the telephone, and came back with a broad smile:

"It's for you, Pierre, your uncle Henri."

You dashed to the phone.

"Hello, Pierre? If I'm not mistaken, you're fifteen today, is that right? Congratulations! You'll gradute when you're sixteen, that's good. Listen, would you like to stop by the house this afternoon, after school? Your aunt would like to see you. We'll have something to eat. You get out at five? After physics? Fine. Then I'll see you at the house at five-thirty. Is there something you'd like? A book, for instance, or anything else? You think it over. See you later."

You came back into the living room.

"Uncle Henri invited me to go there after school."

"That was very nice of him," your mother said; "remind him that we expect them here for lunch Thursday."

I stood up; I buttoned my jacket.

"We'd better be leaving, so you can see your uncle at the lycée before going there after school. What are you studying now? Rabelais? Goodbye, Anne, goodbye, Jean, it's agreed then, tonight Pierre's my guest; I'll take him to a restaurant. He'll come next door around seven."

The four of us went downstairs, walked along the apse of Saint-Sulpice, glimpsed, in the Rue Saint-Hilaire, your Uncle Henri who was coming from the other direction, having just left Claude and François at the door of the elementary school. We reached the concierge's lodge first. I let you go in, waited for him, watching you all climb the stairs toward your respective classes.

He greeted me,

"So it seems our nephew Pierre is fifteen today. I had forgotten all about it. But we'll have a bite together this afternoon."

"You'll spoil him."

He climbed up the stairs in his turn; I crossed the courtyard to join my seventh-graders.

Your brother Jacques, who, your parents had decided after a trip, would learn Italian and not English like you and your older brother, handed in his homework to Monsieur Bonnini:

"Answer a letter from an Italian friend who has asked you to describe your family."

Your uncle was now listening to Denis Régnier read in a low, carefully modulated tone, obviously enjoying the sound of his own voice:

". . . all the sorts of herbs and flowers that grow upon the ground; all the various metals that are hid within the bowels of the earth; together with all the diversity of precious stones that are to be seen in the Orient and the southern parts of the world: let nothing of all these be hidden from thee."

Your older brother, in the amphitheater, all the curtains closed, was watching in the darkness while Monsieur Hubert was demonstrating the existence of a focus for spherical mirrors:
coming from a projector enclosed in a metal box, two parallel rays, illuminating the chalk dust he dropped through them, reflected on a strip of concave metal and met.

I question Jean-Pierre Cormier, half hidden by Michel Daval, about the Renaissance. He answers me:

"It's a change in teaching."

"What do you mean?"

"Monsieur Jouret told us that."

"Monsieur Jouret is certainly right, but you must still explain to me what he meant, so that I can see whether you have understood him."

"It's the revival of Greek and Latin studies, of the humanities?"

"Didn't people study Latin in the Middle Ages?"

"Oh, yes, classes were all taught in Latin. But no one studied Greek any more, without which a man may be ashamed to call himself a scholar."

"I see Monsieur Jouret is having you study Rabelais. Now tell me, Monsieur Cormier, why did people suddenly start wanting to learn Greek? Why does Gargantua insist on it so much in his letter to Pantagruel?"

"Because they wanted to rediscover Classical times."

"Had they forgotten all about them?"

"No, but the people of the Middle Ages didn't actually look at the texts or the statues; they were satisfied with what was said in the schools."

"And that wasn't enough any more?"

"No, because of the taking of Constantinople by the Turks, because of the discovery of America."

"What do you mean?"

"Well, they were forced to realize that the world wasn't the way they thought it was."

"And it was this change in the face of the world that necessitated a change in teaching, which took a long time to come about, which is perhaps only beginning even today. Thank you."

Monsieur Hutter, the German teacher, is at the other end of the floor, with his tenth-graders. I now know his degree of relationship with his homonym, Francis Hutter, in the first row in front of me, beside Alain Mouron, in front of Michel Daval. One must go back rather far: Frédéric Hutter, grandfather of Monsieur Alfred Hutter, had a first cousin, Émile Hutter, great-grandfather of Francis. They had never seen each other before meeting in class.

He is the one I am questioning now. He raises his head, startled.

"Well, stand up!"

He brushes back the reddish lock that was hanging over one eye.

"What were the consequences of the Renaissance in the fields of art and literature? Your book won't tell you anything. I've already asked you to close it, and your notebook too during recitation. This goes for everyone. Well? I'm waiting. What do you know about the painting of the Sixteenth Century?"

"Every country started imitating Italian painting."

The door opens, an old man in a smock comes in, carrying a tremendous ledger bound in black cloth.

"Just a minute, please."

I add my signature to your Uncle Henri's under the names of the absentees: Philippe Guillaume and André Knorr. There is a typed sheet that I pick up and read to you:

"Abbé Gollier, chaplain of the Lycée Taine, reminds you that the class in religious instruction for the eleventh grade meets every Tuesday from five to six."

I initial this sheet. The old man leaves for the next classroom, where your Uncle Henri is.

"All right, Hutter, what can you tell us about this Italian painting? You must know some of the names at least."

All eyes turn toward him, mocking. He begins moving his fingers, bites his lip, frowns; the others laugh. Then he blurts out:

"Leonardo da Vinci."

"Fine. Now tell me about Leonardo da Vinci . . . You don't know anything? You don't know where he was born, where he died, how he lived, the names of some of his paintings, what else he did besides paint picures? No? Tell me about some other artists, then."

He lowers his head, glances right, then left, as if seeking help. Why did he sit in the first row if he wanted prompting? He probably knows something, but his mind is confused for the moment; I can tell that he won't say another word, that he's resigning himself to whatever I'm going to say to him, that he'll make up for it another time. I'll try to remember to question him again on Saturday, or even tomorrow, in geography, about the year, the seasons, the day, the hour.

"I'm obliged to give you an F. You can sit down."

That was Tuesday and, in the following hour, in the amphitheater on the top floor

(through the window you could see the sun already setting, and the zinc roofs with occasional bright yellow patches, and the clouds moving faster over the chimneys; Monsieur Hubert's face and lab coat were silhouetted on one side by a luminous strip; he was setting weights on a little tray hanging from a cylindrical spring with an indicator that shifted along a graduated vertical scale),

Alain Mouron, exhausted by the day's study, unable to understand why the professor was making so much of notions that seemed quite simple and ordinary to him, began to pencil in a detail of the first illustration of the chapter being discussed, two circles representing the spheres of a dumbbell held at arm's length by a muscular man in a bathing suit, with the caption:

"The athlete provides a *muscular effort*",

these two last words underlined.

Monsieur Bailly had gone to meet his two sons at the door of the elementary school.

They walked down the steps of the Saint-Hilaire métro station. He handed in their tickets to be punched; they waited on the platform of the Auteuil line. A man was sleeping on a bench under a big poster advertising powdered soup, a North African, his face almost entirely concealed by strips of adhesive tape that formed a kind of mask with two eye holes. Many students were coming and going, their arms full of books, especially groups of Africans and Orientals. The train going the other way, toward the Gare d'Austerlitz, came into the station, stopped, started again. There were almost as many people as before on the platform, but they weren't the same ones, and all, or almost all, headed quickly toward the exit.

What Michel Daval was looking at was not the spring (dynamometer) with which Monsieur Hubert had just been playing, but the Atwood machine which he had used the hour before, with his seniors, to check the first law of dynamics, and which he had pushed over to the end of the long counter, near the sink; on each side of the pully the copper weights on nylon strings swayed gently, which was noticeable only because of the vibration of the tiny image of the windows that was reflected in them.

But a word in Monsieur Hubert's speech broke the spell of this fascination; the teacher had just said that the unit of force is the kilogram-force or weight, that is, the weight in Paris of a cylinder of iridized platinum, kept at the International Bureau of Weights and Measures in Sèvres, for this reminded him that there was also a standard meter made out of iridized platinum which was kept there too, and he wondered what the word iridized could mean, hesitating to ask, for no one in the class had had the courage to do such a thing, since Monsieur Hubert had never encouraged them to speak, and finally looking in his textbook where he found the following note:

"Alloy of platinum and iridium, about 10% iridium."

Iridium, what was this element he had never heard of before, even in science-fiction stories, except by way of this obscure adjective that had never concerned him up to now? Why had they combined it with a metal as precious as platinum? Why did this kilogram have to be made out of platinum? Was it only to show that it was a unique, irreplaceable kilogram, one that had to be guarded as carefully as a royal crown or a talisman?

He imagined it in a glass case in the middle of a huge crypt, closed away behind enormous doors with terrible and complicated locks, around which circled relays of picked guards, armed with powerful revolvers,

gleaming in the darkness and the solitude broken only by the visits of a few scholars permitted to contemplate the iridescent radiance due to the 10% of this mysterious iridium.

He felt as if he had just discovered—by accident, by the inadvertence of a textbook—one of the most significant secrets of science (which of his classmates even suspected its existence?). Did the teacher, Monsieur Hubert, really know, having passed the word by without seeming to attach the slightest importance to it?

" . . . all the various metals that are hid within the bowels of the earth . . . "

31

A moment ago, your Uncle Henri, in the Rue du Pré-aux-Clercs apartment, closed his big Racine, the Firmin Didot 1837 edition, in which he had just finished rereading *Iphigénie:*

" . . . Recompense Achilles, and repay your kindness."

He looked at the endpapers whose pattern reminded him of the sudden spattering of a glass covered with a thick layer of dust, the once violet leather that had turned olive-green on the back. He looked at his watch; he still had about ten minutes before leaving. He filled and lit his pipe, picked up one of the compositions your class had handed in the day before, on the subject:

"Describe the one day of your vacation . . . "

read a few lines of it, but it was too boring right now; he put it back on the pile, leafed through the latest *Match* in the dining room near the radio, not stopping at any picture, uncertain how to use these few moments of respite (your Aunt Rose had gone out);

he put on his raincoat, walked down the six flights, and sat down on the terrace of Le Rouquet, at the corner of the Boulevard Saint-Germain and the Rue des Saints-Pères, to drink a cup of coffee.

In the gym, you were stretching your muscles as far as you could to climb up a rope that you couldn't grasp between your feet (you had the wrong kind of shoes); the rope wriggled like a snake, and the knot at its lower end beat the sawdust in the pit; you still had more than a yard to go before you could touch the hook screwed into the big green metal girder; Monsieur Moret, in blue shorts and a sweat shirt, his legs bare like the scout leaders, little Monsieur Moret who is the oldest of all your teachers after Monsieur Martin, was showing the boys in another group the exercises he wanted them to do on the parallel bars.

In one of the classrooms on the first floor, I was telling my eighth-graders about Justinian's attempt (it was our second history lesson) to reassemble the fragments of the divided Roman Empire; I tried to make them grasp a little of the poignant Byzantine splendor by describing my dream of Constantinople and Santa Sophia.

And now Alain Mouron, alone at his desk in front of me, for Francis Hutter is absent, like André Knorr, is carefully writing in his neat notebook, in an elegant but already quite cursive and illegible handwriting, how to take bearings:

" . . . to determine the meridian, one must know Greenwich time when it is noon where one is, which is simple provided the weather is good; it must be true noon, of course, astronomical noon, the moment when shadows are shortest, not the conventional noon of time zones. We already know that a difference of one hour denotes a difference of 15 degrees . . . "

He stops writing; he is wondering: But how do you find out Greenwich time? He hears me mention the radio. But what if the radio stops working? What if you're lost at sea or in the desert, on a big ship or in a plane lost after a storm, and you have to determine which port or oasis is closest, supplies and courage are running low, then there's no way of knowing, all the maps you have are of no use, all this work of discovery and surveying; you have to start off at random, like the first men on earth; you risk dying of hunger a few miles from the richest stores . . .

The measurement of latitude; on the blackboard I draw a sextant; he no longer understands what I am saying, he has missed too many things; he is waiting until I am through with the parallels before he starts writing again.

Monsieur Bailly has just returned to his apartment in the Rue Pierre-Leroux, after buying a pack of cigarettes (Wednesday is his day off); sitting at his desk in front of the mail that has accumulated and which he must answer, he lights a cigarette. Couldn't he have left last night too, taking advantage of these two days, Wednesday–Thursday, escaping Elizabeth as Elizabeth had escaped him for Orléans, Sunday–Monday, taking refuge with Claire? He would have had to ask his cleaning woman, who comes in mornings only, to keep her afternoon free so she could pick up the children, since today Elizabeth stays at the Aulnoy lycée until five.

" . . . A terrestrial globe"

(pointing to the one which is gathering dust on the cabinet and which no one ever uses)

"is a faithful but inconvenient representation; we must have maps, but since it is impossible to make the slightest fragment of a plane surface coincide with that of a spherical body, there is necessarily a transposition, a projection, by means of various systems, all of which have their disadvantages, always distorting certain aspects, so that one must always choose, in studying any region of the earth, the system that suits it best, and always be cautious about maps that claim to represent the entire earth, always try to keep uppermost in your mind the kind of corrections that must be made in them. . . . "

Michel Daval thrusts his hand into his briefcase to take out a pencil sharpener in the shape of a tiny globe, rolls it on his notebook with the palm of his hand, continues writing, but no longer manages to follow the lines, senses that I am watching him, closes his hand over the pencil sharpener (the expression "Mercator's projection" makes a zigzag, the last letters growing larger), straightens up, sets the pencil sharpener down in front of him, underlines what he has just written with a straight line, looks up at me, waits a moment, wonders if it will fall, yes or no, leans over his notebook again, nudging you with his elbow, as if you had just disturbed him.

▓▓▓▓▓▓▓▓▓▓▓▓▓ MONSIEUR BONNINI, facing his seniors for the first time, after congratulating the newcomers on passing their eleventh-grade finals and deploring the failure of those who are repeating the year, after giving some advice and encouragement, has them write on a sheet of paper he passes around the class their name, date of birth, address, and their father's profession,

"We'll begin this year with several cantos of the *Purgatorio*."

Denis Régnier, standing up, his finger tips pressing on the desk,

"It's called the Middle Ages because it comes between two great periods."

"Is that a good enough reason? The Seventeenth Century, which we will be studying, comes between the Sixteenth and the Eighteenth Centuries; yet we don't call the Seventeenth Century the Middle Ages. How does it happen that it is just this thousand-year period which we call by this name?"

"Between two periods that are alike?"

"Do you think so? The late Roman Empire and Europe of the Renaissance?"

"Probably not . . . "

"Well then?"

"People were trying to imitate the men of ancient times, and everything that had happened since didn't interest them any more."

"Perhaps, but why? What had happened? Thank you, you can sit down,"

which he did, leaning back, raising his chin a little, pressing the top of his desk with both hands, a gesture that probably comes from his mother's side, since it is also exhibited by Monsieur Hubert,

who was talking about rectilinear movement to his eleventh-graders in the amphitheater, where you examined him for the first time during the next hour

(last year, you were still studying only "natural sciences", not physics and chemistry; you had only passed him in the halls, or on the way home from school),

examining, too, this new classroom with its long counter like the bar of a café, provided with a sink and a gas ring, the blackboard much

35

larger than those in the regular classrooms, in two parts that you could move up or down as you wished,

with these steps, these black blinds, that sheet of cardboard like a map but representing no country, divided into squares filled with figures and letters: H, He, Li, B, with concentric circles in the first column, only one around a black dot in the first row, two around the second, and so on, the caption above: Periodic Chart of the Elements,

while I am getting to know my seniors, more or less recognizing certain faces I had seen two or three years before in my eleventh-grade class (but not last year, since I wasn't teaching any senior classes then), the five who were repeating, who again, in this first lesson of the year, listened to me speak of the great natural divisions of the United States, of its mountains, its rivers, its climate, its population, its history and its cities.

The next day I met with my seventh-graders again

(the various stone ages, the invention of pottery, the discovery of metals, all those tremendous obscure migrations, the caves and their paintings, the changes of climate and fauna; and so on down to the first inscriptions),

for I teach your class on Wednesday afternoon only every other week, alternating with Monsieur du Marnet, my new mathematics colleague,

whom you saw for the first time, who reminded you what an algebraic number is.

Your Uncle Henri, on the other side of the wall, was describing the life of Racine, and the legends about Iphigenia.

He had mentioned the play to Monsieur Hubert, who on Sunday, in his apartment in the Avenue Émile-Zola, tried to read:

"Yes, it is Agamemnon . . . "

The raindrops bounced against the windows. His wife, ten years younger than he, pregnant for the first time, was knitting a baby sweater.

Denis Régnier was watching the people in the Rue du Cardinal-Lemoine, pulling their raincoats around them or taking shelter in doorways and closing their umbrellas.

Monsieur Bonnini, on the other side of the street, ten numbers farther down, two stories below, in his room overlooking the courtyard, the light on, sitting beside his wife, who was lying pale and thin on her bed, was silently pasting into an album the photographs he had taken on their vacation.

Then, while the Empire clock on the mantel in your Uncle Henri's study was striking four, the rain having stopped for a few minutes just then, I struggled out of the leather armchair and said goodbye.

Micheline Pavin had arranged to meet me at the Royal-Saint-Germain at five. I still had over three quarters of an hour to linger along the quays, looking in the antique-shop windows.

Sitting with the Bisons, on the wet ground at the intersection of three paths, having won the game, you waited for the rest of the troop; the Chamois arrived with the leaders.

The next day, I ate lunch with Micheline Pavin in a restaurant in the Rue des Saints-Pères. It was one-thirty, we were smoking, finishing our coffee, I looked at her eyes, her lips, her neck; she smiled at me. I saw that the minute hand was approaching 10 and that I would have to go.

The clock chimed twice from Saint-Germain-des-Prés, from Saint-Sulpice, from Saint-Hilaire, the echoes reverberating in the courtyards of the lycées, and Monsieur Bonnini, his face sad, terribly worried by his wife's health, which was growing worse, stepped up onto the platform to discuss with his seniors:

" . . . Guai a voi, anime prave!
Non isperate mai veder lo cielo!"
(. . . Woe unto you, perverted souls!
Never hope to see the sky again!)

Denis Régnier was examining the profile of Caesar he had drawn on his sheet of paper, and was not satisfied with it; the forehead was probably too low; the eyes should have been more prominent.

He sharpened the tip of his charcoal with some sandpaper, underlined eyelid and pupil, but this gave the imperator a stupefied expression quite different from that of the model, and he felt that the very face he was drawing was mocking his lack of skill.

The bell rang; his classmates were beginning to put away their things. Abandoning any hope of improving his drawing, deciding that the others must have finished theirs and that consequently there would be a different model next time, Denis wrote his name at the top and to the left, adding his grade: "Eleven."

Then Jean-Pierre Cormier, a short, dark boy with a lock of hair hanging into his eyes, always wearing last year's jacket, the elbows patched with leather ovals, a little too tight across the shoulders now, his yellow-and-green striped tie already dirty, badly tied, showing his collar button,

while pretending to pay close attention to what I was saying about time zones, keeping his eyes fixed on me, slowly nodding as though in approval, pretending to write but hiding his notebook behind Michel Daval's back, tried to catch the words the latter was whispering to you about me.

I hear from Monsieur Hutter himself, who was amused by the interest I take in the relationships within this class, that his paternal grandmother was named Cormier, Régine Cormier, so that it is quite possible that there is some connection between Jean-Pierre and himself, though he was unable to tell me any more about it, his father having completely lost track of that branch of his family. He promised me to do a little research. It would be odd, if this investigation leads to something, to see them become interested in each other, grow closer, simply on account of this curiosity I showed for a relationship they themselves were unaware of. For now they are still strangers to each other; it is only because of me that the name Jean-Pierre Cormier came to Monsieur Hutter's attention, when I showed him the list of the eleventh-grade pupils, the list of their teachers, and the exceptional group of cousin-relationships which I had succeeded in uncovering, for this boy is not studying German, but Italian with Monsieur Bonnini; so they have no class together.

Monsieur Alfred Hutter, at this moment, on Monday, October 11, during the second afternoon class, was explaining to his seniors something by Goethe, and Jean-Pierre, once the conversation between you and Michel Daval was halted by the apprehensiveness you felt toward me the day before your birthday, your particular desire on that day to get into the good graces of an uncle living on the same floor as you and your parents, took out of his briefcase his Italian textbook, slipped it discreetly under his geography textbook.

I had just drawn a diagram on the board to explain the time zones, how it is midnight at the antipodes when it is noon in Paris, and it was when I turned around that I saw the furtive movement of that hand, of that arm hiding itself behind Michel Daval's shoulder, which itself was half concealed by that of Francis Hutter in the first row, who was looking at his book open to an illustration on this same subject, comparing this diagram with mine, making an obvious effort to understand,

38

then looked at the face of the clock I was pointing at while explaining that an hour corresponded on the clock face to thirty degrees, but that if the twenty-four hours of the day were put there as sometimes happens, and not only half of them as is customary, then each one of them would occupy exactly fifteen degrees, like each of the zones on this great clock which is the earth.

And during the English class, Alain Mouron went on examining this diagram that had remained on the blackboard, the circle representing the terrestrial equator, another, smaller circle underneath, then the sun surrounded by its beams, one of them longer than the rest, ending in an arrow with the word noon, and at the top the word midnight almost at the edge of the board.

At his left, on the other side of the window, between two branches, just above the roof behind which it was soon going to set, the real sun had just appeared between two clouds, shining on his book open at the first page of selections from *Julius Caesar*, and the shadow of a bar outside the window striped the dictator's face with a broad, oblique band.

It was no longer Francis Hutter sitting at his right but one of the students of another eleventh-grade section; in front of him, at the desk, his uncle, Monsieur René Bailly, was asking with a bored look for volunteers to read the roles of Brutus and Cassius.

Since no hand was raised, his eyes swept over the whole class, row after row, resting a little longer on Alain Mouron, then on Michel Daval, finally selecting two students from the back of the room. There was a noise of pages turning.

"I see you were occupying yourself with other matters, Monsieur. Let us have a sample of your talents."

The voice began, trembling, hesitant, stumbling over each syllable.

"One would think you had never read English before."

All the students' faces turned toward the victim.

"Well, Cassius, what are you waiting for?"

Monsieur Bailly stood up; he was holding the book in one hand, in the other a black wood ruler with copper corners, one end of which rested on his desk.

All the students' faces were bent over their texts.

"And now, can you translate these few sentences for me? Can you show me whether you've understood anything of what you've just read?"

39

Alain Mouron glanced at his cousin Michel Daval behind him, gesturing with his hand and making a face that said as clearly as any words:

"He's in a bad mood today, watch out."

Michel Daval, with a twisted smile and a slight shrug of his shoulders, answered wordlessly:

"You know he never asks us any questions."

They both looked at the clock, examined the diagrams I had left on the blackboard, avoided the eyes of their uncle who had turned toward them momentarily; both boys bent over their texts, listening to the word-by-word translation being stammered from the back of the classroom by a student from another eleventh-grade section whose name they didn't know yet.

Michel Daval couldn't help reading ahead, as though drawn on by this text he had prepared, not that this was his habit, but because what little he had understood at sight had given him the incentive to look up the obscure words in his dictionary; he had written in his notebook a brief glossary for this page:

"endure: supporter

raw: âpre

gusty: orageux";

he was not listening to the corrections his uncle might be making; he read the whole assignment for that day, then reread it, translating a few snatches of it to himself, fascinated:

"*I was born free as Caesar . . .*
. . . and we can both
Endure the winter's cold as well as he . . .
. . . and this man
Is now become a god, and Cassius is
A wretched creature and must bend his body
If Caesar . . . "

He was forced to stop now and then, to leave gaps in his translation and his reading; there were difficulties he could not negotiate, but he persisted, although once past this line:

"*If Caesar carelessly but nod on him*",

the page of his open notebook left him without any recourse. The obscure passages grew more numerous, longer and closer together;

he was obliged to give up; he found himself stopped as though by a wall.

He began leafing through his textbook, *Anthology of English Literature*, looking for a picture, and found one several pages farther on, badly printed, almost unrecognizable, especially since in order to see it properly he would have had to turn the book around, a gesture which Uncle René Bailly would certainly have considered quite insolent,

"The death of Caesar, after Rochegrosse",

which he couldn't examine, study at his ease, until the next day, in his room where he had gone to "take another look" at his afternoon lessons, while his parents were drinking their coffee:

to the left, the pedestal of a statue of which only one foot could be seen, to the right, stools overturned; that black spot with an arm coming out of it must be Caesar; and where were Brutus and Cassius in that mass of folds and heads? Looking closer, he managed to make out the daggers in certain hands; one of the faces looked a little like his cousin Mouron, another, very dim, with graying hair, reminded him faintly of Uncle René Bailly,

who in the apartment building next door, one floor above, was sitting on a Louis XVI armchair covered in faded cretonne, stirring his two lumps of sugar in his coffee cup with a stainless-steel coffee spoon beside his wife who was standing, swallowing a last mouthful, her hat and gloves already on, before taking the children to their respective schools.

Alain Mouron, in his big bedroom, took out of one desk drawer the books he would need this afternoon: *Sixteenth Century French Authors, A New Course in History, Eleventh Grade, XVII and XVIII Centuries*, the thin *Physics Textbook*, all carefully covered in strong navy-blue paper with white labels.

Out of another, wider drawer he took the French composition he would hand in to your Uncle Henri, looked at it a moment, reread the first lines, added a circumflex over the first *a* in the word *château*, underlined his name in red ink, then in green ink, wrote underneath in large, elaborate letters: "eleventh-grade", crossed out the circumflex he had just added over the *a* in *château*.

Beside him, during French class, Francis Hutter was studying his secondhand textbook, protected by the dreary cover advertising a bookstore, the pages already covered with annotations made some other year by some other student during the course given by some other teacher, listening to the voice of a classmate behind him whose name he didn't know yet:

" . . . and by frequent anatomies get thee the perfect knowledge of the microcosm which is man."

"Let's stop there, and see if you've looked up all the difficult words."

Francis Hutter was writing new paraphrases in the narrow, already crowded margin. Just after the word "microcosm" in the text, the figure 12 referred to this commentary at the bottom of the page:

"The microcosm opposed to the macrocosm",

under which Francis' unknown predecessor had added in pencil the following explanations:

"microcosm: micro:small, kosmos:world
man is a microcosm
macrocosm: macro:big",

so that after your Uncle Henri asked Denis Régnier what these two words meant and Denis said nothing, Francis Hutter raised his hand and gave an answer which earned your uncle's congratulations:

"That's something you should all have known, without even having to consult a dictionary. Microcosm, in fact, comes from these two Greek words that you've all known for a long time."

But since micro and kosmos were written in Roman script in his textbook, Francis Hutter had not realized he did know them, and would never have been able to say what language they came from; relieved that the teacher, Monsieur Jouret, your Uncle Henri, hadn't discovered this serious lacuna, he rewrote them in his textbook in Greek characters.

Monsieur Alfred Hutter was making his seventh-graders decline the German articles.

"In sum, let me see thee an abyss of learning . . . "

"What does that word sum mean? What is a sum in arithmetic? The result of a process of addition. Gargantua says to his son: 'If you add together all that I have just told you, you will obtain the following sum: "an abyss of learning." ' We often say someone is a well of learning. Who can explain this expression? You"

(he looks at the seating chart spread out on his desk)

"Cormier? It's not so difficult, after all. What is a well? A place that gives us water. What is an oil well? A place that gives us petroleum, the precious substance hidden in the 'bowels of the earth.' A well of learning is therefore someone who can give us learning, the knowledge we need. But notice that Rabelais does not say a well of learning, he says an abyss of learning. Exactly what does this word abyss mean? All right, Cormier, tell us!"

"It's something very deep, a crevice in a mountain or a hole on the bottom of the sea."

"That's right, it's a hole, a cavern, a bottomless pit whose capacity cannot be measured, in other words an inexhaustible reservoir, like the inexhaustible bowels of the earth where Rabelais tells us the precious metals sleep . . ."

Monsieur Tavera is with the six tenth-graders taking Spanish.

I am asking questions about the Reformation, about Luther and Calvin. I call on Hubert Jourdan, who is behind you, at the rear of the class, and who looks so much like Monsieur Tavera that I must inquire one of these days about the names of both sets of ancestors;

and I also think I recognize, between this Hubert Jourdan and Monsieur du Marnet, who has just drawn an isosceles triangle on the blackboard for his ninth-graders, a certain family resemblance, not in the features (and of course it would never have occurred to me to look for some relationship between du Marnet and Tavera), but in certain gestures, certain expressions perhaps secretly transmitted without anyone's ever actually noticing, over perhaps a dozen generations, which would take us back to a common ancestor (one out of 1,024 is enough) at the beginning of the Eighteenth Century.

That was Tuesday the twelfth.

Monsieur Bonnini left the lycée at four; he walked down to the Boulevard Saint-Germain which he followed as far as the Rue du Cardinal-Lemoine. He was walking very slowly, worried about the condition in which he was going to find his wife. The situation couldn't go on this way. The doctor would certainly announce that she had to be taken to the hospital at once and be operated on as soon as possible. Fortunately, Geneviève, her sister, was with her. He stopped to buy a package of tobacco and matches. He would have liked to bring some flowers, find a way of pleasing her, of bringing a smile to her unrecognizable face, but he had thought of it too late; he would have had to go all the way back to the Boulevard, and he was too tired.

He climbed the five flights, stopping to catch his breath at each landing, his hand on the shaky banister, glancing at the desolation of the courtyard through the cracked panes, repaired with strips of tape, and the red wallpaper, torn in places, showing the dusty plaster underneath,

and he turned the brass knob in the middle of the dark-brown door. The hall was already dark; he turned on the ceiling light, a globe of dirt-streaked milk glass hanging from three brass chains.

His wife was awake, sitting up, leaning back against her pillows, breathing heavily, her hands spread out on the sheets, their nails white. Geneviève, who was knitting a black sweater beside her, stood up, saying that she would make tea for both of them.

He sat down, took one of his wife's hands in his own and caressed it gently. She turned her head toward him, with a smile that betrayed a terrible exhaustion.

"The doctor will be here at five. He telephoned after you left. What did you have your students read today?"

"Oh, the usual routine. My seniors have begun the *Purgatorio*, the first passage they have in their book, and my tenth-graders . . . my tenth-graders . . . "

Geneviève came in with the tray for the tea.

Denis Régnier was watching Monsieur Hubert make the same gestures he had made a year before, at the same point in the school cycle, opening a box containing lead weights, another containing copper weights, a third, flat box containing weights made out of strips of aluminum varying from one milligram to five decigrams, which he picked up with tweezers like the ones Denis used for his stamp collection.

Then he arranged his history textbook and his *Sixteenth Century French Authors* to make a support for his physics book, incidentally constituting an effective rampart against the teacher's indiscreet glances,

took out of his jacket pocket a little notebook in which strips of celluloid contained his duplicate stamps,

and began examining them one by one, which gradually attracted the attention of all his neighbors.

Monsieur Hubert put away his aluminum-strip weights.

Once the box was closed, he declared in a voice suddenly much louder, as though to wake up his audience:

"Now we're going to talk about the dynamometer",

and he turned around to write this word on the blackboard in large capital letters, repeating each syllable distinctly.

"Those of you who are studying Greek will immediately understand what this word means. Suppose one of you eleventh-grade gentlemen dazzles your colleagues by your learning, shows them that the study of the language of Homer can also be of use to physicists ..."

Your Uncle Henri went home to the apartment in the Rue du Pré-aux-Clercs to wait for you. Your Aunt Rose had already been there for a quarter of an hour with the two younger children whom she had called for at the door of the elementary school at four; she had taken them to a shop on the Boulevard Saint-Michel to buy winter boots. They had not yet unwrapped them; they put them on for him to inspect and then changed into their slippers.

"Good God, I don't know if we have any cookies left, I forgot to buy some on the way home from the shoestore! I'll run out to the bakery now. Fix the cups meanwhile, so he'll think everything's ready."

You let your two brothers walk home down the Rue Saint-Sulpice, you followed the Boulevard Saint-Germain where you caught up with your cousin Gérard who, because the eight-grade classrooms are on the ground floor, had a head start.

You poked his shoulder at the Carrefour de l'Odéon. He turned around, very surprised.

"I'm coming to your house."

"You are?"

"Didn't you know? I'm coming over because it's my birthday. I'm fifteen. How old are you?"

"Thirteen."

"When'll you be fourteen?"

"Not until after Christmas."

"What grade are you in?"

"Ninth."

"You'll be fourteen in the ninth grade, and I'm fifteen in the eleventh. You're not so far behind."

Your Aunt Rose was coming down the stairs.

"Go on up, children, your uncle's waiting for you: I have to run an errand, I'll be right back."

Climbing the six floors, you thought about what present you would ask your Uncle Henri for, then you decided he would be sure to think anything you really wanted was too expensive; it wasn't worth worrying about, encouraging hopes that could never be realized. It was the first time your Uncle Henri ever felt the need to give you something for your birthday, and you knew it was because you were in his class. So you decided that the best thing would be not to talk too much, to wait and see what would happen, and to answer his questions as vaguely as possible.

Sitting at my desk in the Rue du Canivet, looking out the window from which I glimpsed, over the roof of the house across the street, between the chimneys, the towers of Saint-Sulpice and the reddening clouds,

instead of preparing, as usual, my Wednesday afternoon's classes: the second history lesson for the eighth grade, Justinian's efforts, the splendor of Byzantium; the third geography lesson for your grade, the representation of the earth, maps and projections; the third history lesson for the seniors, the growth of capitalism, the development of the railroads and the industrial cities.

I began writing up these notes about our class, which are meant for you, Pierre, though not as you are today—not only because you would probably be unable to read them and be interested in them, but also because they are not yet in condition to be read, because you must wait until they are completed, corrected, which may take quite a long time—

which are meant for you when you will finally be able to read them, for that Pierre Eller who will apparently have forgotten all about this October 12, 1954, the events which occurred on it, the knowledge that we attempted to give you on it,

these notes which I hope, at that time, will be a literal description, without any intervention on the part of my imagination, a simple account of precise facts, but that wouldn't have permitted me to give an adequate representation,

for to describe the space in which these facts occur, and without which it is impossible to make them appear, it is necessary to imagine a quantity of other events impossible to verify,

consequently these notes in which for your sake I have started to imagine our class while trying to rely as much as possible on what I know with certainty, on the little I could prove before some pitiless judge, and which—because of certain special circumstances, particularly the fact that among the students and their teachers there exists a remarkable number of rather close family relationships, we might call them extramural relationships—allows me to obtain a good deal of information that is much more varied and voluminous than what can ordinarily be known with certitude by a teacher about the occupations and the feelings of his students or his colleagues,

to imagine this class while describing it, as I already used to imagine it before, merely seeing it, merely watching you boys listening to me, but without my realizing it.

I am absolutely certain, for instance, that on Wednesday, October 13, your friend Alain Mouron went at two in the afternoon to the gym on the street floor of the Lycée Taine, a room I know, which I can visit again, where I can sit down and make a precise description of its iron pillars, its sawdust, its skylight, the streaked paint on the walls;

I know exactly which people were with him there, that is, I know their names, I have the list of students, and I noted those who were absent that day;

I can describe the features and the clothes of the gym teacher, Monsieur Moret.

The sky had cleared, the sun came out, the sawdust danced in the beams.

You yourself told me that some of you had climbed up the rope, that another group had worked out on the parallel bars; but how could I find out which Alain Mouron did during this hour? How could I find out if he talked, what he said, if the teacher reprimanded him?

Among these few certainties appears an element of irremediable doubt, which can be reduced only by multiplying my references, specifying the situations in greater and greater detail, clarifying one after the other every group of probabilities.

I know, in the same way, that Monsieur Bailly was not at the lycée during this hour, since he is off all day on Wednesday. He was obviously very eager to meet that woman he is seeing more and more often, Claire Duval. He telephoned her in the apartment on the Avenue Émile-Zola. Yes, she was hard at work, he mustn't disturb her. Or else the line was busy, a customer no doubt, her business was going very well these days, Hermès had ordered scarves from her (check if she has a telephone . . . Oh, certainly!). He would call back later. He couldn't concentrate on his reading. There was a pile of letters on his desk that he should have answered long since. He couldn't concentrate on writing. He turned on the radio, tried various stations, then turned it off. He started reading the newspaper, then went out

47

to buy a pack of cigarettes at the corner of the Rue de Sèvres and the Rue Vaneau.

As for Michel Daval, he probably doesn't like gym much, he doesn't belong to the Scouts or any other club, his chest is narrow but his movements are quick, and his eyes have that intensity that doubtless allows him, when the goal seems worth the trouble, to exert all his energy and do better than many of his huskier schoolmates,

the rope must be a torture to him, unless he has made it part of one of his fantasies, a creeper in the virgin forest or a serpent to wrestle with in order to save some lady explorer in distress or the children of a black prince, or a rope attached to an interplanetary rocket, let down to permit Space Lieutenant Michel Daval to accomplish the most dangerous rescue . . .

If that was the case, his hands seized the rope, his teeth locked, he looked down at the sawdust beneath, where you had just landed; and the dust you raised was the earth's atmosphere, through which he tried to make out the outline of the continents.

There was only a yard left before he reached the hook, and he wondered if he could make this effort, if he wasn't going to have to give up.

Breathing heavily and regularly, rising only a few inches farther each time, he finally touched the metal, let himself slide down, exhausted but happy to have fulfilled his mission, suddenly rediscovering the real world when he touched ground, realizing that he was the last one, that all his schoolmates were already lined up and that the gym teacher, Monsieur Moret, who didn't know his name yet, was whistling at him.

Monsieur Hubert, in the amphitheater under the roof, was explaining to his seniors the transformations of weight appearing within a system of movement, whether elevator or interplanetary rocket.

Denis Régnier, as usual, wasn't listening to me.

I was trying to explain that it is impossible to represent the earth exactly without distorting it, just as it is impossible to represent reality in speech without using a certain kind of projection, a system of points of reference whose shape and organization depend on what you are trying to show, and, as a corollary, on what you need to know

(this latter, obviously, I didn't tell you in class, it's an idea that came to me as I was writing),

and that our habitual representation of what is happening in the contemporary world, and of universal history, is constantly distorted by the primacy, in our minds, of the cylindrical projection, the so-called Mercator projection, used in almost all planispheres, those found in the offices of navigation companies as well as in schools or dictionaries, and which has the peculiarity of considerably enlarging the surfaces of countries in the temperate and polar zones to the detriment of those in the equatorial zone,

so that we must often make a considerable effort to appreciate the true relation of masses which exists between nations like France and England on the one hand, for instance, and India or China on the other.

Denis Régnier glanced in my direction to see if I was watching him; he winked at Jean-Pierre Cormier, who had passed him, across the row, the German notebook of Jean-Claude Fage, sitting right behind him.

He kept it on his knees a minute, bent over his desk as if he were writing diligently, whereas he was making a checkerboard out of the squares of the little Mercator projection in his textbook, glanced again in my direction, passed the notebook to his neighbor Bernard de Loups, who was impatiently waiting for it and who began to copy it at once.

If I didn't interfere, it's not only because Denis Régnier is a rather good student and because he's already heard and taken notes on everything I had said about this subject the year before, but also because I had already begun writing up these notes, and was consequently taking a new interest in the behavior of your classmates, in their games which I didn't want to disturb. I would have to keep a close watch on myself, for if I let myself merely observe them without interfering, their conduct would be transformed—and disastrously for me; they would take advantage of me and abuse the situation as soon as they had realized what it was, which they would certainly do right away.

At best, if I credited them with the most favorable intentions in my regard and a desire to collaborate in this work which I am dedicating to them as to you, which I dedicate to them through you, at best they would become little actors, trying to attract this extramural attention to themselves, and in their desire to play a larger part in the book, they would see that some of their tricks amuse me, and all of them interest me, and do everything in their power to discover new ones that might be still more dangerous.

Monsieur Bonnini wasn't at the lycée either; he is off Wednesday too. But what he was waiting for was the ambulance that was to take his wife to the hospital where she was to be operated on.

Breathing heavily in her sleep, from time to time her hand contracted, then relaxed, and afterwards she heaved a deep sigh that seemed to scrape her chest.

Geneviève was almost through packing the suitcase.

I went upstairs to tell my seniors about the development of capitalism in France during the second half of the Nineteenth Century, the progress of the railroads, the growth of the cities, the birth of the great stores, but I had difficulty getting through this hour, for I had not been able to review all these subjects either last night or this morning, busy as I had been writing up these notes.

I had moments of painful vagueness, and since I am not in the habit of improvising from the textbook, my students certainly noticed it, which, at this time of the year, was irritating. I must now correct this impression and take the class in hand again.

I will not put myself in this position again. However eager I am to get down what I know, what I've seen, what I imagine distinctly —which is in danger of fading, of growing vague—I resolved, after this irritating hour, never again to encroach on the time devoted to the preparation of my classes, and henceforth this time will be established in my week's schedule as strictly as the hours of these classes themselves.

You had reached the Rue du Canivet apartment before your brothers. Shut up in your room, you took off your shoes, stretched out on your bed and began reading Number 11 of the magazine *Fiction*, on the cover of which was printed Michel Daval's name and address.

After examining the table of contents, your first choice fell on a story by Fritz Leiber, "The Game of Silence":

"Lili felt a thrill of excitement when the American soldier stuck his broad white face and his gun through the bitter-smelling oak leaves and put his finger on his lips, just as if he knew the game of silence . . . "

When your Uncle Henri arrived at the Rue du Pré-aux-Clercs apartment with your two youngest cousins, your Aunt Rose said:

"Would you mind taking them to the barber after they're through eating? They can't go to Jean's for lunch tomorrow with their hair looking like that!"

"Wouldn't it be better if they did their homework for Friday tonight, and I took them to the barber tomorrow morning?"

"Tomorrow morning I have to take François to the dentist, and I don't know how long that will take."

On Thursday, your Uncle Henri and your Aunt Rose, after leaving your parents, took their three youngest children, Lucie, Claude and François, to the Jardin des Plantes.

The sky was overcast; they stood in line a long time to get into the vivarium. When they came out again, a few drops of rain were beginning to fall.

In the headquarters of the Bison Patrol, an attic room overlooking the Seine and Notre-Dame lent by the parents of your second in command, a room with bare walls you were supposed to decorate, and with no furniture except some old trunks you used as chairs, you and your friends were playing Concentration:

on a purple scarf with two red stripes around the edges, you had arranged twenty different objects: a handkerchief, a piece of string, a box of matches, a penknife, a button from one of the back pockets of your trousers, a stamp, a five-franc piece, a notebook in which you had copied out the words of the songs you had been taught, a pebble, the key to this room, a nail you had pulled out of one of the walls, a little blue pencil with a chewed-off point, a safety pin, a whistle, a shoelace, an electric light bulb (the one from the ceiling), a tin spoon and fork, a marrowbone,

all this covered with another scarf at the moment you opened the door to let in your six friends waiting silently in the hall,

who were entitled to examine the collection for three minutes, which you timed watch in hand, then the objects were concealed again, each boy having taken out of his pocket a little notebook and a pencil or a ballpoint pen and trying to enumerate what he had seen.

In the Rue du Pré-aux-Clercs, but not in your Uncle Henri's apartment, two numbers farther down, in the waiting room of my dentist, Monsieur Hubert, the brother of Monsieur Hubert your physics and chemistry teacher, I looked at magazines in the company of an old lady and a girl in a raincoat, both of whom had come before me, though not together, and who therefore would both be taken care of before it was my turn.

I walk into the classroom and I step up onto the platform, I call the roll. There are only two absentees: Laurent Garrac and Georges Tannier. My notebook is open to the page of your class: to the left, the list of your names in alphabetical order: Abel, Armelli, Baron . . . , then the columns, each devoted to one hour, where I mark absences and the grades I give you. I began at the top for history recitation, at the bottom for geography, and according to this system, it should be your turn now, but I hesitate, I am suddenly disturbed, I don't know how to look at you, what tone to take.

I find a way out in the fact that Abel and Baron were absent on Saturday the ninth, and consequently have no grade yet either; I ask the former to give me a brief description of Europe and its religious divisions in 1600; I ask the latter what he knows about the Hapsburgs, particularly Philip II.

Then, deciding that it is extremely dangerous to let the degrees of relationship that unite us, and particularly the relation—so special, so curiously intimate—that derives from the text I am writing for you, interfere with my work, even for so slight a question, even on a point that I alone can detect at this point (the students are so watchful for anything they can interpret as an illegitimate favor, that I can't take too many precautions),

I control myself:

"Eller, give me more details about France at the beginning of the Seventeenth Century."

I make my expression severe, I watch you, I wait, but there is not the trace of a smile of complicity on your face; it is as if you didn't recognize me; I am at this moment no more to you than the teacher who is grading you, and you expect no indulgence on my part; on the contrary, the only difference I can detect between your attitude and that of your classmates is a more evident apprehensiveness, and I understand why: it's on account of the others,

for, either you must show them that our relationship doesn't have any effect on you and that consequently you can take advantage of the situation, declaring war on me in class, either openly or under cover, getting bad marks or leading some conspiracy, which is impossible on account of your genuine respect for me, the real friendship we have outside of school,

or else you are obliged to behave, you can no longer permit yourself any digressions, you can't provoke a single sarcastic remark from me without making yourself ridiculous in their eyes, without their feeling the power I have over you and beginning to imagine the various unpleasantnesses, the long and complicated consequences, the shame within the family circle that would result from your weaknesses.

They all know now that I'm your uncle, they all watch you even when their eyes are on me, and since you take some time to answer, since you speak slowly and in a low voice, with many hesitations, spacing out your words, leaving rather long pauses between your sentences, I should like to help you by reformulating my questions so they can guide you more closely, so they somehow force your knowledge—the blurred, scattered memories—to reassemble, to re-awaken, but all these eyes, all these ears inhibit me.

The hints I could give to others without their being even noticed would in your case immediately provoke smiles, winks, a secret and lasting scandal that would persist all year, attached to both our faces; consequently it is with a real sense of relief that I finally hear you telling me about Henri IV and giving an intelligent explanation of the Edict of Nantes.

On the other side of the wall behind me, your Uncle Henri passes between the rows to collect from each desk the French compositions whose subjects he assigned fifteen days ago; he puts all these papers striped with lines of writing away in a worn file, takes the names of those who have not handed in their homework, and declares that this time he will be lenient and still accept the compositions handed in tomorrow.

▓▓▓▓▓▓▓▓▓▓▓▓▓▓▓▓▓ WITHIN THE GROUP formed by the students of this class with their teachers, there are three groups of three people connected by degrees of relationship which I know exactly,

first of all, the one formed by us, your Uncle Henri, you and I,

the one formed by Monsieur Bailly and his two nephews, which is one degree more remote,

and the one, obviously much more distant, formed by Denis Régnier, who is repeating the year (he's not the only one, there's also Bruno Verger, who was with me last year, Georges Tannier, who was at the Lycée Buffon, Francis Hutter, who was in Bourges), Monsieur Hubert and Monsieur Bonnini.

I have succeeded in identifying a fourth group (it is the resemblance of names that put me on the track), but it could be of only slight use to me, since its members do not see each other outside the lycée, at least for now. Monsieur Hutter, the German teacher, had never met young Francis before having him in his class, was unaware of his very existence; as far as he's concerned, at least, he knows—and has told me, in detail—what their genealogical connection was, while for Jean-Pierre Cormier this remains vague and is perhaps even illusory. I complete this fourth triad by employing a hypothesis which only an accident could enable me to verify; how can I find out, as a matter of fact?

I have already situated the activity of all these people during the second hour of the afternoon, from three to four, on Monday, October 11, 1954, the second Monday of this school year, the day before I began to write up these notes, exactly twenty-four hours before this pivotal lesson on the discovery and conquest of America.

Now I must go on, indicate where these other three people were and what they were doing at this moment, in this zone whose duration is so carefully charted—these three others whom I have already brought on the stage and who form a fifth group, within which I can only suppose a relationship, of a much more remote degree than that of the preceding group—a forgotten relationship—basing my hypothesis on two resemblances, one quite striking, the other much more vague.

Monsieur du Marnet was with his ninth-graders. I know that on

Monday he is teaching them arithmetic, before initiating them into algebra, and he must still have been dealing with the decomposition of a number into primary factors,

calling them one after the other to the blackboard, making them divide by two, then by three, then by five, and so on, enormous, specially calculated numbers of which he had found a list in a collection of problems.

Hubert Jourdan, who has the same nose, the same forehead, the same color eyes and hair, the latter thicker, without that bald spot in the middle, was listening to me explain to your class what an hour is, what time is, that the pivotal moment, the one from which one measures, noon, is in principle the one moment of the day when the sun is highest, the shadows shortest before beginning to grow again,

but that this is true only at the center of the time zones, and that the limits of the latter are distorted by political frontiers, so that one sets one's watch according to the time in a place often far away from one's own country, so that the time of clocks and radios coincides only rarely with that of the stars,

and especially since, in some cases, considerations of habit, a whole series of constraining customs, the slow shift toward evening of all activities, effect a general transposition, whether during the summer or during the whole year as in France today, so that without suspecting it we regulate our whole lives not according to the noon of our own sky, but according to that of Prague and Trieste;

and he was scratching behind his right ear with his forefinger pointing down, a gesture also characteristic of Monsieur Tavera, the Spanish teacher, who has the same schedule as Monsieur Hutter, and who therefore at this moment was in one of the classrooms upstairs with the students taking Spanish,

but though I can read English and Italian, though I know a few words of German, I don't know any Spanish, and consequently it's very difficult for me to reconstruct the way it's taught. To complete this description of our class, I must begin a serious study of everything that can be learned by its members.

The next hour, Denis Régnier, stammering, translated the beginning of Cassius' speech, his last year's notebook on his desk, open to the notes taken then that he had not bothered to reread.

> "I know that virtue to be in you, Brutus,
> As well as I do know your outward favor."

"Just what does that mean, your outward favor?"

"Well, it's a poetic expression; it means the consideration he has for others."

"It does? Very ingenious. Tell me, Régnier, you were in the eleventh grade last year. We studied this passage together, didn't we?"

"Yes, Monsieur."

"Apparently it hasn't done you much good. Don't you see that beside the word favor there's a tiny four? You don't wear glasses, you have good eyes!"

"Yes, Monsieur."

"Well, you ought to know that this little number refers to an explanation at the bottom of the page, which you will be good enough to read aloud."

"Favor: personal appearance."

"That you don't prepare your lessons is so much the worse for you, it will earn you bad grades and all kinds of inconveniences, as you know—it's at your own risk; but that you aren't capable of taking advantage of what's under your own nose is enough to make me despair!"

The whole class gave a little laugh of complicity which was immediately hushed.

"All right, now go on!"

Next door, Monsieur Bonnini made your six classmates studying Italian read the one sonnet from the *Vita Nuova* that was in their textbook:

"Tanto gentile e tanto onesta pare . . ."
(So gentle and so pure appears . . .)

I met him on the stairs after my tenth-grade class, stopped him to ask permission to consult his assignment lists, asked him several questions about the authors he was studying, the curriculum he intended to follow. He answered pleasantly, talked to me about his wife's illness, left me once we had reached the street.

I went into the Café Taine to telephone Micheline Pavin; we arranged to meet for dinner.

Back in the Rue du Canivet apartment, I prepared my lessons for the next morning:

the rotation of the earth for the seventh grade (not difficult, review at an elementary level, with more drawings on the blackboard and little stories, the ones I had told you this afternoon), the climate and the vegetation of Africa for the eighth grade (this was different: something that is not reviewed during the entire course of secondary studies, and of which I have therefore had no occasion to speak for a year),

the topography of France for the tenth grade (which we review in the twelfth grade, but I have no geography seniors this year, I had none last year).

The next day, Tuesday, in the apartment in the Rue du Cardinal-Lemoine, after watching his wife sleep in the room with the drawn curtains and smelling of herb tea, Monsieur Bonnini closed the door behind him and joined his two children, Isabella and Giovanni, in the dining room, where they were already turning their spaghetti around their forks.

The bell at the beginning of the afternoon; Monsieur Tavera went into the seventh-grade classroom.

Hubert Jourdan, from the back of my classroom, followed on the sunny page of his textbook what his neighbor, Jean-Claude Fage, was reading aloud:

" . . . for from henceforward, as thou growest great and becomest a man, thou must part from this tranquillity and rest of study . . . "

The bell rang at the end of the hour; Hubert Jourdan immediately closed his book, but your Uncle Henri's hand went up,

"One moment, please, Friday we will finish the reading and explanation of this letter, and you will also prepare for me—please make a note of this—'The study of Gargantua according to the discipline of his schoolmasters the sophisters', down to the end, page thirty-two: 'the cork of his shoes swells up half a foot high.' I should also like to remind you that tomorrow I want to see in your notebooks a précis of the first preface to *Britannicus*, with the usual explanation of all the words that you found difficult. Class dismissed."

The students were shouting in the courtyard.

Monsieur du Marnet erased the subtraction exercises his eighth-graders had just performed on the blackboard. He looked at his schedule and headed toward his ninth-grade classroom.

The Saint-Hilaire chimes rang three times. The bell of the Lycée Taine rang.

I know that Jean-Claude Fage, at the back of the classroom beside Hubert Jourdan, behind Jean-Pierre Cormier who is listening to me say:

"Today I should like to review how an event of great significance occurred—the sudden multiplication by two of the dimensions of the universe, the discovery and conquest of America . . . ",

is not the first cousin of his homonym, Henri Fage, that they didn't even know each other before meeting in class.

Of course the fact that they're both named Fage could be a simple coincidence, Fage could be a surname taken at different times, in different places, by two people without the slightest relation to each other;

it's even possible that originally there were two different surnames which were gradually distorted until they became more and more like each other;

and even if there had been a common ancestor, how far back would you have to go? There may have existed, at the end of the Fifteenth Century, two brothers or two cousins named Fage, who parted at the very moment when Columbus' ships left Cadiz for the first time in search of Cathay, and who never saw each other again, whose descendants never had any connection until the day when two of them converged on Paris, two of the children, or grandchildren (or who knows?) of the latter converged on the Lycée Taine and this eleventh-grade class.

Consequently, picking any teacher at random, for instance Monsieur Martin, who is at this moment teaching the ninth grade how to draw, it is quite possible that one of his eighteenth-century forebears met a Monsieur Fage of the branch to which Henri belongs, that another, in the Seventeenth Century, maintained a correspondence with another Fage from the branch to which Jean-Claude belongs, and that consequently, without any of the three realizing it, there is a closer link between these two pupils than the person, the common ancestor, to whom the identity of their name refers, if that ancestor even exists. One can even suppose alliances, marriages . . .

Since I began this description by taking you in groups of three, arranged according to the decreasing closeness of the degrees of relationship which constitute them, why not continue by associating Jean-Claude and Henri Fage, as the identity of their surnames suggests, and by adding to them, in order to complete the triad, any teacher, for example Monsieur Martin, merely by postulating among them a genealogical link even more remote than that which certain resemblances suggest between Monsieur du Marnet, Monsieur Tavera and Hubert Jourdan.

Henri Fage is sitting behind you, near the window, at the same desk with Jean-Pierre Cormier; he is hiding from me, I have a strong suspicion he isn't listening to what I am saying about Marco Polo, about India and China, about that distant splendor that reached Western Europe and lured men to travel.

I have the pleasure of feeling all the rest, around him, in this corner of the class which I keep under my eyes, captivated by my description, whether they have their eyes on me, on their notebooks in which they are writing, on their books that they have stopped reading, on the clouds in the sky, or on that old yellowed globe, forgotten on top of the cabinet.

He is studying something, probably his physics lesson for the next hour; his lips stir, his brows contract. I try to draw him away from it, I fix my eyes on him, raise my voice; I want to force him inside the circle of my discourse like the others.

Soon several of his schoolmates' heads turn toward him with an abrupt movement. His neighbor, Hubert Jourdan, nudges him with his elbow. He straightens up with an irritated expression, realizes that he is the center of attention, leans back over his desk, begins writing with exaggerated diligence.

Then his posture becomes more natural. He is listening now. I hold him for several minutes.

That was on Tuesday, October 12.

The Saint-Hilaire chimes rang four times.

In the amphitheater, Jean-Pierre Cormier, who was watching the movements of Denis Régnier sitting in front of him in the row below, gradually stuck out his elbows and leaned on his forearms, moving his head forward to try to see, despite his rather weak vision (he wears strong glasses), which stamps were in the notebook.

"What are you doing up there? Yes, I'm talking to you, at the back there; stand up! What's your name?"

"Cormier."

"What are you looking at over your friend's shoulder?"

"I can't see what's written on the board, Monsieur."

"Then why did you sit in the last row? There's still room down front. Take your books and come down here. I don't want this to happen again!"

Monsieur Hutter was reading *Egmont* with his seniors.

For Francis Hutter, who discovered that physics was a bore, the Cormier incident was a welcome diversion; he followed his classmate's descent and installation in the first row with interest. Then, when Monsieur Hubert turned back to the blackboard on which he had already drawn two axes of co-ordinates, and started talking again about dynamometers, elongations of springs, and curves of calibration, he read on the open page of his textbook that the weight of an adult man varied from sixty to a hundred kilograms, the weight of an empty freight car from ten to fifty tons, and instead of continuing to write in the margin of his notebook, he drew a tiny man, consisting of a dot and several lines, beside a tiny freight car.

He covered this first creature with ink and drew another inside the freight car.

Then came the weight of the Eiffel tower: eight million tons. He hitched the freight car to a tiny, carefully detailed locomotive, with piston rods and a plume of smoke, and framed the whole thing by the arch of an Eiffel tower whose flag he had to color in with the help of a red pencil he dug out from the bottom of his briefcase.

Looking up, he saw that the figure on the blackboard was now complete. Monsieur Hubert was talking about abscissas and ordinates, about the point M, and the force F. All of which reminded him of something, and he wished he had kept his notebooks from last year.

He would have liked to start taking notes again, but now the page was so full of illustrations that he would have to write on another and copy onto it what was already on this one.

Luckily it was one of those spiral-binding notebooks you could tear the pages out of without any difficulty. He would take care of that tonight; he would ask to borrow a friend's until tomorrow morning.

Monsieur Hubert was talking about initial points, intensity of forces, vectors.

After the weight of the Eiffel Tower came that of a trans-Atlantic steamer: fifty thousand tons. He drew the shoreline, made a little loop to represent a dock against which the waves were beating, and then a steamship with three smokestacks and a flag.

"A large transport plane, the Lockheed Constellation, weighs ninety-five tons."

The latter began to fly above the shore, decorated with brilliant cockades.

As for the tensile force of a horse, it averages seventy kilograms, but can increase to four hundred.

Four hundred, Francis thought, that's a tremendous difference.

He sat for several moments with his pen motionless, no, drawing a horse was really too hard, and he furiously crossed out everything he had just drawn.

The Saint-Hilaire chimes rang five times.

Going down the stairs, Francis Hutter stopped his usual neighbor in class, Alain Mouron, to borrow his physics notebook.

"What for?"

"To copy today's lesson."

"I didn't get it all."

"You got most of it."

"You won't be able to read my writing."

"All right, if you don't want to lend it to me, I'll ask someone else."

"Don't get mad. All I meant was that my notebook isn't a model."

"Well, who should I ask? Your cousin? Daval's your cousin, isn't he?"

"He's not a first cousin, he's just a cousin; but if you think he took a lot of notes . . . "

"Well?"

"Just use your book."

"But what if he looks at my notebook?"

"Where were you last year?"

"I was in Nancy. You had to have your notebook, and I had my physics one all done—I'm repeating, you know, I was sick . . . but I left it in Nancy."

"You come from the country, all right. With all the students he's got, you don't think he's going to bother taking the notebooks home with him! Don't give it a thought."

"Were you here last year?"

"No, I was in Bourges."

"That's the country too."

"I know, but my cousin told me what to do."

"Was he here then?"

"Not in this lycée but here in Paris. He lives near our uncle—you know Bailly, the English teacher."

"Do you know him well?"

"A little; and my cousin—you know, they live in the same street, the houses are right next door."

"Even though the German teacher's named Hutter and I think we're distantly related, I don't know him at all. Are you through?"

"No, I've got Abbé Gollier's class. Don't you?"

"Me? I'm a Protestant."

61

"No kidding!"

"What do you mean, no kidding?"

"Sorry, I didn't . . . "

"Well, see you tomorrow."

Alain Mouron crossed the courtyard on his way to Abbé Gollier's class, where the latter had already begun speaking, standing in the middle of the room, a sheet of paper in his hand.

Alain gently closed the door behind him; he went to sit down on one of the chairs that was still empty, looked at the furniture, the books in the shelves, the pictures on the wall, his classmates all around him, and he noticed that you, the leader of the Bison Patrol in the troop he belonged to, weren't there; that meant you thought the scout chaplain's lectures on Thursdays or Sundays were enough; Abbé Gollier's course was unnecessary; Alain Mouron decided he wouldn't come next week.

In the apartment in the Rue Pierre-Leroux, Monsieur Bailly stood up, furious, and went to the back bedroom.

"René, aren't you ashamed of teasing your little sister like that? You, Georges, what are you doing on that bed? Get down off there! Have you finished your homework for tomorrow?"

"She's the one who's bothering us!"

"Really! All right, Nisette, stop crying! Put your doll in your carriage and come back to the living room with me. Why did you need to bother with these two big blockheads anyway? Each of you sit down at your own desks; I don't want to hear another word. What homework do you have to do, René?"

"I finished my physics analysis, but I still have the problems."

"And the lessons?"

"A little history and some grammar."

"What about you, Georges?"

"I finished my copying; I have the exercises, I don't know how to do them."

"Just ask your brother to help you. Hurry up now; do you know what time it is? Almost five-thirty. I'm leaving the door open. You come and show me your notebooks when you're through."

He went back to his study. He opened the file that holds his notes on Wordsworth, a projected dissertation virtually untouched for years. Little Agnès, beside him, was undressing her doll.

The key turned in the lock of the street door. At the same moment Georges cried out:

"Papa, René won't let me work!"

Elizabeth Bailly, taking off her coat at the same time, rushed to the back bedroom and gave each of the boys a slap. Then she went into the living room where her husband was standing, waiting for her, hands spread wide, palms up.

"Do you imagine the children will work if you don't watch them? Anyone would think you'd never taught school! Agnès, come over here. You mustn't distract your father."

"This apartment is really too small. We can't go on like this."

"There's nothing I'd like better than to find another place, but I just don't have time to deal with it now. All right, Agnès, did you hear me?"

The little girl began to cry.

"Oh, now don't start that again. Come here right this minute. We'll go see what's happening in the kitchen."

"Oh, leave her here. Anyway, I have to go out. I have an appointment."

"You're terrible. How do you expect . . . "

"All right, all right, I know. Do whatever you want. See you later."

He took his raincoat off the hook, but only put it on after he had slammed the door behind him.

He turned into the Rue de Sèvres; the lights in the shop windows were being turned on. He went into a café to telephone Claire, who wasn't there; he decided to take a walk around Saint-Germain-des-Près to wait until she was likely to return.

Michel Daval didn't know what to do with his hands. Sitting on a chair in Abbé Gollier's study, he was listening to the latter describe the various parts of the Mass; but there was no way of taking notes or reading in secret or making little drawings. He twisted his fingers around the handle of his briefcase. stretched his neck to the right to try and see the face of the clock ticking on the desk, on top of a pile of books bound in black cloth, looked at his classmates one after the other, trying to find a reason to smile, to seem one of them. The daylight was growing dim. The ceiling light had had to be turned on. Through the barred window, the gray plaster wall could still be seen.

Abbé Gollier turned around, raised his hand as if he were in the pulpit, examined his students' faces one after the other, and their hands, Michel Daval's were hidden under his briefcase until it fell to the floor with a thud, opened; the *Sixteenth Century French Authors*, the *New Course in History for Eleventh Grade*, the *Physics*

Textbook and the October issue of the magazine *Fiction* fell out on the unwaxed floor.

Abbé Gollier waited until the interruption was past before discussing communion.

The next Wednesday, I too had in my briefcase that *Physics Textbook* for the eleventh grade, and its twin, the *Chemistry Textbook*, as well as the *Physics Textbook* for seniors, which I had also bought that morning, because I knew, having consulted my colleagues' schedules, that it was this class that Monsieur Hubert had been teaching the day before, Tuesday the twelfth, between three and four, and I wanted to be able to grasp what he was doing, where he was at that moment, where he was coming from when he met you the following hour—a book by the same author as yours, but much thicker, and obviously much more detailed.

I also had the Italian textbook Monsieur Bonnini uses.

After eating lunch in a Greek restaurant in the Rue de l'École-de-Médicine, I brought this entire harvest back to my apartment in the Rue du Canivet and put it on my big desk beside the pile of schoolbooks I had already bought in order to prepare these notes, the *Sixteenth Century French Authors* and its brothers, those of the Seventeenth, Eighteenth and Nineteenth Centuries, and the *Anthology of English Literature* Monsieur Bailly uses.

I took my own class books, the ones I needed for my afternoon classes this Wednesday the thirteenth, since I had neglected to prepare these classes, too busy, the day before, getting this project under way, counting on the fact that I had already given similar courses so many times:

the *Medieval Europe* for the eighth grade, with the picture of a Gothic hall with two rows of pillars printed on the cover in blue and yellow on a gray background,

the *New Course in Geography* for your class, with the photograph of a valley bordered with terraced rice paddies,

Contemporary Civilization for the seniors, a paperback book with a drawing of the Eiffel Tower,

and I walked past Saint-Sulpice toward the lycée.

Monsieur Bonnini went to buy a new suitcase for his wife, for the one she had taken with her to Provence had lost one of its metal corners on the way home, and he wanted her to have something suitable for her stay in the hospital.

His daughter went with him, her time still free since courses at the

Sorbonne hadn't started yet. He wouldn't have been able to decide by himself; they went from shop to shop along the Boulevard Saint-Germain, he didn't even see the articles offered for sale. She finally decided on a rather expensive one made of black leather lined with silk. When they brought it back to the apartment in the Rue du Cardinal-Lemoine, Geneviève, who had already laid out the nightgowns, the bathrobe, the toilet articles and a few books on the dining-room table, had a fit of nausea.

He decided: "We should never have chosen this color, this black." He sat down in an armchair, his hands on his knees. He stared at the floorboards.

Denis Régnier was waiting in the gym for the bell to ring, for this class to be over at last.

He watched his schoolmates play; he was panting so hard his chest hurt around his heart, and he was ashamed of this fatigue, of this pain, of this incapacity.

He sensed a few ironic glances, and he began to burn with a terrible desire to be strong, to be able to fight, to avenge himself on the others' superiority, their ability to climb the rope he had never reached the top of, to balance, arms rigid, on the parallel bars. It was as if he had drunk a mouthful of acid.

He clenched his teeth. He would have liked to see them fall and break their bones, or a leprosy eat away their skin, find a way—a drug, a trap—of making them as fallible as he, the repeater, not the only repeater in the class, actually, but for all his last year's professors, "the" repeater,

to lure them into an impasse, leader of a gang over whom he would have complete authority because of some knowledge, some exceptional weapon, some superiority recognized in the boldness of his plan, his scorn for law and order, holding them at his mercy, seeing the fear in their eyes, forcing them to beg him for favors.

"All right, go get dressed," Monsieur Moret shouted.

Denis Régnier went to put his jacket back on; he felt in his inside pocket for his notebook of duplicate stamps. He was back among his classmates who jostled each other toward the door, but he no longer understood why he had been so furious with them just now, thinking as he climbed the stairs:

I mustn't bother about gym any more; what's gym? Just fix it so that the teacher has no reason to be mad at me. I'll never be first in anything. Just fix it so I don't have to repeat the eleventh grade again.

My father's left my mother, and he doesn't care about me; he always tells me I'll never be good for anything, but someday I'll be good for telling him I despise him and that new wife of his who keeps trying to get around me. And I'll make these boys envy me with my stamps. The bell.

Jean-Pierre Cormier, who had laid on his open textbook the notebook of duplicate stamps Denis Régnier had just passed him, taking advantage of one of my moments of inadvertence, examined at close range the stamps slipped under the five little strips of transparent paper on the double page:

to the left, at the top, under the inscription Panama, a Prussian-blue rectangle, with the portrait of a general, tiny palms embroidered on his collar, a huge medal on his chest, and underneath, his name: Simon Bolivar,

in the second row, two stamps from San Salvador, a country you could make out next to Honduras on a gray 15-centavo stamp from the latter country, in the row underneath,

as, lower down, around Bolivia, in a sky-blue 25-centavo stamp from that country, Peru, Brazil, Argentina and Chile,

then, at the very bottom, Bolivar again, on Colombia, but he looked no more like the one on the Republic of Panama than the bust of Caesar in the geography classroom looked like the picture in the English textbook;

to the right, in the top corner: United States, three rows down, Philippines, then Alaska,

here, just one stamp, purple, three cents, a landscape:

in front of a snowy mountain, a few pines, a little village, and a tiny laborer in the middle, pushing his plow behind an animal that was either a horse or an ox.

That was the first time Jean-Pierre Cormier had ever seen a stamp from Alaska; folding back not only the notebook but the page of the geography book on which it was resting, he pointed to it and questioned Denis Régnier with a look.

The latter answered with a movement of his lip that congratulated him on his taste, raising the thumb and index finger of his right hand to indicate that he had no intention of trading such a stamp except for two others.

Jean-Pierre Cormier shrugged. It was at this point that I intervened, getting off my platform and walking down the row to their desks.

"You will both spend two hours here tomorrow. Give me that. Oh, it's yours, Régnier! I'll give it back to you Saturday, after you've taken your punishment."

I went back to my desk.

"The Mercator projection is made with a cylinder, but one can also use a cone . . ."

Not another whisper could be heard. All heads were bent over the notebooks. Jean-Pierre Cormier glanced right and left several times, parading an indifference he didn't feel, but meeting no response he leafed through his textbook, then resigned himself to writing in his notebook: "conic projection"; a few minutes later, correcting himself, he added an s to the word projection.

What was Monsieur Hutter making his eighth-graders do?

Francis was far away, in a Lorrainese cemetery, under trees whose last leaves the wind was tearing off, sending them fluttering past the orange hills beneath the shreds of clouds; he was wearing a beige raincoat with a black armband, walking beside his brother Jean-Louis and his sister Adèle, following his father and mother, both of them grief-stricken,

staring at the pebbles in the path, sincerely trying to remember something about this grandfather shut up in the box they were going to let down into the grave at the end of the path.

The clock in the steeple said five minutes to four above the wall and the branches; his mind turned back to the bell that would end the geography class, to his neighbor at the desk, Alain Mouron, whose afternoon would be over, whereas his own, an ordinary Wednesday, would be continued for another hour, an hour of German with that Monsieur Hutter who was a distant relative, but whom he hadn't seen at the funeral, who still didn't know about the death of this grandfather, who would probably not receive the announcement until the next day.

Alain Mouron walked past the porch of Saint-Hilaire, he walked past a clothing store decorated with big mirrors, he saw himself reflected in one, stopped, examined his gray-blue eyes, his thick lashes, his rather long nose, trying out several smiles, giving himself a severe look, then a playful one; he noticed, behind his own shoulder, the faces of several people walking by, an old lady who looked scandalized, a tall, fat man in a gray overcoat who laughed at him, a North African whose cheeks and forehead were covered with adhesive tape, making a kind of knight's helmet with two slits for eyes that stared at his reflection as though trying to hypnotize him.

He started walking again, running his finger along the walls, and he remembered his hair. His father had told him today for the third time that he must go to the barber.

The next day was Thursday; the day after that, they would go to the playing field in the morning; there was only a little Greek to prepare (that was the hardest), Homer, the *Odyssey*, the beginning of Book VI, starting where they had left off this morning, Ulysses hidden in the reeds had fallen asleep covered with leaves, that was hard, the next page was called Nausicaa's Dream, what was she going to dream about?

from the beginning down to line 23, old Jouret didn't do things by halves, a little Greek, if you could call it that;

then some grammar to learn, of course, still those damn verbs, a little Greek . . . ,

and a little French, but that was nothing, all he had to read was "the study of Gargantua according to the study . . .", well, something like that, there were a lot of incomprehensible words but . . .

but, but, but . . . ;

so there was no need to be in such a hurry; it would be better to take advantage of the good weather, spend some time looking for a nice barbershop, in other words, one where there were a lot of magazines, more than in the one on the Rue du Pré-aux-Clercs, where there was really nothing to do while you were waiting except twiddle your thumbs . . .

He decided on the Rue Saint-Sulpice (what did that North African want, anyway, with his black look between the strips of adhesive tape, his nose covered with tape, his hungry stare?), and he finally pushed open a glass door on which was written in old enamel letters: HAIRCUTS FOR LADIES AND GENTLEMEN.

Three men in white smocks were wielding their scissors. Four people were already waiting on straw chairs, but on a little rattan stand there was a big pile of old magazines with torn covers.

As he was beginning to look through them, he noticed that in front of the mirror, on one of the chairs, that boy getting a shampoo was one of his classmates, one of the ones in back, whose name he didn't know yet.

He kept winking at him, but the other boy didn't even look at his reflection, he was carefully following the slow course of a fly across the ceiling.

He jumped to his feet when the barber took away the white towel, wet now where the little hairs stuck to it, stopped a minute at the cash register to pay, then vanished outside. Alain Mouron went back to his pictures of the United States, a highway intersection outside New York, the Brooklyn Bridge, shoeshine boys, the iron balconies of New Orleans, the many-colored clothes on a university campus, a trolley in San Francisco.

René Bailly, alone in his Rue Pierre-Leroux apartment, turned around in his living room, stopping in front of his wife's desk, a little mahogany Directoire piece with two drawers (his own, bought before his marriage, was walnut-stained maple and covered with scratches), two locked drawers that fascinated him,

(he looked for the key along the shelves of the little bookcase beside it, behind the books, in the bedroom cupboards, the mirrored wardrobe, under the piles of his wife's lingerie, her stockings, trying to put everything back in place, in the kitchen, opening the larder, the tea can, the sugar can, coming back to the living room),

"She must have taken the key with her in her bag; if only I could know if it was still in the lock last week; did she happen to suspect that today I would feel like looking? maybe it was when she came back from Orléans that she decided she'd better take precautions; but that means she really has something to hide, letters she wants to keep and that she doesn't want me to read."

Then he hunted up all the keys in the house, those to the cupboards and those to the drawers, and he tried them all, one after the other. Some went in, but couldn't turn. He put them back, and this took him a long time.

It was too late to telephone Claire now. Quarter to; it was time to go to the Aulnoy lycée to call for little Agnès who must have been waiting a good quarter of an hour already. The boys, René and Georges, were coming out of the Lycée Buffon at this very moment; they wouldn't be surprised to find no one there, would start home, and if they took their time, there was a chance he would meet them at the Duroc intersection or in the Rue de Sèvres; otherwise they would find the apartment locked.

Out in the street, he caught sight of his nephew, Michel Daval, who was on his way home, going into the building next door, his briefcase under his arm, obviously quite light, since all he had inside was his notebook and his *Geography Textbook*; he was looking through another book that he was holding in his hands, and when he passed his uncle he blushed and tried to hide it; too late; Monsieur Bailly, with a teacher's reflex, snatched it away; he read the title:

"The Odyssey, Homeric poem, Volume One, Books One to Seven, translation by Victor Bérard."

"Now there's good reading for you, my boy! And what does Monsieur Jouret think of that?"

"Someone lent it to me."

"Oh, someone lent it to you? You just went and bought it on your way home from school, didn't you? Don't bother trying to lie. Well, you'll go far, my boy!"

"Don't . . . Don't . . . "

"Hurry up now, go home, your mother must be wondering what you're up to. You're lucky I'm in a hurry, otherwise I'd come up with you."

He handed back the book and walked off, taking long strides, his expression severe. Michel Daval remained stunned for a moment; he couldn't understand why his uncle, who had just found him out, had left him this book he hid in his briefcase before climbing the stairs.

In the apartment, his mother greeted him with loud cries:

"Well, where have you been? We were expecting you. Don't you leave the lycée at four on Wednesdays? We have news for you."

His sister Lucie was standing behind her, beaming.

"You found an apartment?"

"Yes, we just found it, near Saint-Sulpice; we went there together, the two of us. We telephoned your father at his office. Of course he has to see it for himself, but we're sure, aren't we, Lucie? He'll like it; it's so much better than anything we've seen for the price. At last we'll have a real bathroom. And it's empty, we could get in right away, it was repainted quite recently. It belonged to an American woman who had to go back to her country quite suddenly. A real piece of luck!"

"Can we go see it tonight after dinner, or when Papa comes home?"

"No, we have to wait till tomorrow. We have an appointment with the agent early in the afternoon, and your father said he would arrange to be free."

On Thursday, before going at three to the attic headquarters of the Bison Patrol on the Quai des Grands-Augustins, overlooking the Seine and Notre-Dame, you went to your room in the Rue du Canivet apartment, worried about how you were going to entertain your classmates. You looked through your little bookcase for the scouting manual, between the *Sixteenth Century French Authors* and the October number of the magazine *Fiction* that Michel Daval had lent you. New to the job, you needed help and advice; you had been second in command all last year, but that wasn't the same thing; there wasn't the same responsibility . . . Your patrol leader had missed only one patrol meeting, because of tonsillitis; you had had to lead the group, but you had asked him for instructions and you had done everything he had told you to do.

Today you would have to decide how to decorate headquarters, set up a schedule; last year, the Bison Patrol had never finished anything; by July, the attic room they used for their meetings still had for its only ornament, along with a few old Louis-Philippe pieces that the parents of the lender had left there—a bed with its box spring, three chairs whose upholstery had a lot of rips, and a shaky stand with a dark-gray marble shelf—a few dried leaves from different trees pasted on a piece of warped cardboard and a collection of knots executed in red and green string, fastened with thumbtacks to a beaverboard rectangle painted black. It was not presentable: they had never dared invite either the leaders or other patrols. They would have to settle this matter, but they would also have to organize a program of studies to help the new Scouts, the ones who had just joined the troop or the movement, to pass the tests that would permit them to take their pledge, and the tests that would entitle them to be Second-Class Scouts, and then First-Class Scouts.

Looking through your manual, you decided to organize a game of Concentration, and you collected various objects which you slipped into the pockets of the handsome leather jacket your parents had given you the day before, on Tuesday, October 12, for your fifteenth birthday:

a handkerchief, a piece of string, a box of matches, a penknife, an ordinary canceled stamp, your wallet, your songbook, the key to the headquarters, a little blue pencil with a chewed-off tip, a safety pin, a whistle.

Closing your desk drawer, you decided you needed something else, and you went to search through the kitchen, taking a jar top out of the cupboard, and from one of the plates next to the sink a bone with a hole in it from which you could later make an elegant scarf ring.

You came back to the living room to say goodbye to the Jouret family and to thank your Uncle Henri once again for the fine pen he had just given you.

On the way, you picked up the little pebble between the roots of a tree.

I was drinking my coffee at the Mabillon, thinking about these notes which I am writing for you, for the person you will have become in a few years, who will have forgotten all this, but for whom all this and a thousand other things, will come back to mind by reading this, in a certain order and according to certain forms and systems that will allow you to grasp and fix it, to situate and appreciate it, which you are incapable of doing for the moment, lacking that system of references which we are trying to inculcate,

so that a new awareness can be born in you, and so you will become able to grasp precisely this enormous mass of information in which, as in a muddy and tumultuous river, you move, ignorant, swept away,

that slides over you, wastes itself, loses itself, and contradicts itself,

that slides over us all, over all your schoolmates and all your teachers who are mutually ignorant of each other,

that slides between us and around us.

My tooth was hurting me despite all the aspirin that I had taken and that made my head heavy, my eyes watery.

Holding my cheek in my hand, I headed down the Boulevard Saint-Germain, swaying along the edge of the sidewalk, just missing the people walking the other way, toward the waiting room of the dentist, Monsieur Hubert, in the Rue du Pré-aux-Clercs.

Alain Mouron had a patrol meeting in the building where he lived, your Uncle Henri's building, next door to the one where I was.

Alone in the apartment, he had opened the door for his classmates, one after the other; they had climbed up to the seventh floor together.

Only one was missing, a newcomer whom they had seen for the first time the Sunday before and who had seemed quite frightened. They tacked on the door, under the visiting card, this little message for him:

You're late; we're on the seventh floor, room 15. Get moving.
CHAMOIS.

Alain Mouron led the way, the bunch of keys in his hand, very much the owner showing off his property; and yet this was only the second time he had climbed up to this room.

He observed the effect that the long, winding corridors made on his friends. He opened the door,

"There it is."

It was an attic room, very small, lit only by a dusty skylight, cobwebby, empty, the walls covered with a mauve-flowered paper, of which a wide flap had come unstuck and fallen back, revealing the swollen plaster eroded by humidity.

"There's no electricity," the leader remarked. "We've looked, but there's just no electricity."

"It doesn't matter; in winter we could bring an oil lamp."

"We'll have to bring an oil stove too, otherwise we'll freeze to death up here. And you know how oil smells! Can we open that skylight?"

"I never tried."

They tried, but low as the ceiling was, they couldn't manage to reach it. They tried boosting each other up, they reached the catch, but hadn't strength enough, in that position, to release it.

"Well, the first thing we'll need here is chairs. You don't happen to have extra chairs in your apartment, do you? Or stools? Or boxes? What about you? Nothing? Think about it a minute! The best thing would be to take big logs. I think there's some wood in the cellar at home, but I don't know if the pieces will be big enough. We could go down and see. And if there are, we'll bring them up, and that'll be that."

Alain Mouron closed the door behind him. The whole patrol went down four steps at a time to look for these logs which were pronounced magnificent, exactly what was needed, and transported to the Rue du Pré-aux-Clercs in a little two-wheeled cart borrowed from the Saint-Hilaire church guild.

Each Chamois carried his log up the stairs. They were heavy and required many stops. It left a lot of dust and splinters on the carpet.

"That's a good beginning," the leader said, "we'll be able to fix this up just right. Bravo Alain!"

Hands on his hips, he surveyed the room around him; it was obvious that from now on he was the true owner. But Alain Mouron was wondering how this would all end, for things had gone much faster than he had thought, and he was careful not to reveal that he hadn't yet spoken to his father.

Elizabeth Bailly had just gone to the Jardin des Plantes with her children. Her husband, who had pretended to start working, spreading out his notes, opening his Wordsworth, as soon as silence had fallen in the apartment, the footsteps fading on the stairs, pushed everything away and reached for the telephone.

"Claire, I have to see you. I tried to reach you several times yesterday. Something new has come up. I can't talk about it on the phone, it's too complicated. Are you free this afternoon?"

"Right now?"

"Yes, I'll take the métro and be there right away."

His raincoat, his cigarettes in his pocket, his plaid muffler, his belt buckle;

the Rue Pierre-Leroux, the Rue de Sèvres, the Vaneau station after the Egyptian fountain, opposite the Lazarite chapel,

the ticket handed in at the window, the blue enamel plaque with the list of stops printed in white, the Auteuil line, the steps, the walls covered with white ceramic tile, the platform with the little booth for the station chief, the big posters advertising wines or detergents;

the train, the doors opening, the sighs of compressed air,

Duroc, Ségur, La Motte-Picquet, Émile-Zola;

the trees covered with yellowing leaves, the wide 1910 or 1920 housefronts, the old elevator.

"You're in the middle of work; I'm sorry to bother you. Let me catch my breath. Yes, pour me a little coffee. Don't bother to heat it again. That bird's lovely—for Hermès too? I think you're making progress every day. About Elizabeth . . . "

In the empty apartment in the Rue Servandoni, Monsieur Daval looked at his watch,

"I have to get to my office. This all looks fine to me. I'd like a little more time to think about it, of course. I'll telephone you tomorrow morning, say, to give you my final decision. I'd like things to be done quickly."

"But of course, Monsieur, it'll be very easy, Monsieur, my client would like to complete the arrangements as soon as possible too, as soon as I have your decision I'll call her lawyer. Goodbye, Monsieur."

"You're not coming, Germaine?"

"No, I'd like to stay a little longer and look around, if you're not in a hurry, Monsieur. We'll measure the rooms, if you don't mind. It's always better to know before rather than after, isn't it?"

"Of course, Madame, do whatever you like, Madame, you are absolutely right; I'll merely ask your permission to leave for a few minutes to make a telephone call."

"Speaking of the telephone . . . "

"Oh, it works, it works; all you have to do is continue paying the rates."

"Well, that's fine, Monsieur, we'll be here at least half an hour; we won't leave the premises. Michel, take that yardstick and let's get to work."

"I'll see you later."

"I'll go down with you. I'll be back directly then, Madame, Mademoiselle, Monsieur."

The three of them were alone now in the largest of the four rooms, the one with two windows overlooking the street, the roof of the building opposite, above which, between two chimneys, they could have glimpsed the windows on the courtyard of your parents' apartment in the Rue du Canivet; but Michel Daval didn't realize this.

He was measuring the length and height of the walls, dictating the figures to his sister Lucie, who was writing them down in a little notebook, while their mother was walking up and down, commenting:

"It's practically new; the paint, the bathroom . . . It's all been put in working order. There's not a bulb in the place, we can't tell how the switches work. Oh, Michel, you go down and buy one when you're done with this room. Lucie and I will manage the rest."

"There, that's done. Do you want the measurements of the mantelpiece and the mirror?"

"Yes, you'd better; we have to find out what we're dealing with; that fireplace is dreadful, but if it's a hard winter we might be glad to have it. Here, take my wallet, and hurry."

Michel Daval went down the stairs four at a time, ran across the Place Saint-Sulpice with a feeling of extreme lightness, banking like a plane, crossing from one sidewalk to the other, narrowly missing the cars whose drivers shouted at him without his paying any attention to them, examining the shop windows; passing the terrace of a café, he recognized, at a round table, the real-estate agent, who was smoking a little cigar, sipping a glass of beer, looking quite pleased with himself, rubbing his hands together with a smile.

Then Michel Daval decided:

"Yes, this is where we're going to live, now it's only a question of days; we'll have to pack, wrap everything up . . . "

He wasn't running now; hands in his pockets, his right hand holding his mother's wallet, he was thinking as he walked, whistling, down the Rue Bonaparte.

Monday, while your Uncle Henri, on the other side of the wall behind me, was making his class read Saint-Simon's portrait of the Princesse d'Harcourt:

" . . . a type of person whom it is agreeable to meet . . . ",
you were looking through your Geography Textbook, stopping at
the chapter I was going to discuss,
   pictures:
   the ice breaking up in the Saint Lawrence near Quebec: a few
roofs with pointed steeples and a weather vane, the white blocks
shifting down the river, and the other bank covered with snow under
a gray sky,
   two landscapes in the same latitude: above, a Nova Scotian village
during the long winter (eastern coast of the continent): low houses
among conifers on a hillside under a cloudy sky, fence posts indicating
the limits of fields or pastures, punctuations on the page of the slope,
striped with long shadows, with the delicate design of some bushes,
probably thorny ones,
   underneath, a pine forest on the dunes near Arcachon during the
mild winter (western coast of the continent): the trees parasols
against the bright sky (that is, dark gray in the photograph, indicating
blue), the sand along the shore gleaming against the calm sea.
   I asked Pelletier to tell me about longitude, how a navigator took
bearings.
   Régnier, remembering his classes of the year before, managed to
get through the Mercator projection.
   Spencer had retained only vague notions as to the representation
of elevations.
   Today, I fascinated my seventh-graders,
   the Pyramids, Luxor, the treasures of Tutankhamen, and the bas-
reliefs of the tomb of Ti at Sakkara;
   I saw their eyes open wide, and the longing to travel spread from one
head to the next, like a fire from tree to tree in a dry forest.
   Your Uncle Henri handed back your compositions on the most
memorable day of your vacation, criticizing your account of the
opening of the cabin in the Herrecourt woods in such a way that
it was not apparent he was one of the actors, not discussing the
facts, or the situation of the places you were describing, which he
nevertheless knew better than you, not pointing out any errors of
this kind, speaking with detachment, as if he knew nothing about it,
merely pointing out errors of language, saying that at this point he
couldn't understand exactly what had happened, whereas he knew
as well as you,

which was natural, of course, if one took the whole class into account, but still seemed unfair to you, disturbed you, gave you a feeling of uneasiness and discouragement, making you worry about your next composition.

While Michel Daval pretends to be listening to me explain the word mercantilism, I know that his mind is elsewhere, that he is with the movers carrying crates, trunks and furniture from the Rue Pierre-Leroux to the Rue Servandoni, where he won't sleep tonight, but certainly by tomorrow; he tries to imagine his new room, the location of his desk and his books.

Monsieur Bailly and his seniors begin *The Rime of the Ancient Mariner,*

"Notice the archaism of all the terms of this title. If we were to translate this as merely: *The Story of the Old Sailor,* (as you will find it in many French editions), you lose all the color, all the unusual flavor of these words. You are now far enough along not to be satisfied with the literal meaning, as it is given by the dictionary, of the object designated, you must also consider the way it is designated . . . "

Alain Mouron writes down what I say about the pirates and buccaneers, his text open under his eyes, with two old prints reproduced on the right-hand page:

"The Mines of the Potosi:

in this mountain of the Andes which they have tunneled through, almost naked Indians are digging out the silver-bearing seams by torchlight; others carry the ore outside, where is it loaded on donkeys,

planter's house in the Antilles:

in the background, the master's house; under sheds, the slaves work at the preparation of the *petun* (tobacco) or the grinding of manioc flour."

▉▉▉▉▉▉▉▉▉▉▉▉▉▉ I HAVE ALREADY situated for this hour from three to four, on Tuesday, October 12, not only all the teachers that you yourself have in class, but also those who teach your classmates, who instruct them in German, Italian or Spanish, except for Monsieur Moret, the gym teacher, and Abbé Gollier, who obviously has a special status:

I have already presented in these notes, brought onto the stage, in a manner of speaking, nine of you out of thirty-one, and what I would like to do, of course, is to furnish portraits of each, locate each of you within the school framework. There are a few others who have more or less stuck their heads in the door, but only incidentally, as a kind of background, without the lens being focused on them yet.

Up to now, I have been able to deal with these characters in triads, two teachers and one student: you, your Uncle Henri, me; Monsieur Bonnini, Monsieur Hubert, Denis Régnier; Monsieur du Marnet, Monsieur Tavera, Hubert Jourdan; or else two students and one professor: Alain Mouron, Michel Daval, Monsieur Bailly; Francis Hutter, Jean-Pierre Cormier, Monsieur Hutter, because of the degrees of relationship uniting them.

After these five groups, I have constituted a sixth one within which these relationships—despite that snare, the identity of two surnames —are of an indefinite degree, equivalent, as far as I know, to those that might exist between any two students taken at random and one of their teachers in any class of any lycée: Jean-Claude Fage, Henri Fage, Monsieur Martin, who, in this regard, are distinguished only by the fact that an external circumstance makes me take them as an example.

It is obvious, therefore, that I must find for your schoolmates, if I want to go on taking them by groups, other principles of connection, but there still remains one possibility that I want to exploit for these two remaining teachers (not exactly teachers, one actually more of a monitor, the other called a chaplain),

which is to present them at the same time as a student with whom I have every reason to suppose that they have still fewer family ties than any of the others, that their common origin is even more remote;

now, the only thing that could justify imagining such a separation,

78

without there being the slightest certainty (surprises will be welcome), is a difference in race;

it is therefore his dark skin that makes me choose Maurice Tangala, considering, unless some correction is brought forward, that there is more likelihood of a relationship among any of your classmates we shall discuss in the pages to come than among Maurice Tangala and Monsieur Moret or Abbé Gollier, almost as much as between Jean-Claude and Henri Fage, less than between Hubert Jourdan and Monsieur du Marnet.

Monsieur Moret is not at the lycée. I don't even know his address, but I can ask for it at the office. I don't think I have ever spoken to him. Is he married? I neglected to notice if he wore a wedding ring. I must get all this in order, but whatever my efforts, I know in advance that I have too few sources of information concerning him ever to manage to find out exactly where he is during this second hour of the afternoon, on Tuesday, October 12; and yet he must be somewhere, he must be thinking about something; he has problems, or plans. You see, if I leave this compartment almost blank it is because I have too few elements to move my imagination in one direction rather than in another, but you know that it would have to be filled somehow.

For Maurice Tangala, it's a different story. He's in the same classroom as you and I; I see him in the last row, beside Jacques Estier, with whom he usually whispers, but he's not whispering now,

for he is a Negro from the Caribbean, and this whole lesson about America, about the discovery of America, about the tragedy of America, America's vengeance, America's riddle, affects him especially,

but even if he came directly from Africa, I think this lesson would interest him differently from the rest of you, for by the mere fact of his color he would attach himself to anything that can separate him from Europe, from the white men, from all of us who differ from him by this detail which is the sign of so many other differences, this pigment in his grainy skin,

this exclusivity of civilization which it continues to arrogate to itself, despite all the proofs which it has unearthed, and which it continues to seek and produce, nourishing this contradiction, this great fissure, this great lie which saps and undermines it.

So for the moment, if I speak of this desire that led Christopher Columbus to sail for the Indies, if I try to rekindle in your minds that obsession with gold and the great shining cities (not yet describ-

79

ing either Mexico nor Cuzco, unknown at the time, making clear that what was in question was Asia, and more particularly China and its silk, Cathay, the character whose fabulous countenance appears among you, by the power of the quotations from Marco Polo which I read to you, being not Montezuma but Kubla Khan:

" . . . A great palace all of bamboo set on gilded and varnished pillars . . . built in such a manner that he can readily have it taken down and carried where he wishes; and when it is reconstructed, more than two hundred strong ropes of silk maintain it on all sides, even as a tent . . ."),

I see his black face, his dark lips smile quite differently from yours.

Abbé Gollier, in his office, is preparing this afternoon's lesson, the first lesson of his course on the Mass, that lesson you will not attend; and he knows there will not be many of you; last week, he remembers, there were only twenty-five students for the entire eleventh-grade. That is why he circulates another announcement.

That was a month ago.

At the end of the physics class, Hubert Jourdan, sitting just behind Francis Hutter, was looking over the latter's shoulder at the drawings by which he illustrated the chart on page 13 of his textbook: order of magnitude of various forces.

After the big transport plane, he was expecting the plow horse and its harness, but instead of this drawing he saw his classmate furiously cross out the little train, the Eiffel Tower and the Lockheed Constellation.

Hubert Jourdan also felt unable to draw a horse, but there still remained another line of the chart without an illustration: tensile force of a locomotive: 4,800 kilograms in movement, 6,300 standing still.

Of course Francis Hutter had drawn one in front of the freight car he had then framed under the arch of the Eiffel Tower, but all that was crossed out now.

That is why, on the same page of his textbook, above the illustration showing a boat in front of a dock and a horizon marked by several trees and triangles that could be interpreted as haystacks or houses, beside the title of the third part of the chapter: the elements of a force, representation by vectors, he began to draw a locomotive with its piston rods; then, as he looked up toward the ceiling where he saw the lamps, he decided that he wasn't sure if he was drawing a steam locomotive or an electric one;

consequently, on the other side of the figure 3 he drew a long rectangle with windows, which he set on two tracks and provided with a trolley sliding, as indicated by a few parallel lines representing not only movement but speed, along a wire supported by pylons with cross bars.

Next week Monsieur Hubert would explain Chapter 3, Concurrent Forces, and would have them write out one of the exercises ending this chapter. A word to the wise, then—those who have prepared them will have a great advantage . . .

The black triangle at the end of the minute hand of the clock over the door covered the figure 11. The bell rang in the amphitheater, as in every classroom.

Monsieur du Marnet, after having looked at the blackboard on which he had just drawn the locus of the equidistant points of two given points, said to his tenth-graders:

"Class dismissed."

Great hubbub of books closing, briefcases fastening, footsteps and conversations. He watched the classroom emptying. The last student, on his way out the door, turned around and hesitated a moment, as if he wanted to ask a question, or as if he were curious to know what this mathematics professor was going to do in front of the blackboard once he was left alone, freed of the obligation of watching and teaching them, what mysterious operation he was going to perform;

but Monsieur du Marnet waited until he was absolutely alone to correct the vertical line he had drawn, and to join to it, with a piece of green chalk he found on the floor, two tiny leaves, one on each side, inspired by lilac leaves, then to erase everything.

He took his hat off the rack, buttoned up his coat, closed his black leather briefcase; as he walked down the stairs and through the hall, he greeted several of his colleagues, including myself, then headed for the Odéon métro stop, where he took the Porte de Clignancourt line to the Château-d'Eau station in order to get to his apartment at number 7, Rue des Petites-Écuries.

In his Rue du Cardinal-Lemoine apartment, Monsieur Bonnini saw the doctor, Monsieur Limours, to the door.

"She must be operated on as soon as possible—it would be best before the end of the week. Do you know a surgeon?"

"A surgeon?"

"You've never had an operation yourself?"

"Yes, when I was a child, the . . . "

"I mean recently."

"Recently? No."

"You have no surgeon in your family?"

"In my family?"

"Yes, a brother, a cousin, anyone?"

"No, I don't think so, no."

"As far as private hospitals are concerned, you don't . . . "

"Private hospitals? No . . ."

"Then the simplest thing is to take her to the city hospital, but you have almost no chance of getting a private room. If you don't mind the ward . . ."

"Yes . . . What should I do?"

"Listen, I want you to know the truth; don't worry, there's a very good chance; I've seen complete cures in cases like this, and very quickly too; but it's rather urgent nevertheless. Do you want me to take care of it?"

"You could take care of it? Now?"

"I still have several visits to make, but I think I can arrange it. You'll be here tonight, of course? Could you have her taken to the hospital tomorrow, in the afternoon?"

"Tomorrow? That would be fine for me, I'm free all day. I have no classes at the lycée, and in any case, you think . . . "

"Fine, I'll telephone you tonight after dinner. You can count on me."

"Thank you. Doctor, you've been extremely kind, and I'm, I'm . . . "

"All right then, I'll call tonight. Don't worry."

"Goodbye, thank you again, telephone as soon as you can . . . "

The doctor made a little gesture with his hand as he was going down the stairs. His head was hidden by a step. Monsieur Bonnini gently closed the door and went back to the kitchen to speak to his sister-in-law Geneviève.

"He seems to be a good man, that doctor. He told me he would take care of everything. She'll leave for the hospital tomorrow. He'll telephone tonight after dinner to tell us exactly . . . All we have to do is wait."

"Fine. All we have to do is wait. I hope it won't be too long."

"I'll go tell her now. It won't come as a surprise. It may all turn out fine, you know. We can hope for the best."

"Of course we can, relax, wipe your eyes before going into her

82

room; you mustn't let her see you with a face like that. What she needs most of all is confidence, and for that you have to have confidence too. You can see he's an excellent doctor, he has a fine reputation, otherwise I wouldn't have recommended him to you in the first place."

"I've never had much to do with doctors up to now. When are the children coming home?"

"They'll be here for dinner; they didn't tell me anything different."

"They couldn't even think of leaving their friends to come home early . . ."

"What good would it do? They're as upset as you are; they don't dare come home because they want to encourage you, console you, help you a little; so they're trying to compose themselves. You should go to her now. She's probably counting the minutes, worrying about what the doctor said. Be careful, your face is more important than what you say to her now."

The patient on the pillow saw the door start to open (she had been staring at it since the doctor left); she sat up, holding her sheet over her chest; with her wide-open, dark-ringed eyes, she questioned her husband, and he read such fear in her gaze that he had great difficulty maintaining the smile he had so laboriously composed.

"Well, it won't be so much after all. You'll have to have a little operation, of course, and the sooner the better. The doctor will take care of everything. He's really very nice, isn't he? Tomorrow, if everything goes all right, we can take you to the hospital. I hope you'll have a room to yourself, but we can't be sure, and next week you can come home."

"The doctor's really very kind, and when will the children be home? Do they know that I'll be in the hospital tomorrow?"

"Don't talk as if you were afraid of the hospital! It's very well equipped—not at all the way it used to be. You have a bad kidney, it has to be taken care of, such things happen every day. Afterwards you'll have to be a little careful, and you'll be in perfect health."

"They didn't tell you when they'd be home. They don't have any classes now . . ."

"No, they don't have any classes; they're with friends, probably; I didn't ask them what they were doing, but there's no reason to change their schedules, postpone their appointments. Thank God things haven't gone that far. They'll be here for dinner, as usual."

"Of course, there was no reason . . ."

"No, we just have to take this precaution, that's all, just a precaution, but we have to take it, you know; I can't not take it."

"So you think I'll be in a ward. I'll have to ask Geneviève to come and help me pack my bag."

"You'll have plenty of time; she'll take care of everything; you know how devoted she is."

"I don't mind at all, Antoine. Come here, I'm tired, Antoine. I really don't think I mind at all, Antoine, I think you're right, I don't mind at all, the doctor's really very kind, he's right to take this precaution. Would you like to read to me a little? It's been so long since we've read together. I close my eyes, but I'm not sleeping; I only close my eyes because the light tires me a little, yes, even that light; but you can turn on the ceiling light to read to me by, anything, whatever you like, what you read to them in class."

Monsieur Bonnini went to get his *Anthology of Italian Literature* out of his briefcase. Back beside his wife, he realized that she had fallen asleep, and he stayed there watching for the moment when her breathing would change its rhythm and in order to soothe her now with beautiful lines.

The next day, on Wednesday the thirteenth, from three to four, Monsieur du Marnet—not with you in the eleventh-grade classroom as eight days before or eight days after—but in the staff room on the main floor next to the seventh-grade classroom, where we each have our locker that most of us never use, and our mailbox where we sometimes find complaints from parents or personal communications from the administration, and where we keep posted, a windfall for me (I had never consulted this elaborately worked out chart before this year), the hour-by-hour schedule of each of our teachers, except for the gym monitors who probably are entitled to come and rest in here, but who never show up (they have their own staff room), and Abbé Gollier,

in this staff room because he hasn't been as fortunate as I, because the principal hasn't managed to make up for the hours he teaches in such and such a class once every fifteen days

(when I'm not with you on Wednesday, I teach history to the seventh grade),

was correcting the exercises he had assigned his seniors on the

Friday before, and which they had handed in on Monday morning. Hubert Jourdan, at the back of the room, between the window and Jean-Claude Fage, behind Henri Fage, listening to me talk about conic projections, about how the shortest route from New York to Tokyo looks on the different kinds of maps, ran his hand through his hair, remembering that his mother, at lunchtime, had made him promise to stop at the barbershop on his way home from school.

As for Monsieur Tavera, the Spanish teacher, since Monsieur Hutter was with the eighth grade on the main floor, he must have been there too, in the room next door, where he apparently had many fewer students to teach.

Both went up to the next floor, and the German teacher came to take my place in this eleventh-grade classroom, but very few of you stayed on, only six, since there are only eight studying German, and out of these eight, Francis Hutter and André Knorr were absent. Jean-Claude Fage came to sit beside Bernard de Loups in the place Denis Régnier had just left,

while Denis walked past the concierge's lodge with Jean-Pierre Cormier, both of them crushed, looking at the bulletins I had signed, condemning them to spend two hours at the lycée the next day making a list of the capitals of all the countries of the world with the number of their inhabitants.

Once they had left the lycée they discovered they were taking the same streets, and asked each other their addresses.

"Rue du Cardinal-Lemoine. Yours?"

"Rue de Jussieu. You take the métro?"

"I don't have to, do you?"

"Yes. The Rue de Jussieu is a long way away, and if I want to get any work done before dinner . . ."

"Tomorrow's Thursday."

"Yes, but we have to come back here to the jail, thanks to that old pig Vernier. For a history and geog teacher . . . "

"Didn't you ever have him?"

"No, did you? Is he always like that?"

"I'm repeating; I had him last year for the same class. I've already heard all his stories about the Mercator projection, conic projections, scales, elevations; I know it by heart, and believe me, the rest of the year won't be any better . . ."

"Take the métro with me; you can get off at Cardinal-Lemoine.

You're lucky to know it all by heart. I would have forgotten it all by now."

"Oh, I don't really know it all by heart, but I remember enough to tell you it's boring."

They went down the stairs of the Saint-Hilaire métro station.

"By the way, how will we find the list of capitals with the number of inhabitants?"

"Oh, it's easy; we just have to do it before we get to the lycée tomorrow. You know, the proctor doesn't care what we do, as long as we keep quiet. Vernier already assigned that punishment last year —not to me, but to a friend of mine. You take a Larousse—you have a Larousse, don't you? And you look up all the names of the countries, and you see: capital, such and such a place. Then you look up the name of the place, and you see the number of inhabitants; then you put the whole thing in alphabetical order."

"But how do you find out the names of all the countries?"

"You look at the maps of the five continents. You learn something too, it's not so bad. But don't get any ideas, you'll be at it all night. We'll check our lists together tomorrow."

They had reached the Maubert-Mutualité station; the doors closed with a sigh.

"What about the stamp?"

"The Alaska one?"

"Yes."

"Vernier has it now."

"But he'll give it back to you Saturday."

"I'm not worrying about that. But I don't trade it except for two others. I'll have to see if you have anything I want."

"I'll bring my notebook tomorrow. We'll have to fix it so the proctor won't separate us. You know him?"

"There's more than one, and there may be new ones since last year, but usually they don't care. Where were you last year?"

"I was at Taine too, but in the tenth grade."

"And you were never kept after school?"

"A couple of times."

"Like me. You know, when there are two of us, it's not so bad. This is Cardinal-Lemoine; I get off here. See you tomorrow. Don't forget your stamps."

A few buildings before his own, Denis Régnier saw an ambulance stop. A little crowd formed. An orderly got out. Denis Régnier went on his way.

The orderly went up to Monsieur Bonnini's apartment; it was Geneviève who answered the door. Yes, everything was ready; the patient could walk down; no need to bring up the stretcher or call the driver.

The Italian teacher supported his wife under one arm, the orderly under the other, and they began—very slowly, step by step—to walk downstairs. Geneviève had stayed out on the landing.

After two floors, Monsieur Bonnini couldn't go any further; he was panting as hard as his wife, and he had to get help anyway.

Finally, though, poor Clara was settled on the bed in the ambulance. Monsieur Bonnini sat beside her, his knees apart, his hands clasped, his head bent forward, swaying each time they stopped for a red light, each time they started again. The clocks were chiming five when they crossed the threshold of the hospital.

I was walking down the Rue Saint-Sulpice, and I had only one idea in my mind: how to keep these notes that I am writing up in your behalf, and in behalf of your classmates too, less directly, and —through you and them—in behalf of all those who were or will have been eleventh-grade students, and even—I think I have to go this far—in behalf of everyone who has any relation with people who have gone through the eleventh grade,

how to keep my work on these notes, that is so new and so ex-asperating, so profoundly tyrannical, as I was already discovering, from disturbing my professional obligations;

for I must prevent any vagueness, any inadvertence such as that which occurred in my senior class the hour before, from ever happening again;

now I realized that not only could I not allow myself to prepare my classes less carefully than before, but that on the contrary, given this new occupation I had imposed upon myself, this new orientation of my mind and my attention, which transformed my attitude during every moment of the day and particularly during classes (since I was looking at my students in a new way, with a new intention, since I was in a sense playing two roles and could no longer give my teaching more than a portion of the effort, the energy that it used to demand),

I had to prepare my classes in much greater detail, devote much more time to them outside my hours at the lycée itself.

87

To accomplish this, I would have to set up an extremely strict, almost monastic regimen, reserve a certain number of minutes for the preparation of classes, a certain number for this narrative, and then keep unwaveringly to what I had decided, without ever permitting one realm to encroach on the other, or else either my teaching would suffer or I would never reach the end of this task begun the day before.

This is why, once I had returned to my apartment in the Rue du Canivet, the first thing I did was to take my schedule, that piece of pink cardboard ruled off in squares, on which the five days of the week are indicated vertically: Monday, Tuesday, Wednesday, Friday, Saturday—Thursday still being free—and the hours horizontally, from nine to noon, and then, after a double bar, from two to five, and within the boxes thus formed, the subjects to be taught—history or geography—and the various grades,

and reproduce it on a much bigger sheet showing the entire week, all seven days, with all their hours from nine in the morning until eleven at night, when I usually go to bed.

Considering the numerous unforeseen contingencies, meetings, visits and delays, I would have to allow a little more than an hour of preparation for each hour of class; consequently, Monday, Wednesday, Friday and Saturday mornings were automatically devoted to the preparation of the afternoon classes, but since the whole of Tuesday morning was spent at the Lycée Taine, I had to shift the preparation of Tuesday's six class hours to Monday night from five to seven, and then, after dinner, from eight to midnight.

The result was that on Monday it would be impossible for me to write a line for myself, for you, one of these lines: I could catch up during the rest of the week, and I regularly devote to this task the two hours before dinner, even on Thursday and Sunday, as if I had gone to the lycée, devoting the two morning of these days to the systematic study of the subjects my colleagues teach, using the textbooks they use, though it was soon obvious that this amount of time was absurdly inadequate, reserving the two afternoons for the indispensable errands.

I drew up this schedule, this regimen, on Wednesday, October 13, and I have kept to it since then without too many infractions; I don't know if I will be able to do so for much longer; there's no need to tell you that it is a terrible, oppressive burden.

And Thursday afternoon, while your physics teacher, Monsieur Hubert, was receiving his parents-in-law, his little cousin, your classmate, his student Denis Régnier, on the main floor of the Lycée Taine, in a classroom which is usually used by the eighth grade, sitting beside Jean-Pierre Cormier who had brought his notebook of duplicates, arranged less strictly, stamps from different countries occurring under the same strip of celluloid, without any concern for geographical classification,

occasionally glancing toward the platform to see if the proctor was still deep in his reading,

examined them one by one with contemptuous looks, and each time checking his list of capitals with the number of their inhabitants which I had asked him to make, to make certain he had included the capital of the country this stamp was from;

indicating, for instance, with the tip of his ballpoint pen, an ultramarine Swiss 30-centime stamp with a waterfall on it, winking to show that he already had it, that it didn't interest him, then consulting his list and checking off Berne, 146,000,

Denmark, 25 öre, pale blue, a jet plane, I already have it, Copenhagen, 1,168,300,

Norway, vermillion, 20 öre, a heraldic lion holding an ax in its paws, I don't have it, there's a little tear in it, it's not worth anything that way, you should know that, Oslo, 434,000,

Republic of Lebanon, the citadel of Tripoli, azure, 25 p., what does p. mean?, maybe . . .

He took it out, set it on the black wood beside the notebook, then looked on his list without finding the Republic of Lebanon; then he signaled to Jean-Pierre Cormier to wait for a moment, he concealed all the stamps under his forearm and looked through his Larousse, which he had bought as a precaution,

R,

Republic (the), a dialogue by Plato . . . , that wasn't it,

Republic (On the), a political and philosophical treatise by Cicero . . . ,

Republic (On the) or On Government, a work of political philosophy by Bodin, who was Bodin?

Republic of France, the French Republic has been proclaimed four times in France. . . .

And the next name was Requesens: Spanish general and statesman.

Wasn't there any Republic of Lebanon?

He took a notebook out of his briefcase, tore out half a sheet, and wrote on it under his classmate's eyes:

"Did you get the capital of the Republic of Lebanon?"

Jean-Pierre Cormier looked at his own sheet and pointed to the line on which he had written:

"Lebanon, Beirut, 201,000."

"Are you sure it's the same thing?"

"Of course."

"You can't tell in those countries . . . "

The proctor had looked up; he concealed a yawn with one hand.

"All right, there."

Denis Régnier added Lebanon between Laos and Liberia and went back to looking at the stamps, thinking:

I made a mistake; it would have been better to leave my list of capitals incomplete, since Monsieur Vernier won't check it anyway, and not show Jean-Pierre Cormier that I obviously don't have one stamp from Lebanon, since I asked him that stupid question.

The latter, in fact, had just written on the half-sheet of notebook paper:

"It's worth two."

And Denis Régnier, while looking at the next stamp,

Luxembourg, the archduchess, cranberry, 30 centimes, Luxembourg, 62,000,

was deciding that what he had to do was get some Lebanon stamps that same night or the next day so he could show them to his classmate Saturday, and that it would impress him more if he slipped them into his notebook of duplicates, as if he had all he needed, at the moment I give it to him, at the end of history class.

Yet he knew only one person who could give him the money he needed for this without insisting on explanations; that was his father, whom he could go see that night, his father whom he had decided not to see any more, whom he had passed judgment on, whom he had found guilty,

who would greet him with his usual, slightly contemptuous smile, who would offer him a cigarette, who would ask him to stay for dinner,

his father to whom he had promised himself he would never speak another word, except to spit his contempt in his face, to whom he had begun writing a letter to explain why he henceforth refused to consider himself as his son, why they couldn't have the slightest connection from now on,

90

a letter which of course has stopped at the first line because he hadn't wanted to tell his mother about it and because he would have had too hard a time turning his phrases by himself,

because, above all, he was afraid that his father's reaction, reading such a letter, would be simply to burst out laughing when he saw the mistakes in spelling.

This father held the keys to the Lebanon stamps, and to obtain them he need only postpone for a day the big explosion, the great noble outburst, the great silence, the great, contemptuous isolation,

as if he hadn't yet made his decision, as if he didn't have to make it until tonight, after having seen him one last time, after having given him one last chance . . .

The pencil point hovered in front of the blurred face of the grand duchess.

Now his father's first cousin, Monsieur Bonnini, was in a hospital ward between two beds, sitting on a white-painted metal chair. His sister-in-law Geneviève, in her black coat and black hat, stood resting a hand on her brother-in-law's shoulder. Isabella and Giovanni were on the other side of the bed, and these four faces, their eyes wide, watched that other face stir on the pillow, yellow, drawn, unrecognizable, the gray hair mussed, the lips twisting, the tiny wrinkles puckering at the temples, smoothing out and suddenly reappearing, the eyelids apparently pasted together, occasionally swelling and then suddenly opening, the pupils empty, wandering, fear gradually accumulating in them, then the lips parting, releasing a groan, and suddenly the whole body shaken, thrown forward, the hands clenched into fists, throwing back the sheets.

The eyes of all the other visitors turned toward her, mothers coming to see their little boys who had been operated on for appendicitis, factory workers coming to see the victim of an accident, the young wife at the bedside of her husband whose leg had been broken in an automobile collision.

Her sister grasped her shoulders, gently laid her back in the bed, and at that moment Clara recognized her family and wiped her hand across her forehead.

"Don't talk, don't even try to talk. It went very well, the doctor told me. You can come home in two weeks. I promise I'll come see you every day. You aren't in too much pain, are you? I can see it hurts less already. Isabella and Giovanni will come too. We had to do it, darling. Go back to sleep now. It's four o'clock, we have to go now. All the other visitors have left already."

The four chimes from the hospital clock, the four from the chimes of Saint-Germain.

In his apartment in the Rue du Pré-aux-Clercs, Monsieur Hubert, not Bernard Hubert, your physics and chemistry teacher, but René Hubert, his brother, my dentist, opened the door and called out:

"Monsieur Vernier!"

He shook my hand as he said:

"Sorry to have kept you waiting."

I had been cooling my heels for an hour and a half, stuffed with aspirin in that little overheated waiting room.

"Sit down. Open your mouth. There it is. Does it hurt much? Oh, it's in bad shape, all right!"

He tapped my teeth with the metal shaft of one of his instruments.

"We'll save the others, but there's nothing to do with this one but pull it out. I'll give you an anesthetic."

He took a syringe out of a metal box and adjusted the needle.

"It's usually just when school begins that I see you. You take a long vacation, you let your teeth go bad, and then you come back here. But this time it's later than usual. You'll have one tooth less."

I heard the bell at the door. The maid went to answer it; she came in to announce the visitor's name, then the telephone rang; she picked up the receiver, listened, answered:

"Oh, fine",

with a smile,

"I'll put him on,"

and, holding out the receiver,

"It's Monsieur Bernard."

"Monsieur Bernard?"

"Yes, your brother."

"Oh, of course!"

I was thinking:

"Bernard Hubert, that sounds familiar; where have I heard that name before? Head tipped back, I stared at the big lamp that lit up my mouth, and the transmission belts of the drill, with their tiny gleaming pulleys.

He hung up; he came back over to the chair.

"Sorry, it was my brother."

He thrust the needle in my gums; he began to push the plunger. I started at his hand that was tense with the effort.

"There! Now we'll have to wait a little while. But you may know him. You're at the Lycée Taine, aren't you? I know there are so many of you that you don't necessarily know each other very well. He teaches physics and chemistry. Can you still feel it when I press? He has one of our nephews in his class, the son of our first cousin, a sad story, she's separated from her husband, divorced; the husband has remarried, the boy goes back and forth, he's quite upset. It doesn't help his school work any. I think he's had to repeat this year. You may have him in one of your classes, or you probably will one of these days. He's a good boy, really. I only see him rarely, because his mother hasn't really seen anyone since all this happened; it's been going on two or three years now. But you probably have so many students . . . it's hard for you to give each of them personal attention. How many of those faces can you see during the week? I think we can start now."

He talked, he talked, I didn't even try to answer him; I took note of all the precious information he gave me. He took his forceps and began wagging the tooth back and forth.

It took quite a long time. He told me to take more aspirin and go to bed early, then he looked at his schedule and gave me an appointment for Wednesday, October 20, after school, around five fifteen. That was annoying, since it would keep me from writing these notes according to the schedule I had so carefully established yesterday; but he explained that he always had a lot of school-children on Thursday, and that he might have to keep me waiting a long time; I agreed with him.

The half-hour chime from the tower of Saint-Germain-des-Prés; the half-hour chime from the great clock of Notre-Dame.

In the attic room on the Quai des Grands-Augustins, you looked at your watch. The game of Concentration had been over a long time, with rather discouraging results. Now you were trying to set up a program of activities for the following meetings. Your friends were all sitting on the floor along the wall, only you, as the leader, had a seat, one of the three old trunks that were in the room.

One boy had been appointed treasurer, another secretary, and the latter was solemnly writing your decisions in his little spiral-bound notebook.

There were two important points: first the fixing up of headquarters, the problem of the seats and the furniture in general (were you going to be satisfied with these trunks? Wasn't there some way to get rid of them, taking them down to the cellar, for instance? there had to be a cellar . . . , oh yes, no one would mind that; you'd have to let someone know, of course; all right, that would clear the floor; and then? making stools? too long, too hard; using logs? it was an old idea, actually, almost all the other patrols were doing it; they should find something else, something original; why not deck chairs, for instance? why not buy deck chairs? yes, why not? they couldn't cost so much, the treasurer would look into it; if everyone was willing to give something . . . why not raise the monthly dues; and last year, what did they use for seats in the Bison headquarters? oh, some old broken-down chairs that belonged to the leader's parents; besides, everyone knew that if the Bison Patrol had distinguished itself in many ways, it wasn't because of the way it had fixed up its headquarters; from that point of view, it was better to start from scratch, everyone agreed on that; so, deck chairs, but they didn't have to buy them all; everyone had some old deck chair at home, in a cellar or an attic, that would do nicely; they could buy some strong material with the patrol's colors and nail it on the wood with upholstery tacks; it would take an afternoon, that was all; everyone was supposed to bring deck chairs; they would have to have them in by next week, to know how many others they would need to buy, add up the accounts, calculate the additional dues; and on the walls? they weren't going to start repainting, they just needed to create a certain atmosphere; how about dried leaves? they crumbled too quickly; knots? everyone was tired of them, and they weren't much use; how about inscriptions? the rules, principles, things like that? that's what books are for; drawings? scenes of scout life? who could make them? photographs? they'd need enlargements, and that cost too much; maps? yes, that was a good idea . . .

"Listen, what we should have is a big map of Paris, like the one in the métro, and a map of the region around Paris too so we can prepare our hikes",

and one of your new members said:

"One of my brothers has a whole collection of Michelin maps."

"That would be great! You think he'd lend them to you?"

"I can always ask him."

"It all depends on the way you do it. You fix it up."),

second, preparation for the tests. It was understood that during the course of this year all the new members were to pass the ones that would allow them to take their pledge, while all those who had already taken it were to become Second-Class Scouts, and those who were already in the second class were to become First-Class Scouts, and those in the first class were to get their certificates, all of which would require everyone's co-operation, and a flawless organization. They would have some leisure time, of course; they could even go to the movies together now and then; but they had to set up some hours for study, the boys who had already passed a test transmitting their knowledge and experience to those who were going to take it.

Consequently it was decided which boys would take the others in charge, and a rotation system was scrupulously noted by the secretary, who was to recopy it on a large sheet of paper in different colored inks, in order to thumbtack it to the wall at the next meeting.

The next day, Friday, October 15, at three o'clock, you were in front of your Uncle Henri in the eleventh-grade classroom.

You had just finished your Greek; he had given you a few minutes rest, but hadn't dismissed the class.

Like you, he put his Greek book away in his briefcase; like you, he took out his *Sixteenth Century French Authors*,

he turned the page of his notebook, considering the alphabetical list of your names, in front of which was a day-by-day column for notes and marks, the one for this Friday the fifteenth being already the eighth, the first seven scattered with capital letters for grades and with tiny a's indicating absences.

He marked three new a's opposite the names André Knorr, Bernard de Loups and Jacques Estier; then he tapped his pencil on his desk a few times, waited for silence, crossed his hands, raised his head,

"Gentlemen, I should like to point out that it is already three minutes after three, and high time we began. Last Tuesday we read together the letter from Gargantua to his son Pantagruel, in which he informed the latter what he wanted him to study. Rabelais wrote the book devoted to Gargantua after the first book of Pantagruel, and certain ideas sketched here for the first time will reappear in the second work, considerably enlarged and developed. What we shall read today is an example of *bad* education. Next Monday we shall consider the detailed program of a reasonable education, reasonable for a giant, naturally. You have already read this text, since you have prepared it, and I am certain that some among you, at certain moments, have recognized yourselves in it. Gargantua first studied under the direction of a very bad instructor; his father, Grangousier, seeks out a good one for him, finds Ponocrates. The latter, before beginning his instruction, wishes to see how far his student has proceeded. Most important, he is not content merely to question him, he observes the way he lives. A bad education produces a vicious way of life, and it is Gargantua's whole way of life, in its every detail, that Ponocrates will attempt to correct. Well, Abel, will you read? I don't think I've heard the sound of your voice yet."

"This done, he with all his heart submitted his study to the discretion of Ponocrates; who first of all appointed that he should do as he was accustomed, to the end it might be understood by what means, in so long a time, his old masters had made him such a sot and puppy..."

"Stop there for the moment, and let me see if you've understood what you just read. Let's start at the beginning; analyze that first expression, that first little word: *this*; give me a grammatical analysis of that word, if you please."

"It's a demonstrative adjective..."

"If it's an adjective, there must be a word it modifies."

"It modifies *done*."

"And what is *done*, then?"

"A verb..."

"And what function does it have in the sentence, if you please? You're not going to tell me that *done* functions as a verb—what verb could it be? No, the verb goes with *he*, in the next expression. By the way, who is *he*?"

"It must be Pantagruel..."

"No, not Pantagruel, Gargantua! We're talking about Gargantua now. *This* is not an adjective, it's a pronoun, and *done* is a past participle; it's as if Rabelais said: Once this thing was done. Now what is this thing that he did? Look at the note at the bottom of the page! Read it!"

"This done: the restoration of the stolen bells."

"Now what's this about the bells? What bells is Rabelais talking about? Abel, Abel, you haven't prepared your text."

"Yes I have, Monsieur."

"What do you mean, yes I have?"

"I can show you my notebook, it has the whole passage worked out."

"I know you can show me your notebook; I saw you just now, while we were doing our Greek. Rabelais is talking about the bells of Notre-Dame de Paris, which Gargantua stole upon his arrival, and there was no need to look any further; all you had to do was look at the top of this very page you're supposed to be reading. Now see if you can make up for it; what does *heart* mean, *with all his heart?* . . . "

You were staring at your open notebook, at the analysis you had made of this passage:

"lines 1 to 5, introduction,
lines 6 to 29, getting up and breakfast,
lines 30 to 47, Gargantua's excuse,
lines 48 to 61, the morning,
lines 62 to the end, lunch."

You had put it on your right side, so that Michel Daval could copy it more easily.

It was another of your classmates you were listening to now, reading:

" . . . Then did he tumble and toss, wag his legs and wallow in the bed some time, the better to stir up and rouse his vital spirits . . . "

while your uncle continued with his questions:

"What does *wallow* mean?"

"What are *vital spirits?*"

You wrote down, docilely:

"Wallow: to roll heavily
Vital spirits: energy . . . "

On the floor above, I was talking about the American Midwest before moving on to the Rocky Mountain region, the old Far West, the Colorado desert, the various national parks, California with Los Angeles and its Sunset Boulevard, with San Francisco and its Golden Gate, its marvelous bridges, its trolley cars climbing the hills, and finally Alaska, describing its gold rush with references to Chaplin's film, for these seniors whom I was to see again the following Tuesday in the same room at four o'clock.

Monsieur Bonnini had just explained to some of them the sixth canto of the *Purgatorio*, describing the meeting with the Mantuan

97

poet Sordello, and he had wondered, as he looked at them, if he could ever read these lines to his wife again.

Denis Régnier, while I was telling your class about the slave trade, the raids on the Sudan, the landing of cargoes in the Antilles, in Brazil and in Virginia, had kept his eyes fixed on this illustration:

the mines of the Potosi, a steep mountain in the form of a sugar loaf, with a gaping wound which it was easy to see never existed in reality but which had been opened by the artist in order to show what was to be seen, and in this cavern communicating with the outside world only by a round orifice at the top, like the mouth of a crater, climbing up and down a rope ladder, like the infernal counterpart of the one in Jacob's dream,

naked men were carrying on their backs sacks filled with ore or bringing them back empty, in attitudes of exhaustion, toward those of their enslaved companions who were wielding picks or shovels, stripped of everything save the signs of their dependence, their abasement, some brandishing torches,

men whose sweat he could see flowing down their limbs to the rough floor of the cavern that had also been hollowed out with pickaxes,

men whose agitation was like the tumult inside a volcano,

whose despised work, whose forced rage, whose ferment constantly kept in check by police and priests the picture did not show, sent out of the crater a little silver transported with great difficulty, with great losses, with great cruelty, to the harbors and then across the sea to Spain,

before splitting open this whole new empire, gradually ripening and roasting an enormous secret vengeance (whose smoke would appear only much later), these men had doubtless not completed their expansion even today;

the phrase of Rabelais he had read the week before ran through Denis Régnier's mind like a tune he couldn't stop singing:

" . . . all the various metals that are hid within the bowels of the earth",

and he thought of his Bolivian stamps, of the hundred-franc pieces in his wallet;

Monsieur Hubert, in the physics amphitheater, had just explained

98

to his eleventh-graders the principal formulas concerning the resistance of the air; he had spoken to them of bellows, of fan blades, of parachutes, of shock waves, of the way the profile of an airplane wing was studied, of the transformations of shape induced by exceeding the speed of sound; he had made several colored-chalk drawings on the blackboard to illustrate his remarks; he had explained the whirling of leaves falling from the trees in the autumn,

of those leaves that you could see at this moment, far beneath you, since you were near the window in the last row of the amphitheater, listening, with all your classmates, to Monsieur Hubert giving you a lesson that interested him much less than the last one, giving you a few elementary notions concerning the pulley, the composition of concurrent forces, making a few summary diagrams on the board, but reluctant to erase the fine drawings he had made before four o'clock,

and you were wondering, under the Mendeleev chart, as you surveyed with delight not the drawings he was making, a few stupid arrows with dotted lines, betraying boredom, even disgust, but the ones that were already there, so interesting and so carefully executed, when you came into the amphitheater after having left me,

when you would finally be leaving this purgatory of platitude, when you could finally enter into this marvelous realm, the profile of airplane wings;

one of those machines, with its wings so carefully designed, whose calculation had required such study, was at that moment passing over the chimneys through the gray and yellow sky.

It was Tuesday, October 19, and I was talking about Canada, kingdom of woods and wheat, empire of ice.

I didn't teach your class the next day. As every fifteen days, on Wednesday from three to four, instead of being with you, I was with my seventh-graders, on the main floor, making them recite the lesson of the day before about the religion, the temples and the tombs of ancient Egypt, before transporting them to the other tip of the fertile crescent, describing the marshes of Mesopotamia, telling them for the first time about the civilization of Sumer, the treasures of Ur, the cuneiform inscriptions, the walls of Babylon, the Hammurabic Code, the wars of Ashurbanipal, Nebuchadnezzar, the ziggurats, the astrologers, the invention of zero, the Hittite lions, King Croesus, the antiquity of Iran, the ceramics of Susa, Cyrus and Darius, the ruins of Persepolis, the enameled bricks, the worship of fire, Ormazd and

99

Ahriman, the towers of silence where the birds of carrion tore apart the corpses.

You were with Monsieur du Marnet; you had handed in your first homework:

algebra:

"Simplify the expressions: $3(a+b+c) - 2(a-b+c) + 5(a-b-c)$ and $(x+y)(a+b) + (x-y)(a-b) - (ax+by)$,

perform this operation: $39 + 65-26$, all over -13",

geometry:

"through the point O intersection of the diagonals of the quadrilateral $ABCD$, extend the parallel to BC which intersects AB at E, the parallel to CD which intersects AD at F, the parallel to AB which intersects BC at H, and the parallel to AD which intersects CD at G;

show that EF and GH are parallel to BD;

what can you say about the quadrilateral $EFGH$ when O bisects AC?";

then he told you about powers, squares and cubes, roots and the operations that you could perform upon them, covering the board with expressions full of exponents and with those big asymmetrical V's that are called, he told you, radicals.

And your Uncle Henri?

I realize that on several occasions I have spoken of our class without mentioning him, thereby contravening the rule of narration I had imposed on myself at the beginning in order to describe this class in all its amplitude, just as I have several times mentioned Monsieur Bonnini and Denis Régnier without mentioning Monsieur Hubert,

or spoken of Monsieur du Marnet and Hubert Jourdan without mentioning Monsieur Tavera; but in this latter case, this is not so serious, for it is understood that the degrees of relationship among these three people are already quite slight, that what particularly unites them is a double resemblance that struck me as quite marked between Monsieur du Marnet and Hubert Jourdan, much more fugitive between the latter and Monsieur Tavera.

They cannot give me any information about each other; if it is therefore natural that this student and his mathematics teacher should attract each other in the course of my description, in the writing of these notes, it is also natural that I should often pass on to someone else, skipping Monsieur Tavera altogether.

As far as Denis Régnier is concerned, one could say that his relationship to Monsieur Hubert, his mother's first cousin, is of the same degree as his relationship to Monsieur Bonnini, his father's first cousin. The fact that he is living with his mother and only goes to see his remarried father occasionally, the fact that Monsieur Régnier, his father, is an object of scandal to the Bonnini family, which has stopped seeing him altogether, would at first appear to link Denis more closely with his physics teacher. Now it is the contrary which is the case, because another element intervenes whose importance, from the point of view of the organization of this narrative, continually increases—the proximity of their residences.

Monsieur Bonnini and Denis Régnier both live in the Rue Cardinal-Lemoine, a few houses from each other, while Monsieur Hubert lives in the Avenue Émile-Zola.

Consequently, in this system of triads which I have employed hitherto, and which I will have to complete in any case in order to bring into the account, one after the other, all your schoolmates, there are dissymmetries so noticeable that they have a tendency to break up these decreasingly solid groups, with their looser and looser internal links, until they become the contrary of links, negative links, as in the case of Maurice Tangala, the Negro, Monsieur Moret and the Abbé Gollier.

I can, of course, go on using these triads, even when they are mutilated, by saying that I will later on fill in the gaps of my account, but I am afraid that the elaboration of this work will take me farther and farther away from these holes I would have left, instead of bringing me closer in order to fill them up, so that I could come back only much later, too late, when my attitude would no longer be the same, thereby cheating whenever I added something to my text.

It is possible that I will be forced, in subsequent notes, to make a general reorganization; yet this new organization must somehow derive from the old one, and consequently I must abide by the old one as long as I can, keeping to its strictness, and—at least until a new solution is clear to me—not permitting the densest of these triads (the one you, your uncle and I constitute) to be broken again,

which an extremely strong local dissymmetry—the fact that I live on the same floor as you, so to speak in the same apartment—will no doubt one day cause to explode,

but in which the degrees of relationship, of frequentation, of information are so solid that it is by means of this structure that links the three of us together that I was able to begin this enterprise,

that I was able to conceive of vanquishing these huge difficulties which were apparent to me even before I decided to write the first line,

these difficulties which now look more and more dizzying on every page, and which are linked to the very contradictions of that society we—students and teachers—constitute,

contradictions which I am trying, by means of this text, to present to you so that within yourself at least some of them may be resolved,

difficulties of expression and representation which I have merely touched on in these pages so far.

My relations with your Uncle Henri are such that I know exactly what he was talking to his seniors about that Wednesday on October 20 from three to four, on the other side of the wall in front of you:

Iphigénie, Act I, Scene 2,

Agamemnon, Achilles, Ulysses,

"What's this, my Lord, can it be that so rapidly . . . "

I know this because he told me, because he allowed me to consult the detailed curriculum he has worked out for himself. Literally, it is all I know, and if I want to continue my description, I am obliged to use my imagination; and I am obliged to continue my description, if not in this case, then in others, so that a representation can take shape within you.

But I must go still further: at the moment I wrote: "That's all I know", I supposed I was telling the truth, but at the very moment I was writing it, I felt that this "literal" truth was immediately and inevitably being transformed into a lie, for it is not true that it is all I know, since I know your Uncle Henri, because he is your Uncle Henri, and because he is my colleague and my friend,

and since, in consequence, I know in what tone he might have read those lines of Iphigénie;

I don't know exactly what gestures he made with his hands at that moment, but I know what kind of gestures;

I think I can see him, I can almost hear him prodding his students, asking them:

"Can one of you tell me where Aulis is?"

and for the next lines:

"Where are Thessaly and Lesbos?"

So not only am I obliged to use my imagination for you, but for myself as well; these words that I wrote or else that I am speaking when I say "that's all I know", these very words have a meaning for me only because I know other things as well, because the other things are present to my mind in varying degrees of verisimilitude;

this fact which is like a peg holding my text together and keeping it from disintegrating, has, in the long run, an existence for me, for you, for us all only because it appears as a focus in the middle of a whole zone of imaginings and probabilities,

and these imaginings are all the stronger and all the more likely since I am capable of connecting this moment of your uncle's life, by grammatical or other categories, to other moments,

this man to other men, this place to other places, this quotation to the rest of the tragedy, this tragedy to others by Racine, this fragment of culture to others,

bringing a little light into this huge confusion where we are struggling, a little light that is shed over this moment, that renders it visible, observable, that is gradually reflected over this moment to light up the obscure present a little

(that was Wednesday, October 20),

and I know by the same means, in the same way, that Tuesday, October 26, in other words exactly fifteen days after this pivot-hour, this history lesson during which I talked to you about the discovery and conquest of America, and that all these explorations in the preceding or succeeding hours must help you to situate,

starting from this place, this time, this milieu in which you will find yourself when you finally read these lines which are intended for you,

I know that your Uncle Henri was once again with his seniors in the classroom behind my back, and that he was returning the corrected compositions they had handed in eight days before, on the 19th, whose subjects he had assigned on the first Tuesday of the school year, on October 5, subjects connected with the curriculum they had followed the year before, in other words, when they were in the eleventh grade, as you are now:

"Education in Rabelais and Montaigne."

"In his preface to *Bérénice*, Racine writes: 'The principal rule is to please and to move. All others exist only to effect this first one.' What is your reaction?"

103

"In his Art Poétique, Boileau states:

'There is no savage fiend or beast or blight
That art cannot transform to please the sight.'

Discuss this notion, making use of examples drawn from painting."

And what I want is to enable you, by means of all the circumstances, all the conjectures which I will have transmitted to you, to represent to yourself, with sufficient exactitude and verisimilitude, what such a class can have been, what he might have said to his French Classics students while you, on the other side of the wall, were listening to me talk about the beginning of the Thirty Years' War;

I should like to be able to restore to your memory this moment, this hour which is already so far in the past for me that, despite the attention I was paying to you, to your whole class, I am incapable of recovering with certainty which gestures you might have made, at which moments you were listening, at which you were distracted.

To help you realize what you yourself have been, in other words, where you come from, in other words where you are going—what is the vector of your present—I must already make a great imaginative effort of reconstruction, I must put myself in your place, try to see myself through your eyes and consequently let you speak, thereby destroying the equilibrium of this narrative.

Here are the facts:

I know that Michel Daval was beside you, his cousin Alain Mouron in front of you, and beside the latter Francis Hutter with his black armband, whom I questioned on that day, and to whom I gave a grade of C

(but just which question had I asked him, and how, in what words had he answered? I would have to write down everything, and I cannot write down everything, I cannot even write down everything I know I might need for this narrative, for this description, this operation I am attempting; hasn't this undertaking which swells and proliferates so terribly devoured me enough already?

what is sure is that the question I asked him certainly concerned what I had talked to you about during the preceding lesson, that is, Elizabeth's successors, the Puritan revolution, Cromwell's dictatorship),

and behind you Henri Fage, but that Jean-Pierre Cormier was absent.

I can therefore reconstruct the whole area around you, I can put you in your seat, say what you could see, tell you with a sufficient degree of exactitude what you were hearing.

Because of everything I know about you, I am entitled to put in your mouth words like: I was thinking this, I decided that,

so that you can recognize yourself or, on the contrary, what would be even better, so that suddenly the denial of some detail might burst out of you during your reading of these notes, consequently making a whole portion of this past, of this instruction that will have passed, rise up before you, so that at last you would seize this possession that is now beyond your reach.

I know that Zola, too, was absent, that I also questioned Garrac and Guillaume, that I gave the former a D, the latter a C Plus, that you must still have been thinking about the French class that had preceded this one, and already about the physics class that was to follow it, that you had your notebook open and that you wrote down as I dictated it:

"The Thirty Years War, part one, Bohemia",

that I explained to you what Bohemia was at the beginning of the Seventeenth Century, reviewed the decision of the Diet of Augsburg in 1555, *cuius regio, eius religio*, that I made you laugh, as I make the eleventh-graders laugh every year, by telling about the defenestration of Prague.

The words I spoke during that hour echo in my mind, and I know that for a long time to come I shall be able to transcribe them virtually when I choose without running too many risks of distortion—long enough, that is, some time still, several weeks or several days; after that, I'll have to imagine them.

That was Tuesday, October 26.

It's a bright November day.

You put away your French books, opened your notebook, your *History Textbook.*

I call the roll, I look at the class:

Abel in the second row, Armelli in the first, Baron behind Armelli and beside Abel, Buret two seats farther back, near the door,

Cormier at the desk beside yours, not Cormier, Cormier's empty seat, and I write an a opposite his name in today's column, Tuesday, November 9.

Also absent: Francis Hutter, Denis Régnier.

105

To catch the unwary, although during the entire month of October I had asked no one who already had a geography grade to answer history questions, I now question the same students I had called on the day before,

Rémy Orland about the youth of Louis XIII (unable to say a word), about Léonora Galigaï (it's as if he were hearing this name for the first time),

François Nathan about Richelieu's early career, about the siege of La Rochelle,

Alain Mouron.

Concealed behind you, you are leafing through your textbook, which I forbade during the recitation of the lessons, and I forego reprimanding you. I do not want to disturb you, I am observing you.

Your eyes slide over the pages and you stop, you begin reading something which is probably not printed like the rest of the text, I suppose it is that reproduction of an issue of Théophraste Renaudot's *Gazette*, which I amused myself by making you decipher Saturday:

"From Constantinople, on April 2, 1631:

"The Kynge of Persia with 15,000 horses and 50,000 foot soldiers lays siege to Dille two days from the city of Babylon; where the great Lord has given the command to all his janissaries to surrender upon pain of death, and continues *nonobstante* this Diversion, waging still a harsher War upon those who take tobacco, whom he causes to suffocate in their own smoke . . . "

On the other side of the wall, behind me, your Uncle Henri assigns his students three new subjects for compositions to be handed in a week later, on Tuesday the sixteenth:

"A modern Persian, with a perfect command of French, writes to one of his friends in Teheran to tell him what he has seen and heard in the Parisian cafés",

"A contemporary of Montesquieu suddenly finds himself transported to modern Paris; back in his own period, he describes his adventures and his surprises to a friend",

"Conversely, suppose that in a dream you were to find yourself in Eighteenth Century Paris for a day; upon waking, you describe your experience to a friend."

II

IN THE FIRST ROW, to my right, Philippe Guillaume's seat is empty; he may be sick, a little grippe, or a few degrees of fever; from his bed, he looks out the window down into the courtyard, glad not to be in school; he feels his hands, no sweat; he decides he won't have fever tonight, which means he'll have to go back to school tomorrow.

Beside this empty seat, Bruno Verger, one of the oldest in our class, born in April '38 (Laurent Garrac in March of the same year, Claude Armelli in February, and only Henri Buret in 1937), which makes him sixteen, while I was just fifteen today,

has stopped taking notes and like the rest of us listens to you reading:

" . . . for by reason of the lightness of the bamboo, the wind would cast it to the ground.

And the Great Khan lives here three months of the year. . . . "

In September, Alain Mouron's father, who was superintending the transfer of his furniture from Bourges to the apartment in the Rue du Pré-aux-Clercs, entrusted his son to Monsieur Bailly, who had taken him along with his own family to Finistère.

It was nice weather during the middle of September, and so it is possible that on the second Tuesday, the fourteenth, at the same time we now come to your history class week after week, Alain could have accompanied his little cousins, René, Georges and Agnès, to the beach.

All four undressed in the green-and-white-striped beach cabin; let's say the tide was out; they built a sand castle and dug moats around it, with canals to bring in the water from the sea, for the tide was beginning to rise. When the towers were submerged, it would be the right time for swimming.

Monsieur Bailly was in his room at the Hôtel de la Plage. His wife had left for a week, saying that she had to visit a sick relative in Orléans, that she was the only one who could take care of her, the other members of her family being so unsympathetic they had virtually refused to have anything to do with her since her divorce . . .

But Alain Mouron knew that his Uncle René didn't believe his Aunt Elizabeth's explanations and that he thought that her famous cousin wasn't so sick as had been supposed, expecting his wife to come home and tell him, as once before, that it had been only a false alarm,

thinking that the family in Orléans hadn't been so narrow-minded and provincial after all, that everyone he had met on visits had really been quite pleasant, that there was another reason for this trip, this absence;

Alain Mouron knew that it wasn't his wife he was writing to in his room, from time to time coming to the window half concealed by pine branches, one of whose panes glittered in the sun, to watch them down on the beach,

but to that woman in Paris he had never seen but whom he had heard his father whisper about once, who was an artist, he had said, who designed silk scarves for some fashionable shop, even did some paintings.

They came home the twenty-eighth, all of them together. The six of them took up almost a whole compartment on the train; there was only room left for an old couple, a farmer and his wife nibbling on Vire sausage the whole trip.

They were approaching Chartres, but the rain was beating against the windows, and they could see nothing.

Madame Bailly had put on her glasses to knit; Monsieur Bailly was deep in an English detective novel. Little Agnès was beginning to get restless. Her father asked if it was time to take out the bread and chocolate; her mother answered that they should wait until four o'clock.

Alain Mouron, near the window, opposite his cousin René, who had just celebrated his ninth birthday the week before, at the seashore, had put up the little table to be able to play cards, an old-fashioned game called Canfield, much enjoyed by the entire Bailly family but which Alain didn't know very well,

and he enjoyed asking help from little Georges, who quite often had occasion to correct Alain's mistakes, with little smiles of triumph,

because Alain was quite preoccupied by his imminent arrival in Paris, his life in this big city which he had visited only occasionally, to spend a few days of vacation, especially at Christmas (he stayed with his father then, in a hotel on the Rue Vaneau), when he had to visit all his uncles, aunts and cousins, the Mourons, the Baillys, the Davals, and the rest,

by this new apartment he had never seen, in a street whose name intrigued him, the Rue du Pré-aux-Clercs, in which he would find some of the furniture that had been in Bourges, but differently arranged, unrecognizable,

by the new lycée where he knew he had been entered, where his Uncle René was an English teacher, might be his English teacher, it wasn't certain, he hadn't been able to promise anything, you couldn't tell for sure until the first day of classes,

where his cousin Michel would be in eleventh grade like himself, but perhaps there would be more than one section.

Still, on Monday, October 4, it wasn't next to his cousin Michel Daval that he was sitting, but near the window in the first row, no

111

doubt by choice, wanting to have every possible advantage for this school year that he suspected would be a difficult one.

It was our first geography lesson; his textbook was still brand new, without a cover, without a name written in it, without holes or scratches of any kind, his fine blue-checked notebook still blank.

On the first page, he wrote in large capital letters:
"ALAIN MOURON
ELEVENTH GRADE
LYCÉE HIPPOLYTE TAINE
GEOGRAPHY TEACHER MONSIEUR ..."

and he leaned toward his neighbor Francis Hutter to ask him, pointing with his thumb, what your name was, which Francis didn't know either. Then Alain turned toward his cousin Michel Daval, then toward me.

Monsieur Bailly, a few classrooms away, was asking his tenth-graders to write their names, addresses, etc., on a sheet of paper.

And the next day, in the same classroom, Monsieur Hutter met with those of their classmates who were taking German, while his distant nephew, Francis, slashed a big *I* on top of the first page of his red notebook and slowly printed the title of your lesson:
"The end of the Middle Ages"
and the name of its first part:
"The collapse of the Roman Empire and the development of Christianity";

Francis, too, during the first mathematics class, on Wednesday the sixth, asked his neighbor Alain Mouron, pointing to the teacher with his thumb, what his name was.

Alain Mouron made a gesture indicating that he should keep still, shrugging slightly, frowning, and went back to writing the rules of multiplication for algebraic numbers: plus times plus equals plus, plus times minus equals minus ..., thinking that he would ask this information from his Uncle René who was at home looking up which scenes of *Macbeth*, which he intended to have his seniors study, were included in his *Anthology of English Literature*,

the moment when the witches, after having recited their spell, fall silent as Macbeth enters and declares to Banquo that he has never seen a day "so fair and foul", still unaware of the truth of what he is saying,

which he could choose as a starting point, permitting him to begin

112

reading the play on Friday (it was hopeless to expect his students to have a complete Macbeth before next week),

then the selections from Julius Caesar, a play he usually taught to the eleventh grade, for which selections would be quite sufficient.

Now he had to find some long Nineteenth-Century poem for his seniors. His book fell open almost of its own accord to The Rime of the Ancient Mariner. It was destiny. They must have known the name Coleridge already. Next week, on October 12, they would still be explaining Keats's sonnet in class, the one on the first time he read Chapman's translation of Homer, then the old sailor, the wedding-guest, the land of ice and its terrifying noises . . .

So it was from this textbook that he had his seniors read, on Saturday, after having urged them to bring a complete Macbeth to class next Monday, knowing quite well that those who hadn't bought it already couldn't have it by then, but hoping that by getting furious on Monday, even pounding his fist on the desk, he would manage to inspire them with enough healthy terror so that the question would be settled once and for all by the end of next week,

that passage where the witches, when the victorious captain asks them "from whence you owe this strange intelligence" and why, on this blasted heath, they stop him with such a prophetic greeting, ordering them, adjuring them to speak,

burst out laughing at this powerless command, vanish into thin air, while the first confirmation of their prophecy approaches in the form of the messengers Ross and Angus, who come to tell Macbeth that he has been named Thane of Cawdor, which makes Banquo say:

"What, can the devil speak true?"

On the other side of the wall, Alain Mouron was listening to you tell us (after calling on Armelli, de Loups and Buret, about what you had told us the Tuesday before) what you would be calling on us about the following Tuesday, the Reformation, trying to make us understand the link between the humanist questioning of the scholastic tradition apropos of the literary, scientific or philosophic texts of antiquity and the questioning of the ecclesiastical tradition by Luther apropos of the sacred texts,

looking at the map of Western Europe on which were indicated the principal centers of this schism: Wittenberg, Geneva and London

(that was Saturday, October 9),

next to Francis Hutter the Protestant, who, the next day, in his apartment on the Avenue Émile-Zola, went to his father's study (his father was out) to look at an old print of Calvin that had been in his family for generations, took out of the bookcase the big old Bible that no one read any more, wondering suddenly what this religious adventure was that he had been told about the day before, about which he might be questioned in two days, how it concerned him, who had practically never gone to church in his life,

and especially what it could mean for this man who had the same name as his, who shared the same family tradition, whom he had never seen before this week, with whom his parents had never had any connection but whom they had found on their genealogical tree,

Monsieur Alfred Hutter, his German teacher, who, in a big apartment formerly occupied by one of his father's cousins, Francis' grandfather's older brother, in the Rue de Jussieu where he had just moved with his three motherless children—Henri who was a senior at the Lycée Taine, Gérard who was in the seventh grade, and Geneviève who was in the eleventh grade at the Lycée Sévigné—

was selecting the German texts he was going to have his seniors read and putting the plays of Goethe back in his bookcase next to Luther's translation of the Bible.

The next day, his son Gérard, on the top floor of the Lycée Taine, under the supervision of Monsieur Martin who had composed a little still life: some books, a bottle and a rag (the bust of Caesar was still in the middle of the classroom),

bent down to pick up a red pencil from the floor, turned it over in his hand, read the name of its owner written in ink on the carefully scraped wood: Jean-Claude Fage,

and since one of the books in the still life had a red cover, he began coloring in the corresponding rectangle on his drawing.

Monsieur Martin approached:

"We'll just work in black and white today, we'll see if you can use wash later on."

Gérard Hutter put the red pencil in the inside pocket of his blue jacket.

Jean-Claude Fage leaned over toward Hubert Jourdan to ask if he had seen his red pencil, because he wanted to underline the subject you had just dictated to us:

"The international date line."

That was Monday, October 11, in the afternoon; up till now, all

114

the little facts you have reported, or that you have made me report, are situated in the afternoon. Isn't it time to begin with the mornings, particularly the morning of Tuesday, October 12, the pivotal day of this narrative or, more exactly, of this investigation?

At ten, Uncle Henri assigned us a Latin translation, a passage from Cicero's *De Signis*, Verrès' pillage of Sicily, which we were supposed to hand in the next Tuesday, then we started the fourth book of the *Aeneid*, nineteen lines down to:

"For him, for this one man, I could perhaps have weakened."

My Uncle Henri left, then more than half my classmates left, Monsieur Bailly came into the classroom, called the roll, recorded Philippe Guillaume's absence, reminded us that we had to hand in, on the following Monday, the translation he had assigned the day before, *The Charm of Winter* by Thomas de Quincey (the assignments were beginning to be a full evening's load), then had us go on with our reading of *Julius Caesar*:

"Let's see, Eller, yesterday we weren't able to finish what I had assigned you to prepare; suppose you start back at Cassius' speech, line thirty-five:

"I, as Aeneas, our greater ancestor . . . "

After leaving the tenth-grade class (the topography of France) you waited for Monsieur Bailly at the top of the stairs, you asked him for the list of the thirteen eleventh-grade students he had in his class and what we were translating right now; you talked to him about Julius Caesar.

The two of you separated in front of the newspaper kiosk on the sidewalk in front of the Café Taine.

You saw me passing with my brothers, little Jacques who was carrying in his briefcase his geography textbook and notebook, that lesson on the topography of France which he would have to recite for you in a week, and Denis, my older brother, who is not in any of your classes this year.

You waited until almost everyone had gone past, looking at the covers of the literary reviews, then you asked the saleswoman if she had the magazine *Fiction*.

She gave you a strange look as she handed it to you; the next time, it would be better to buy it farther away from the lycée.

Gradually catching up with us, you followed us to the Rue du Canivet.

Everyone was waiting for you in the dining room. There were several big packages at my place and, on the sideboard, a cake with fifteen candles of various colors stuck in it.

In the same row with me, André Knorr's seat is empty; he was absent yesterday too. His neighbor, François Nathan, with kinky hair and dark skin, is listening to you read:

" . . . sometimes in the palace of marble, sometimes in the bamboo palace . . . "

▥▥▥▥▥▥▥▥▥▥▥▥ LAST YEAR, you didn't read that passage to your eleventh-graders, including my brother Denis, you didn't spend a whole lesson on the discovery and conquest of America;

on Tuesday of the second week, since you had almost the same schedule as this year, only a little less conveniently arranged (instead of giving the tenth-graders their geography lesson on Tuesday from eleven to twelve, you had to come back to the lycée for them on Wednesday morning at the same time, that is, for us, since I was in that class); from three to four, you gave an account of Europe in 1600, Elizabeth, Philip II, Ivan the Terrible, Suleiman the Magnificent, Henri IV, and by then I had finished my day, I was going home to the apartment in the Rue du Canivet, after Monsieur Bailly's English class.

I remember how surprised my brother Denis and I were when we had seen him arrive in the middle of August, with his wife and his three children, at the Hôtel de la Plage, at Saint-Cornély. We were coming down from our room in bathing suits, and we saw them, with all their luggage, in front of the porter's desk; we couldn't believe our eyes and wondered how we could avoid being recognized during the three days we had left at the hotel.

You were coming back from Bourges, where you had gone to spend a long weekend on the estate of one of your friends, taking advantage of the occasion to see the old city, its cathedral and the house of Jacques Coeur; you were beginning the second part of the Description of the World by Messer Marco Polo, also called the Book of Wonders, "in which are recounted all the deeds of the Great Khan", while daydreaming about your coming trip to Greece.

Several weeks later, in Mykonos, with Micheline Pavin, you ate broiled lobsters in a little restaurant, watching the boats tossing in the sparkling harbor.

"Why go back to Athens tonight, we should spend a few days here, go back to Delos tomorrow . . . "

I was leaving Paris, I was going to join Uncle Henri at Les Étangs where I was supposed to spend the end of September; my brother Denis opposite me was reading a detective story; as for Jacques, he had stayed in the Rue du Canivet apartment because of a bad cough.

117

He came to join us with our mother and father the following weekend. He still had to rest, he stayed stretched out on his bed when we went to the station with them (a good two kilometers' walk), on Monday afternoon, all of us together, my brother Denis, Uncle Henri and the four cousins, even little François whom we soon had to take turns carrying on our shoulders.

You were walking through the alleys of the old part of Naples with Micheline Pavin, the boat that was waiting for you in the harbor was supposed to leave for Marseille at four.

The two of you glimpsed the shores of Provence through the portholes during lunch the next day.

At Les Étangs, Uncle Henri sitting in the middle of one side of the table, Gérard at his right, Lucie at his left, Aunt Rose opposite, Claude at her right, François at her left, we cousins at the two ends, Denis opposite Jacques and me (Jacques was still quite pale) we watched the thirty-nine candles on the cake burning.

Denis gave our uncle the book on Italian painting that our parents had brought for him, carefully wrapped in its brown paper, Gérard gave him a blue and black tie, Lucie gave him a package of English tobacco.

Then Aunt Rose exclaimed:

"Claude, François, where are your presents?"

The two children stood up, blushing, and went to get the drawing they had hidden on the sideboard behind a big platter, one representing the cabin we were building, and the other the cake itself with its thirty-nine lighted candles.

Since it was a holiday, we older children were allowed to have coffee and even a little cognac in Uncle Henri's study. On his big black desk Aunt Rose had arranged a magnificent bouquet of field flowers that we had all gone out to pick together.

Then Denis gave the signal to leave. Jacques decided he had rested enough and that in any case, since it was a holiday, he was entitled to see the cabin, but Aunt Rose was adamant: he had to go back up to his room, at four, he could come with the two little children, who would show him the way, and bring us something to eat.

On the doorstep, we announced the big news we had been keeping in reserve; despite all our efforts, we hadn't been able to finish the cabin for our uncle's birthday, but the work had advanced quite far anyway, and we hoped that the grand opening could take place the next day.

118

You had accompanied Micheline Pavin to her cabin, you went back to your own to pack your things and close your suitcase. A stiff breeze kept the boat dancing.

Michel Daval tossed on the floor the issue of *Fiction* he had just finished reading lying on his bed in the warm, dry room, then ran downstairs, shouting at his mother that he was going out to play with his sister Lucie.

"She must have gone down the hill with the others."

"I know, I want to use the cart."

The Bonnini children, a boy and a girl, often joined this group, but they had gone to visit their grandparents in Italy just then. The teacher was walking with his wife near a fountain.

As a matter of fact, it was only the next Tuesday that the opening of the cabin could have taken place: we had had to repair the damages caused by the storm. My brother Jacques, completely recovered, had helped us a lot, and he was the one who made the coffee that day, and Aunt Rose said it was perfect.

You were proctoring the entrance exams for the Lycée Taine, thinking about Micheline Pavin, whom you hadn't seen again since your return from Greece, resolving to telephone her at her office once the ordeal was over,

which you did the next Monday. She was in Paris this time, she had come in that morning, but since she was having her apartment repainted, she had asked for a week's extension which had been granted, for business hadn't really started yet; she wouldn't be back until October 4, the day classes began; no, she didn't have a telephone number yet; you already knew her address.

When you left the telephone booth, you wrote the following letter:

DEAR MICHELINE PAVIN,

We promised to meet again in Paris. I tried to reach you at your office. Could you give me a call one of these days, and we'll have lunch.

Yours cordially,

PIERRE VERNIER

My parents had taken Jacques home, and Denis and I had stayed on with the whole Jouret tribe, supposedly to help pack and take care of the younger children during the trip back the next day.

It certainly was a chaotic business. We had to eat in a rush.

The little children, Claude and François, were wildly excited. Aunt Rose told them to go with me to Monsieur Moreux' house, while I reminded him we were expecting him with his cart at 3:45 at the latest. Gérard and Lucie had been requisitioned to dry the few dishes we had used. Denis was helping Uncle Henri bring down the bundles of sheets and blankets from upstairs.

In a restaurant in the Rue des Saints-Pères, you were trying to look objectively at Micheline Pavin, who had telephoned you at my parents' even before having received your letter, and who had already lost her tan from the trip (Delphi, Delos),

studying her smiles, the way she fluttered her eyelashes, smoothed her hair, noticing her hands, her nails, her movements in wiping her mouth with her napkin, lighting a cigarette.

The chimes of Saint-Germain-des-Prés rang two o'clock.

"Why don't you come have coffee at my place?"

"Can you make coffee?"

"It's not such an accomplishment, after all. If the prospect alarms you, remember that I rent a room from one of my sisters; she's certain to be in, she came home yesterday from a weekend in the country; she's a splendid cook and particularly good at making coffee. You have nothing to fear."

"I wouldn't like to bother her. If she can lend us her kitchen for a second, I'll show you that I can manage pretty well too, but usually sisters don't like lending their kitchens to their brothers' friends."

"We'll manage, you'll see. Come on."

Boulevard Saint-Germain, Rue Bonaparte, Place Saint-Sulpice.

On the way to your room, you decided that if you really wanted to live with this woman, you would have to find another apartment.

Of course, the bed wasn't made very nicely. You went to look for my mother who, a few minutes later, though you usually never let her come into your room, even to straighten it, brought in a tray with two cups, the coffeepot, the sugar bowl and even two bottles, cognac and Cointreau, with two liqueur glasses, which you hadn't thought of asking for.

She didn't say a word, as if she had been a servant; you didn't dare introduce her. She inspected your friend with a good deal of curiosity and interest; she closed the door behind her without making a sound.

I had come back to my uncle's house with the two youngest children, Claude and François, my mission accomplished. Denis and Uncle Henri were tying up the wicker hampers. I was asked to close the upstairs blinds; at each window, I said goodbye to the garden with its fruit trees, to the fields strewn with big haystacks, to the woods in which the Baron d'Herrecourt had allowed us to build a cabin and which were already changing color, to the ponds that were sparkling in front of the Bresles hills, to the steeple among the lindens, its weathercock gleaming like a golden accent.

Monsieur Bonnini had gone back to Paris a week before. His wife's health had grown worse again, and she had spent the afternoon in bed.

Michel Daval was coming up the Rhône valley with his big sister and his mother, who was saying to him:

"You know, I just had a letter from Henri Mouron, yes, you know, Uncle Henri Mouron, my cousin who lost his wife; he was in Bourges, but he came to Paris to see us last year with his son Alain, remember? Well, he's moved to Paris; he's found himself an apartment in the Rue du Pré-aux-Clercs, and Alain has entered the Lycée Taine in the eleventh grade, like you. You'll probably be in the same class."

"With Uncle René too? He's Uncle René's nephew too."

"Just like you. You may all find yourselves in the same classroom next Monday."

"He was nice, wasn't he?"

"Your uncle's counting on you to show him around a little."

"I'll be new at the Lycée Taine too."

"You know the neighborhood though. I think he's a bright boy. You could help each other."

"What about Uncle René? He's supposed to be tough."

"You have to work hard; he'll probably keep an eye on you if you're both in his class, but he'll be kind to you too."

"Maybe Alain won't be taking English."

"Henri doesn't say."

On Sunday, walking down the Champs-Élysées, Micheline Pavin: "So work begins tomorrow?"

"For you too. Are you going back to your office?"

"You can telephone me there. How many hours of class do you have a week?"

"Eighteen."

"And you complain!"

"You can't imagine how tiring it is."

121

"Still, you don't have so much homework to correct in history and geography."

"No, that's not it; there are the preparations, of course . . ."

"But you must know it all by heart, after all this time."

"No, and yet I'm lucky enough to have the same courses as last year, my schedule's almost the same, only it's a little more convenient this year. I used to have to go to the lycée two mornings a week—now it's only one."

"Are you going to start that project you mentioned to me, that description of your class?"

"I don't know yet."

Now that I was the leader of the Bisons, I was at our headquarters, near Saint-Hilaire, taking my Scouts' names, addresses, dates of birth, fathers' professions.

The day school started, my two brothers and I told how our first morning had gone. I had the most interesting story since I had been with Uncle Henri two hours; Denis hadn't had Uncle Henri as a teacher last year because there had been two eleventh-grade sections.

I prepared my briefcase for the afternoon. I was supposed to take my drawing board, some paper, some charcoal, but we always pretended not to know what we needed, waiting until the teacher asked us to supply ourselves with these things.

Alone in a little restaurant at the Carrefour de l'Odéon that was not full of students yet, thinking about Micheline Pavin, about the dishes she had made for you, hoping that she would invite you again some evening and deciding that if you began to see a lot of her you would probably have to postpone the execution of that literary project you had talked about together and which she encouraged you to carry out,

you looked at your watch; it was time to go back to the lycée for your first class of the year, history for the ninth grade, the discovery of America, then the topography of the earth for us eleventh-graders (I had already had you as a teacher last year, I was used to you in this role, it didn't bother me the way it did in Uncle Henri's case); history for the tenth grade, including my brother Jacques, the American Revolution and the Declaration of Independence.

In front of the concierge's lodge, Monsieur Bailly:

"Oh, Vernier, here you are back again; well, ready for another year? You must come and have lunch with us one of these days."

"How is Madame Bailly?"

122

"Her work gets more and more wearing."

"It does for all of us."

"I'm afraid it bothers her a lot more than me. You have a splendid color."

"It's the trip to Greece."

"Oh! . . . Congratulations, you'll have to tell us all about that. You don't happen to be free tomorrow, for instance? If there's something else on, I'll let you know tonight. You're still on the Rue du Canivet?"

The bell rang. On the ground floor, you asked the ninth-grade class to write their names, dates of birth, addresses, fathers' professions, on a seating chart, then, after the usual advice, you told them about Marco Polo, you read them the description of Cambaluc, today Peking,

"It is within these walls that the palace of the Great Lord . . . ",

you told them about the voyages of Díaz, Vasco da Gama and particularly Christopher Columbus,

a lesson you had carefully prepared, realizing that the following week you would be teaching it to us with more details and commentary, because you intended to use this hour as the pivot for that essay in description you talked about with Micheline Pavin.

Two floors higher, under the skylight, Monsieur Martin:

"You are certainly old enough to understand that you can't make a drawing without a sheet of paper and without a board to tack it on. I congratulate those of you who remembered to bring these indispensable supplies; I want all the rest of you to have them next Monday, or else be prepared to be kept in after school. For today, we shall confine ourselves to a small sketch. I shall hand out pieces of Ingres paper, which you can prop on your notebooks. We shall try, this year, to draw the human face. You see this plaster head, it is one of the portraits of Caesar; you will make some sketches of it, and then one in full scale. Please note where you are sitting so that you can take the same places next Monday."

First geography class: you were describing for us the inside of the earth: its core of nickel and iron, its viscous envelope of silicon and magnesium, its broken crust of silicon and aluminum; Michel Daval, while carefully taking notes in his notebook that was still neat, was adding some more shadows to the pencil sketch he had made of Caesar's head.

123

A few classrooms away, Monsieur Bonnini was looking at the newly painted walls.

The next morning, Monsieur Bailly dictated a passage from one of Coleridge's lectures on *Julius Caesar*.

I waited for Denis when school was out, but he had already met a lot of old friends, and he walked past me with two tall boys, nodding his head at me and saying:

"My brother."

They seemed to recognize me. Jacques was coming from the other end of the floor, and you were following a few steps behind him. Denis had passed Jacques on the stairs and indicated him with the same gesture of his head,

"My other brother."

Jacques waited for me; we walked down together. We turned behind Saint-Sulpice, and reached the Rue du Canivet apartment long before Denis. We sat down without him. My father was furious,

"A good start!"

My mother tried to calm him down. Denis came in with his head in the air, after we had started the dessert.

At the door of the eleventh-grade classroom, you had met your colleague Bailly.

"You have a nephew in your class, Vernier; but just think, I have two of them, not so close as yours, they're both the sons of first cousins, Alain Mouron and Michel Daval; they're both in the lycée for the first time. I never had any relatives in my class; I know you're used to it; you've already had one of your nephews in the eleventh grade, and as for the one you have this year, his brother Pierre, you were already his teacher last year; but you know, I'm rather curious to know what effect this will all have."

"It depends on your relations with them outside. You know I have this project, it's still quite vague, I don't know when I'm going to start on it, to write the description of a class. If you could give me some information about the occupations and opinions of your two nephews, you'd be doing me an enormous favor."

The métro at Saint-Hilaire; Odéon, Mabillon, Croix-Rouge where there's no stop, Sèvres-Babylone, Vaneau where you both got off; the statue of the Egyptian, the shops and cafés; you both turned into the Rue Pierre-Leroux, went upstairs.

Madame Bailly had gone to pick up the three younger children at their elementary school; dinner rather gloomy; once inside the door, your colleague lost his good humor, he didn't say a word all through lunch.

Madame Bailly was watching you; their relations were growing more and more strained, it was as if they kept trying to avoid looking at each other, and the three children took advantage of it to play all sorts of tricks on each other.

In the métro, after coffee, Monsieur Bailly recovered his cordiality. Your briefcase was very heavy, since it contained, in addition to the morning's textbooks, those for the afternoon as well.

At the desk behind mine, Jean-Pierre Cormier wrote from your dictation:

"Part Two, the division of the Roman world into two rival empires, its religious expression in the Great Schism."

On the main floor, Monsieur du Marnet was breaking down the numbers 1,492 and 1,954 into primary factors for his ninth-graders.

On Wednesday morning, Denis walked past me again with his friends. I didn't wait for Jacques, deciding he would be perfectly capable, now that he was in tenth grade, of walking home to the Rue du Canivet alone, and I followed my older brother, at a slight distance.

He went into a café, sat down at a round table near the window.

I crossed the street, watched him for a while.

He didn't suspect I was there; they ordered three glasses of beer, he took out his wallet to pay for his share.

I decided that next week, as soon as I was fifteen, I would also be entitled to a little pocket money.

They came out, I hid in the shadow of a doorway. They walked past me; one of the tall boys offered Denis a cigarette; I had never seen him smoke, I had never smoked myself. He couldn't help coughing, but he got over it quickly. It couldn't have been the first time; he had probably started with them last year.

I made a detour through the Rue de Vaugirard, running, because I wanted to get home ahead of Denis, and I succeeded, but too late all the same; everyone was already sitting down at the table.

When Denis came in, my father exploded:

"I'm reminding both of you that we eat lunch at twelve-thirty around here; there's no reason to be late; I don't want you to be hanging around the streets like this."

Jacques was the picture of a clear conscience. Denis sat down

125

without saying a word and slowly unfolded his napkin, staring at me, I wondered for a moment if he had seen me.

The three of us left together, we crossed the sunny Place Saint-Sulpice without a word, we passed the morning's café without either of us seeming to notice it.

My briefcase was light, only the math textbook and the notebook.

Sitting on a café terrace, sipping your coffee, you saw us, glanced at your watch, called the waiter, caught up with us as we were going into the lycée, where we separated, Denis and Jacques going upstairs, while I went to the gym.

Turning left into the courtyard, you went to teach your ninth-graders the Italian wars, Pope Julius II, Chevalier Bayard *sans peur et sans reproche*, the Battle of Marignan, Charles becomes Emperor.

An hour later, Michel Daval, next to me, was staring at our math teacher whose name we didn't know yet and who reminded us that for division, the rule of signs is the same as for multiplication: minus divided by plus equals minus, minus divided by minus equals plus.

In the Rue du Cardinal-Lemoine apartment, sitting beside his wife, who was napping, the shutter closed and the room lit only by a little lamp, Monsieur Bonnini was rereading the first two cantos of the *Inferno*:

"*Nel mezzo del cammin di nostra vita . . .* "

to be ready to discuss them with his seniors on Friday.

Uncle Henri, whom I was beginning to get used to in his role as a teacher, and whom I hadn't seen outside the school since we had got back from Les Étangs, had assigned us the *Épître à Lyon Jamet*.

That was just after the Greek lesson; we had stayed on, he at his desk, I in my seat.

He began by reminding us of the composition we had to hand in the next Tuesday; he looked at the seating chart and suddenly raised his head in my direction, but winking, as though to avoid seeing me:

"Tell me, Monsieur Mouron, what do you know about Clément Marot?"

It was as if he had first intended to question me, and then at the last moment changed his mind, the choice falling on the boy sitting just in front of me.

You talked about prehistoric France, the stone age, the Lascaux cave paintings, carved reindeer horns, the discovery of metals, megaliths and the invention of writing.

On Saturday at noon, coming out of math class, I saw my brother Denis and his two tall friends walk past again, and I followed them as carefully as I could, but this time I think he suspected something and looked behind him several times. Luckily I had taken the precaution of crossing to the other side of the street. They went into the same café. I walked on, turned around a few steps farther, and saw that they were coming out, that Denis had a pack of cigarettes in his hand and was offering them around.

I walked home wondering how much the pack cost, and how much Denis could buy every month with the allowance my parents gave him, the same sum they would soon be giving me, once I was fifteen, the following Tuesday, five hundred francs, supposedly so we could buy our own métro tickets for the scout hikes and our own school supplies.

He certainly couldn't buy a lot of beer or cigarettes with that, five hundred francs, which was what he had had last year at the same time, when he was still fifteen, but maybe his allowance had been increased now that he was sixteen, maybe he got a thousand francs a month, I couldn't find out, he had never mentioned it to me, and it all was done so secretly; maybe it would be increased again after November 10, his next birthday, but in any case he couldn't go on being so generous with his friends for long.

Leaving the house after lunch, I noticed the pack in his pocket, and the box of matches that he took out, playing with it for a minute, tossing it and catching it, crossing the Place Saint-Sulpice, watching me out of the corner of his eye as though to tease me. I didn't say anything, I knew he would finish by offering me one.

On the Boulevard Saint-Germain, on the same café terrace, at the same table maybe, but not alone this time, with a woman we had never seen, you didn't notice us, and you came to the lycée late, after having walked her back to the métro stop, running like a student when you heard the two chimes, to get to your ninth-graders who were beginning to be noisy, so that you had to pound your fist on the desk in order to make them be quiet, ashamed of resorting to this method,

"This year, we are to study Europe."

Its situation, its small size, its historical importance, the role it still played, the changes that were in store for it; then you came back to the apartment with us.

Michel Daval, while you were talking to us about Luther, crossed out with a kind of fury the name of Ignatius Loyola, written in on the map showing the chief centers of the Reformation, beside the city of Rome.

Two classrooms away, Monsieur Bonnini was making his seniors read the passage where Dante asks Virgil what men are lamenting so loudly and the Latin poet answers that they are the ones even Hell rejects because they have lived without infamy and without praise, without even any hope of dying, their blind lives so base that they are envious of any other fate.

Sunday morning, the patrol's first hike, we walked through the transfer tunnel of the Denfert-Rochereau métro stop, following close behind Jacques' Tigers, followed closely by the Chamois.

While we were waiting for the train at Massy-Palaiseau, the first drops began falling. I still had my blue canvas jacket that wasn't even waterproof any more, greatly envying those of my classmates who had leather jackets, and I had already suggested to my mother that she give me one for my birthday.

In my pocket, the instructions; we tried to decode them in the train, but it was only at lunchtime, in the cold and already soaking woods, that we managed to find the key.

My Uncle Henri told you that none of the boys would be there because Gérard, his older son, had joined the Saint-Hilaire scout troop this year, the Squirrel Patrol, and that he had left with Jacques and me,

"Pretty bad weather for eating outside",

and that the other two had been invited by their Grandmother Jouret. Yes, Lucie was there, she came to say hello to you.

You went into Uncle Henri's study for coffee and began talking about the lycée, about the curriculum and about me.

Jean-Pierre Cormier, during the afternoon, went to a movie to watch outlaws galloping through the woods of the Rockies, dismounting, lighting a fire and making themselves coffee. Monsieur du Marnet, with his wife, had visited his parents-in-law, whom he hadn't seen since school started.

On Monday, the routine had already begun; a whole week of classes had passed. We had grown used to our schedule and we knew that in the morning Greek would be followed by Latin, the text of Livy in the big *Latin Literature*, Hannibal crossing the Alps.

Uncle Henri reminded us that for the next day we were to prepare the beginning of the fourth book of the *Aeneid*, the first nineteen lines, from:

"But now for some time while the queen had been growing
more grievously lovesick..."

with a note explaining that the word cura, which ordinarily means
"illness" or "care", meant love,
down to this line in Dido's speech:

"For him, for this one man I could perhaps have weakened",

and that we were supposed to continue our reading of Livy for
Wednesday.

The bell rang; some of the boys left the room and came back in
at the second bell.

We were through with Clément Marot. Uncle Henri told us about
Rabelais' life, made us read the episode that led Gargantua to the
death of his wife, Badebec, reminded us that tomorrow we were to hand
in our composition on the one most remarkable day of our vacation,
asked us to prepare the letter Gargantua sent to his son Pantagruel
to give him a curriculum for his education.

In the Rue du Canivet apartment, you were preparing your three
classes for the afternoon:

for the ninth grade, the conquest and exploration of America,
which was particularly important to you, because you wanted to talk
to us about it the next day too, in the second part of that hour which
could be the point of departure for your description,

for us, the earth in space, its motion, the measurement of time,

for the tenth grade, the beginning of the French Revolution and
the Declaration of the Rights of Man.

You went to lunch in the restaurant on the Rue des Saints-Pères,
and you decided that there couldn't be a better place to take me to
dinner the next evening.

During the afternoon, Henri Fage turned around toward Jean-
Claude Fage, who is no more related to him than I am, to take back
the red pencil he had handed him so he could underline the subtitle
you had dictated to us:

"The year."

In the courtyard, Monsieur Moret was making all his eighth-graders
breathe rhythmically.

Monsieur Mouron had already put on his overcoat when he came
into his son Alain's room and opened the shutters.

"It's five to eight already, hurry up, the coffee's on the stove."

129

He slammed the hall door behind him. Alain had difficulty opening his eyes, he had gone to bed late the night before, staying up over his French composition. He was alone in the apartment; the cleaning woman wouldn't be there before nine. He threw back the sheet and blankets, buttoned his pajama jacket and went to the bathroom. There was no hot water.

While drinking his coffee at the kitchen table covered with an almost new oilcloth that still had a strong smell, he read his homework over and added a few commas. It was for the afternoon. He had not had time to finish his Greek and Latin preparations for the morning, it was only English that he wasn't worried about, with that passage from *Julius Caesar*, wasn't very worried about; for the rest, he would have to hope he wouldn't be called on.

When he reached the lycée, several minutes after the bell, the janitor, still indulgent at the beginning of the year, didn't take his name.

"All right, all right, hurry up there!"

The halls were empty and silent. Only one other pupil, an older boy, was climbing the stairs. Alain Mouron opened the door to our class cautiously. Uncle Henri looked up.

"What's your name?"

"Mouron."

"Oh yes, Mouron, of course! I don't need to tell you, Mouron, that you're late for the second time. If this happens again, I shall have the painful duty of carrying out my threat. No, I don't want any excuses. Go to your seat, please, you've disturbed the class enough as it is."

Ulysses finally approaches the mouth of the river on the island of the Phaeacians. He has just implored the god Poseidon to take pity on him.

Another boy was reading, whom my uncle was correcting. Francis Hutter showed the line to his neighbor:

"His whole skin was swollen; the sea streamed from his nose and mouth . . . "

And so on down to Ulysses' fear that he might drowse off and be devoured in his sleep by some wild beast.

"Tomorrow we shall finish this fifth book, which will make a somewhat longer assignment; excellent for your Greek. Ulysses will hide in a thicket camouflaging himself as well as possible, and yield to his exhaustion."

130

Some boys went out, came back. We switched from Homer to Virgil. After assigning the lines of translation we would have to hand in the following Tuesday (the homework was beginning to mount up), he asked Michel Daval to translate:

"But now for some while the queen had been growing more
  grievously love-sick,
Feeding the wound with her life-blood, the fire biting within her.
Much did she muse on the hero's nobility, and much
On his family's fame . . . ",

but Michel Daval, who had already been called on in Latin the week before, had decided there was no need to prepare this passage, and I had counted on the fact that my uncle wouldn't have the heart to risk giving me a bad mark on my birthday, so that I was no help to Michel.

I saw that my Uncle Henri loved what he was reading to us, that he would have liked to communicate this love to us, commenting in detail on these words my neighbor was stumbling over, exasperated to be forced to deal with only the most elementary corrections;

I know that Michel Daval was furious with himself, that at this moment he was really sorry to be incapable of reading better.

He had to continue, advance, clear away difficulties, amid increasing boredom. It didn't go much better with Pelletier or with Orland. Uncle Henri's features began to droop with exhaustion. He looked at his watch, the bell was about to ring.

Christopher Columbus, his first crossing of the Atlantic, his first landing on the islands of the New Indies, full of unknown dangers, in those Antilles he had taken for Cathay; at the back of the class, Louis Pelletier, afraid of being called on by Monsieur Jouret the next day, is copying, hidden behind the broad shoulders of Bernard de Loups, out of a page from a notebook brought by Rémy Orland, his neighbor, the notes taken by the latter's older brother two years before, when he was in the eleventh grade with Uncle Henri as his teacher, on Hannibal's crossing of the Alps.

Rémy Orland is drawing in the notebook's margin a little galleon on the prow of which he writes Santa Maria, inspired by a picture he saw on a Spanish stamp, the waves of the sea, the steep coast of an island.

During the evening, you began writing that text I am continuing, or more precisely that you are continuing by using me, for actually,

131

it's not I who is writing but you, you are speaking *through* me, trying to see things from my point of view, to imagine what I could know that you don't know, furnishing me the information which you possess and which would be out of my reach.

You were addressing this text to me, you were writing it with the intention of making me read it, once it was finished, once I would be in a position to understand its interest and all the words in it, once I had finished climbing that ladder of secondary education, and you still didn't suspect, waiting for me in the Rue du Canivet, on that Tuesday, October 12, 1954, that you were going to introduce me into it in this new manner, making use of me as a narrator, and this by making not the Pierre Eller who I was on that day, who certainly wouldn't have been able to express himself in this way, but the Pierre Eller who I might be in a few years, do the writing.

You had arranged to meet me at seven, but since Uncle Henri kept me quite a long time, it wasn't until seven-fifteen that I reached the Rue du Canivet apartment, ringing at your door this time instead of at my parents'.

You left your typewriter and opened the door, you showed me, without making me read them, the few pages already written, giving me a brief explanation of your intentions and asking my help.

Obviously you wanted to avoid any misunderstanding, it was not at all a question of spying or tattling, and you promised to make no academic use of any information I gave you. To rid me of any such hesitation, you insisted on the fact that I could delay giving you such information as long as I liked. It was only a matter of reporting to you, so to speak, the tiny events of the class, of allowing you to consult my notebook regularly, of giving you my impressions about my classmates or your colleagues.

I felt that there was something a little dangerous here, that I would have to be careful never to let this kind of secret mission be known, and that excited me a lot; it was a game much more serious than any of those my scout experience had accustomed me to, or than my brothers, my cousin and I had invented during our vacation.

Before going out, we had sealed a kind of pact. Provided with a role and something like a new point of view, it was then that I really felt I was fifteen, that I had crossed a threshold. There had been the presents, the first allowance of five hundred francs which had been given to me; now there was this beginning of a singular adventure which I didn't understand very well, except that you attached a great deal of importance to it and that because of it you were beginning to attach a new importance to me as well.

In the restaurant on the Rue des Saints-Pères I could choose from the menu myself for the first time, and afterwards, on the Boulevard Saint-Germain, in that café where we used to see you on the terrace quite often when we were going to the lycée after lunch, you bought me a glass of beer and even a cigarette, without suspecting what this meant to me, in other words, that I didn't have to wait for Denis' generosity, deciding that last year, in November, when we had celebrated his sixteenth birthday, he had probably not been entitled to such ceremonies.

We met again the next day in class.

(Monsieur Martin, under the skylight, had asked each of his tenth-graders to draw the first letter of his name and to decorate it as he chose; the bust of Caesar was waiting for us);

the representation of the earth,

you were commenting on those figures that looked so peculiar to us in our textbook, showing what orthographic or stereographic projections are, explaining their uses to us,

when at the back of the class, Jean-Claude Fage heaved a deep sigh, making us all turn around to laugh at him.

"Is it as boring as all that?"

"Oh, no, Monsieur, not at all."

Without a trace of insolence, upset, in fact, at having disturbed the lesson, but his attention was beginning to wander, and he was not the only one, as you had sensed yourself.

Once this slight disturbance was silenced with a movement of your hand, you let several moments of silence go by.

"Now, write the subtitle: scale representation."

On Thursday, Francis Hutter, a black armband stitched on his blue coat sleeve, sitting in the train beside his brother Jean-Louis, his sister Adèle, his mother in a black veil, and his red-eyed father, watched the Champagne landscape slide past as they returned from the village where they had just buried his grandfather.

The German teacher was taking a walk with his daughter Geneviève and his son Gérard in the Jardin des Plantes, from the monkey house to the lion house; a faint sunbeam cast the shadow of the bars on the animals inside.

On Friday, on the other side of the wall in front of me, Monsieur Bailly, after having collected the translations, a passage from a lecture

133

by Coleridge on *Macbeth* (five or six boys, including my brother Denis, who declared that they hadn't been able to finish it, would be kept in if they didn't hand it in the next day, and anyone who didn't have a suitable complete edition of the play by Monday would also be kept in),

"Now let us look at our texts, those of us who have nothing else, on page one hundred and seventy-seven. The notion of the murder begins to dawn on Macbeth. He is so absorbed by his new feelings that he no longer pays any attention to those around him, and Banquo is obliged to remind him of the present."

In front of the wall, in front of the platform, Alain Mouron was reading:

"Ponocrates remonstrated with him that he ought not to eat so soon after getting out of bed . . . ",

and on Monday he was writing from your dictation the definition of climate; his uncle at the other end of the floor was reading the *Jungle Book* with his tenth-graders;

and on Tuesday, Monsieur Hutter being with another tenth-grade section, Francis, wearing his black armband, not writing for the last few minutes, his eyes fixed on the textbook illustration, a planter's house in the Antilles, with its sheds and its courtyard, its various palm trees, its black slaves wearing long drawers, drying tobacco leaves or shredding manioc (manioc?), many details remaining obscure, what was bubbling in the pot in the middle, what were those cakes arranged on the roof of the hut,

was dreaming that he was walking in the back door of the residence of this planter whose tiny white figure he made out near a bush, not a rosebush, but some flower that was bigger and more heavily perfumed;

and inside this house, there were furnishings quite like those he had seen in his grandfather's living room, the day of the funeral, last week, but all made out of silver;

the walls were covered with ceramic tiles with blue designs on them representing episodes from the Bible whose titles were written in German in an old-fashioned script,

the windows overlooked huge fields of tobacco whose leaves and flowers swayed under the warm wind; there were clouds of parrots and parakeets that flew into the air from time to time;

in the distance, the harbor with big sailboats, full of silver ingots,

134

that were about to leave for Spain; and out of some holes in the mountains rose the songs of the slaves and the sound of their pickaxes.

"What am I talking about, Hutter?"

He stood up, dropped his book.

"About America."

"But what about America?"

"About the slave trade."

"Show me your notebook. I see. You'll have to bring this up to date, my boy. Just ask your neighbor to help you."

You were looking at his black armband, you didn't feel like punishing him, he sensed it, decided that he would have to copy everything over anyway, and that it was therefore no use, for the rest of the hour, wearing himself out writing down what you were saying; besides he had completely lost the thread of your lesson, companies, freedom of the seas, international law, but since he was in the first row and wanted to be a good student and in your good graces, he would at least have to pretend to be taking notes; that is why he wrote on a blank sheet of his notebook:

"The planter is sitting near his window. The planter is smoking his pipe. The planter has buried his grandfather the week before. The planter knows that slavery is forbidden. The planter knows he is damned."

Hypnotized by the sentence he had just written, he straightened up, covered it with his hand, for his neighbor Alain Mouron was turning his head toward him as though trying to read it. He carefully crossed it out, then the whole of his text to the top of the page. He put down his pen, stared for a long time at these black lines.

"Monsieur Hutter, I'm sorry, but you'll have to come in next Thursday."

On Wednesday, Alain Mouron, after having satisfactorily extracted the square root of 2642 at the board, went back to his seat and took out his ink bottle in order to fill his pen.

Badly corked, it had spotted his notebook and the cover of the magazine *Fiction*, which he took out for a second to dry it with his blotter, and which Francis Hutter looked at with envious eyes.

A few minutes later, bending down to put back his briefcase that had fallen over onto his foot, he generously took this copy out again and laid it on his neighbor's knees

135

(Monsieur du Marnet, at the board, was correcting the numerous errors of Bernard de Loups),

scribbling these words in pencil on his notebook:

"Something to read when you're kept in. Give it back soon; not to me."

Under the shiny October rain, Monsieur Bailly was pacing up and down the Avenue Émile-Zola, unable to make up his mind to go into his mistress' house, for he had come to tell her that he had finally decided on a divorce, that he had had a hideous scene with Elizabeth, but that the best way to get things over with, since he hadn't managed to obtain any real evidence against her, was to make the court decide that the offenses were on his side

(he would therefore need her complicity, he would also have to find a lawyer who would co-operate),

and now that he was about to tell her this, to take the first steps, it seemed monstrously clumsy and painful; he suddenly felt that it wasn't worth the trouble, that perhaps everything could be settled equably, which would be so much simpler for the children.

He was supposed to be at Claire's at three; a clock in the window of a grocery store already showed half-past three; she must be getting worried; he entered the building, composing his features.

And the senior boys, the following Tuesday, didn't understand why he suddenly grew so nervous when he explained the passage where the wedding guest hears the music without being able to go in to the festivities, constrained to listen to the ancient mariner, the old man with glittering eyes, telling about his voyage to the land of ice and terrible noises.

Alain Mouron took notes from your dictation:

"Development of the Thirty Years' War; the mercenaries; Wallenstein."

Now you are questioning him about Richelieu's work, particularly about his colonial policy; he is somewhat at a loss, for like the other two, Nathan and Orland, you had already called on him the day before, in geography.

Monsieur Bailly, after having collected the homework, proceeds to the second part: the fog lifts, the boat enters the Pacific Ocean, heads north to the equator, stops in a dead calm.

||||||||||||||||||||||||||||||||| In 1952, in the class Joseph Jourdan and Philippe Fage were in, after having asked questions about the Renaissance and the Reformation, you gave an account of Europe around 1600 and finished your lesson with descriptions of Philip II and Henry of Navarre.

On the main floor, a teacher whose name I have forgotten was making us reduce to primary factors several numbers, in particular the number 1952.

Then the vacation; my father, having scheduled his for September, took my brothers and me to a little village in Provence, Saint-Florentin.

You were in Saint-Cornély, in the Hôtel de la Plage, which Monsieur Bailly had recommended to you.

For my brother Denis, who was fifteen, for François Cormier, Bertrand Fage, Denis Régnier, who got sick soon after and had to repeat, the end of the Middle Ages, the taking of Constantinople by the Turks and the discovery of America.

I was thirteen, I had finished my day at school, I went home to the apartment in the Rue du Canivet with a light briefcase, only my notebook and my English textbook, without my written work for the next day, just preparations in Greek, Latin and French.

I was fourteen the next Monday. I went into English class proud of my new briefcase with its yellow leather buckle and passed it around among my new classmates,

sitting near the window but in the third row, beside Henri Fage who soon exasperated me because he talked all the time.

A few classrooms away the earth in space, the measurement of time, what a day is, an hour, a month, a year, a season.

The next afternoon in the seventh grade, Egypt, inundations of the Nile.

Alain Mouron, in Bourges, didn't have the same schedule I did. Since he would have thought it was peculiar if I had asked him how his classes had been arranged last year, and since you had told me you would like to know, I had to use strategy; I stole one of his tenth-grade notebooks that he used for his rough drafts and in which I had noticed that he had pasted his schedule for the week. So, on the afternoon of October 13, 1953, after a geography class, he studied mathematics for an hour, probably watching his teacher whose name he has no doubt already forgotten, explain, drawing the figure on the blackboard, that the geometric locus of the points equidistant from two given points is the perpendicular raised at the mid-point of the line jointing these two points.

At the Lycée Taine, Uncle Henri was reading to his seniors the passage in Saint-Simon about the death of Monseigneur the Dauphin.

The wheel of the school year with all its months, down to the last lesson, has revolved. The day before July 14, we were already on our vacation; the prizes had already been awarded that morning. You were hearing orals at the Lycée Buffon; I was preparing my sleeping bag and my camping kit to leave with the Saint-Hilaire troop. We had talked about it, my brother Denis and I, one afternoon at Saint-Cornély, it was raining; in the hotel living room, a little girl was playing exercises on the piano, Jacques was reading *From the Earth to the Moon* in the Green Library series, and we were sitting on rattan armchairs, absorbed in magazines abandoned there by various guests.

"I left the troop; 'I'm supposed to become a scoutmaster in September, but I wonder if I should bother. There are the finals at the end of the year, I think I'll have to work pretty hard for that. Of course you'll only be in eleventh grade. You'll be able to be patrol leader without worrying about anything."

I stood up without answering him, I went to sit down at the other end of the room, I was annoyed.

To get out of the rain, you went into a bookstore on the Boulevard Saint-Germain, and after looking through several books, you bought the *Description of the World*.

The following Monday, you visited the house of Jacques Coeur. It was a beautiful day, even in Saint-Cornély. While the three of us were on a huge boulder that we had covered with imaginary houses, this unevenness a living room, that one a bathroom, a fish pond, a garden, a prison, we noticed, swimming a little farther down the beach, two of those girls we wished we had known better, who might have peopled our wet mineral city, whom we might have adorned with necklaces of seaweed.

We had named this reef our Indies; we were watching for ships of pirates coveting our gold mines and our rum springs.

Coming back from Bourges (the leatherette seat, warmed by the sun, was sticky), you opened the *Description of the World* to Chapter 75: in which is described the city of Ciandu and the marvelous palace of the Great Khan.

At Les Étangs, Uncle Henri, probably walking alone in the birch woods, plunging through the huge ferns as through the dense waters of a calm river full of fish.

Alain Mouron was taking a nap in the hollow of a big, dry rock from which he could see the steeples of Saint-Florentin and Saint-Gatien, in the middle of the tremendous, scorched landscape, dreaming of life in the open air, of camps, of explorations, of campfires and songs around them while the crickets chirped.

At the end of the month, my brothers and I met back in vacation-deserted Paris: we didn't know what we were going to do with our afternoon. Once we went to Versailles. There was a huge crowd in the park. We went for a boat ride on the big pond, and Jacques managed to fall in. He knows how to swim, of course, but he caught cold because he couldn't change clothes before he got back to Paris.

You were at Delphi. You didn't meet Micheline Pavin until the following Monday, on the Greek ship that was taking you to Mykonos; she was looking in her *Guide Bleu* for the name of the islands, you helped her.

I was packing my things with Denis, for we were supposed to leave the next day for Les Étangs to spend the end of the vacation there. Jacques still hadn't recovered from his cough.

On the way back from Delos, you gave your hand to Micheline Pavin to help her out of the boat full of tourists. You found a cool restaurant and you went in and ordered lobsters. The fatigue of the trip, the tossing of the little boat, the heat, all this made you silent.

Uncle Henri, with his two older children, started for the station to meet us when we got off the train, crossing the big linden woods, the old paths of an estate whose grounds was covered with soft moss; a little farther on the trees were mostly oaks; since there was plenty of time, they stopped and made little men with acorn heads, supposedly for Claude and François, who had stayed home to play in the garden.

It was raining in Saint-Cornély. Young René Bailly, who had celebrated his ninth birthday at lunch, had received, among other presents, a parcheesi set; Alain Mouron was trying to learn the rules

139

and teach them to his little cousins. On the other side of the wall, they knew that their mother was packing her suitcases, for she was going to leave them soon to go to Orléans.

It was Sunday that we went to see the baron, the owner of the woods, to ask permission to build a cabin, Denis, my cousin Gérard and I; Jacques had come the night before with our parents, but they had made him take a nap.

A reddish-brown dog barked when we made the gate creak; in the hall, we felt the black-and-white tiles give slightly under our feet. The baron received us in his mournful study, with a slow-combustion stove for the winter, a worn carpet with big rents in it, showing the unwaxed floor with deep holes burnt all over the surface.

You were crossing the isthmus of Corinth with Micheline Pavin. The boat was running through the huge trench.

You ate lunch in Naples the next day, in a modest restaurant near the National Museum, then you began walking through the old alleyways.

After their nap, Alain Mouron took his little cousins to the beach. They undressed in the green-and-white-striped cabin; the four of them holding hands, they waded into the foam. Little Agnès, who had been very cheerful up to this point, began screaming.

Alain took her in his arms, consoled her, while keeping an eye on René and Georges who were splashing each other happily, made a hole in the sand and discovered a little gold shell which he gave her and which calmed her; she carefully washed it off.

Alain Mouron decided that his uncle had invited him to take care of the children, because he knew his aunt wouldn't stay with them during all of September.

Uncle Henri was walking in front of us on the path to the station with my father. We had passed the tall lindens; then came the oaks; then the path turned around the pond and the willows hid them.

Both of them, carrying their coats on their arms but wearing their hats, were making broad gestures with their canes. We caught up with them on the platform, sitting on a bench near the shed for the wheelbarrows and the lanterns. A cart went across the bridge. The train came, my parents got on; my Aunt Rose took the suitcase from Denis and handed it to my father.

Then I realized something that I had never really understood before, the fact that they were brother and sister.

The train left, we watched it growing smaller; my uncle kissed my aunt affectionately.

Then the next day was his birthday, and when lunch was over he blew out the thirty-nine candles.

Alain Mouron, at the little table the Bailly family had chosen long before his arrival, was looking at the other tables, the other boys, the girls he dared not speak to, still feeling obliged to take care of his cousins; it was the price of his keep.

He went upstairs to put them to bed while his Uncle Bailly was drinking his coffee, then went down to the living room of the hotel, sat in a rattan armchair

(through the window, he saw the other boys and girls leaving in a group on some excursion, squeezing into two huge convertibles; he hadn't dared ask his uncle's permission to join them, and the latter, silent, lost in his thoughts, shifting the care of his children onto his nephew now that his wife had left, hadn't probably even noticed his desire),

went back to the pile of magazines.

His uncle came over and interrupted his reading; at three-thirty, he went upstairs to wake his cousins, help Agnès to get dressed.

Uncle Henri had stood up in his study and was watching Denis and me go down the path to the Herrecourt woods; he took his pipe out of his pocket, stuffed it with English tobacco. The bouquet of wildflowers trembled in front of the open window.

Denis Régnier was coming back from Savoie with his mother and his sister. He had to take the entrance examination; he was holding his geography book, but he couldn't read a single word.

Now Monsieur Hubert happened to be on the same train, he was coming back to Paris to correct this examination and the second baccalaureate session.

Jacques came to join us with the two little Jouret children, Claude and François, who had served as his guides through the woods, bringing us in a hamper the buttered bread and apples that we ate in the cabin, almost finished now except for the roof that we had to cover with ferns. The walls were already well insulated, and it felt safe inside, we had put in a window that had a spendid view, the quicksilver of a pool showing through some birch trees.

Each of us armed with a penknife, we cut ferns until nightfall.

The boat came into the harbor of Marseille. You walked down the gangplank behind Micheline Pavin, whose suitcase you were carrying with your own. Since neither of you knew the name of a hotel, you told the taxi driver to take you to the station.

In the twilight, we gathered up our tools. Only half the roof was covered, but the wind was getting cooler; the little children were beginning to be frightened. We headed back to the house; we still hoped that the cabin would be finished the next day.

But there was a terrible storm that lasted until dark, and we had to spend the afternoon playing lotto in the dining room.

The weather was beautiful in the Rhône valley between Valence and Lyon. Micheline Pavin, opposite you, was reading a woman's magazine.

" . . . for it is the greatest city to be found in the world, and one can taste there so many pleasures that one imagines oneself to be in paradise . . . "

The entrance exams began on September 20; you proctored Denis Régnier. My two brothers and I, with Gérard and Lucie, were cutting ferns to finish the roof of the cabin at last. They were damp, but that didn't matter much now, it was almost time to go back to school.

On Tuesday, still proctoring the exams, you began thinking about the year that was about to begin again, about this life of sterility and solitude that was waiting for you. There were two ways for you to escape it: literature or marriage.

Uncle Henri drank his coffee with us, in the cabin that was finally finished. The sun on that day had almost dried the already yellowed ferns. Alain Mouron, in the hotel living room, was thinking of his life in the big city.

On Sunday, September 26, the big trunks were packed under Aunt Rose's supervision. Uncle Henri, having nothing to do, walked back and forth smoking his pipe. You were wandering through one of the Greek rooms of the Louvre.

You went to the lycée the next day to ask the principal what your schedule for this year would be. It was the same as last year's, save for one point, which made a great improvement: the tenth-grade geography class on Wednesday morning was shifted to Tuesday.

You went into the Café Taine to try to telephone Micheline Pavin, who was supposed to have returned to Paris.

Madame Bailly, back from Orléans, was supervising the packing at Saint-Cornély. It hadn't stopped raining since morning.

Uncle Henri, for the last time that year, was walking alone through the woods, in the fine rain that he scarcely felt, while we were packing.

On the twenty-eighth, the whole Bailly family ate an early lunch; they were to take the one-thirty train. The manager of the hotel took them all in his car with the luggage. Alain Mouron got on the train first and discovered a compartment with only two people in it, an old peasant couple who were eating Vire sausages.

With the help of my brother Denis, Uncle Henri brought down from upstairs the bundles of sheets and blankets; then they tied up the rattan hampers.

Denis Régnier had come back from his father's in tears, his mother tried to comfort him, he described the whole scene to her.

He had told his father that he had failed his entrance exams, and instead of feeling sorry for him, his father had burst out laughing.

"I don't understand," he had said, "why your mother insists on wanting you to continue that ridiculous secondary education . . . "

Monsieur Hubert was walking slowly with his pregnant wife, near the Pont Mirabeau.

Monsieur Moreux helped us load the trunks on his truck. I sat beside him near the steering wheel, Denis squeezed against me, slammed the door, and the whole Jouret family were packed in the back with the luggage, like sardines.

We couldn't find a compartment for all of us; Uncle Henri and Aunt Rose sat on one side with the two little children; Lucie and Gérard sat on the other side; Denis and I stood up in the corridor.

In your room, you were talking to Micheline Pavin about that work you are writing; you drew diagrams on sheets of blank paper showing her how it was organized; you showed her your history and geography textbooks one after another.

At five o'clock, the two of you went to a café in Saint-Germain. She asked you to come to her apartment for dinner.

Aunt Rose took out of the hamper some slices of buttered bread and apples. The landscape rolled past. We were coming back to our parents, to the Rue du Canivet, to the Lycée Taine. We didn't say a word. It was raining.

The next afternoon, Denis, Jacques and I went to get the list of the textbooks we would need for this year. Mine was almost the same as Denis' from last year. He would give me his eleventh-grade *Anthology of Greek Literature*, his *Sixteenth Century French Authors*,

143

his *Seventeenth Century French Authors*, his *General Geography*, his history textbook. I already had the *Anthology of Latin Literature* and the *Anthology of English Literature*; *Physics, Chemistry* and *Mathematics* had changed; we would have to line up in some bookstore to buy them.

Jacques' list was almost the same as mine from last year.

You leafed through those history and geography textbooks piled on the table, thinking it would be necessary to review it all, to bring to your classes some new yeast or else risk asphyxiating yourself and boring us to death.

On Saturday you rang at Uncle Henri's door; Aunt Rose told you he had gone with the children to the stationery store. We ran into them, in fact, in a big store where we were all looking for the same things: notebooks, pencils, erasers, ink, penwipers . . .

On Sunday, drinking coffee with Micheline Pavin, you asked her if she'd like to go to the movies. Yes, but to see what? The easiest thing was to take the métro to the Étoile, then to walk down the Champs-Élysées and trust to the whim of the moment.

She had rested her hand on the edge of the table, and you were hesitating whether or not to take it.

Uncle Henri asked some of his son Claude's classmates to the house to celebrate his tenth birthday.

Alain Mouron, in the headquarters of the Saint-Hilaire troop where he had come for the first time that day, met the members of the Chamois Patrol he was going to belong to.

Back in the Rue du Pré-aux-Clercs apartment the next day, after his first morning at the Lycée Taine, he told his father that he had had a class in Greek, one in Latin, and that he was supposed to have had one in French after that, with the same teacher, but that there had been a mistake, that this teacher had left the school and that they had spend the hour under the supervision of a proctor.

Yes, he was in the same eleventh-grade class as his cousin Michel Daval, and he had recognized one of the leaders of the scout patrol he had joined the day before.

He didn't suspect that this literature teacher was two floors above him in the same building, collecting the impressions of his children as to this first morning of the school year, Gérard in the ninth grade, Lucie in the eighth, Claude and François in the sixth and fourth grades; Aunt Rose had picked them up at elementary school because

Uncle Henri, relying on the faulty schedule he had been given, had gone home at eleven. But the principal had telephoned while he was still at the dinner table and asked him to stop in at two to arrange this detail.

Alain Mouron put his new geography textbook, the English textbook he had already used in Bourges, and two blank notebooks into his briefcase.

And while Monsieur Hubert, in his amphitheater which Denis and the seniors had just left, was taking the names, addresses and various other information from his eleventh-grade class before warning them against the uncertainty of physical dimensions and initiating them into the calculation of errors, we had met—Alain Mouron, you and I —and Denis Régnier, in the same classroom as last year, was listening to you read for the second time while you reviewed the history of the earth, checking in his notebook that the names of the various ages and geological periods had not changed, staring at the photograph of the Grand Canyon with the different strata through which erosion had cut so sharply, until the bell rang, indicating the change of subject.

For you, it was a question of walking to the other end of the floor to teach the tenth grade, including my brother Jacques, requesting the usual information, establish the seating chart before telling them about the American Revolution, while I had to wait here for the English teacher; I didn't know yet that it would be Monsieur Bailly, like last year.

After the bell, I met Jacques on the stairs, Denis caught up with us in the hall. We walked home, exchanging our impressions of our new teachers. You followed us a quarter of an hour later, because of the many people you had had to stop and greet.

The next day, Uncle Henri already knew that it wasn't Tuesday but Monday that he would be teaching us French at eleven, and he went home to the Rue du Pré-aux-Clercs apartment delighted to have escaped an hour of work.

Alain Mouron took down the English dictation, then passed it to his neighbor—not Francis Hutter but a classmate from another eleventh-grade section.

When he came home to the Rue du Pré-aux-Clercs apartment, the cleaning woman was getting lunch ready. When she got around to pouring out the coffee, she explained to him what he would have to heat up for dinner that evening, then left.

Aunt Rose brought in a big platter of fruit.

Hubert Jourdan, near the window at the back of the class, sensitive to the bright sunlight, exploded into a magnificent sneeze; it was just the beginning of the year, you only laughed at him, and you won a good deal of sympathy by your indulgence. Raising your forefinger like a conductor to obtain silence, you dictated to us the title of the third part of the lesson:

"The Moslem threat."

Monsieur Tavera had assembled his few tenth-graders in the classroom next to Jacques'.

Exhausted after your six class hours that day, instead of heading directly for home after leaving school you made a long detour to the Île de la Cité, the quays of the Seine and the Louvre as far as the Pont-Royal; a marvelous evening sky over the Tuileries and the Gare d'Orsay, the dome of the Grand Palais transparent; you lingered in the little streets and only got back to the apartment in the Rue du Canivet after six-thirty.

Still no written work to do, but already preparations for the next morning, Uncle Henri's classes, the beginning of Hannibal crossing the Alps, and lines 400 to 416 of the fifth book of the *Odyssey*.

Now since the three of us had only one Bailly Dictionary and only one Gaffiot, we fought over which of us would have it first and wasted a lot of time waiting for each other to be through, so that I still hadn't finished my Homer when you came for dinner.

I had sensed, the year before, that Denis no longer had quite the same intimacy with you, that he always kept quiet at table when you were there, and I kept still that evening; I had already had you as a teacher the year before, but this year was more serious for all of us, even Jacques didn't say anything; our parents were rather surprised; you looked worried.

No French preparation to do that night, because Uncle Henri, the next day, told us about Racine's life and reminded us that next week we would have to buy a copy of *Britannicus* in some convenient edition, Larousse, Hatier, or any other,

which Alain Mouron wrote down in a little account book that he took out of his inside jacket pocket, and I envied him,

for if he had an account book, that meant he already had an allowance like my brother Denis, whereas I wouldn't have any until after next week, when I would be fifteen, and I didn't know how old he was, but I had the impression he was younger than I.

When he got back to his apartment, Madame Davez told Alain Mouron that his father had telephoned that he wouldn't be home for lunch. He ate quickly, then left to explore the banks of the Seine, a blank notebook and his mathematics textbook in his briefcase.

When Aunt Rose came in with her big soufflé that was beginning to fall, she saw the ink spots all over Gérard's fingers and told him to go wash his hands; Uncle Henri looked at his own hands, they were covered with chalk.

The mathematics teacher, whose name none of us knew yet, consulted the seating chart he had just made us fill out,

"All right, you, Denis Régnier, you were here last year, you shouldn't have any difficulty with this, you go to the blackboard."

Monsieur Hubert was talking about circular movement.

After your history class with your seniors, the world after 1848, back in the Rue du Canivet apartment, thinking about the dinner of the evening before, you decided that things couldn't go on like this, that you would have to try to re-establish the situation in one way or another, either by no longer taking your meals with my parents, though you were afraid of being alone, or by finding a way to forestall this transformation of our relationship, which the projected work might help to accomplish.

For this evening, there was still one solution, to telephone Micheline Pavin's office and ask her if she was free. No, she had to go out with a friend from the office. When then? Perhaps tomorrow evening; she would call back.

Since the next day was a Thursday, I felt completely free that evening, as if the vacation had started all over again. Of course, in principle, I could have gotten ahead, so to speak, begun that composition Uncle Henri had already assigned us, but I didn't have the heart. Denis had just come home with Jacques; they both threw their briefcases on the couch. Denis took out a detective novel and went to read in the dining room, Jacques took out a tiny transparent envelope with two stamps in it.

Lying on the bed, leafing through my geography textbook, the Grand Canyon, the Midnight Sun at North Cape, the Pointe du Raz . . . , I saw him closely examine the two little rectangles of paper and put them in his album.

147

Denis dashed in; he was looking for an eraser.

"You want stamps? I'll bring you some."

I sat up on the bed, waiting to see what would happen. He came back with a cardboard box full of old envelopes on which was printed: Albania, Algeria, America . . .

"Here."

When he went out, he gave me a nasty smile. Because the year before, when I saw that he was no longer interested in his collection, I had begged him to give some of it to me. He had made a lot of promises and had extorted all kinds of things from me by this blackmail.

And now he was giving it all to Jacques! I was furious. I tried to take it away from him, shouting that it belonged to me, but he didn't see it that way. Mother had to separate us.

After having fumed alone for a long time in the dining room, I came back into the bedroom.

"All right, I'll give them to you, since you want them so much; I'll help you put them in."

That Thursday, no scout meeting, the leaders supposing that we had too much to do during that first week of school. Actually, we still didn't know what to do with ourselves. It was raining. Visiting other cousins with the Jourets, we played parcheesi around a big table. We laughed a lot, but it wasn't really much fun.

In front of your piles of textbooks, you scribbled the diagram of our degrees of relationship: on the top line, your name, Pierre Vernier, then that of my mother, nee Anne Vernier, that of my father, Jean Eller, that of Aunt Rose, nee Rose Eller, that of Uncle Henri Jouret,

on the line beneath, connected by a vertical line to the St. Andrew's cross uniting my father and my mother, my name, Pierre Eller, between those of my two brothers, Denis and Jacques, to whom, the next day, you gave his second history lesson, the problems of the Old Regime.

Alain Mouron, when Uncle Henri called on him, said that Clément Marot was a poet of the early part of the Sixteenth Century who had followed François I to Italy, that he had suffered for his religious opinions, that he had written ballads, epistles and a translation of the Psalms at the end of his life.

"Well, that's not too bad. You had to prepare one of those epistles, the one to Lyon Jamet, who can tell me who this person was? All right, Monsieur Knorr."

The next morning, Alain Mouron, although he didn't have to come until ten for the gym class, was late to school. We were already running in the sawdust track around the gym.

Then we all went up together to Monsieur du Marnet, the relation of two segments or two vectors. We had managed to find out his name; Alain Mouron wrote it down on the cover of his notebook under the title Geometry.

Uncle Henri, free all day long on Saturday, had got up late and went to the elementary school to call for Claude and François. Gérard caught up with them in the Place Saint-Germain-des-Prés. Aunt Rose had already gone home with Lucie, who set the table, cut the bread and served the tuna fish.

The Council of Trent, the Counter Reformation, Denis Régnier who had heard it all the year before and of course forgotten it, was staring in his textbook at the double page of maps in various projections showing the routes of the chief voyages of discovery, that of Vasco da Gama to the East Indies, which you had not told us about, that of Christopher Columbus to the West Indies, which you were going to tell us about the following week, in much greater detail than you had done the year before, that of Magellan and of Sebastián del Cano around the world.

Monsieur Hubert's wife, her belly enormous now, was resting on her bed with Monsieur Hubert beside her reading a detective novel before coming to give us our first chemistry lesson.

Art and thought in the middle of the Nineteenth Century for your seniors, Darwin, Pasteur, Taine, Marx, visiting the Louvre to see Courbet, Daumier, the Jeu de Paume to see Manet, Degas, Monet, going to the Opéra to hear Wagner when a German company came, your last lesson of this first week. In two days, it would all begin again. You went to your café on the Boulevard Saint-Germain, ordered a beer, filled your pipe, watched people going past.

After having taken a cup of tea (Mother always makes tea on Saturday because Father is home), I shut myself in my room with Jacques, and knowing that tomorrow I would be too tired after my scout hike to work seriously, I prepared for Monday morning the rest of Hannibal crossing the Alps and the twenty lines of the fifth book of the Odyssey (really, Uncle Henri was pushing pretty hard),

"He could endure it, but the backwash rolled upon him again . . . "

Luckily Denis took pity on me and took the translations he had used last year out of his bookcase and gave them to me.

On Sunday morning, Alain Mouron, in his scout uniform, went to Mass at Saint-Hilaire, two rows in front of me.

He decided to take Communion, like several of our classmates, but he hadn't thought of bringing breakfast along, probably supposing he could get some *café au lait* in a neighborhood bar, but since his patrol leader, the second in command and most of the other Chamois had eaten all they needed before leaving home, he was told quite sharply, when he asked where he could get something to eat, that he should dig into his own knapsack or else buy a croissant at some bakery.

After a lot of consultations and arguments, once the last instructions were received, the Chamois Patrol set off ahead of ours for the Odéon métro station to reach Denfert-Rochereau.

In bed, Uncle Henri saw that it was ten, time to get up, shave and dress in order to be ready when his children came back from Mass with their mother.

Only the three youngest were there. My uncle asked what Gérard was doing.

"You know he went off with his Scouts. Since I have to fix lunch, don't forget that Pierre Vernier's coming, why don't you take the children to your mother's, and give them a little walk on the way?"

So instead of going directly to the apartment in the Rue Guynemer, Uncle Henri, holding Claude and François by the hand, walked down to the Seine, but it started to rain, so he quickly turned up the Rue Bonaparte, taking shelter in doorways and advancing in this way by little dashes.

The children were soaked by the time they reached their grandmother's, for neither of them, save in their Cub uniform, would have submitted to the humiliation of wearing a hat.

Old Madame Jouret quickly dried them off with magnificent bath towels.

"Will you stay for a while?"

But he looked at his watch and answered that he couldn't, that he was expecting someone for lunch, one of his colleagues.

In the afternoon, Hubert Jourdan went to see a movie, *Strangers on a Train*, with his brother Joseph.

Monsieur Tavera, in his studio apartment on the Boulevard Montparnasse decorated with superb rugs, was receiving his daughter Gisèle, who was in his former wife's custody. He had a cupboard full of toys and costumes for her to play with. The rain was making a loud noise on the skylight; heavy drops were falling into a pot near the stove.

Since the rain that had seemed to be stopping had started in again, keeping you from lingering along the quays, you took shelter in the doorways of the Rue de Beaune, thinking about me, about my brother Jacques, my cousin Gérard, Bison, Squirrel, Tiger, in the soaking woods.

You went into the Royal-Saint-Germain to wait for Micheline Pavin.

You ordered some tea and then you talked to her about that conjunction of family relationships within your eleventh-grade class, about this opportunity not to be missed, this constellation which couldn't reasonably be expected to reproduce itself in some future year; consequently it was now or never that you should undertake the description.

"Yes, of course, you must begin it."

"I'm afraid it will take me a long time, that my classes will suffer for it."

"Excuses . . . "

"I'm almost frightened, really . . . "

"Of failing?"

"Yes, because of the number of things I'm going to have to learn about."

"But isn't it mostly what an eleventh-grade boy is supposed to know?"

"The thing is, I'm not a student and I'm going to have to know it —and understand it—in an entirely different way."

"Isn't that what you want to do, what you told me about?"

"I keep hesitating, I have the sense . . . "

"Oh, I know you, you like to take things too seriously. You want encouragement? I'll give it to you. You need help? I'll do anything I can. Between the two of us . . . "

"Seriously?"

"What else can I say?"

"I need one more thing, without it I'm helpless."

"Tell me what it is. Please! I hope it won't be something too outrageous."

"It is outrageous."

"What?"

"I have to be ordered."

151

"Ordered?"

"You have to order me to start on this venture."

"You certainly like to use dramatic words."

"I'll do anything you tell me to if you're able to give me this order, and then I'll be able to bring the attempt to its conclusion, in spite of and against everything. Only you can discover in me . . . "

"Don't tremble like that. All right. I order you to begin this work, I forbid you to abandon it so long as I'm not satisfied with it. Is that enough for you? It's not so hard, you know; I'm sure you'll do it wonderfully. I look forward to it with great pleasure."

"You're going to be disappointed."

"I'll take the risk."

"And now what would you like?"

"To go for a walk in the rain."

Bursts of laughter; the other customers turned around as the two of you left the café. Night was falling.

We were heading as fast as we could for the station through the darkening woods, then the village, most of us tired, my left shoe soaked (I had stepped into a puddle).

We got there just in time; the train was full; other scout troops and youth groups were packed into the steaming cars, some singing.

We went off in different directions at Denfert-Rochereau. I gave my Bisons the assignments for Thursday's meeting. Jacques and I went home, exhausted; I was carrying his knapsack; he was too tired, but he seemed pleased with the day.

Our parents had already sat down at the table with Denis. We went to take off our shoes and socks and put on our slippers before coming to eat the soup that was getting cold.

"What a sight you are! The first hike of the year, you're already covered with mud. You really needed another jacket, didn't you."

I didn't answer my father, but this remark filled me with joy, because I interpreted it as the sign that I would have a new jacket, maybe a leather one, the day after tomorrow, for my birthday.

When Monsieur Mouron wakened his son, Alain was still stiff in the joints; he stood up, waited until the door was closed again, then fell back on his bed, stretching luxuriously and closing his eyes

(on his chair, his uniform, the blue sweater with the insignia, the shorts, the belt with the leather buckle, the scarf with the ring made out of a braided thong in a Turk's-head knot);

when he opened them again, he realized with horror that it was

152

already twenty to nine. He rushed to his closet to put on his long pants, his jacket, a clean shirt and a tie. He scarcely washed, didn't bother to comb his hair;

Greek Literature and Latin Literature, Sixteenth Century French Authors and the corresponding three notebooks;

he swallowed his café au lait without heating it up or putting sugar in it, ran the whole way, but it was already ten after nine when he got inside the lycée. Luckily the janitor was looking the other way.

"What's your name?" Uncle Henri asked.

"Alain Mouron."

"Oh, yes, Alain Mouron. Listen, I know it's hard to get up in the morning, but it's something you have to make yourself do. I see you didn't even take the time to comb your hair. Now let's get on with our work."

Francis Hutter stood up to let Alain Mouron get to his seat. Alain winked at me.

Ulysses is clinging to a rock to resist the wave that is sweeping him away, then manages to swim to the mouth of a river, where he addresses this prayer to its tutelary god:

"Hear me, Lord, whoever you are."

Several of us were half asleep. We were a little wider awake for Livy, like Hannibal's soldiers in the Alps, like the soldiers on a secret mission that we had been the day before, in the Verrières woods.

We are annoyed with Uncle Henri—Monsieur Jouret to everyone except me—for getting through the thickets of these long sentences so easily, for knowing his way among all these subjunctives and these imperfects, obviously amused by our mistakes, but exasperated by our slowness, our yawns.

When the clouds opened, revealing a triangle of blue sky, he too stopped talking to look out the windows, then he rapped on his desk, but that moment of relaxation was enough to give the boy who went on reading, Maurice Tangala, the Negro, new resources of courage and confidence.

And while Maurice Tangala was turning to the definition of the tropics during the afternoon, dreaming of that Africa he had never seen, looking at the patches of sunlight on heads and books of his classmates near the window, Abbé Gollier, in his study, was preparing his senior class.

As night was falling behind the towers of Saint-Sulpice, after finishing a quick review of your next day's morning classes, you hurried on

153

to prepare Egypt and the inundation of the Nile, the Atlantic seaboard of the United States, and especially that lesson for us, from three to four, on the discovery and conquest of America, that was to act as a point of departure and a fulcrum.

You took the *Marco Polo* under your arm, to show Micheline Pavin which passages you wanted to read us during this essential hour.

After having eaten dinner with my parents and my brothers, I had to get started on that composition Uncle Henri had assigned us for the next day. I chewed my pencil a long time, letting a lot of memories run through my head. It would probably have been best to choose a day when I wasn't with Uncle Henri, but it was getting late, and what I remembered best was still the inauguration of our cabin in the Herrecourt woods near Les Étangs.

I slept badly that night; I woke up with a start at four in the morning; I turned on my bed lamp and looked at the clock; Jacques turned over in his bed and asked me thickly:

"What's the matter?"

"Nothing. Go to sleep."

I turned the light out, but put it back on again a little more than an hour later, my mind troubled by the notion that I hadn't done my Greek, Latin, English or French preparations, I hadn't studied either my history or physics lessons. I hoped you and Uncle Henri wouldn't be so cruel as to question me on my birthday, but Monsieur Bailly and Monsieur Hubert, if they were supposed to know my date of birth, both of them having made me write it down during our first class, would certainly pay no attention to it. Jacques didn't move; I turned out the light, waited, didn't fall back to sleep.

For you, too, the day that was about to begin would be different from the others, was to transform your life. You opened your eyes at quarter of six, turned on your bed lamp, opened your window.

It was still dark. The street was empty. You went back to bed. *Marco Polo* was on your night table. The magnificence of Kubla Khan.

Michel Daval was sleeping peacefully in the Rue Pierre-Leroux apartment. His mother turned on her light at seven-thirty, for it always took her a long time to get up.

Monsieur Bailly got up. His wife was still asleep in the bed next to the one he had just left. She started, saw what time it was, pulled on her bathrobe, went to wake the children.

Monsieur Bailly went into his bathroom, began shaving, ashamed of his face that fascinated him in the mirror. He had plenty of time; he didn't need to be at the lycée until eleven, when he would be teaching our class.

Amerigo Vespucci and the other navigators.

One beside the other in the first row, Claude Armelli and Gabriel Voss, the former short, with black hair and bright eyes, the other boy tall, blond, freckled, his eyes a strange green color, their hands lying almost parallel.

"Pre-Columbian civilizations, the condition of the New World at the period of its discovery."

Claude and François, in pajamas, came in to say good night to Uncle Henri in his study, interrupting his reading of *Britannicus*, the first preface to which he had assigned us for the next day. Lucie came in at the end of the second act,

"*Destroy the wretched to secure ourselves*",

still dressed, of course,

"All through with your homework? You've studied all your lessons? All right, hurry up now, get into bed",

Gérard came in when Burrhus, left alone on stage says:

"*So at last, Burrhus, Nero shows his hand*",

to confess that he was having trouble with his first Latin translation of the year, the one he had to hand in the next day; but his father was adamant and ordered him to come and show him his work once it was done.

He came in at ten of ten, his expression downcast; his father looked at the page and allowed him to go to bed, saying Gérard shouldn't be surprised if he got a bad grade on his work.

Alain Mouron was looking through the Gaffiot dictionary for the obscure words in Hannibal crossing the Alps, then he picked up his *Britannicus*,

"*Of all the favors I have done for Rome . . .*",

before going in to say good night to his father, who was smoking his pipe, alone, listening to a concert on the radio.

The next morning, my uncle called on me to explain the passage in Livy. No use saying I had been unable to prepare anything because of all that had happened the day before; he should have suspected as much; he couldn't know, of course, that I had spent the evening with you, and that we had made a pact between us that made me consider him and all my classmates with a new curiosity. Luckily Michel Daval had a translation, but since Francis Hutter was absent, he had a lot of trouble keeping it out of sight.

During French class I could relax, my uncle wouldn't call on me for several days. Michel Daval, listening with one ear to the explanation of the first preface to *Britannicus*, was furtively finishing the October issue of *Fiction* that was lying on his knees, a magazine I had never seen, but of course I immediately felt a wild desire to know, because of our conversation the night before, what my neighbor had been reading recently, and I asked him to pass me the issue, which he did, asking me not to keep it too long.

In a big bookstore, you were standing in line to buy secondhand copies of the textbooks we use, eleventh-grade physics and chemistry and also senior physics, since that's the class Monsieur Hubert taught on Tuesday from three to four, as well as the Italian books Monsieur Bonnini uses, then you ate lunch in the Greek restaurant on the Rue de l'École-de-Médecine.

How and with what instruments, surveyor's poles, theodolites, aerial photographs, a map is made. Henri Fage, just behind me, was looking in our textbook at the three maps of the Mans region on different scales; they particularly interested him because he had spent his vacation at Saint-Mars-la-Brière, whose name wasn't mentioned on the bottom map, but showed on the one in the middle and was cut off by the frame of the map at the top.

In the courtyard, Monsieur Moret was making my brother Jacques and his classmates do deep-breathing exercises.

On Thursday, before lunch, home from the barber, I prepared my afternoon scout meeting.

Deep in *Sixteenth Century French Authors*, my assignment list in front of you, which you had carefully copied, you read with particular attention, since it was our program for the hour which had immediately preceded that of the discovery and conquest of America, the letter from Gargantua to his son Pantagruel:

"Now it is that the minds of men are qualified with all manner of discipline . . . "

Since your tooth was beginning to hurt you again, you went to the bathroom to take two aspirins. Then, before going to lunch alone in the Rue des Canettes, you rang at our door; my mother answered and you asked her to give me my assignment list, which surprised her a good deal, but you decided not to give her any explanations.

On the stairs, you ran into the entire Jouret family, who were coming to lunch with us.

Jean-Pierre Cormier, during the afternoon, kept his eye on the proctor, but he had the satisfaction of having scored a point against Denis Régnier. Now he was counting on having the Alaska stamp by trading his Lebanon stamp for it. He would have to be pretty shrewd, but the breach had been made and solid commercial relations, based on reciprocal esteem, could soon be established. Monsieur du Marnet and his wife were visiting the Jardin des Plantes.

Wednesday morning, October 15, was devoted to outdoor activities, I came home for lunch not from the lycée but from the Croix-de-Berny stadium by the Sceaux train, as though from a scout hike. More than half of our classmates got off at Denfert-Rochereau to take a métro, but we had gone on as far as the Luxembourg stop. When I reached the apartment in the Rue du Canivet, everyone was already eating his salsify. Then all three of us took our books.

You had eaten lunch at Monsieur Hubert's for the first time. You had cautiously asked him a few questions about his teaching methods, about what he thought of his pupils. He had been amused by your curiosity. His wife was very tired; the blessed event would not be long in coming.

"There's still another month to go, supposedly."

You both took the métro to the Saint-Hilaire stop; you separated at the lycée stairs at the second floor; you went to lecture Jacques and his classmates about the Revolutionary societies, Cordeliers, Feuillants, Jacobins . . .

Then Michel asked me if I had finished the issue of Fiction he had lent me. No, but I could give it back to him the next morning.

" . . . a memory equal in capacity to the measure of twelve skins and twelve casks of oil . . . "

Monsieur Bonnini, his eyes even more sunken, was making his seniors translate:

> "My son, spoke the courteous master,
> Those who die in the wrath of God
> All meet here, whatever their origin . . . "

But he wasn't listening to them; he was reading to himself:

"*Figliuol' mio, disse il maestro cortese . . .*",

as if it were a journey he was remembering, and a good many of the boys in his class, hanging on his lips and his blank eyes, were listening to him mourn in front of them, by the intermediary of Dante.

You saw Micheline Pavin again the following Sunday for the first time since the preceding Monday, since that decisive class, since you had embarked on the writing of this work, which had been your principal concern, of course; she was delighted when you told her about its progress, gave you all the encouragement you desired when you told her about the difficulties you were beginning to encounter, showed only a slight anxiety when you showed her how heavy the week's program was, and it was she who decided that you would have to arrange for your meetings in advance.

The two of you were walking together along the Seine, you had decided to take dinner together every Tuesday (after the six hours of class and the two hours of writing you planned on, it was absolutely necessary, she said, that you have some diversion) and also every Friday, a quieter day, when you could talk a little about this work. And on Sundays . . . it would depend on which ones.

I didn't have any scout hike that day; without letting anyone in my family know, you had made an appointment to meet me at the Royale-Saint-Germain at four, because Micheline wanted to meet me.

How hard it was not to tell my brother Denis about it all! But how would I have gone about it? He had kept away from me the days before, and now I was the one who was hiding from him, since I had agreed with you that I would give you an account, bring you my harvest of information, on the way home from school, and I didn't want him to see me or ask me questions. I was sure I couldn't explain things properly to him, and that he would make fun of me, that he would mention it to our parents in some stupid way that might embarrass you as well.

Now on that Monday, one of his new friends was probably absent. I was surprised to find him at the bottom of the lycée stairs, waiting for me with Jacques. We started walking home together. I was desperately trying to think of a way to ditch them. Luckily I caught sight of Alain Mouron on the other side of the boulevard, and I said I had to go over and ask him something.

They paid no attention. They let me run off. I followed them at some distance. I waited on the stairs, in the Rue du Canivet apartment building, until they had slammed the apartment door.

It was only then that I went up and into your apartment, where you were waiting for me impatiently, since you had been invited to lunch with Monsieur Hutter (last year, you saw very little of your colleagues, with the exception of Uncle Henri and Monsieur Bailly); I told you about my difficulties, I let you copy the new page of my assignments, I told you that the issue of *Fiction* was now in Alain Mouron's hands, and that Francis Hutter had gone to his paternal grandfather's funeral in some village in Lorraine. You asked me to come back in the afternoon.

"It seems inevitable," my father said when I walked into the dining room, "there's always one who's late." I mumbled something about a friend, thinking to myself that I'd have to find a better solution.

You were introduced to Madame Hutter and her daughter Geneviève; Henri is one of your senior students; Gérard is in the eighth grade. You and Monsieur Hutter talked about Francis, about the death of his grandfather (a first cousin of Monsieur Hutter's father), about his parents, his brother, his sister.

The four of you took the métro together; Henri Hutter went up to the third floor, his father to the second, Gérard Hutter turned left in the courtyard, you turned right where Gérard Jouret, Jean-Louis Hutter, Claude Jourdan and their classmates were waiting for you to speak to them

about the transformation of European society after the discovery of America, about the rise of the cost of living,

quotation from Jean Bodin:

"It is incredible and nevertheless true that there has come from Peru, starting in the year 1533 . . . more than a hundred million gold francs and twice as much silver . . . ",

the remarkable development of the international bankers, Fugger, Medici, the fall of the standard of living in the poor classes.

Temperature and its variations during the course of a year or a day, depending on the region; Michel Daval, his mind preoccupied with his coming change of address, whispered to me that everything in his apartment had already been packed, that he would be sleeping the next night at his new address in the Rue Servandoni, and I had no scruple about listening to him instead of to you; I knew that you wouldn't punish me, that you wouldn't punish him unless it were absolutely necessary, all too pleased to hear from me, a few minutes later, information of such importance for your undertaking, but Michel Daval didn't know about that and took the greatest precautions, with long moments of apprehensive silence, and I couldn't reassure him, let him in on my secret; on the contrary I had to pretend to be afraid, pretend to conceal the fact that we were talking.

Since he couldn't bear to talk any more, Monsieur Bonnini made his tenth-graders translate a passage without using their dictionaries, a text taken from a newspaper, which he slowly wrote on the blackboard.

The next day, instead of listening to Caesar's speech, I was thinking of how to give Denis a likely explanation of my previous day's behavior. He had seen that I was avoiding him; then he had discovered that I was hiding so he would pass by without seeing me. That was nothing in itself, but since it would certainly happen again, I needed an excuse.

"Well, I see you're like Cassius, you have a lean and hungry look, you think too much, think about your text instead."

And I read:

"He thinks too much, such men are dangerous."

I was a little startled, I couldn't help applying this remark to you, especially because of that new, starved look in your eyes now. I forced myself to drive this all out of my mind and to concentrate all my attention on the passage from Shakespeare, but it was no use, your thin face, your eyes that were brighter, deeper than before, came back to disturb the printed lines.

Coming out of the lycée, you gave me a scarcely noticeable wink, which I answered in the same way. I let you walk off. Denis walked past me with his classmates. He offered them a cigarette. That gave me an idea; I would make him think I didn't want him to see me smoking.

Jacques had joined me; I couldn't get rid of him. I decided I wouldn't stop to see you before lunch, only in the afternoon, that would be simple, neither Denis nor Jacques stayed at the lycée until five.

So on that day, it was only Denis who was late to lunch. I wasn't very hungry, I knew you were waiting for me, I wondered if I would be able to make you understand why I had to take so many precautions about my brother, whether you would make fun of me or decide to do without me since I was having so much trouble. I would have to be careful, protect myself on all sides in order to preserve this exciting complicity.

After half an hour, you decided to come to our apartment to see if I had come back, but you sensed how odd this curiosity would seem, and while I was agonizing at the table, you simply decided I must have forgotten, that in any case it was unnecessary for us to see each other twice a day, that we would have to arrange matters more economically, and you went off to lunch in the Rue des Canettes with, in your briefcase, the eleventh-grade history textbook in which, while you were telling us about the corporations, Jean-Pierre Cormier, behind me, was studying an illustration showing the Foire Saint-Germain. Monsieur du Marnet was telling his ninth-graders about the nature of the right triangles.

On Wednesday, you and I ate lunch together at my parents', I was sitting next to you, on the excuse that I was your favorite, Jacques to my right. My parents gave you a book about Spanish painting. At dessert, my mother went to the kitchen to bring in the cake, made a sign from the door, and I went to join her; I was the one who lit the thirty-five candles you blew out shortly afterwards with an embarrassed smile. Because of the occasion, we were all allowed a little cognac; we left for the lycée in great excitement.

Your first afternoon hour, as it was every other week, was history for the tenth grade: Charles V, François I, Henry VIII. Monsieur Moret was making us do calisthenics in the courtyard,
"One, two, one, two, now standing where you are . . . ",
Marking time with a shrill whistle.

Then Monsieur Bonnini went home to the Rue Cardinal-Lemoine with his older son whose nineteenth birthday they had celebrated so sadly. Geneviève, opening the door, asked them:
"How was she? . . . Did she at least recognize you?"
"Oh, yes, yes, she looked comfortable."
Michel Daval was explaining to me how his new room in the Rue Servandoni apartment was arranged.
"Are you going to stop talking?"
"But Monsieur, I wasn't saying anything."
"What do you mean, you weren't saying anything? Come to the

blackboard for the moment, and if you don't recite satisfactorily you'll be kept in tomorrow."

He didn't recite satisfactorily.

The following Monday, after having noted the absentees, Tannier and Zola, you asked us to take a blank sheet, write our name and class at the upper left, then write as the title: Geography Quiz.

"You will please answer the following questions:"
(you wrote them on the board)
"1: What is an isotherm?

2: What are the hottest and coldest points of the globe, and why?

3: What is an inversion of temperature?

You have a quarter of an hour; afterwards we shall discuss atmospheric circulation, in other words, the wind."

The first question didn't give me too much difficulty, a line joining points of equal temperature, whether extremes or an average; all I could remember about the second was that the coldest place was in Siberia, that the hottest place must be in the Sahara and similar deserts; but to find out what an inversion of temperature was, I had to look at what Michel Daval was writing next to me—he didn't know either—or what Alain Mouron was writing in front of me.

On Tuesday, Jacques was sick, another cough. He didn't go to school, stayed in bed, ate virtually nothing for lunch.

We each went in to talk to him a little, and you came to find out how he was and brought him some mint drops.

Then you told your seventh-graders about the Hebrews, their religion, their sacred books which constitute the Bible.

Uncle Henri gave us a new French assignment:

"What do you think of Rabelais' ideas about education? Compare today's education with the kind Rabelais opposes and the kind he proposes",

to be handed in on Tuesday, November 9,

before making us read what we had had to prepare for that day, the praise of the marvelous herb called Pantagruelion, that is, hemp,

" . . . without it, kitchens would be a disgrace, tables repellent. . . . "

After that, Monsieur Bonnini made his seniors write out in class the translation of the passage from the Purgatorio about the Valley of the Princes; Michel Daval, beside me, was taking down from your dictation:

"The Scandinavian invasions."

162

There were three days' holiday for All Saints' Day; you took advantage of it to make considerable progress in the writing of this work and the study of our textbooks.

Consequently, on Tuesday afternoon, All Souls' Day, you reread Racine's *Iphigénie* which Uncle Henri was making his seniors study. I was camping with the other patrol leaders on the grounds of a little Seine-et-Oise château. The rain had forced us to take refuge in an abandoned stable. There was a big shaky table, crates that we used as stools, an old wood stove on which we boiled water for tea.

The following week, the routine resumed without a hitch.

When you came into our classroom, you noted the absence of Francis Hutter and Denis Régnier, you called on Rémy Orland about clouds and their various systems, François Nathan about rain and other forms of precipitation: fog, hail, dew, mist and snow.

The photographs illustrating the next lesson, climates and types of weather:

two views of the New Hebrides, one of Saint-Pierre-et-Miquelon: tiny house on the oblique horizon above dwarf pines, another taken in Mexico, a hedge of tall succulents like candles.

My brother Denis was sick in his turn, a good dose of grippe, beside his bed the phonograph he himself had assembled out of spare parts. It scratched a lot, but he was very proud of his handiwork and turned it up as loud as it would go. We could hear it in the dining room during lunch.

"He's going to wear himself out with all that noise."

"Let him alone, it's nice for him. As long as the neighbors don't complain . . ."

Coming up to get your books for the afternoon, you stopped to give him a little 45 repressing of Duke Ellington that delighted him and that he immediately tried on his machine; unfortunately something was wrong with the speeds. He stopped everything and started to take the machine apart, scattering parts all over the bed.

All of which interested me a lot, but it was time to go back to school, I ran, and passed you in the street, you were with Jacques.

On the way in, you gave me a wink. We had an appointment for after class, a reconnaissance meeting.

Written quiz for the seventh grade:

"What do you know about Crete?

What do you know about the Phoenicians?"

163

before telling them about the Homeric poems and in particular the travels of Ulysses. Claiming that it was to reward them for good conduct, you read them, in Victor Bérard's translation, Ulysses' arrival on the Island of the Phaeacians:

"But Pallas Athena then had her design . . . "

We handed in to Uncle Henri our composition on Rabelais' ideas of education; he told us about Calvin's life.

Now Monsieur Bonnini, dressed all in black, is continuing the reading of the *Purgatorio* with his seniors.

Michel Daval is drawing a pair of spectacles on Lebrun's portrait of Turenne.

I say now, but it isn't really now, just as I'm not actually doing the writing; that hour was over long ago, and this present tense I'm using is like the pier of a bridge connecting these other present tenses:

the one in which you are writing, the one in which I and my classmates will read you,

at that central hour which is becoming more and more remote and which you distinguish from all the rest, which surround it with ever-increasing density,

by utilizing for it a motionless present-tense narrative,

whereas for this particular hour, the middle of the afternoon of Tuesday, November 9, 1954, the next time you come back to it, focusing your mind on another student and another professor, since you will want to situate it, too, among other hours, not only after those which preceded it, but before those that have followed it,

you will make me describe it in the past.

IN OCTOBER 1953, Monsieur Bailly had almost the same schedule and consequently on Tuesday afternoon, between three and four, he was with his seniors, and the second Tuesday of the school year, October 13, he was probably making them read Keats's sonnet on first looking into Chapman's translation of Homer,

" . . . Or like stout Cortez . . . ",

unless he had already started on the Ancient Mariner.

Vacation came for him too, and on August 10 he arrived with his wife and three children at the Hôtel de la Plage. Denis and I had already been his students, but he didn't recognize us as we were walking down toward the water, preoccupied as he was by getting the luggage in and registering.

The porter took them up to the third floor, where two connecting rooms had been reserved for them.

His wife left for Orléans on September 7. He watched her packing her suitcases without helping her. The rain was beating against the window panes. On the other side of the wall, Alain Mouron was explaining to the three children, in professorial tones, the rules of the parcheesi game that had been given to little René for his ninth birthday.

Madame Bailly closed the clasps.

"There, now I'm ready."

"You have to say goodbye to the children. With this weather, it's better if they stay here; luckily we have Alain to keep an eye on them."

He opened the door.

"Mother wants to say goodbye."

Everyone stood up, betraying a little impatience.

"Stay where you are, go on playing, I'm just coming in to kiss you. I'm going to Orléans, and I'll be back very soon. You won't even notice that I've gone."

Georges and Agnès, the youngest, sat down again obediently. Alain Mouron felt embarrassed, leaned on the bed and looked out the window through the rain at the shining cedar branches, the blurred stones in the little wall beyond. René burst into tears.

"Now be good on your birthday," his father said, then to his wife:

165

"I think it's time."

He closed the door again, picked up the two suitcases, walked down the stairs, put on his raincoat that was hanging in the vestibule, near the porter's desk.

He walked out into the rain without turning back toward his wife who was following him. It took only ten minutes to reach the station.

She climbed into the train; they did not wave goodbye to each other.

Instead of returning to the hotel, he walked through the village, his hands in his pockets. For the first since he had been in Saint-Cornély, he systematically explored the bars and the brands of beer sold there.

On Monday the thirteenth, he received a letter from her saying that, contrary to what had been agreed upon, she couldn't come back to Saint-Cornély on the fifteenth, her visit to Orléans had turned out to be much more complicated than she had thought at first.

She gave no hint as to what the complications could be, but they must have involved that physics and chemistry teacher who had already come to visit them several times in Paris.

Their big mistake, he decided, rereading the letter in his room after lunch, wondering how he was going to answer it and especially how to tell the news to the children, had been for two English teachers to marry. If the disciplines had been different . . . He knew that he was deceiving himself; his dissertation was proceeding slower and slower; what he wanted to know was whether this teacher from Orléans, whose name he kept forgetting, had some projects under way, quite close to completion, which might suddenly bring him, in the near future, that notoriety on which he himself no longer counted, on which his wife had counted so much for him;

and he was wondering as he looked out the open window, under the big cedar branch beyond the little wall, on the gold beach between the sparkling rocks, at his three children wading in the foam under the surveillance of his nephew Alain,

who suddenly took little Agnès in his arms, apparently to comfort her,

tiny, thin, silent figures amid the noise of the leaves and the waves,

what would happen if that brilliant young teacher were transferred to Paris the following year, and especially if he were transferred to the Lycée Taine.

Hoping against every probability for a telegram countermanding the letter, he had preferred to wait before announcing the news, and on Tuesday at lunch, since no one had referred to Elizabeth's return the next day, he had not dared bring up the subject, trying to convince himself that his children had forgotten the date, that they weren't paying attention to it any more, that the start of school was still too far away for them to have already begun counting the days, looking at the calendar every morning; but such forgetfulness, already unlikely in the case of little René, was quite inadmissible for Alain Mouron, whose calm, sad eyes hadn't stopped watching him.

He had gone upstairs to put the children to bed (what a good idea to have invited him, but if he hadn't been here, perhaps Elizabeth would have had more scruples about leaving the children alone with their father; her smile had been so strange when she had welcomed him, this little orphan cousin, she had taken such care to instruct him in a baby-sitter's responsibilities),

now he was coming back down; Monsieur Bailly, who was finishing his coffee, watched him cross the hall, go into the big, cold living room that was almost always empty.

He wiped his mouth and went to join him. He sat down in another rattan armchair opposite him, the two of them alone between the moist, dirty walls near the window overlooking the deserted garden with the patches of sunlight shifting on the gravel with the movement of the branches against the blurred horizon of the sea.

"I received a letter from your aunt, she still doesn't know when she'll be back."

"I see."

"I know it doesn't matter so much for you . . . "

"Oh, I . . . "

"Yes, that isn't what I meant, but you understand me."

"It's the children?"

"Well, you see, she told me—perhaps she told you too—that she'd be coming back tomorrow, Wednesday, but I don't know if she told the children the same thing, and even if she did, whether they remember. She writes that they need her so much in Orléans that she won't be able to get back here until the twenty-sixth. If the children do expect her tomorrow, we'll have to tell them, of course. Otherwise, it would be better just to tell them that . . . "

"They didn't tell me anything."

"We'll see, enjoy your reading."

But some two hours later

(in the dining room at Les Étangs, my Uncle Henri was calmly taking tea with your Aunt Rose, both of them alone in the house, since they had just sent my brother Jacques with the two younger children, Claude and François, to take us our tea at the cabin we were building in the Herrecourt woods),

Alain Mouron, who was sunbathing on the sand

(there was a cool breeze),

saw little Georges Bailly coming out of the water shivering, his teeth chattering;

he rubbed him hard with a bath towel and told all the children to get dressed again;

and waiting outside, since they wouldn't all fit in the beach cabin, he heard Georges ask his older brother René what time their mother would be coming the next day, and the latter answer that he would ask Cousin Alain, which he did as they were walking back to the hotel.

"Tomorrow? But she's not coming back tomorrow, she won't be back until next week."

"What?" little Georges exclaimed. "I know it was tomorrow. We're supposed to go meet her at the station."

"Who said so?"

"René did."

"She told us that the day she left."

"No, she said she'd probably be back on a Wednesday, but she never said which Wednesday it was, maybe the one next week, and even then it's not sure."

"But we'll be going back to Paris after that."

"Don't worry, she'll be here before we leave for Paris."

"But I was sure it was tomorrow. Father told me it was tomorrow too."

"When?"

"I don't know any more, it wasn't long ago."

"I was just talking to him about it, he told me it would be next week."

"It must be that cousin who's sick."

"Yes, that's it."

"Father must have had a letter."

"Yes, he had a letter."

"It's been a long time since we've had one."

"She probably sent you kisses in the one she wrote Uncle René."

"Then why didn't he show it to us?"

"Does he show you all the letters he gets?"

"All the ones Mother sends us kisses in. And if he knows when she's coming back, he better tell us, because we thought she was coming back tomorrow; that's what René heard . . . "

"Yes, that's what I heard, and I thought you heard it too, Alain; so if she's changed her mind, it must mean that something's happened . . ."

"Now, Agnès, don't start crying! We better go see Uncle René all together right away, and he'll explain anything you need to know."

They went up to the room, hung their bathing suits and towels on the rack next to the sink, knocked at Monsieur Bailly's door, but he wasn't there. Then Alain began to get worried: he took Georges and Agnès by the hand and went looking for his uncle through the streets of Saint-Cornély; it was a beautiful day, but the wind was getting colder, the sun's horizontal rays lay in patches on the granite walls, the sea was lapping at the pebbles; bird cries; bicyclists returning from their rides; they found Monsieur Bailly in a harbor café, Alain had caught sight of his face behind the glass; after a moment's hesitation, he went in, pushing his cousins in front of him: a jukebox was screaming out an old tango.

Monsieur Bailly was alone at his table, they surrounded him, silent, he told them all to sit down.

My Uncle Henri was waiting for us at Les Étangs, was smoking his pipe upstairs, watching the evening slowly spread over the fields and woods. My Aunt Rose had already gone out to the kitchen to make dinner.

At the turn in the road, near the three oaks, he caught sight of us coming with the basket full of tools. One or two stars were coming out. There was a spectacular sunset, clouds heaped up under the Bresles hills, and gusts of wind were making the wash hanging near the gooseberry bushes flap loudly.

But while it had rained the next day over half of France, it was beautiful in the Rhône valley that you were riding through, opposite Micheline Pavin, the sun falling on the pages of your book between Avignon and Valence, at Chapter 135 where those idols of Cathay are described whose function is to bring about the recovery of lost articles.

In Saint-Cornély it was raining hard, and Alain Mouron had a lot of trouble keeping his three cousins quiet. Luckily there was that parcheesi game little René had been given for his birthday. None of them wanted to take a nap. They had already been shut up all morning, and all three were on the brink of tears. Agnès hadn't wanted to play, was scolding her doll at the other end of the bed. The worst was that on the other side of the wall they could hear Monsieur Bailly walking up and down and muttering to himself.

René cast the dice, shouting:

"Double sixes!"

"You're cheating," Georges replied.

"Liar!"

"I saw you."

"What did you see?"

"Alain, he was cheating, wasn't he?"

"Start over."

"Why start over? I got double sixes."

"All right, you can still start over, it's only a game."

"He's a bad sport!"

"I'm a bad sport, when you're the one who's cheating!"

"I didn't cheat, I'm starting over, double sixes! There you see, I didn't cheat."

"All right. My turn."

"Oh, no it isn't, I still have another throw, I had double sixes."

"Then I can't ever play."

"Be patient."

"You're always the one who wins in these games."

"That's not true, the day before yesterday you won, didn't he, Alain?"

"Yes, but I didn't cheat."

"I didn't either! You stop saying that!"

The door opened. Monsieur Bailly, furious, clenched his fists, then relaxed and said very gently, with an ironic smile:

"Will this nonsense be over soon?"

He closed the door behind him. Alain Mouron asked his two cousins:

"Want to play some more?"

"No," little René said, "it's too silly. I have an idea."

"What?"

"Let's write Mother a letter."

"Who's going to write it?"

"We'll all do it together."

"No."

"No? You don't want to write Mother?"

"If I want to write Mother, I'll write my own letter."

"Oh, all right, if that's the way you want to do it. We'll see."

"What about me?" Agnès said, coming closer, holding her doll by one arm.

"We'll write yours together," Alain Mouron answered. "We'll go out to buy postcards at the tobacco store, put on your raincoats."

He knocked at the door. Monsieur Bailly cried out in an almost harsh tone of voice:

"What is it?"

"We're going out to buy postcards."

"Don't let them get all messed up in the puddles!"

Scenes you reconstruct from what I told you about what Alain told me.

And Uncle Henri, in the dining room at Les Étangs, smoking the tobacco his daughter had given him the day before, was playing lotto with us while the rain was beating on the windows and the thunder was growling.

It rained almost every day until the end of September, particularly in Brittany. The rain beat on the window panes of the dining room, while Monsieur Bailly was rereading the letter he had received from Paris at the same time as the one from his wife, mailed from Orléans, notifying him that she would be arriving on Friday night to spend the last weekend and pack up. Through the glass door he caught sight of his nephew Alain, alone in the living room.

It took all day Monday to pack the luggage. Not even a half hour was left over. There was a terrible commotion in the two adjoining rooms, and Madame Bailly kept going back and forth from one to the other.

"René, bring me your trousers, no, not you, your son; Georges, bring me yours, but hurry up now; look, here's a hole, I'm not surprised, I'll bet you've been walking around with that for three days before anyone noticed it."

"No one noticed it."

"You think so? How people must have laughed. Poor René . . . "

"But I don't have a hole in my trousers, that's Georges'."

"I'm not talking to you, I'm talking to your father. Oh, stop crying

171

over a thing like that, if you want to cry you better go somewhere else, you hear me? Go into the bathroom or somewhere, anywhere where I can't hear you, and don't come back until your eyes are dry. Poor René, I really wonder what got into our heads the day we gave that child the same name as yours, it gets more and more inconvenient. Hand me your shirts. Oh, he's sniveling behind the door. Listen, René, since you don't know what to do with yourself, stop walking back and forth like a caged animal and take that boy somewhere. Georges and Alain will be enough to keep Agnès from getting under my feet. If you take your raincoat, take his too."

Monsieur Bailly closed the door behind him, he wiped little René's nose, pulled on his raincoat.

"It's raining a little, but it doesn't matter, we'll walk around the streets for the last time, tomorrow night we'll be in Paris; we're going to look at the houses and church and the rocks, and then you can have an orangeade or whatever you like."

The next day the hotel dining room was still empty when they came down to lunch, all six of them; the two trunks were in the vestibule, with Alain Mouron's medium-sized suitcase and the three small ones belonging to the children; Monsieur Bailly kept looking at his watch; he caught sight of the manager's car out of the window; he quickly wiped his mouth, tossed his crumpled napkin on his plate where half the piece of camembert he had helped himself to was still lying, clapped his hands, as if he were in class, to make everyone hurry. A waiter brought the farewell piece of prune tart; the three children each took a piece that they swallowed while their mother and Alain Mouron helped them into their raincoats.

And that afternoon the train in which they were traveling gradually caught up with our train. When we asked Uncle Henri, standing in the corridor, if he wanted something to eat, he answered:

"No, thank you",

and it was as if we had wakened him from a dream

(he wasn't thinking about the Rue du Canivet, but about the Rue du Pré-aux-Clercs; he wasn't thinking about my classmates but about his colleagues),

he stuck his head in the compartment door and shouted to Aunt Rose:

"I almost forgot: I have to reserve places for the dining car, if there's still time."

He came back a quarter of an hour later, triumphantly brandishing a fan of thin blue tickets.

"It's for the first service, at six-thirty. Here, there are eight of them."

Now it was at six thirty-five that the train in which the Bailly family and Alain Mouron were traveling was supposed to arrive at the Gare du Maine, so there was no question of going to the dining car, it was long past teatime, the children had started playing cards, but they were half asleep and little Agnès groaned a little, her head in her mother's lap, and the latter's severe features softened.

Alain's mind was elsewhere: could his father leave his work in time to meet him at the station, guide his first steps as a citizen of Paris? He had written that he expected to, but that something could come up, and that Alain mustn't be too disappointed if he didn't come; Alain should go home with the Baillys to the Rue Pierre-Leroux where his father would pick him up before dinner.

He was repeating to himself: he won't be able to get away, it's highly unlikely that he'll come, it's probably much easier for him to go directly to Uncle René's, his office may be far away from the Gare du Maine, it's almost not worth looking for him on the platform, I'll look anyway because it would be so stupid to miss him if he did come, making him to go to Uncle René's anyway, missing my arrival in the city of Paris by my own fault. If he's there, I'll see him, I won't rush toward him, I'll wave, I'll tell Uncle René he's here, I'll wait until they've spoken to each other, I'll say goodbye, I'll kiss the children, he'll take my suitcase, we'll watch them leave and afterwards he'll take me to dinner; but he won't come.

Georges was saying to him:

"Aren't you playing?"

The lamp was turned on. The rain had stopped. Twilight was falling over the suburbs. The train slowed down. They had to put on their raincoats, take the luggage off the racks.

Alain leaned out the window, he saw no one. On the platform, he saw no one. His Uncle René said to him:

"I wouldn't be surprised if he couldn't come, you'll come home with us, it will be a big help anyway."

But he was there, just behind the barrier where you turn in your ticket, in the crowd, and Alain Mouron pushed his way through the backs and arms to reach him.

"Oh, there you are! But where are your cousins?"

"They're coming."

"We'll take them to their taxi."

"Are we going to have dinner with them?"

"Oh, your aunt has enough to handle with her children . . . Well, was it a good trip? The children not too tired? I bet they'll be glad to get to bed."

They walked to the taxi stand as if it were Monsieur Mouron who was the Parisian of long standing, as if the Baillys were the country cousins.

"We'll expect you for lunch tomorrow," Aunt Elizabeth shouted, waving her hand out the window of the taxi.

"Are you glad to be here? Tomorrow we'll have dinner at home, you'll meet Madame Davez who comes to clean the house in the morning and who will make our meals, but tonight we'll treat ourselves to a restaurant."

The next day, you took lunch with us. That was the first time I had seen you since you were back from Greece, and after Father left, while you were sipping a second cup of coffee in the living room, the three of us, Denis, Jacques and I asked for details about your trip, because the stories you had told us during the meal were far from satisfying us.

So you told us about the boats, the harbors, the streetcars of Athens, the menus in the restaurants; then Mother came and interrupted you, reminding us that we had to go to the Lycée Taine for the lists of our textbooks we would be needing for the year. She took the coffee tray to the kitchen and you went back to your room.

It was arranged that we would go to Uncle Henri's after school, and that the next day, Thursday, the four little Jourets would come for lunch with us in return.

While we were standing in line outside the secretary's office, Uncle Henri was at the barber's in the Rue du Pré-aux-Clercs, Monsieur Dumarnet (I think he's a distant cousin of our math teacher, who writes his name in two words: du Marnet), quite short at the temples, where it was beginning to gray, not too short in front where it was getting thin, a shampoo but no massage.

Just as he was coming out, Alain Mouron went in; it was their first encounter, they didn't know they were living in the same apartment building a few steps away, they didn't know that starting the following week they would find themselves in the same classroom together eleven hours a week.

The day school started, Monsieur Bailly, Claire's arm in his, was walking down the Champs-Élysées, looking for a movie.

"Elizabeth is in a state; she's checking all the coat buttons. René's starting fifth grade, Georges third, Agnès second; well, she's past kindergarten, we had to buy them all new books, even René's are too old for Georges. When I left the house, just before telephoning you, they were arguing over the color of the covers. Yesterday Elizabeth bought them big blue, green and pink sheets of paper; I don't know why she didn't take them with her to choose; she's like that, she always thinks she can impose her will on people for everything, but now her own children are beginning to resist, and as for me . . . It's easy to predict the result, no one wants pink paper. Agnès was in tears; Georges was mean enough to tear up a sheet René was beginning to fold; Elizabeth slapped him a couple of times and locked him in the bathroom where he had nothing better to do than turn on all the faucets full blast, then I got mad, we decided on a compromise by letting him have the green paper René had begun to fold, I made René understand that he was a big boy, that he had to give in to his little brother's whims, and I promised Agnès I'd buy her some yellow paper as soon as I could, and that seemed to quiet her down. You see what a life it is; she has nothing better to do than get out of the house; tomorrow she'll go back to her lycée and I to mine, until the day she finds some excuse to spend a weekend at Orléans, because I'm absolutely sure, now, that she's sleeping with someone in Orléans, which would remove any scruple of mine, if I needed any excuse, but I don't, I only need to look at you, your eyes, your patience, I'll have to bring the children here little by little, there's no question of separating them from her completely, but you'd be so different for them, you'll bring them something so different; I'd like them to be able to stay with you from time to time, alone, one or another, in turn, quietly, to have a taste of this different life, as soon as possible. Then tomorrow, I go back to the lycée too, at ten in the morning, to see the new ninth-graders, take their names, make a seating chart; then it will be my seniors at eleven, and in the afternoon (Monday will be like last year, my busiest day; there are very few changes in my schedule), the seniors, the ones I've already taught in the eleventh grade and the ones I've already taught as seniors but who failed their finals; I have the lists, I went to pick them up yesterday morning, but I still haven't studied them. What's the use? Tomorrow will be soon enough."

And the next day, after that first senior class where he had found certain pupils he had already had as seniors the year before, including some who had failed the second part of their exams, Monsieur Bailly went to the elementary school to pick up his two boys, René and Georges, after their first morning of this new school year, and took them back to the Rue Pierre-Leroux apartment where little Agnès was waiting for him.

"What is it, darling?"

"You told me, you told me, for covering my books . . . "

"But you know the stores are all closed on Monday; I'll bring you some tomorrow. Yellow, hum? You'll come buy it with me."

"Almost all the girls already have their books covered, and the teacher told us the stores were open."

"But I can't come for you tonight, your mother will come. If I find a store open, I promise I'll bring you back the prettiest yellow paper there is; see, I'm putting it down in my new notebook."

"Oh, I'll ask Mother, and we'll choose it together."

That evening, Uncle Henri was taking tea in his study when my cousin Gérard came home to the Rue du Pré-aux-Clercs apartment.

"Well, how did your first Greek class go?"

"You know the teacher, the same one for Latin and French, Monsieur Laret. He's young, he looks nice, he only told us about the alphabet and the marks, the rough breathing and the smooth breathing, he told us there were accents too, but that we wouldn't bother with them now. We have to learn this alphabet by heart for tomorrow. That's all the work I have for the moment."

"How about some tea? Go get a cup, and you can get settled somewhere to learn the letters, then come and say them for me."

Uncle Henri went back to getting his class notebooks in order, copying our names in alphabetical order in front of the columns corresponding to the days, the hours when he would call on us, where he would put marks, and the homework he would assign us and correct:

"Abel, Joseph, born January 15, 1939,
Armelli, Claude, born February 25, 1938,
Baron, Charles, born May 8, 1940 . . . "

Alain Mouron, alone in the apartment he and his father live in, sitting in his room on a new chair, at the desk he had last year in Bourges, opened his assignment sheet: for the next day, Tuesday, Greek preparation assigned by Monsieur Jouret, page 14, the beginning of a selection from the fifth book of the *Odyssey*,

"Ulysses, rescued, approaches the coast of the Phaeacians",

from the beginning to line 399, almost a whole page.

He read the first line without understanding a word, stood up to get his Bailly Dictionary out of his cupboard where he had put it away the day before; the mauve back, covered with red inkstains, with its green label on which the letters had faded, tore in his hands.

He began figuring out the words, one after another, making a list on the page of his notebook:

"*Autar:* but
Athènaiè: Athena
Kourè: daughter ... "

So that meant:

"But Athena, daughter of Zeus, felt differently."

That made one line, there were sixteen others left. He carefully filled two pages of his notebook while the daylight was fading. His father came home at quarter of seven and asked him to hurry up with his work, since they were going out for dinner that night to the Davals'. Alain decided that his cousin Michel, the Parisian, who was probably better at Greek, could help him finish this preparation.

He was hoping that on other days he could go faster; the difficulties he had just encountered discouraged him tremendously.

Gérard Jouret was knocking at his father's study, where his father was copying, for the third time, the names of the boys in our class into another notebook:

"Pelletier, Louis, born August 6, 1939,
Régnier, Denis, born December 14, 1938",

(in the left margin, he wrote the letter R, repeating)

"Spencer, Robert, born January 20, 1939"

(in the first column to the right, he wrote the letter a, absent) . . .

"Well, it took you long enough to learn the Greek alphabet."

"I did some other things too."

"Do you know it now?"

"Yes, I can say it to you."

His eyes closed,

"Alpha, beta, gamma, delta, epsilon ... "

"Very good, but what I want to know is whether you can read. Come here. This is a passage from Homer which I've assigned my eleventh-graders—including your cousin Pierre, for tomorrow morning. Now read that off. What's bothering you?"

"Do you pronounce a u the way we do or as separate letters?"

"The way we do, and o u too; you see how easy it is?"

"What about a i?"

"Like eye. There are some differences, otherwise it would be too easy. Now read me the line."

"*Autar Athènaiè, kourè Dios, alla noèsen.*"

"Very good. You see? Soon you'll understand what that means."

"Does Pierre understand what it means?"

"I'll find out tomorrow, if I call on him. He'll probably make a few mistakes; there are lots of things he doesn't know yet."

"Is he a good student?"

"I hope so. I don't know yet."

"Denis wasn't in your class last year?"

"No, there were two eleventh-grade sections."

"But Jacques will be next year?"

"Yes."

"And me the year after that?"

"We'll see. Is that all you have to do? I'd like to finish this before dinner."

The next morning, Monsieur Bailly had called an eleventh-grader to the board and made him write the entire text of the dictation, correcting each error.

"Exchange papers. We'll give a grade of twenty, take off one point for each mistake. Make your calculations rapidly."

Someone raised his hand.

"Yes?"

"What about punctuation?"

"Forget about punctuation this time. I'll take the grades now. All right. Abel?"

It was the boy next to him, Charles Baron, who answered:

"Nine."

"Baron?"

Abel answered:

"Seven."

"Daval?"

I answered:

"Eleven."

I saw him blush with relief. I still didn't know he was Monsieur Bailly's nephew. It went on down to Bruno Verger and Gilbert Zola. The bell rang just as we were finishing.

Monsieur Bailly collected our dictation, put away his big red book and dismissed the class.

Jean-Claude Fage, after noting the date the Turks captured Constantinople, didn't put away his books and notebooks in a briefcase to walk up to the amphitheater, but tied them in a long strap he held by one end and carried them up the stairs that way, sometimes knocking them against a step.

I was beside him; we had already been together the year before, in tenth grade. When we were passing other students coming down, he dropped the strap. I picked up the pack of books, and I saw that on the cover of his books was written not Jean-Claude but Bertrand Fage, Lycée Taine, Eleventh Grade, School Year 1953–1954.

"Is that your brother?"

"Yes, he just passed us."

"Maybe he knows my brother Denis."

"Maybe. Say, isn't the literature teacher your uncle too?"

"Who told you that?"

"I don't know, but isn't that true?"

"Yes, it's true."

"What a family!"

And that evening, before dinner, Gérard Jouret was asking his father, whom he had just interrupted in the preparation of the life of Racine that he was going to tell us about next morning, and his seniors next afternoon

(his profile silhouetted against the darkening window):

"I'd like to know something."

"Yes?"

"Monsieur Vernier, your friend Monsieur Vernier, the history and geography teacher, is the uncle of Denis, Pierre and Jacques?"

"That's right."

"And you're their uncle too."

"Just as their father, Monsieur Jean Eller, is your uncle."

"Then why isn't Monsieur Pierre Vernier our uncle too?"

"No, he's not your uncle at all; I'll explain it to you: your mother is Uncle Jean's sister, Monsieur Vernier is Aunt Anne's brother, you see?"

"So for us that doesn't count?"

"He's just Monsieur Vernier. You knew that, why are you asking about all this in the first place?"

"Because the boy next to me asked."

179

"Who is that?"

"His name is Claude Jourdan and he had a brother who's in the same class with Pierre; so he asked me and I was thinking about it now because I have to learn a lesson for Monsieur Vernier tomorrow about the discovery of America."

Alain Mouron was visiting his cousin Michel Daval, in the Rue Pierre-Leroux; they had decided that it was much easier and more sensible to pool their efforts and share their work, particularly for the preparations that looked hardest to the country boy.

They had drunk their tea under the discreet supervision of Lucie Daval, who had then left the room. The difficulty was to get settled, because there was only one desk in the room, and it was much too small for both of them to be able to work at it comfortably.

After a vain exploration of the apartment, Michel decided that it would be best if Alain were comfortably settled, since he was the guest and was doing the Greek preparation, which was the hardest, so it was only natural that the hardest should be done by the one who was the most comfortable.

As for Michel, he was used to working flat on his bed, that didn't bother him at all, he would do the Latin.

So each boy armed himself with his dictionary.

Ulysses caught sight of the land and the forest, leaped ahead to gain his footing. After that came line 400, and darkness fell again.

"All'oté tosson apèn..."

Nothing; whatever little Greek he had learned in Bourges he had forgotten during the vacation, but he couldn't show that to Michel sprawling on the bed behind him, chewing his pencil and leafing through his Latin textbook so casually.

The words one by one.

All'

Oté

Tosson...

The pages, the columns on the pages, all those quotations, alphabetical order: pi, rho, sigma, tau...

"But since he was far away..."

And he continued his exasperating work until six-thirty, while Michel Daval was whistling, stood up, walked around the apartment, came back and collapsed again on the bed, sighing:

"What a bore, this Livy!"

"I'm through," Alain Mouron said. "I have to go home."

"Wait till I copy out your notebook. I haven't finished yet, but it's only the last few lines I'm missing . . . "

"Did you understand it all?"

"Just about. You know, you don't have to make a translation; I bet you're giving yourself too much work. You looked up all the words!"

"How else can you understand what it means."

"Sure you can, you don't need to do all that."

"You can read that and understand it?"

"You don't have to go that far."

"And you can explain what the Livy's about?"

"More or less. Let me use the desk to copy out your vocabulary."

Alain Mouron, standing beside him, looked at his cousin's notebook, five or six words scribbled in it, which he compared with the passage from Livy, trying to read it, but even then he understood nothing. He would have to go on working after dinner. This collaboration didn't look very promising to him.

Uncle Henri was rereading the Victor Bérard translation of the lines in question.

"He was already within shouting distance: he saw the surf that was thundering on the rocks . . . ",

checking certain words in the Bailly Dictionary, adding some new annotations and corrections in the margins.

The next day, Monsieur Bailly had no class. He has postponed his preparation until the afternoon and reopened the file containing his index cards relating to that dissertation on Wordsworth which grew more unlikely every year. He would have to go call for his two boys at the elementary school; he closed his file, thinking: I'll have to ask Claire's advice.

That afternoon, at the end of our first mathematics class, while Alain Mouron, Michel Daval, myself, all his neighbors, were putting our things in our briefcases as fast as we could, for that bell indicated not only the end of a class but the end of the afternoon for us, Francis Hutter remained in his seat, took out a new notebook and his textbook of German authors. He still didn't know that the teacher he was waiting for had the same surname as his own; he hadn't seen him yet.

The latter had just met his eighth-graders.

181

That day, it was Michel Daval who went to Alain Mouron's. Sitting in the dining room, each at one end of the table, they had put between them, as a snack, a package of cookies they had found in the kitchen.

They were doing their homework for the day after the next, Friday, in order to be free for all of Thursday, which they would be spending together, for Alain had no scout meeting that day.

Now on Friday, there were only two afternoon classes, the morning being devoted to open-air activities (the gym teacher had arranged to meet them in the lycée auditorium to take them to the Gare du Luxembourg where they would catch the train for the Croix-de-Berny station),

Greek, French, a dozen lines of Homer and the *Épître à Lyon Jamet* by Clément Marot.

Alain would have been glad to have Michel do the Greek this time, but Michel got out of it by saying that since it was the hardest and the most boring task, it would be better for the one who had everything else taken care of to do it.

"Why do I always have to be the one to do the dirty work? A French preparation's nothing!"

"That's what you think."

"It's nothing compared to Greek."

"If you wanted to do it fairly ..."

"Fairly or not ..."

"If you don't want me to do it for you, I'll do it at home and get Lucie to help me. It's not my fault if you have only one Bailly dictionary ..."

"You're kidding."

"Sure."

"Well, at least do it well, the *Épître à Lyon Jamet*."

"Perfect, you'll see."

Uncle Henri was checking the translation of Sophocles' *Antigone* in the Guillaume Budé series.

Then came dinner time. He heard Aunt Rose:

"Claude, François, have you washed your hands? We're sitting down to dinner."

He went to the bathroom himself. When he came out, his wife brought in the tureen. Unfolding his napkin, he asked:

"Tomorrow we're all going to Denise's, aren't we?"

"No, just the children, at least for lunch. We'll pick them up there at the end of the afternoon."

"Has everyone finished his homework? They'll be exhausted after that little family orgy."

Monsieur Mouron had come home.

"Well, how's the Greek going? Give my best regards to your parents, Michel. Oh, that's right, we'll be seeing them tomorrow. Good night, Michel, enjoy your dinner. And now, Alain, clear that table for me and set it while I find out what Madame Davez has fixed for us out in the kitchen."

After eating your lunch alone in a restaurant in the Rue des Canettes, you went back up to the apartment in the Rue du Canivet, and we passed you on the stairs as we were reluctantly coming down to take the métro to visit Aunt Denise.

Aunt Rose had said to Uncle Henri:

"While the children are at their aunt's, we can clear out the kitchen cupboard."

Empty jars, cans, old dishes, they washed them all, then put things back in place after spreading fresh sheets of oilcloth on the shelves.

Michel Daval had decided to take Alain Mouron to the Vincennes zoo, but the rain ruined his plans.

"Do something," his mother said, "don't just stand there sighing out the window."

"We could go to the movies."

"Do you want to go to the movies? Alain, I'm asking you, answer me, don't be so shy."

"I'd like to."

"Did you go to the movies often in Bourges?"

"No, not very often."

"But do you like the movies?"

"Oh, yes, I like them a lot, but there aren't many movies in Bourges."

"I can't remember any more if your father enjoys movies or not."

"My father? The movies? He loves them, he's always telling me we should go more often."

"What have you seen since you've been in Paris?"

"Oh, we haven't had time to go yet. We're still fixing up the apartment; it's not finished yet, you know."

"Of course it's a little silly to send you to the movies when we asked you over so we could show you something of Paris, but it's the best solution today, even so. Unless we were to go to the Louvre . . . "

183

"Oh, Mother, it's too late; they close around four; we'll go another time, maybe next Thursday."

"No, next Thursday I have a scout meeting."

"Well, the Thursday after that, we have time, the whole year . . . "

"But if it's good weather, it might be better to go to the Vincennes zoo."

Right, we'll only go to the Louvre, or some other museum if you'd rather—you know, in Paris there are plenty of museums—if it's bad weather. This time we'll go to the movies. You better give us some money, Mother, because Alain may have some money in his pocket, but I don't have any left."

"I don't want Alain to spend his money; you take him, Michel."

"Well, what shall we see?"

The next day, Monsieur Bailly dictated to his seniors a passage from a lecture by Coleridge on *Macbeth* and asked them to hand in the translation on the following Friday, October 15, adding that those who weren't on time would not only get a zero but would be kept in the following Thursday.

A brief discussion of Shakespeare, obtain a suitable edition if possible for the next day, the selections in the textbook would not be enough, prepare scene three of the first act, down to where Ross, one of King Duncan's two messengers, declares to the victor that he has been made Thane of Cawdor, that is, confirms the first of the witches' predictions.

It was almost ten the next morning when he reopened the *Complete Works of Shakespeare* and the witches began speaking.

"*Act One, Scene One. Scotland. A desert heath. Thunder and lightning. Enter three witches. First witch:*

> "*When shall we three meet again*
> *In thunder, lightning, or in rain?*"

They have met Macbeth, and he has begun killing, first King Duncan, then his friend Banquo; and when the clock on the mantel showed him it was time to pick up his two boys at the elementary school, he had reached:

"*A cavern. In the middle a boiling cauldron. Thunder. Enter the three witches.*"

At the next history class, you would be telling us about the dis-

184

covery and conquest of America. Francis Hutter underlined the end of that day's chapter in red ink:

"the Renaissance and the Reformation",

then he carefully dried his page with a pink blotter, considered his work and, content, closed his notebook and put it away to go, with the rest of us, to our first chemistry class.

Monsieur Hutter was talking with his elder son along the quays of the Seine. He wanted to take advantage of the splendid weather to visit Notre-Dame.

Before dinner, Gérard Jouret went into his father's study.

"Are you through with your homework? You have a scout hike tomorrow, I think."

"Yes, there was a little Greek grammar, a little Latin grammar, and a history lesson for Monsieur Vernier."

"You know, Monsieur Vernier's coming here for lunch tomorrow; if he mentions you, I want to be able to tell him you did your work well. What were you studying?"

"The Italian wars."

"Bring me your textbook."

Ferdinand of Aragon and Isabella of Castile, Maximilian I, Pope Julius II, Charles VIII, Louis XII and François I, Emperor Charles V; then it was the turn of his sister Lucie, who also had a history lesson for Monday, the Empire under Justinian, the basilica of Santa Sophia in Constantinople.

Claude came in to show his problems, François his grammatical exercises on possessive adjective.

Alain Mouron finished his preparation of Homer; Michel Daval had told him he would do it on Sunday night, not having any scout hike.

" . . . Then, have pity on me, Lord, I declare I am thy suppliant."

Setting the table while his father heated up the soup; and as the two of them were eating in silence,

"Would you like to go to the movies? It's about time we started to find out where the neighborhood houses are."

"I went to the movies with the Davals Thursday."

"That's right, what did you see?"

"A western."

"Where was it?"

"The Sèvres-Pathé."

"We'll find another one. Go get the newspaper for me—it's in my overcoat pocket. Did you finish your homework?"

"Sure."

"Don't leave anything for tomorrow, because you'll be so tired when you come home from your scout hike you won't be able to do anything, and I don't want to keep you from doing your work."

"No, I don't have any written work, not yet, just preparation, a few lessons, it doesn't even take long."

And he was thinking:

"There's still that damn Livy and the passage from Rabelais and the geography class in the afternoon: representation of the earth, and the scene from *Julius Caesar*; but I'll telephone Michel tomorrow night after dinner, and he'll give me a quick explanation of what it's about . . .

"Well, we could go to the Bonaparte, it's not far, just opposite Saint-Sulpice. But the starting times are eight and ten; it's too late for the eight o'clock show, and I think ten's too late for you. What time is your meeting tomorrow morning?"

"Nine o'clock Mass at Saint-Hilaire."

"That's all right. You'll be in bed by twelve-thirty. We still have a good hour; let's see what's on the radio."

"When will the telephone be installed?"

"They promised it in a month. Take an apple, it's good for you. Oh, that's right, you have to take lunch with you for tomorrow. I hope Madame Davez has remembered."

Monsieur Bailly's alarm clock went off at eight; Elizabeth wasn't there; that's right, she was at Orléans, yes, Orléans. The children were beginning to wake up. She had got everything ready for breakfast, she had left him a list of everything he had to do, on his night table, under the alarm clock.

"The milk is on the stove, turn on the gas, light it, make sure the milk doesn't boil. For lunch, ask the children to set the table; don't forget that the whole Daval family is coming. Madame Doignet will be here for cooking and washing up, she has all the instructions . . ."

The children got dressed by themselves, helping each other; they were putting on their Sunday clothes; usually they went to Mass with their mother at Saint-François-Xavier and Monsieur Bailly stayed in bed until they came back, but today? That was something that hadn't been anticipated, that wasn't on the list.

All three knew that their father never went to Mass and they were probably wondering what he was going to do; they had washed more carefully than usual, and had pulled on their gloves without being told.

Everyone ate breakfast, and Monsieur Bailly, holding Agnès' right hand and Georges' left, little René leading the way, walked to Saint-François-Xavier, not getting there until quarter after nine.

Georges discovered that he had forgotten his missal.

"I don't have mine either," his father answered, "the important thing is that you say your prayers properly."

They were already at the Offertory; the organ was thundering; they got mixed up in their genuflections.

Michel Daval was opening his eyes. His mother, at the door of his room:

"If you want to go to ten o'clock Mass, you better get up now; don't forget we're going to the Baillys' for lunch, and since your Uncle René is your English teacher, I think we'd better not be too late."

During the afternoon, Monsieur Martin took his two children to the Vincennes zoo. Jean-Claude Fage was saying to his brother Bertrand:

"What's the matter with Mother these days?"

"What's the matter with her? She's in a bad mood; it comes over women now and then."

"Do you know a lot? Of women, I mean?"

"Listen, I decided: No complications before exams, and if you'll take my advice you'll do the same thing."

"If you want to give me advice, I'd rather have it about that bastard Homer."

"I can't do a thing for you. I didn't have such a fanatic last year as you do now, and I never translated your bastard Homer. If you let Jouret give you such terrible assignments without saying a word, it'll go on all year long, and you won't be able to do a thing about it. If I were in your place, I swear I'd do something to stop that guy."

"But you always do your Greek homework."

"Listen, I'm supposed to graduate this year, I have the baccalaureate exams coming up, and besides, I like it."

"I like it too."

187

"Then what are you complaining about?"

"I like it, but I don't understand it."

"You do your job, I do mine. Do you have Vernier for history and geography too?"

"Yes, tomorrow, for the structure, yes, that's it, structure and history of the earth."

"Watch out for him; he looks harmless but don't get him mad. I never saw anyone smile so much about keeping you in. It's almost four; if you're through with your little job there, I think it's time to go to the movies."

Before dinner, Uncle Henri asked Gérard how his hike had been.

The rain, the game, the Tiger Patrol, the leader of the patrol, the other leaders, Chamois, Squirrels, including me, Bisons, but Aunt Rose, hearing his voice, came into the study:

"What a sight you are! You can tell about all that later. You start by getting undressed and taking a bath."

Uncle Henri went back to the Victor Bérard translation:

" . . . the immortal gods as well, do they not respect a poor shipwrecked sailor . . . ",

fuming as usual over the latter's bad taste, all those wretched lines of blank verse, thinking that this time he had probably given his boys too strong a dose, and that there would be very few, the next morning, who would have done their whole preparation very carefully.

Lucie was the only one of the children who ate dinner in her regular clothes; the three boys were in their pajamas, half asleep over their soup, even Gérard, and they went to bed as soon as the last mouthful was swallowed.

After his bath, Alain Mouron brushed and folded his uniform, then put on his regular clothes. On Sundays, Madame Davez didn't come during the day and consequently there was no dinner ready, which was why the father and son went to the restaurant in the Rue des Saints-Pères for dinner, ladies in evening dresses, gentlemen laughing out loud, talking about plays, Italian dishes, Italian wine, of which Alain probably drank a little too much *cassata* for dessert.

At nine-thirty, he asked if he could make a telephone call. Madame Daval answered. Michel was going to bed, but she went to call him.

"It's Alain Mouron. How are you? The hike? Yes, it was all right, but the weather wasn't so good, you know. Did you finish your work for tomorrow? The English? Oh, good! Let me have your notebook tomorrow, I'll copy it at lunch. The worst is the Latin; if you could tell me what it's all about . . . You didn't finish it? Yes, I finished my Homer last night, but I don't have my notebook here, I'm calling you from a restaurant."

That night, Michel Daval heard his parents' alarm clock go off in the next room. His Greek grammar was on his night table because Uncle Henri had told us to review the first declension and he had sincerely intended to do it before getting up; he turned on the light, opened the book, glanced at the page in question, closed the book, turned out the light, turned over, pulled the covers over his shoulders and went back to sleep.

Monsieur Bailly had slept badly; in an irritable mood, he put on his slippers and went down the hall to shave, lit the gas under the milk and the coffee, went into his sons' room, opening the shutters as noisily as he could, then into his daughter's room, awakening her very gently.

In the kitchen, the milk was boiling.

The three children came in to eat their breakfast.

"At least you could comb your hair!"

They had to hurry. Since Elizabeth was in Orléans, they would have to stop first at the Aulnoy lycée with Agnès before they went on to the boys' elementary school.

That afternoon, to my right, in the first row, Philippe Guillaume was still there; the sweat may have already been coming out on his forehead, he was probably beginning to feel the first touches of the grippe that was going to immobilize him for several days.

The seasons, their inversion from one hemisphere to the next, the difference between the length of the days, and of the nights.

Bruno Verger, beside him, tall, with almost red hair, the beginnings of a beard that he would soon have to shave once or twice a week, was chewing his pencil as he listened to you, terrestrial zones, tropical, temperate, polar, without taking notes, because he too was repeating, but from another lycée and his notebook was already full.

Leaving the table, Uncle Henri kissed Claude and François, who went to bed without making too much trouble, for once. Aunt Rose had sat down next to the radio to knit some warm socks for Gérard who, like Lucie, was pretending to study his Greek and Latin grammar while listening to the detective program.

189

In his study, Uncle Henri, after lighting his pipe, looked through our textbook for a passage to be translated that he would assign us tomorrow, to be handed in the following week,

after several hesitations, decided on a passage from the *De Signis*, Verrès pillage of Sicily,

"Venio nunc ad istius . . . "
(I now come to this man's . . .),

then took his Rabelais out of the bookcase to read the chapter of *Pantagruel* from which we had a passage to prepare for the next day, pages 25 to 27 in our *Sixteenth Century French Authors*,

starting from

"Pantagruel studied very hard . . . "

down to

" . . . his spirit among the books was like fire among the heather, so indefatigable and ardent was it",

got up from his armchair, refilled his pipe, went to join Aunt Rose in the dining room, to tell Gérard and Lucie it was high time for them to go to bed.

Alain Mouron, after having said good night to his father, slipped into his bed, and, since he hadn't had time to do his French preparation, because he had had trouble enough finishing his composition, our first of the year, about the one day of his vacation that had seemed most remarkable to him, the day of his arrival at Saint-Cornély,

this because he hadn't dared write the truth for fear of seeming ridiculous, for actually the one moment that had been happiest and most exciting was the moment of his arrival in Paris,

he read Gargantua's letter from

"Now it is that the minds of men...",

down to the signature.

During the night, turning over suddenly, his hand brushed the book off onto the floor.

Uncle Henri felt Aunt Rose getting up. A child was crying in the next room.

"What was it?"

"Claude. A nightmare. I gave him some water. He went back to sleep."

Denis Régnier was dreaming about marvelous stamps from Troy, with the walls, from Ithaca, with the boats, from Carthage, with Hannibal, and from Utopia—enormous ones with Gargantua, and a bloodstained Caesar from the Roman Republic.

Monsieur Bonnini, unable to sleep opened his shutters and waited for the dawn.

In the first row, close to the door, Paul Coutet is leaning over his notebook to copy the diagram of the two Americas on the blackboard; you have just superscribed three ovals on it, in which you are writing in capital letters:

"Incas, Mayas, Aztecs";

Gilbert Zola, his neighbor, looks up.

Pyramids, temples, gold, feathers.

That was months ago.

At ten that night, Monsieur Bailly had not yet come home to the Rue Pierre-Leroux apartment. Since Elizabeth had left him with the children on his hands for two days, she could take care of them by herself now for a while. After dinner, he and Claire decided to go see a Hitchcock movie. He scarcely glanced at the screen. He was caressing her hand and from time to time kissed her nails. Coming out, walking down the Champs Élysées as far as the Place de la Concorde,

"I don't know how this business of ours is going to come out."

"What business?"

"This business between the three of us, Elizabeth, you and me, or rather the four of us, because I'm sure that there's this man in Orléans . . ."

"How could it turn out, and why do you even want it to turn out? It'll go on like this for a while, and then you'll make up with her; we'll see each other less and less . . . "

"Why do you talk to me like that? I was hoping that at least you . . . "

"You want me to tell you that I love you? Oh yes, I love you; let's take advantage of it now, when we're sure of it. You know you have no way of getting away from her; you know you have only vague suspicions."

"That's just what may change."

"We'll always be at the same point."

"I made a mistake, I made a terrible mistake in marrying her; for years I knew we weren't happy, but I pretended, I kept up appearances, you understand? I was trying to convince myself; I kept telling myself: 'It may be a little hard to admit, but this *is* the happiness people talk about, this is all it is, I couldn't have done better'; I fed myself on absurd illusions like that, until I met you, and then I understood that if I had waited it would have been a whole other life we could have had together. And now you tell me it's irreparable?"

"Look, I love you, we love each other, we're happy just walking together like this; you feel a kind of terror thinking about the moment when you'll be going home. Your wife will be asleep in her bed, alone. You'll be careful not to make any noise so as not to wake the children, and especially not to wake her; and you'll go to sleep in your own bed, alone, beside hers, not much farther from her than when you still had your double bed; and I think about that moment with horror too, in a few minutes, in the Vaneau métro station where you'll leave me and walk down the platform while I'll stay on the train to the Émile-Zola stop, and then I'll walk up to my studio alone. If only . . . "

"Yes?"

"Let's talk about something else."

"But what did you want to say?"

"Nothing, nothing, really; let's walk a little faster, I'm beginning to get cold."

"Listen, tell me what you're really thinking."

"If only I was sure that . . . "

"Sure that what?"

"Why aren't you satisfied . . . "

"You were sure she was unfaithful to me?"

"No, it's only too likely that she's unfaithful to you, even if . . . if I begin to make jealous scenes . . . but she's much too subtle, I suppose, for you to get any proof, that's not what I wanted to say, unfortunately."

"What do you mean unfortunately?"

"Well, since you really want to know, here, here's what I was going to say, but first I want you to know that I love you, that I don't love anyone but you, that I know—I know it, you hear—that you love me; what I was going to say is this: if only—that's it, I began like that, didn't I—if only I was absolutely sure you haven't said that to any other woman since your marriage. There, that's what it was. Are you satisfied?"

"You're crying, darling, calm down. There, that's better. What's the use of all this? And besides, if you were absolutely sure of it, what difference would that make?"

"None."

Monsieur Daval burst into his son's bedroom.

"Turn out that light. It's almost midnight! Tomorrow you won't be able to get up again."

Michel waited until it was quiet again, until the hall light no longer showed through the crack under his door.

Then, turning the light back on, he took out from under his sheets the yellow-covered magazine he had bought that morning and went on reading the story by Fritz Leiber, "The Game of Silence."

" . . . the soldier slowly let go of his gun and raised his hands toward her in a gesture of interrogation . . . "

At the end,

" . . . Lili realized that in a moment she would be capable of speaking",

it was quarter to one; too tired to begin "Wolves Don't Cry",

"The werewolf is a familiar creature in the traditional paraphernalia of the fantastic . . . ",

he laid down the magazine near the lamp which he turned out, and fell asleep murmuring:

" . . . all the various metals that are hid within the bowels of the earth."

We had gone back to the apartment in the Rue du Canivet. You reread a few notes already taken for this work that was advancing, covered several pages with indications for organizing your narrative.

Jacques and Denis were asleep in our room. I undressed in the dark. I couldn't get to sleep. I was fifteen. I was the possessor of a secret. You had confided a mission to me, I wondered what I should do to obtain all the information you wanted; get myself invited by my neighbor Daval, by his cousin Mouron who is a Scout in the Saint-Hilaire troop; have them come here for a meal, for instance, or on the pretext of working together they would give me information about Monsieur Bailly almost without suspecting it; then I would wait for further instruction.

Three o'clock by Saint-Sulpice.

At eight-fifteen, just before leaving his apartment, Monsieur Mouron awakened his son, who this time leaped out of bed at once.

His Greek grammar open under his bed lamp while he pulled on his shirt and pants, he read aloud the table of the third declension which Uncle Henri had assigned us to review for that morning.

193

In the bathroom, a little water on his eyes, promising himself he would wash more thoroughly at lunchtime, a comb through his hair.

He drank his *café au lait* cold, he didn't have time enough to heat it up, then ran down the stairs four at a time.

It was a beautiful day; the morning sun was shining through the yellow leaves. Crossing the Place Saint-Germain-des-Prés, he saw that it was only ten to nine.

A good thing he hurried anyway; his alarm clock must be fast, he slowed down, lingering in front of the shop windows, particularly in front of the maps and globes in the Taride store.

But at the Carrefour de l'Odéon, nine o'clock was chiming.

He would have to sneak in past the janitor, endure Monsieur Jouret's sarcasm. This time he would certainly be kept in, with all the humiliation this implied, not so much in the eyes of his class-mates as in the eyes of the other Scouts of the Chamois Patrol, since being kept in would prevent him from coming to the meeting.

His father would receive the news with that mournful resignation he knew so well.

But by a miraculous coincidence, Monsieur Jouret was late too. He was coming from the elementary school where he had left his younger sons; they met in front of the janitor's office.

Embarrassed smile; he was puffing too, he had just been running, which was a little ridiculous at his age.

Alain let him go ahead. They walked into the class one after the other. There was another late-comer that morning, François Nathan, but my Uncle Henri didn't say a word.

"Abel?"

"Here."

"Armelli?"

"Here."

"Baron . . . "

André Knorr and Francis Hutter were absent; Philippe Guillaume had come back.

"All right. Now, today you were going to review the third declension . . . "

Octave de Joigny, Laurent Garrac, Bertrand Limours.

"For Friday, you will review the declension of adjectives. We'll move on to our dear Homer. You were to have prepared lines 474 to 493 of Book Five, that is, the end of Book Five; the day after tomorrow, we shall begin Book Six, Nausicaa's Dream. Who can give us a résumé of the preceding chapters, so to speak, especially of what we read yesterday? All right, Mouron."

"Ulysses has come out of the river; he's on the shore now, but he's afraid of catching cold and also of the wild beasts, wolves . . . "

"That's right. We stopped at line 473:

'Deidia mè thérèssin élor kai kurma génomaï',

I am afraid lest of wild beasts the food and prey I become, and now what is going to happen? Monsieur Limours, I believe I have never heard you read Greek; would you give us that pleasure?"

Ulysses hid himself in an olive thicket and fell asleep there.

"For Friday you will prepare the beginning of Book Six, down to line thirteen. The hour is up. Those who wish to leave the room for five minutes may do so."

Rémy Orland, Louis Pelletier, Robert Spencer stammered through Chapter 34 of Book XXI of Livy.

"For next Monday, you will prepare Chapter Thirty-five for me. The hour is up. Those of you who want to leave the room . . . "

Representation of relief, cross-hatching and isobars, Maurice Tangala, at the back of the room, was humming a tune he had heard in the street while passing a café with a jukebox on, adding new notes at each chorus. Jacques Estier signaled to him to keep quiet; some of their neighbors were beginning to hear him, to turn their heads.

The Abbé Gollier, in his study, was preparing his senior class in religious instruction.

At six, since it was almost dark, you got up to close your shutters, after having turned on your desk lamp. It was still a lovely clear day, there was a breath of warm wind, the sky was green behind the towers of Saint-Sulpice, with long, luminous streaks; a few noisy birds were flying overhead, and the exclamations of the children crossing the square answered them in the soft hum of the cars.

Back at your desk, you considered this schedule you had just drawn up to permit you to complete this work, every hour of every day of the week, or just about, with its assigned task, and suddenly it occurred to you that there wasn't much room in all this for Micheline Pavin . . .

There were the evenings, except for Monday; you would talk about that together in a little while . . .

195

Then, driving away this thought, you picked up the file in which you had put away the notes taken the night before, and in accord with this new schedule, you continued your researches and your writing until seven,

reminding yourself what had happened exactly a week before yesterday's class which you had decided would be the decisive one, the discovery and conquest of America,

that is, the end of the Middle Ages, and you began the account,

indicating at the same time, according to the information he had given you on Sunday, what Uncle Henri was doing then,

then you went on to what had happened exactly two days before this pivotal hour, that is, that conversation Sunday between the two of you, while I was participating in a scout maneuver in the Verrières woods, in the rain, with my new patrol,

and you went on to the description of Monday afternoon, taking into account what had happened to the three of us between two and three,

what had happened between three and four to three others, Monsieur Bailly and his nephews . . .

Your tooth was beginning to hurt again. You telephoned from our apartment to your dentist, Monsieur Hubert, who gave you an appointment for the next day at three o'clock,

to Micheline Pavin, who had left her office. Had she made an appointment to meet you at that café on the Champs-Élysées at eight, or hadn't she?

We were sitting down around the table. Jacques and Denis were talking a lot. Papa made them keep quiet because he wanted to hear the news on the radio. I felt my five-hundred-franc bill in my pocket, and I wondered what I was going to have my Scouts do the next afternoon.

After dessert, I went to our room. Denis came in, I told him right away I had work to do,

"Tomorrow's Thursday."

"I know, but I have to get my meeting ready."

"Oh, that's right, you're patrol leader now; that's going to be some patrol!"

"As good as yours was last year."

"Oh, I don't care about any of that stuff now, they wanted me to be one of the scoutmasters, but I have too much else to do."

196

"What do you have to do that's so important?"

"I have to get ready for my finals."

"Is that all?"

"What do you mean, is that all?"

"You're not going to spend all your time all day and all night, Thursday and Sunday included, on that?"

"Listen, you've gotten pretty nosy since you've become patrol leader. You think I'm going to hand you a list of my activities? You think I need all that scout stuff to keep me busy? You think there isn't anything else to do?"

"Oh, I have other things to do, but that doesn't keep me from scout work if I want to."

"What do you have to do that's so important, except for your school work? I went through eleventh grade, don't forget, and I know it's not so hard."

"Your record in eleventh grade isn't so much to brag about."

"You're getting to be a real little headmaster, aren't you? Well, outside your homework, your classes (and I know how well you do that) and your burdensome responsibilities as patrol leader?"

"Outside that, I keep myself informed."

"Perfect! And how long have you been doing that? A long time?"

"Oh, no, just recently."

"Well, with your permission, I'm going to do my Latin translation, and I promise you it's a tough one, you wouldn't understand the first line. Since it's the first one of the year . . . "

He sat down at his desk. He picked up the Gaffiot dictionary. I heard him sighing behind me, leafing through the pages.

Once I was sure he had stopped watching me, I took out of my briefcase the issue of *Fiction* Michel Daval had handed me that morning. Actually I would have plenty of time, the next day before lunch, to prepare my patrol meeting.

The first story was called "The Rhu'ad"; it looked long and not very promising.

The second, "The Train 1815", was by Claude Farrère, of the Académie Française; what? Of the Académie Française? I didn't believe my eyes; then this magazine was something quite different from what I had expected! If he belonged to the Académie Française, his story probably wasn't what I wanted.

The introduction to the third story, "The Game of Silence",

"Fritz Leiber, who first followed in the footsteps of his father, a celebrated Shakespearian actor . . . ",

That sounded better.

"Lili felt really excited when the American soldier stuck his broad white face and his rifle . . . "

After a while, Denis turned around.

"You working?"

"Are you?"

"I'm tired of it. I'll do the rest tomorrow."

"I'm staying here."

"Preparing your patrol meeting?"

"Yes, and I'm reading, I may read them something."

"A scout novel?"

"I don't know yet, that depends. You going to the dining room?"

"I'm going to see what's on the radio."

When he had closed the door behind him, I breathed a sigh of relief; he hasn't seen what I was reading; I was afraid of his comments.

"Lili looked at the viscous thing she was holding in her hands, wondering if you got the same feeling from cancer . . . "

Alain Mouron didn't get out of bed until nine. His father had wakened him at the same time as usual before leaving the apartment, but since there was no school, he didn't get up until he heard Madame Davez' key turn in the lock.

She was opening the shutters in his father's room when he crossed the hall to go to the bathroom in pajamas and slippers.

"Goodness, Monsieur Alain, you're not dressed yet? Well, you're right, after all they make you work so hard in school. You haven't had your breakfast yet? Should I heat it up now? It'll be ready in no time. You have a bathrobe, don't you? In any case, your father has one. I'll go get it for you, here it is."

She toasted two slices of bread for him in the oven.

"The two of you get along all right heating up what I fix for you, don't you?" she asked as she was buttering the toast, "tell me how you do it. Still, it's a little sad, you know, a man and his son all alone like that in an apartment in Paris. I do everything I can to make it easy for you, but all the same, it's not the same thing. Has it been long since you lost your mother?"

He was a little shy at first, then he began talking about his life in Bourges, about his memories. At ten-thirty, Madame Davez exclaimed:

198

"Goodness, how the time passes! We go on chattering and the housework doesn't get done; I think it's time to get ready, Monsieur Alain."

When he came out of the bathroom, she was cleaning his room.

"Come here and let me fix your tie."

"I'm going out; I'll be back before noon."

"Enjoy your walk, my boy, enjoy your walk."

Uncle Henri was reading some of our compositions on the most remarkable day of our vacation. Michel Daval's was set in Provence, Denis Régnier's in Savoie, Francis Hutter's in the Basque country: Uncle Henri thought of pinpointing the distribution of his students' vacations on a map, and wondered what results might appear if he were to do the same thing every year.

Hubert Jourdan's composition described a hunt in Sologne, on an enormous estate bordered with thickets and ponds, the return to the chateau in the evening, with the partridges, the pheasants and the hares, the photographs, the long, elegant dinner with all the cousins in the big, fake-Gothic dining hall.

Now on this Thursday afternoon, Hubert Jourdan was with his two young brothers, Claude and Charles, visiting the uncle who owned that estate and listening to a discussion of his grandmother's illness while preparing the tableaux vivants that were to be shown to the grownups at teatime, as they had done several times during vacation.

Monsieur Tavera, in his studio, was taking advantage of the light to get on with his still life—a bowl, a guitar and a partridge—that he had begun the day before.

You came back to the Rue du Canivet apartment, exhausted by your session at the dentist's. Your jaw was hurting, you took some more aspirin; then, to try to keep to the schedule worked out the day before, you went back to your manuscript and when you reached my Uncle Henri in the middle of Wednesday afternoon, seniors, Iphigénie, and you and I at the same moment, representation of the earth, you wrote in the present tense, although not only was it not the same hour, but already not even the same day,

then, like someone who takes a deep breath before going on with his story, you tried to situate it more richly, more profoundly,

the preceding day not sufficing any more than the preceding hour, the week any more than the day,

in the intention of making me feel, later on, when I should come to the reading of this work for the writing of which you are now using my eyes, my feelings and my voice, augmenting them with everything you know and guess,

how this hour and the hours before, already touched on, were situated among other hours, just as my eyes among other eyes,

you tried to remember what you had done, seen and thought, in the middle of the afternoon, a month before that class on the discovery and conquest of America, the second Tuesday in September, the fourteenth,

but soon, despite all your desire to get on, the words began to blur before your eyes, to fade in your mind,

and since evening was falling, your head dropped on the paper, you fell asleep.

I had led the Bisons to the troop headquarters near Saint-Hilaire. The meeting ended with the study of the anthems we were to sing at the next Sunday's Mass (I had learned them all the year before), then with the chaplain's address.

At seven, we broke up; the troop leader reminded the patrol leaders and the assistant leaders that we would have a special meeting on Sunday at ten.

My brother Jacques was already far down the street ahead of me; I didn't catch up with him until we reached the Place Saint-Sulpice.

When we got home, Mother brought in the soup, then, rubbing her hands over her apron,

"Go knock at Pierre's door, I think he's coming for dinner tonight."

I knocked; you didn't answer. I opened the door; your room was dark. I turned on the ceiling light: I saw you were asleep, your head lying on your papers; I called you, I shook you, you woke with a start, rubbed your jaw, looked at me suspiciously, murmuring:

"What's the matter?"

"Are you coming to eat? Dinner's on the table."

You looked for a few seconds at the unfinished page, you followed me without a word.

Friday morning, Alain Mouron, like the rest of us save for the three absentees that day, André Knorr, Bernard de Loups and Jacques Estier, ran through the fine drizzle in the Croix-de-Berry stadium, then played on the side opposite mine during the football game.

Uncle Henri was preparing his afternoon classes, an hour of Greek, from two to three, with us, for which he had assigned us the first twenty-three lines of Book Six of the Odyssey, which was why he had turned to the Bérard translation:

"Now, while far away, the hero of endurance, Ulysses . . . "

to

" . . . She had assumed the features of one of her own companions, dearly loved by her, the daughter of Dymas, the famous navigator",

and the Bailly Dictionary for the indispensable checking,
an hour of French with us, from three to four, for which we were to prepare the passage from Rabelais:

"Gargantua's Studies according to the Directions of his Tutors, the Sophists",

for which he reread the whole of Chapter XXI of Book One, smiling at what had been censored by the editor of the classroom selections,
comparing the notes of the two editions, which took him some time, so that he was not able to prepare his third afternoon hour, from four to five, with the seniors, during which he was supposed to have them read a passage from Sophocles' *Antigone* in translation, consequently relying on his memory.
for he heard his children coming home from their various lycées, Claude and François accompanied by Gérard, and Aunt Rose was through setting the table.
Consequently, a few hours later, after having finished with Francis Hutter, he was having Denis Régnier read:
"Then he studied for a miserable half-hour, his eyes fixed on his book, but—as the comic poet says—his soul was in the kitchen. . . . "
Monsieur Hubert, in the physics lab next door to the amphitheater, was supervising his seniors' first session of practical work.
You went down to the main floor to give your eighth-graders their third history class,
"Mohammed and the Arab conquest."
Instead of going straight back to the Rue du Canivet, you went to the barbershop on the Rue Saint-Sulpice; it wasn't allowed for in your schedule, and yet it would make you lose at least an hour every two weeks.
Six o'clock was chiming when you sat down at your desk.

I was rereading the notes I had taken Tuesday on the discovery and conquest of America,

then, postponing the preparation of the passage from *Julius Caesar* for Monsieur Bailly, the beginning of Cassius' speech:

> "*Why, man, he doth bestride the narrow world*
> *Like a Colossus . . .* ",

since Michel Daval had asked me to give him back the issue of *Fiction* the next morning, I immediately went on with my reading,

" 'Mrs. Hinck',

by Miriam Allen de Ford,

Miriam Allen de Ford is familiar to the readers of our other publication, *Mystery Magazine* . . .

I should prefer, if possible, a woman who was older, more settled in her . . . "

At the beginning of your class, on Saturday, I was afraid of being called on. You began by asking Paul Coutet what he knew about Christopher Columbus, pitiful, *F*; Michel Daval about the pre-Columbian civilizations, I prompted him cautiously, and he got off with a *C*; Octave de Joigny about Hernando Cortez, not brilliant, *D*.

I realized you were going alphabetically and since the one of my classmates who immediately preceded me, Bernard de Loups, was absent, the question about Pizarro would fall on me.

But this time you spared me. You looked at me for a second; we were already so closely linked by our pact that you didn't want to expose me before my classmates to the humiliation of a bad grade; you sensed my mute supplication, warning me, without any possible doubt, by your expression, that during the next history class, the following Tuesday, you couldn't avoid calling on me.

Then you told us the title of the day's lesson:

"Europe in 1600."

All of us noticed that this was the title of a chapter in our textbook; we were pleased, that would make it easier to learn.

Then on Sunday you met Micheline Pavin again, you told her at greater length than on the telephone about your long walk on Wednesday night, the details of the week, and you got around to what was concerning both of you most of all, this text that was by then already quite voluminous.

Uncle Henri took his children to the Naval Museum. Almost next door to our house, Alain Mouron was visiting the empty apartment in the Rue Servandoni with Michel Daval, his sister and his mother, who were going to move into it the day after the next.

It was Alain Mouron whom Uncle Henri asked to read the beginning of the French text we had been assigned to prepare for that Monday:

"How Gargantua was so disciplined by Ponocrates that he did not waste an Hour of the Day."

" . . . In the meantime my lord Appetite came in, and when the happy moment arrived they sat down at the table."

"Well, we're all hungry now; the bell will be ringing in a few minutes, and we too, like Gargantua and Ponocrates, will be sitting down at the table. May I remind you that tomorrow you'll be handing in your compositions on the one day of your vacation that seemed most remarkable to you, and the day after tomorrow we'll read together the second preface to *Britannicus*, so that it will not be until Friday that we will continue reading this text. We shall try to go quite fast; I therefore want you to prepare the rest of this passage, yes, down to the end, page thirty-seven of your book,

' . . . this done, they went to their rest.' "

Then Uncle Henri walked back to the Rue du Pré-aux-Clercs apartment, followed a few steps behind by Alain Mouron, who, while Madame Davez was setting the table, went on reading *Fiction*.

Having finished "The Game of Silence" he went on to "Wolves Don't Cry":

" . . . and, for the first time, he wondered if he was really what he thought he was, a wolf, for he was aware of a salty moisture appearing at the corners of his eyes.

And wolves don't cry."

When he heard his father turn his key in the lock, it was almost one; he would therefore have no time to study his geography lesson, the representation of the earth, or, more serious, to finish his English translation, from which the last two sentences were missing.

What a mistake to have decided to sit in the first row, right under the teacher's nose! It had been a case of overenthusiasm. Luckily, it was Monday; that meant they would have drawing class to begin with,

203

and in that classroom, with that teacher, Alain Mouron could sit where he wanted. He would ask me to pass him my homework for a few minutes, so that he could finish up. I had given him so many signs of friendship these last few days that I wouldn't refuse him this little favor. But he suddenly remembered that I was a Scout in the same troop, that I was even a patrol leader, and that consequently I might raise moral objections. It would be better to ask his cousin Michel, who wasn't bad in English, wasn't a Scout, didn't seem to have too many prejudices. He would copy those two sentences while Monsieur Martin was correcting a portrait of Caesar at the other end of the room.

There was also the end of Cassius' speech and Brutus' reply, but since his Uncle René had called on him Saturday and he had done well, it was likely he would leave him alone this afternoon.

Now, while next door to the drawing classroom, Monsieur Hubert, in the physics amphitheater, was handing back the first homework he had assigned his seniors,

Denis Régnier, back down on the floor below, with the rest of us, occasionally checking to see if the notes he had taken in your class the year before had too many mistakes in them, copied the English notebook Michel Daval had just given him in exchange for the promise of serious advantages in the stamp trading, while you were defining the word isotherm for us and were asking us to look at the two maps illustrating page 58 of our textbook.

After having described the Reign of Terror to the tenth grade, you went home to the Rue du Canivet apartment to spend the rest of the day, according to the schedule you had established for yourself, preparing the heavy teaching load you had the next day, these six hours that were awaiting you:

the movement of the earth around the sun for the seventh grade (not much, it was the end of the class you had taught us the Monday before),

the population of Africa for the eighth grade (required serious review),

the climate and vegetation of France for the tenth grade (not too hard, but boring),

this before dinner, then afterwards:

the religion and monuments of Egypt for the seventh grade (it would be interesting if you could bring in pictures, slides), history for us in the eleventh grade, the most important for you on account of this book, the one you would have to prepare most carefully, European mercantilism, the textbook said, Europe exploits the world,

and Canada for the seniors.

Leaving English class, I had accompanied Alain Mouron to the Rue du Pré-aux-Clercs. At his door, I expressed my surprise:

"But this is where my uncle lives too!"

"Your uncle?"

"Yes, you know, Monsieur Jouret's my uncle; I call him Uncle Henri. It hasn't made things any easier."

"And Monsieur Vernier's your uncle too?"

"Yes, Uncle Pierre. What a spot to be in! Luckily, I have fewer classes with him, and besides, history and geo isn't so important."

"If he heard you . . . "

"You know, teachers don't kid themselves about what they're doing."

"Are you going up to your uncle's now?"

"Not on your life!"

"You want to come to my place? No one's there. My father's at his office and Madame Davez only comes in the mornings. I live alone with my father; he's a widower—for a long time, almost since I was born. If you come up, we'll make tea. Usually I do my homework with Michel Daval, my cousin, not a first cousin, but a cousin; only it's hard to do a Latin translation with only one dictionary between us; besides, even though I like him, he's not so good to do homework with . . . These days, all he thinks about is moving, he's going to live in the Rue Servandoni."

"Yes, I know, it's near where I live."

"It's not far from here either. All right?"

"I don't want to keep you from working."

"You won't. Come on."

"I have my Latin translation to do, and since he's my uncle, you can bet he keeps an eye on me."

He had the Cicero text, I had the Gaffiot Dictionary. We got through it quite fast. We fixed it so that each of us would touch up the style in his own manner when he copied it out, so that the collaboration wouldn't be too obvious. It was much more comfortable working here than in the Rue du Canivet. How quiet it was!

"Yes, I think I'll work much better with you than with Michel.

He couldn't care less. If you want to come over from time to time, we could help each other."

"Yes, I'd like to."

"Yes, but tomorrow there's the class in religious instruction . . . "

"I don't want to keep you from going to that."

"You weren't there last Tuesday."

"Oh, you know, with the sermons from the troop chaplain, I think it's enough, when there's so much work . . . "

"You think? You can come tomorrow if you want. We'll see how it goes. Anyway, tomorrow Michel's moving even if he doesn't go to Abbé Gollier's class."

"Right. I have to get home now. My family must be wondering what I'm up to, I didn't tell them I'd be out."

On Tuesday morning, while Monsieur Bailly was continuing his explanation of Caesar's words, I noticed, thinking about you and this enterprise you are making me share, how Alain Mouron behaved with his uncle, deciding I would question him about Monsieur Bailly tonight.

My Uncle Henri was at home correcting the French compositions he was going to hand back that afternoon, transferring the grades to his notebook. It was Alain Mouron who got the best grade. Aunt Rose came in with her market bag full.

"You know, here's one of the eleventh-grade themes. I assigned them the usual description of the most remarkable day of their vacation, you know, the classic subject. This one's about his arrival at the seashore, at Saint-Cornély. Isn't that where the Ellers went?"

"Yes, and Pierre Vernier went there last year too. Is it by your nephew Pierre?"

"Oh, no, he wrote about the opening of the cabin at Les Étangs. This boy's named Alain Mouron, he's a good student. He describes the hotel, without giving the name unfortunately, but what he says about it seems familiar."

"But isn't that where Monsieur Bailly used to go?"

"That's right, and in his composition he mentions an uncle who's a teacher. I know what it is, he's related to René Bailly somehow; probably he went there with him; I'll have to tell Vernier about this, he'll enjoy it."

"Just ask him to come to dinner some night. Here are the children, back already; it's quarter past twelve. I'll have to hurry."

Alain Mouron was reading in his *History Textbook*:

" . . . conquistadors, toward them sped the galleons loaded with gold, silver, and the wealth of the New World . . . ",

then, in his *Physics Textbook*:

" . . . the weight in Paris of a cylinder of iridized platinum called a standard kilogram, kept at the International Bureau of Weights and Measures, at Sèvres."

Madame Davez, setting the table, came in from time to time to read over his shoulder; she watched him with a broad smile, and finally said:

"How hard you work!"

Which kept him from diving into the issue of *Fiction* he kept hidden in his briefcase.

Hierarchy of the guilds, masters, companions, apprentices. Jean-Claude Fage murmured to his neighbor Hubert Jourdan, absent that morning, in mourning this afternoon, armband, black tie, his darkest suit:

"Well, if it was for your grandmother's funeral, your parents could have got you off for the day! Did you know her well? Did you like her?"

At the other end of the floor, Monsieur Tavera was teaching his tenth-grade Spanish class.

You left the lycée exhausted. You couldn't help stopping in a café on the Boulevard Saint-Germain for a beer. When you reached the Rue du Canivet, you felt so worn out that instead of going straight to your room you stopped in to see us, and my mother immediately realized you wanted a cup of tea.

Jacques and Denis had come home: you asked if I was there.

"No, not yet, on Tuesday he comes a little later, I think there's the class in religious instruction."

"Oh, yes, he has religious instruction."

"Won't you come for dinner tonight?"

"I can't, I have a date with Micheline."

"Oh, give her my best."

You went back to your work, gradually bringing in new characters grouped according to their degrees of relationship, Francis Hutter, Alfred Hutter, Jean-Pierre Cormier.

When I came home, at quarter of seven, I stopped in to see you, and you asked me if I was coming home from the class in religious instruc-

207

tion, which surprised me, because I had told you the day before about my visit to Alain Mouron, and I had seen you write down what I was saying and consequently you should have supposed I was coming from his house. Noticing my startled expression, you searched your memory and said of your own accord:

"Oh, yes, I remember, you told me you'd be going to Alain Mouron's."

At that moment, I realized that I had acquired a power over you, that the role you were making me play somehow abolished the tremendous distance that usually exists between uncle and nephew, between teacher and pupil.

"Yes, that's what we said, but we decided to go to the Rue Servandoni to watch the moving vans delivering the Davals' furniture. It was almost over; they were empty. Michel was on the sidewalk, in front of the door. His mother told him not to go up to the apartment now, he couldn't show it to us, but he would be eating there and he would sleep there; the other apartment, in the Rue Pierre-Leroux, was already empty and it will stay empty for a while because the new tenants intend to have it completely repainted. He promised to show us his new home tomorrow night."

It was getting late. You told me that my parents must be waiting for me and that you would have to get ready, since you had a date.

Leaving the lycée, Wednesday morning, I reminded Alain Mouron that we were going to visit Michel Daval's new apartment at four.

"Tomorrow's Thursday, we have plenty of time."

He was feeling bad, kept poking in his mouth with his fingers because one of his teeth was hurting.

"You should see a dentist; I know it's no fun . . . "

"Oh, it's not that bad, and besides, I'm supposed to go to the barber today."

"You won't have time to go before lunch."

"No, I'll go after class this afternoon."

"What about Michel Daval's apartment?"

"That's right. I'll put that off till tomorrow. I'll tell him this afternoon, no, you tell him during math. Did you finish your homework?"

"Yes. I'll tell him. Take some aspirin."

Back in the Rue du Pré-aux-Clercs apartment, he told Madame Davez about his tooth hurting, and she told him he should see the dentist too. When his father came and saw him holding his cheek,

"You better see the dentist. Madame Davez, do you know the address of a good dentist?"

"Oh, I never have much trouble with my teeth, you know; I have a cousin in Bourg-la-Reine . . . "

"Let's see. The Davals still don't have a telephone in their new apartment. I'd better call René, he'll know."

So Monsieur Mouron telephoned Monsieur Bailly, his first cousin, who gave him the address of a dentist, Monsieur Hubert, brother of the physics and chemistry teacher,

"Particularly since he lives so close to you, in the Rue du Pré-aux-Clercs."

Aunt Rose was asking Uncle Henri:

"What time did you invite Pierre Vernier for?"

"Oh, Lord, I completely forgot to say. I'll try to catch him this afternoon."

"You know, he's a bachelor, he hasn't any regular time."

"No, he eats at his sister's every night at eight, I think."

"He's just as likely to come at eight-thirty, and I'd rather the children didn't eat too late."

"Tomorrow's Thursday . . . "

"Even so."

"If I can't reach him at the lycée, there'll still be time to telephone him."

After his coffee, the compositions of the seniors who had chosen: "Education in Montaigne and Rabelais."

After his coffee, Monsieur Mouron telephoned Monsieur Hubert, the dentist, who asked:

"Couldn't he come this afternoon?"

"What time does school get out?"

"At four."

"I have an appointment at five-thirty," the voice in the telephone said, "if your son could be here at four-thirty, that would be fine."

"At four-thirty? Did you hear that, Alain? Fine, Monsieur, and thanks."

He hung up.

"And I want you to have your hair cut by the time you get home tonight."

"I won't have time to do any work!"

"You have all day tomorrow; you don't have any scout meeting, do you? So you'll have plenty of time."

Alain put his textbook, his notebook, his mathematics homework in his briefcase beside the issue of *Fiction* which he had almost finished.

Then, while Monsieur Hubert, the physics and chemistry teacher, was reminding his class in the amphitheater that the kilogram is the mass of a cylinder of iridized platinum kept at the International Bureau of Weights and Measures in Sèvres, and added that the mass of a cubic decimeter of pure water at four degrees Centigrade is not exactly a kilogram, but only 0.999973,

while Monsieur du Marnet was explaining Thales' theorem to us: when two straight lines are parallel, they determine proportional corresponding segments on any two secants,

Denis Régnier was carefully studying Jacques Estier's duplicate-stamp notebook that Maurice Tangala had passed to him by the intermediary of his neighbor Bernard de Loups, who had returned to the lycée the day before after several days' absence.

Uncle Henri looked for you when our class was dismissed, but you had been teaching your seventh-graders, the great empires of the near east, Assyrians, Chaldeans, Hittites and Persians, and he caught sight of you just as you were going down the stairs to your seniors, dashed toward you while we watched with delight, stared back at us, stopped you, wished you a happy birthday.

"So now you're thirty-five. You don't look it. We expect you to-night, you know?"

"That'll be fine, but don't go to any trouble. It won't be too much for Rose? How are the children? Gérard seems to be starting the year very well. I'll be there at seven-thirty."

"Seven-thirty, quarter to eight. We like to eat early because of the children."

He had finished his afternoon's work, as had I. When I reached the stairs, the two of you were almost the same distance from the landing, a dozen steps above, a dozen steps below. The bell was ringing. You hurried off to ask questions about the Second Empire, about Jaussmann's transformation of Paris.

Then the Italian *Risorgimento*, the unification of Germany.

Alain Mouron had told me, during gym class, that he had a dentist's

210

appointment at four-thirty, but before he left, we had to settle the matter of the visit to Michel Daval's apartment; unfortunately Michel had had the bad luck to get kept in for two hours.

"That doesn't matter, you two come for tea anyway. You don't have any scout meeting, do you? And there's not much to do for Friday. I only got two hours. I'll be home by four-fifteen, four-thirty."

"Fine, I'll tell you all about the drills in Paris."

"Is the trouble with your teeth contagious?"

"I don't think so."

"I keep feeling there's a decaying place right here. Where does your dentist work, anyway?"

"Near me, in the Rue du Pré-aux-Clercs."

"Ours is on the Boulevard Saint-Germain. Where's yours, Daval?"

"I don't go very often; my teeth are good."

"Everyone goes; you'll see."

"The one my sister and my parents use is on the Boulevard Saint-Germain, a Monsieur Fage."

"Near the statue of Diderot?"

"That's right."

"It's the same one."

"Maybe we'll meet there."

"See you later, I have to go now. Good luck."

"You too."

We let him go, then we went back together toward Saint-Sulpice; from now on we were neighbors.

"You poor guy, you have to go back to the lycée tomorrow."

"Don't worry about that, I have something to read."

"Something good?"

"I'll show it to you."

He took out of his briefcase the October issue of the magazine Galaxie.

"Is it as good as Fiction?"

"About the same. Hubert Jourdan gave it to me."

"Did you know his grandmother died? That's why he was absent yesterday morning."

"He gave it to me before. He has a big allowance!"

"Do you still have both your grandmothers?"

"No, only one, my Grandmother Mouron."

"The same grandmother as Alain Mouron's?"

"No, it's more complicated than that; my Grandfather Mouron, who's dead now, was the brother of Alain's grandfather."

"And is Alain's grandfather dead?"

"You sure ask a lot of questions!"

"I don't mean to be rude . . . "

"No . . . let me think. No, he's not dead at all! He lives in Bourges; I don't think I've ever seen him."

"And does your grandmother live with you?"

"Oh, no! She has her own apartment, she lives there with an old cook; it's full of lace; and she's Monsieur Bailly's aunt too, you know, Uncle René we call him at home. Wait till I figure it out; Monsieur Bailly's mother was my grandmother's sister, the sister of my grandfather who's dead, and of Alain's, the one who's still alive."

"And is Monsieur Bailly's mother still alive?"

"Yes, we still see her sometimes at my grandmother's; we call her Aunt Rose. Here's where I live; I'm still not used to it. You see, my grandmother hasn't come here yet; we're having her Sunday. Don't you want to come up now?"

"No, tomorrow will be fine."

I wanted to see you, I knocked at your door: you weren't there. I went to my own room. I heard the telephone.

"Hello? Who's there? Pierre Vernier speaking."

"Hello, Uncle Pierre, it's Pierre."

"What are you doing tomorrow afternoon? If you don't have a scout meeting, I'd like to see you for a while. We could go out and have something to eat later in the afternoon."

"No, I can't; I have to go to Michel Daval's, he's showing Alain Mouron and me his new apartment."

"All right. Well, how about earlier in the afternoon? I'm having lunch at the restaurant in the Rue des Saints-Pères, you know, where I took you for your birthday: come meet me there around two."

"Fine."

My mother was coming into the room; I hung up. I told her that it was for you, that you wouldn't be coming to dinner. She stared at me for a minute.

"You have a funny look on your face."

"I know, I have a toothache."

"Well, then you should see the dentist, and the sooner the better."

"I don't know his number."

"I have it, don't worry; I'll make an appointment. Hello, yes, Monsieur Fage? It's Madame Eller; I'd like to make an appointment for my son Pierre. Yes, as soon as possible. Wait a minute. You don't have a scout meeting tomorrow, do you? No. All right, then, three o'clock, that's fine."

"I have to see someone at three."

"Who?"

"A classmate."

"Oh, well, someone from school, you can postpone it."

"But it's very important . . . "

"Have you any other time free, Monsieur Fage? Well, then it's settled, three o'clock. All right, Pierrot, you have to go then!"

You were going into the office of Monsieur Hubert, the dentist, who told you as he was washing his hands:

"You're following one of your students, Monsieur Vernier—young Alain Mouron; he told me he was in your class and in my brother's as well."

The next day you walked me to Monsieur Fage's house,

"You don't know what time you'll be leaving your friend's?"

"No."

"Don't rush anything. Be discreet. That's the main rule of the game. Tonight, at your house, we obviously won't be able to discuss anything. Next Sunday you have a scout hike. What time do you leave the lycée tomorrow?"

"At four."

"I'm off at five, and you'll probably go work at your friend Mouron's. Stop at my place before dinner, without making any noise about it", before walking back to the Rue du Canivet in the rain, trying to make up the time you had lost on your schedule.

I hadn't noticed the resemblance between the name of the family dentist and that of my two classmates who sit behind me, Henri and Jean-Claude; now I saw lying on a rattan chair in the hall, while the maid was showing me into the Empire waiting room, the *Sixteenth Century French Authors* we used with Uncle Henri, open to the passage of Rabelais we were assigned to prepare for the next day, easily identifiable because of its illustration:

213

"*Le jeu du paume,* from a Sixteenth-Century print",
the last part of the chapter:
"How Gargantua was so disciplined by Ponocrates that he did not
waste an Hour of the Day",
with a pencil stuck in the book to keep the place.
I didn't mention it to the dentist, and he asked me about my school
work, but without any details.
Yes, on Sunday there was a patrol hike and I was the one who organized the games. We went to Versailles, the weather was wonderful, and we walked around the big pond.
Walking along the Seine, you were telling Micheline Pavin about
the progress of your investigation; at the Place de l'Alma you went
into a café to drink a beer and find a movie in the *Semaine à Paris.*
The next day work continued, the return to the lycée, for you only
in the afternoon, at two, ninth grade, including my cousin Gérard, the
Renaissance, the transformation of science, literature and art, with the
reading of the passage of Rabelais cited in the textbook about the
pedantry of the Parisians:

" . . . which reaches the point of extravagance. When I arrived . . . "

Alain Mouron, ahead of me, had answered the first question of your
written quiz:
"What is an isotherm?";
he didn't have too much trouble answering the second, why the
lowest temperatures of the globe are recorded in Siberia, the highest
in the Sahara;
the third seemed much harder: what was meant by inversion of
temperature?
Especially since you had stood up, had rapped on the desk with a
ruler:
"All right, all right, you should be through by now; hurry up!"
Suddenly he remembered that it was something to do with the habitual relation of temperature and altitude, and he wrote:
"It's when it's colder lower down than higher up."
Then he handed in his sheet.
The next day, instead of going toward the Boulevard Saint-Germain, he came with me and Michel Daval to Saint-Sulpice. He was
going to lunch with his cousin, he explained to me, because his father
was invited to a banquet.

"Of course Madame Davez came this morning and she could have made me some lunch just as well as for the two of us, but it wouldn't have been much fun."

"The next time, ask me; we'll eat together."

"Yes, I'll arrange that, I don't know when, but I meant to tell you, I mentioned you to my father; he told me I could ask you over whenever I wanted; and since Madame Davez didn't make any lunch this morning and she's coming tonight to make dinner, if you want to come, and your parents will let you, just tell me this afternoon."

He had a heavy briefcase, because he had brought not only what he needed for morning classes, but for afternoon classes too. While Monsieur Daval, Madame Daval and their daughter Lucie were drinking their coffee and Michel was getting ready, he checked to see that he had everything. It turned out he was missing his *Sixteenth Century French Authors*. Despair. No question of going back to the Rue du Pré-aux-Clercs, he had already been late this morning for Greek, which had earned him two hours next Thursday; if it happened again this afternoon, the two hours would become four and there wouldn't be the slightest hope of getting this penalty diminished for good behavior.

Now two hours after school was bad enough, but from a Scout point of view it would eliminate only the patrol meeting early in the afternoon; he could meet the others, and me in particular, for the troop meeting at five, but if he had to stay in four hours, he would only have time to go straight home, covered with shame.

Alain almost had tears in his eyes. He was asked to explain what the matter was. Monsieur Daval assured him there must be a Rabelais in the house somewhere, if that was all it was.

"There's a Rabelais all right," his wife answered, "but all the books are still in the crates."

"A Rabelais here!" Lucie Daval said, "It's the first I've heard of it! I remember I wanted to read it once . . . "

"You don't think we'd leave a book like that around the house!"

"Why aren't I entitled to read it, if you give it to Alain?"

"Now you know that's not it at all; be reasonable; your cousin forgot his textbook; he'll bring back the Rabelais tonight after religious instruction, won't you, Alain? As for you, if you really want to read Rabelais, you're old enough now."

"Me too," Michel said.

"You have your textbook. But with all your speeches and reproaches, I still don't know where that book can be. Lucie, you look in that crate, Michel, take that one, and Alain, you come and help me."

"I'm going now," Monsieur Daval said, "don't be late."

"How dusty these books get! The room's going to be filthy! Oh, the apartment's still far from being presentable. I don't know when we can start entertaining. Oh, here it is: Rabelais, *Complete Works*, it's an old edition without any notes; you'll manage, won't you? You're lucky! Next time, try to keep your wits about you, and be sure to bring this one back at six. Now it's time you were going, children."

Uncle Henri had just put into his briefcase the French compositions he was going to hand back to his seniors,

education in Rabelais and Montaigne,

a sentence from the preface to *Bérénice*,

two lines of Boileau in the *Art Poétique*,

and had taken out the Greek translations we had handed in that morning.

Since he was trying to find a way to get Alain Mouron out of the two hours after school he had had to give him, he called on him first.

Michel Daval whispered:

"Chapter Fifty-one, Book Three."

"Daval, I must ask you to be quiet or stay in too. Have you found the place, Mouron? What is this chapter about?"

"About Pantagruelion."

"And what is this Pantagruelion?"

"It's hemp. Rabelais writes in praise of hemp."

"Very good; read us the first paragraph."

"The plant Pantagruelion got its name in all these ways—always excepting the mythological one ... "

He stopped because he recognized nothing from the passage he had prepared; and none of us recognized anything he read. In our books, the text began this way:

" ... without it, kitchens would be a disgrace, tables repellent. ... "

In front of the first word there were three dots, indicating a cut. Michel Daval whispered:

"Farther on."

Uncle Henri calmed the disturbance. Alain Mouron looked at the beginnings of paragraphs:

"Others we have heard, at the moment when Atropos . . . ",

that wasn't it,

"Pantagruelion is also called by similarity . . . ",

that wasn't it either; everyone was waiting; Michel Daval whispered:

"Without it, kitchens would be a disgrace . . . "

"All right," Uncle Henri said, "I see you have a complete edition there, which rarely happens with young people your age; I congratulate you on wanting to refer to a proper text, but I fear that certain passages will cause you enormous difficulties; if you have prepared the whole chapter, that's splendid, but you could have checked against your textbook as to just what was asked of you."

"Oh! I only prepared the assign . . . "

"Monsieur, it's because he had forgotten his book . . . "

"Keep still, Daval. Now find me the beginning of our passage: Without it, kitchens would be a disgrace . . . ;

have you found it? Now begin!"

During history class, Denis Régnier said to his neighbor Bernard de Loups:

"Do you know what's the matter with Cormier?"

"No."

"Who knows him?"

"I don't know."

The end of the hour; *Wallenstein*, the death of Gustavus Adolphus, it all seemed more and more remote and vague to us. You waked us up telling us that next Saturday we would have a written quiz for which you were asking us to review everything we had done since the beginning of the year. You would give us our grades on the geography quiz the next day. All of this provoked, of course, many protests; but the bell put a stop to them.

Denis Régnier went over to Henri Fage, the neighbor of the absent Jean-Pierre Cormier, to ask if he knew what had happened to him, if he was sick or what? But Henri Fage didn't know anything.

Monsieur Hubert, after dismissing his seniors, stopped the metronome he had turned on for them. Looking out into the courtyard, we saw that one of the tenth-grade classes was being photographed; soon it would be our turn.

We sat down in the rows of the amphitheater, we arranged our notebooks and textbooks as though for an ordinary class, but we were all waiting for the principal to come in and ask us to go downstairs for this little ceremony. Monsieur Hubert calmly called the roll.

"So Jean-Pierre Cormier and Gilbert Zola are absent; they'll be missing from the photograph, since it's today that the *camera oscura* is supposed to immortalize the features of this collection of studious young men."

This was said to make us laugh; we laughed. Then he asked us questions about pulleys, about the composition of forces, without giving us grades on our answers.

"Today we shall discuss the moment of a force in relation to an axis."

We all heard the footsteps in the corridor. The principal came in.

"There must be no disorder. You will go downstairs without making any noise, and you will then come back as quietly as possible."

There was a little table in the middle of the courtyard, in front of chairs, the photographer's enormous apparatus with its black cloth. Monsieur Hubert sat down in the middle, looking pleased with himself. I was behind him, Alain Mouron to my right, Hubert Jourdan to my left with his black armband, and next to him Francis Hutter with his black armband too.

I said to Alain Mouron:

"It's all right for tonight."

"What do you mean?"

"I'll explain."

The principal, his hands crossed behind his back, was looking in our direction. The photographer exposed two plates. We walked back up to the amphitheater and had to listen to the discussion of the moment of a force.

After having described the Soviet economy to your seniors, you went home to the Rue du Canivet as fast as you could, impelled by that demon which was gaining more and more control over you as the written pages accumulated on your desk, eagerly awaiting my report.

I was with Alain Mouron in front of Abbé Gollier's study.

"I've got to go, because of the Rabelais."

"What are you talking about?"

"I went to Michel's for lunch, and I left my *Sixteenth Century French Authors* at home, so they lent me the complete works, but they made me promise to return it right after religious instruction. If I

218

go before it's over, my aunt will ask me a lot of boring questions, if I go after, without having been to class, Michel will be suprised to see me and give the whole thing away, and that'll be even worse."

"Go, then, if you have to."

"Yes, but Madame Davez told me to let her know as soon as possible if you were coming."

"And six-thirty isn't soon enough?"

"I don't think so."

"Then write her a note and I'll take it to her, since I can't go to the Abbé's class anyway. I have an appointment. She's at your house now?"

"She must be. She didn't do the housework this morning; only don't you think she'll think it's funny to see you bring my note and then see you coming back for dinner?"

"Don't worry, I'll fix that."

He scribbled a few lines on a notebook sheet that he folded twice and handed to me, then he went into the abbé's study.

I ran off to tell you about it.

"The best thing would be to have Denis take the note." (Jacques was in bed.) You asked me to tell him to come in.

"Denis, could you do me a favor? This is an urgent letter, I have to have it delivered as soon as possible. Pierre can't because he's having dinner with one of his schoolmates tonight, and he has to do his work before."

"I have work for tomorrow too."

"But you could do your work after dinner."

"Madame Davez, at Monsieur Mouron's, Twenty-six Rue du Pré-aux-Clercs, third floor. You know, it's your Uncle Henri's building."

"It is? I hadn't noticed."

The next day, in the geography class on alternate Wednesdays, with one absentee, Jean-Pierre Cormier, you handed back the quiz we had taken two days before, then you told us about clouds and rain, fog, hail, dew and snow.

Denis Régnier tapped the shoulder of François Nathan sitting in front of him, and cautiously passed him the October issue of *Galaxie*, pointing at Michel Daval, to whom François Nathan handed it across the row, while you were drawing on the board the diagram of a storm system, and Michel turned around to pass it to Henri Fage behind me, pointing to Hubert Jourdan wearing mourning at the back of the room, who by a sign indicated to Henri Fage that I was the goal of the trajectory.

Henri Fage tapped me on the shoulder and passed me the magazine, while you were asking us to look out the window and tell you what type of clouds were floating across the sky,

on the cover was the wreck of a plane or a rocket (how could you tell which?) and a metal cabin suspended by cables, inhabited by a pilot looking around and furnished with two long, jointed arms ending in elegant pincers, amid fish and bubbles,

and on the back, an advertisement, two profiles, a man and a woman, drawn on the sky above the sea,

"Each Friday rÊVEs",

only the three center letters of this last word standing on the horizon reflected in the water,

which I put in my briefcase before writing from your dictation:

"Types of rain."

Then came the first vacation, All Saints' Day. With the other patrol leaders, all in uniform, knees bare, I walked on the rain-beaten road (the clouds hanging low in the sky were incontestably nimbus), my hands in the pocket of my leather jacket; the many passing automobiles spattered us.

Not quite recovered from the slight case of grippe that had kept you in bed the day before, you had stretched out on your bed after having eaten lunch with my parents, and you were asleep.

On All Saints' Day, at Micheline Pavin's,

"I have to be going now."

"What's your hurry?"

"You know."

"Your book?"

"Of course."

"Is it coming along?"

"Yes, it's coming along; of course it's coming along, but so slowly. I'm getting behind."

"Behind what?"

"Behind what I wanted to accomplish by now, and I'm trying to hide it from myself; there are so many things I'm starting to take short cuts over. This stupid little grippe hasn't helped any."

"Take your time."

"No, I can't take my time, don't you see: there are thirty-one boys in this eleventh-grade class, and up to now I've only brought in seven, and brought in is all, since what I've written about them up to now doesn't constitute a portrait at all—seven students and nine teachers."

"You should be finished with the teachers."

"Finished! When you say . . ."

"At least you've mentioned them all."

"Almost, the only ones left are the ones who have a rather marginal position: Monsieur Martin, the drawing teacher, Monsieur Moret, the gym teacher, and Abbé Gollier, the chaplain . . . "

"There's no Protestant pastor, no rabbi?"

"Not at the Lycée Taine. And you see, I'm up against an enormous difficulty with the last of my colleagues whom I brought into account, a difficulty I had foreseen, of course, but which I thought I could solve more easily; since certain pupils in this class are taking German and Spanish, I have to mention the hours when they are studying these two languages and the professors who teach them, Monsieur Hutter and Monsieur Tavera; now I can do pretty well in English or in Italian, but I know almost no German or Spanish; the best thing would be to learn both these languages."

"That might take you quite some time . . . "

"And then there's math, God knows the math they learn in the eleventh grade is simple enough, but you have no idea how abstruse the textbook my nephew uses can seem to a history and geography teacher."

"And how is your nephew, by the way?"

"He's on a scout hike."

"It can't be very comfortable out there today. All right, I won't keep you, I see you're beginning to get quite nervous, looking at your watch every other minute. Your work calls, dear Schoolmaster, but couldn't you allow yourself a few minutes' diversion this evening all the same, to take me to the movies as you promised? To make up for the Sunday date your illness canceled out?"

"Of course! Where shall we meet?"

"Come to dinner here; for once you can take advantage of the fact that I have time to cook for you."

"You're really so . . . "

"Tell me something, my dear Schoolmaster, hasn't it ever occurred to you that you might be dealing with me on somewhat more intimate terms?"

"Not yet!"

"Not yet? When?"

"Well, when I've finished my work."

"I may have to wait a long time."

"No, once it's really started..."

"It's not really started yet?"

"No, I'm still marking time, I wonder if I haven't begun badly, if I shouldn't try the whole thing over from the beginning, but I'm already in so deep ... I have to get out of it, you see, I have to get somewhere, there's no other way..."

"Don't worry, I have no intention of getting in your way. I'll wait..."

"Yes, it's a matter of a few days of good work..."

"Tonight we'll talk about something else."

"Of course, yes, how kind you are ... How patient and indulgent! I'll walk over tonight, to air out my mind a little before I come up."

"Better hurry now; work well, get a good start . . . Till tonight."

My cousin Gérard had the same kind of grippe that my brother Jacques had caught first and that you had just recovered from.

Agnès Bailly too, which is why her mother, who stayed home to take care of her, asked Alain Mouron, who had come to their house for lunch because his father was working that day, to take his two cousins for a little walk despite the rain, to the Naval Museum or the Army Museum, or perhaps the Museum of Natural History; he didn't know these museums yet, did he? They might interest him.

He decided on the Museum of Natural History. When the three of them came out of the Trocadéro métro stop, they saw that the museum was closed on Tuesdays. There was nothing else to do but go back to the Rue Pierre-Leroux.

The next Sunday, there was a scout hike; we had carefully worked out a complicated game with many coded messages on the theme of the conquest of America; I had suggested the idea; some of us were to be the Aztecs, the other Cortez' men; but although I had already returned to class the day before, my father, seeing that I was still somewhat tired by the grippe I had caught in my turn, coming back from the last hike, had absolutely forbidden me to go. Jacques, who had got over his long ago, would tell me about it.

As for Denis, he was feeling logy, had eaten almost nothing at lunch, and his face was red; he had stretched out on his bed with a detective story he wasn't even reading. When Mother came into the room, she put her hand on his forehead.

"You better take your temperature, I think you're getting it too."

You were saying to Micheline Pavin:

"I've begun to study, to study like an eleventh-grader; I do all the homework—my nephew Pierre brings me the subjects. Since Bailly is making them read *Julius Caesar*, I reread it, Jouret makes them read *Britannicus*, I reread it; only you see, since Bailly is making his seniors read *Macbeth*, and Jouret is making his read *Iphigénie*, I have to reread them too, and as soon as I can, very carefully; that's why, for today, I think it would be better if we didn't go to the movies together. I have to cross this barrier, you understand, I have to get these chief elements in hand: afterwards, it will go by itself."

"I understand, I promise you I understand very well; yes, go back home and start reading *Iphigénie* or *Macbeth*, but our date for Tuesday still stands?"

"Of course."

"What's the matter, Pierre? Did I hurt your feelings? What is it you want me to say? I promise you I have every confidence in you, I have complete confidence in you, I know it's all for your work . . . "

"What do you mean, Micheline? I . . . "

"You don't need to tell me, I know. On Tuesday—we won't go to the movies Tuesday, isn't that it?"

"If you like. I'll do whatever you want."

The next day, for the ninth-graders the Counter Reformation, the Council of Trent, Ignatius Loyola, Philip II.

Then, while Uncle Henri, in the classroom next door to ours, was making his seniors read the thirty-sixth Persian Letter:

"Coffee is widely used in Paris . . . ",

the janitor came in, with not only the register as usual, but also with a package of photographs including one of the senior class and passed it around the class, asking each of those who wanted a copy to write his name on the back,

and ten minutes later started all over again with us.

Alain Mouron wrote his name at the top right, with the new pen his father had given him at lunch for his fifteenth birthday (he also had a new briefcase and a new scarf),

and on the next day, Tuesday, while Madame Davez was serving the coffee, he finished copying the composition he was to hand in at two:

"What do you think of Rabelais' ideas about education? Compare today's education with the kind he opposes and the kind he proposes."

My cousin François was in bed. Doctor Orland was saying:

"It's nothing, just this little 'flu bug that's going around; I don't need to give you another prescription, it's exactly what his brother had, but since he's younger, he has a little higher fever, that's all",

to my uncle, who, after having told us about Calvin, reminded us that for the next day we were to prepare the second scene of Act II of *Britannicus*:

"*The gods be praised, my lord, Junie in your hands . . .*"

At the bell, Alain Mouron, who hadn't had time to learn his history assignment (since you had called on him the day before for geography, he wasn't very worried), hastily refreshed his memory in his notebook and his textbook:

Louis XIII and Richelieu, illustrations: portraits of the prince and his minister, the siege of La Rochelle from a print by Callot (all those tiny boats, all those tiny soldiers like ants on the shore), a page from Théophraste Renaudot's *Gazette*:

"The Kynge of Persia with fifteen thousand horse . . . ",

that would be all right . . . , leafed through the next chapter, which more or less corresponded to the lesson you were going to teach that day:

The Peace of Westphalia (what was Westphalia?), on one page portraits of Condé and Turenne, ratification of the Treaty of Münster by G. Terborch, on another the Feast of Saint Nicholas, by Jan Steen, Dutch interior by Pieter de Hoogh, the West India House in Amsterdam. That should have been interesting, but the caption said merely: "Describe this print."

Why? Was it a riddle? How would Monsieur Vernier describe it? For the time being it was more discreet to go back to Richelieu, you never knew: proscription of dueling, persecution of the Protestants, the *Journée des Dupes*, Samuel de Champlain and Canada, the Compagnie des Îles, Martinique, Guadeloupe, Santo Domingo, tobacco, sugar cane, Negro slaves . . .

Denis Régnier, in his bed in the Rue du Cardinal-Lemoine apart-

ment, was sorting the latest stamps he had obtained from his classmates to whom you explained what Westphalia was, talked about the
development of Holland as a mercantile power, about the East India
Company, and without thinking of making us describe or of describing to us the West India House in the textbook, about the found-
ing of New Amsterdam that was to become New York.

Monsieur Hubert got involved in the description of the different
forms of energy and their transformations that he was writing out
for his seniors:

"Tribo-luminescence: transformation of mechanical energy into
luminous energy; if, for instance, you break a lump of sugar in the
dark, you will notice a bluish gleam; anyone can make the experiment . . . Where was I? Tribo-luminescence; yes, we've just discussed
it . . .",

his confusion increasing during the next hour, apropos of pairs
of forces, making us do excercises dealing with bicycle gears, screw-
drivers and corkscrews. His wife was at the clinic.

The British Isles for the seniors, then you went back to the Rue
du Canivet apartment where you quickly got down to this work, for
you would have liked to reach, according to your schedule, the second
hour of the afternoon of that Tuesday, November 9, exactly a month
after the original hour,

but the pages that concern the three of us at that moment, and
which seem to have been written the same day because of the present
tense you use in them, were actually written only several days later,
like those concerning, at that same hour, Alain Mouron and Monsieur
Bailly, then Michel Daval and Monsieur Bonnini, written at an increasingly great distance from what they are describing,

in that intermediary present, a stage that navigates, that shifts
between the presence of that past with which it is concerned, and
this present where one is in order to examine and to write it if one
is the author, in order to reconstitute it by reading it if one is a
reader,

coming closer and closer to the narrative present attached, from
the start, to the discovery and conquest of America, distinguishing
itself increasingly from the real, literal present.

I was with Alain Mouron; it had become a habit I was already trying
to break in order to explore more deeply, so to speak, my other classmates; but this habit was extremely useful to me from an academic

point of view, for Alain Mouron was greatly my superior in Latin and in Greek, and helped me a lot with my preparation and written homework.

The next day, Tuesday, Michel Daval showed me that he had bought the November issue of *Galaxie*, which I asked him to lend me, and he promised to as soon as he finished it himself.

Absent: Denis Régnier, Francis Hutter and Jean-Pierre Cormier; you asked Hubert Jourdan what the different types of climates were; you asked André Knorr about the action of the climate on the flora and fauna of a region; you asked Bertrand Limours about the watershed system.

Details about equatorial and tropical climates.

The following Tuesday, November 16, Jean-Claude and Henri Fage absent, after having questioned Octave de Joigny, Michel Daval and Paul Coutet about education, agriculture and the clergy under Louis XIII, you told us about European civilization in the mid-Seventeenth Century, the condemnation of Galileo; the janitor came in with the package of photographs we had ordered, one for you, one for me, one for almost all of us, except Jean-Pierre Cormier and Gilbert Zola, absent at the time the picture was taken, and except Denis Régnier and Francis Hutter, present in the picture but absent the day they had been ordered.

The pictures had to be paid for at once, and since many boys had forgotten to mention the matter to their parents, they did not have enough money with them, which provoked all kinds of negotiations among neighbors, but even these were insufficient, so that the janitor left with the two prints intended for Jean-Claude and Henri Fage and with four others whose presumptive owners had not been able to pay for them and which would be at the janitor's office at their convenience, when they had enough pocket money.

Quickly, with Michel Daval's help, I wrote on the back the name of each of my classmates where his face was.

It was three-thirty when you went on to tell us about painting.

On Tuesday, December 14, for the history composition, absent Abel, Baron, Spencer, the discovery and conquest of America, the Thirty Years' War, Holland in the Seventeenth Century.

I wrote my name at the top left of my paper, Pierre Eller, and I began chewing my ballpoint pen.

That is far away and I loathe it.

Today, Tuesday, October 11, 1955, I am a senior, in French class; our teacher, Monsieur Devalot, is making us read Saint-Simon's passage on the revocation of the Edict of Nantes,

"Without the slightest excuse and under no necessity, and the various proscriptions rather than declarations that followed it . . . ";

and it's been a long time since I renounced all collaboration in that work which you continue, more and more deceptively, fraudulently, to designate me in the first person, which cannot go on much longer because . . .

A few classrooms away with your eleventh-grade boys, including my brother Jacques—your schedule has remained virtually unchanged since last year—you are talking about the discovery and conquest of America.

||||||||||||||||||||||||||||||||||||||| LET'S GET BACK to Monsieur Bailly, who, in the middle of September, on the day he had received the letter from his wife informing him that she wouldn't be back from Orléans the next day, Wednesday, but instead on Sunday the twenty-sixth, had left the hotel, while his children had gone to the beach, accompanied by Alain Mouron,

had fled the hotel and after having pushed into the mailbox his letter to Claire, had gone to think things over in a café in the harbor, where a jukebox was screaming out an old tango,

hoping that their young cousin would have learned about and somehow explained to the children their mother's delay.

He had ordered a beer and half finished it (it was a beautiful day, the masts of the boats swayed on the low water; a landscape painter on a campstool was brushing in a water color in front of a huge pile of rigging, with a whole audience of vacationing ladies in print dresses and hats behind him), when he saw the door open and Alain come in, his face serious, followed by René, Georges and Agnès.

"They'd like to know what Aunt Elizabeth said in her letter."

"Well, unfortunately, Cousin Louise has gotten worse and worse. Mother sends you all her love and promises to be here Sunday, you know, not next Sunday, but Sunday the twenty-sixth; she'll be here to do the packing; we'd have a hard time managing all by ourselves, wouldn't we?"

The children burst out into an embarrassed laugh.

"Look at that boat coming in with its sail patched. Aren't you thirsty, any of you? We can have a little something here, then we'll go for a walk around the point before sunset."

The next day, alone in his room, looking at his calendar, he notice that it was his wedding anniversary, his tenth.

And on Tuesday the twenty-eighth, he reached Paris with his wife and children. Alain Mouron joined his father who was waiting for him; they arranged to meet the next day at lunch, then the taxi drove off; if wasn't far from the Gare du Maine to the Rue Pierre-Leroux.

The concierge came out to say hello and give them a package of

letters. The apartment was cool and smelled musty; it wasn't completely dark yet, but there was no use opening the shutters now.

The three children collapsed on the chairs of the study that were
still swathed in their slipcovers. Madame Bailly sent her husband out
to the Rue de Sèvres for some bread; the rest of the dinner would
come out of cans.

Then the next day, Monsieur Mouron and his son had come to
the Rue Pierre-Leroux apartment for lunch, and afterwards Monsieur
Mouron had gone to his office and Alain had gone to find a barbershop.

Monsieur and Madame Bailly had then taken their children by the
hand and begun visiting the large shops, looking for notebooks, penwipers and, for little René, a new briefcase, since it was understood
that he would give the one he had used to his sister Agnès, who
would eventually take hers to the Catholic Charities, because it was
no longer suitable for the daughter of two schoolteachers.

The evening after the first day at school, there was a great commotion in the Bailly apartment. Monday, that year, was the busiest
day of the week for Monsieur Bailly, who had that morning met his
ninth-graders, including my cousin Gérard, and during the afternoon
his seniors, including my brother Denis whom he had already had the
year before, and his tenth-graders including my brother Jacques, and
then finally our class.

Luckily for the whole family, his wife didn't begin working until
Tuesday.

He shut himself up in his study, letting his wife deal with the
children, copied the class lists, finishing just before dinner with ours.

The next day, after his wife had come in that evening, he told her
that he had to go out, an appointment with you, his colleague Vernier,
as he told her, to talk about a project . . . And it is true that you had
arranged a meeting, but not until the next day, and even if it had been
true, Madame Bailly wouldn't have believed it.

"Go ahead, you know I'll take care of the children; you know I never
stop you from doing your work."

At seven on Wednesday evening, you waited for him in a café at
the Sèvres-Babylone intersection. Since it was impossible for you to
receive all his family, you had decided to take him to a restaurant to
be able to tell him about your project for a description of a class, but
he had had quite different ideas; seizing this excuse not to eat at home,
he had planned an evening at Claire's, intending to introduce you to

her. This is why, after having drunk a glass of beer, you walked together to the métro, and took the Auteuil line to the Émile-Zola stop.

On Thursday, Madame Bailly having declared that she had too much work and too many letters to write to be able to take the children out, Monsieur Bailly went with them to the Jardin des Plantes.

And on Saturday night, Elizabeth Bailly went back to Orléans, having categorically refused to show her husband the alarming letter concerning her cousin Louise, declaring that if he couldn't trust her in such a simple matter, in an obligation so elementary, living with him would be quite impossible; and he was thinking, looking out the window, watching her walking toward the Rue de Sèvres with her suitcase in one hand, accompanied by little René who was carrying another smaller bag, that if it had only been a matter of living together, just the two of them, it wouldn't have been so complicated, but unfortunately it was a life for five that they were leading, and that when she left him alone this way he had to take care of the three children all by himself; and though he declared he would have no difficulty with meals, he thought of the coming weekend with terror; how long would it be before his courage gave out and he asked Claire to come and help him?

On Sunday, after the Davals had left, he couldn't stand it any longer; Claire came to fix dinner, she put the children to bed; he had had to explain to them that she was one of their mother's friends, and of course it was preposterous to ask them to keep her presence in the house a secret; he was forced to trust to chance, to their forgetting, to their discretion.

Once the lights were out in their rooms, Monsieur Bailly led Claire into his own, but she wasn't willing to lie down on that bed; they left the apartment stealthily.

On Monday the eleventh, while you were keeping us quiet with a gesture of your hand, reminding us that you would be questioning us the next day about the Renaissance and the Reformation, André Knorr had his wrist in the doctor's hand; his mother was standing in front of the window, the shutters half closed.

That evening, Madame Bailly came back from Orléans. Claire hadn't been able to come to help with the dinner; Monsieur Bailly had been obliged to manage by himself with the leftovers in the refrigerator. The children hadn't stopped asking questions about their mother's return; they didn't want to go to sleep without having seen her, as if they were afraid she had left for good. They were all in pajamas and bathrobes in the study, and their father was reading them a story.

When Madame Bailly came in, she slammed the door so loud that all four of them jumped.

"What? Not in bed yet? They have to go to school tomorrow, you know! What were you thinking of?"

"Elizabeth!"

"Yes, oh yes, it was very nice of all of you to wait up! Now be good; I'll come in to kiss you when you're in bed ... "

"Well, how's Cousin Louise?"

"Much better, really much better."

"So you won't need to go back to Orléans for the time being?"

"Just what do you mean by that?"

"Nothing, I ... "

"Do you happen to think you have something to reproach me for?"

"Elizabeth ... "

"All right, let's be honest with each other, for once; you know perfectly well that it wasn't only for Louise's sake that I went to Orléans ... "

"I beg your pardon?"

"Yes you do, René, yes you do," she went to close the door, "you know it as well as I do, it was to get away from all this for a minute, yes, has it ever occurred to you that I might need to, sometimes? Don't you have anything to say? Don't you believe me? You think this is a nice way to greet your wife when she's back from a two days' trip during which she did nothing but take care of someone else, leaving behind her ... Why are you laughing? You're hateful ... "

"Listen, Elizabeth, you're tired from your trip ... "

"I know what you're thinking, well, there's one thing you're entirely mistaken about ... "

"What's that?"

"Poor Louise was really miserable ... "

"But she's better now."

"Yes, she's almost recovered ... "

"No fear of a relapse?"

"There's always a possibility, you never know ... "

"And naturally, in case of a relapse, you're quite ready to go and take care of her again?"

"Selfish!"

"I simply said that you were ready to go and take care of her."

231

"Do you think you're funny?"

"Me?"

"I have to teach tomorrow morning."

"So do I."

"You don't start until eleven."

"Elizabeth, forgive me, don't take what I'm going to say in bad part; you can understand that this weekend wasn't easy, and that I've left work for you, the sink is full of dishes, I know I need a woman in my life, you know it too. That isn't what I meant. No, let me talk a little; it's natural that we should quarrel sometimes, it's natural that . . . No, listen, you're tired, you get some sleep and tomorrow . . . This is what I wanted to say: do we have to keep on arguing like this all the time? Couldn't things be done some other way? Are you crying now?"

"Don't kiss me, please, don't kiss me . . . "

"Now what does this one want? Go to bed, René!"

"It's not René, it's Georges; you're crying, Georges, what's the matter? You can't sleep? Come with your mother. You see, she hasn't even been able to take off her hat yet; the others aren't asleep either? All right, get into bed . . . They've heard everything, aren't you ashamed?"

"Elizabeth . . . Elizabeth . . . Elizabeth . . . "

A few hours later, during the night, Monsieur Hubert awakened; his wife had got up to get a drink of water.

A few streets away, Francis Hutter was turning over in bed, he was about to land on the beach of the Phaeacians, the waves were breaking over him, carrying him out to sea . . .

"Hear me, Lord, whoever thou art . . . "

The river god . . .

Monsieur Hubert turned on his bed lamp; his wife was groaning in her sleep, her swollen belly raised the sheets, he caressed her shoulders.

"Our world hath of late discovered another (and who can warrant us if it be the last of his brethren . . .)",

near the wall, behind Paul Coutet, Henri Buret is carefully cleaning his nails. Beside him, Robert Spencer is looking in his physics textbook at the lesson we are to study for the next hour: the different states of matter,

" . . . the wonderful magnificence of the cities of Cuzco and of Mexico, and amongst infinite such like things, the admirable Garden of that King. . . . "

That was last year.

The next night, the insomnia of Monsieur Bonnini worrying about the insomnia of his son and his daughter, his sister-in-law's movements, his wife's panting,

the dreams of Denis Régnier, stamps and power, stamps of one kilo of iridized gold, kept in the bowels of the earth in Mexico and the naked slaves carrying knives and gold tweezers, bursting into Monsieur Régnier's apartment in the Rue du Pré-aux-Clercs.

Uncle Henri sleeping peacefully, Aunt Rose pulling the blanket up over his shoulder.

Alain Mouron wakened with a start at quarter of four, watched several patches of light glide across the ceiling.

The day began around seven, a gradual dawn, a fine morning. The sun's reflected ray penetrated the blinds, brightly striping the chair on which Michel Daval had laid out his clothes.

Elizabeth Bailly's right hand, knotty and dry, her arm crossing the narrow aisle between the two beds, was caressing the skinny chest of her husband who was overwhelmed by a tenderness so unexpected after all the suspicions, all the scenes of the previous days;

but her entire body, absurdly armed with a coarse nightgown which the movements of sleep had raised to her chest, wriggled away as though in a convulsion of disgust; she opened her eyes, saw her husband; she turned over, drew away to the far edge of her bed, clutching the sheet in her fist.

The English teacher made neither sound nor gesture; he stared at the back of her neck, with its dry and whitening hairs,

"Now I know she was unfaithful to me at Orléans, I know that if I want to look, even here, I'll find proof, and I'm going to spend the day finding it, for I was hoping against hope that this caress, which reminded me of years gone by, was intended for me, that her body still maintained some accord with mine, but that look when she awakened showed me without any possible doubt that this wasn't so; I wonder if I caressed her too, in my sleep, if I betrayed myself by the same movement of withdrawal."

The alarm clock went off at eight. Madame Bailly got out of bed, opened the blinds of their bedroom, went into the other rooms to open the other blinds and waken the children, then turned on both faucets in the tub.

Monsieur Bailly put his feet in his slippers, pulled on his bathrobe, went into the dining room where he began setting the table for breakfast, for he had to wait until his whole family was through in the bathroom before shaving.

The representation of the earth; in the first row, Philippe Guillaume, back after only one day's absence, was dreaming about Brittany as he looked at the illustrations on the last page of this chapter, an aerial photograph of the Pointe du Raz, with its fields, its paths, its cliffs and fringe of foam,

and another photograph of the same site taken from directly above, with the lattice work of waves and the village like a handful of rock salt,

Lescoff, as the third picture under the other two was called, the simple caption identifying this photograph,

but it was the illustration on the page opposite that was attracting the attention of the boy to his left, Bruno Verger—a map of the island of Borneo with the indication of its principal products: rice, rubber, oil, and the disturbing silhouette of Celebes to the lower right,

while you were making Denis Régnier and Jean-Pierre Cormier come to your office to tell them what they would have to do tomorrow while they were being kept after school.

After dinner, Uncle Henri took his Rabelais and began with the prologue:

"Most noble boozers, and you my very esteemed and poxy friends . . . "

looked through the first chapter: of the genealogy and antiquity of Gargantua, then the corrective conundrums found in an ancient monument, how Gargantua was carried eleven months in his mother's womb (not for the eleventh-graders; and he smiled at the notion that one of them might find a complete Rabelais in his parents' library and dip into it out of scholarly zeal),

so that, when Gérard came in to say goodnight before going to bed, he was only up to Chapter VII: how Gargantua received his name, and how he gulped his liquor,

while Alain Mouron, two floors below, armed with his Larousse, was preparing Chapter XXI for the day after the next, or rather what was quoted from Chapter XXI in our textbook:

"After this, Gargantua was eager to put himself at Ponocrates' discretion. . . . "

The next morning, since his children were not going to school, Monsieur Bailly did not get up until eight-thirty. His wife had already gone out, taking her bag with her. The coffee and the milk were cooling on the dining-room table.

Michel Daval didn't get up until nine-thirty; his mother brought the café au lait steaming hot into the dining room when he came in, his face washed but still unshaved.

That afternoon, Jean-Claude Fage,

" . . . but for a beginning, his tutor ordered him to go on in his usual way. . . . "

His brother Bertrand was there, as well as his sister Gabrielle; the oldest child, Andrée, had gone out with a school friend; Madame Fage was in a bad mood, something must have happened, she hadn't eaten lunch at home, had come in only at three o'clock, and consequently hadn't seen her husband all day long, it was Andrée who had done the cooking and set the table; Madame Fage was doing nothing; she was standing at the window with a book in her hands, cutting the pages with her forefinger without looking at them; she was waiting for someone.

" . . . Ponocrates protested . . . "

Someone rang; Gabrielle got up to answer the door.

"You haven't finished your work, have you? Stay where you are, I'll answer it myself."

A few moments of expectation and immobility,

" . . . Gargantua replied: 'What! Haven't I taken enough exercise?' "

then Madame Fage came back with a smile:

"I have to go out; I left two thousand francs on the mantel; when you're through with your homework, you can go to the movies, if you want to. Dinner's ready in the refrigerator. Be sure not to come back too late for dinner, you know how fussy your father is about being on time; Andrée will be here, you'll help her; if I can't be here on time, I'll telephone."

They heard the door slam: they knew the face of the man who had rung, they had often seen him in the street, but they didn't know his name.

Bertrand said to his brother Jean-Claude:

235

"It's getting worse and worse."

"Andrée won't be here for dinner, she'll telephone too."

"We ought to go for a long walk after the movies and not come back until nine; when Father comes in he'll find the house empty, it'll give him a surprise."

"We could go to a restaurant instead of the movies; two thousand francs ought to be enough for the three of us."

"Don't be silly."

"But if we go to the movie house across the street, it'll cost us two hundred francs each, what'll we do with the rest?"

"We'll split it up, five hundred for you, five hundred for me, four hundred for Gabrielle."

"That's not fair!"

"What do you mean, that's not fair? You're the youngest and you're a girl. Girls don't need money."

"I'll tell Father."

"What'll you tell Father? That Mother had a date with her boy friend? He knows all about it—he couldn't care less."

"He does not."

"I suppose you know more about it than I do . . . Listen, are we going to the movies?"

"I'm not going."

"Then you'll stay here alone. Why don't you want to? She's just like her mother! We'll go to the movies, and we'll be back when we can."

"And what if Mother telephones?"

"No one'll be here."

"And when'll we be back?"

"We'll see."

Monsieur Martin was taking his two children, Daniel and Gilberte, for a walk in the Bois de Boulogne.

My cousin Gérard came back from our scout meeting, and the whole Jouret family sat down around the table.

Uncle Henri resumed his reading at Chapter XI:

" . . . From his third to his fifth year, Gargantua was brought up and disciplined . . . "

Alain Mouron had cleared the table and gone out with his father to the movies. At the corner of the Rue du Pré-aux-Clercs and the Boulevard Saint-Germain, they passed the tall North African wearing a beret, his cheeks and forehead covered with adhesive tape, which made a kind of pinkish mask with two wide slits for eyes.

They had decided on one of the movie houses in the Rue de Rennes, where a Technicolor Western was showing.

The next morning, Friday, October 15, Monsieur Bailly, looking for a barber, decided against those on the Rue de Sèvres, started for the one on the Rue du Vieux-Colombier but turned left down the Rue Bonaparte, came back along the Boulevard Saint-Germain, stopped in the Rue du Pré-aux-Clercs to look at the house his nephew Alain lived in, whom he had not yet visited, the whole family was invited there for that evening, realized that it was also the house his colleague Jouret lived in, noticed Monsieur Dumarnet's shop and, since it was already quarter of eleven and he still had to correct the exercises he was to hand back to his ninth-graders early in the afternoon, went in without looking any further.

Francis Hutter had returned to the lycée wearing the darkest of his suits, a black tie and a black armband. Uncle Henri had called on him to read and explain:

"After having taken a thorough breakfast he went to church . . .",

went on to Denis Régnier,

" . . . then he studied for a miserable half-hour. . . . "

Francis was carefully writing down the explanations in the margin with a pencil that suddenly snapped in two.

" . . . The cork soles of his shoes swelled up half a foot."

That was the end of the hour.

"For next Monday, the eighteenth, you will prepare the following text: how Gargantua was so disciplined by Ponocrates that he did not waste an Hour of the Day; it's a little too long for us to be able to read it all at once; we certainly won't get through more than the first part, up to page thirty-six line eighty-three: which showed him the art of horsemanship. After the description of a bad education, Rabelais gives us one of an ideal education; we shall see what we ought to think about that."

The bell rang. Francis Hutter stood up to let Alain Mouron get by, sat down again, sharpening the two pieces of his pencil, to wait for the German teacher who was climbing upstairs from his seventh-grade class.

Since, the evening before, Uncle Henri had stopped at the end of Chapter XV:

" . . . and that they should all go to Paris together to learn what the young men of France were studying at that time",

and since he had hurriedly reread Chapter XXI for us during the morning, neglecting for the moment the correction of our compositions on the most remarkable day of our vacations, he turned back to Rabelais to fill the remaining gap.

Alain Mouron had prepared, before dinner, with Michel Daval, Cassius' speech about Caesar; there remained, for the morning, the mathematics assignment: algebraic numbers (review), for the afternoon, the history assignment: the discovery and conquest of America, and the chemistry assignment: natural water, pure water, mixtures and pure bodies, the composition of water.

At two, you asked my cousin Gérard to describe Europe's location, then you talked about the continent's relief.

Uncle Henri was taking his other sons for a walk in the Luxembourg. It was still a fine day, but cool. While watching the boys playing with hoops, he went on with his reading.

Alain Mouron, in front of me, was taking down from your dictation the subtitles of the assignment, Europe in 1600:

"England, the Low Countries, the Scandinavian countries, Italy, Poland, Germany, Switzerland, Russia, Turkey. . . . "

Under his textbook, he was concealing the issue of *Fiction* I had just given back to Michel Daval and which the latter had passed to him between classes.

On Sunday afternoon, Monsieur Bailly went for a walk with Claire in the park at Versailles, and on Monday morning, after having left his ninth-graders, he collected his seniors' homework, a translation of the first page of De Quincey's chapter on Coleridge in his *Recollections of the Lake Poets*, which he had dictated to them the Tuesday before, after having them explain Keats's sonnet:

"Much have I travell'd in the realms of gold . . . "

then he spent the whole hour telling them about Coleridge, and it was as if he were talking about an old friend, asking them to look for the next day at the first six stanzas of *The Rime of the Ancient Mariner*.

During the afternoon, Francis Hutter, after having listened to you comment on the two maps of isotherms—January, July—in our text-book, showing us how these more or less parallel lines were curved by the continental masses, pointing out those two regions of extreme heat, in the Sahara and central Asia in summer, and the region of extreme cold, in Siberia in winter, bounded by the isotherm of January minus forty,

then, on the next page, those two juxtaposed photographs of landscapes of the same altitude, a Nova Scotian village buried in snow, the pines on the beach at Arcachon in the sunshine, adding parenthetically that for these pictures to be really informative, it should have been stated at what time of the year they had been taken,

lastly explaining the phenomena of inversions of temperature,

put his things away in his briefcase and stood up to go home, for since he was through with German he had ended his school day, while all his neighbors, Alain Mouron to his left, Michel Daval behind him, Bruno Verger to his right, were all taking English and remained in their seats, waiting for Monsieur Bailly.

Monsieur Hutter was finishing the dictation of a German passage to be translated by his seniors.

At seven, Alain Mouron and I had finished our Latin translation. I told him that I had to go home to eat dinner, and we agreed to work together the next evening, cutting religious instruction, of course. We still had to prepare, this evening: seventeen lines of the Odyssey, eighteen of the Aeneid and thirty-three of Julius Caesar, as well as studying, for you, Europe in 1600, the Hapsburgs, Henri IV, and, for Monsieur Hubert, the measurement of forces.

After having corrected ten more of the most remarkable days of our vacations, Uncle Henri looked in a corner of his bookcase for his notebooks of the preceding years to find us a Greek text to translate: he decided on a passage from Plutarch's life of Caesar.

Homer, "Nausicaa and Her Father", according to the subtitle given in the textbook; Bérard translated:

"But Aurora, mounting her throne, wakened the maiden in her lovely veils . . . ";

Virgil, "The Triumph of Love", according to the subtitle given by the other textbook; André Bellessort translated:

"Anna answers: 'O thou whom your sister loves more than light . . . ' ";

and for the seniors:

"The revocation of the Edict of Nantes . . . and the various proscriptions . . . that followed it were the fruits of this dreadful conspiracy . . . "

Alain Mouron, once he was alone, set the table and then, waiting until his father got home, continued reading *Fiction*:
"But if he wasn't a wolf, then what was he?"
The next day, Tuesday, once his other eleventh-grade class had finished Caesar's speech about Cassius:

> "*Come on my right hand, for this ear is deaf,*
> *And tell me truly what thou think'st of him*",

Monsieur Bailly assigned us for Saturday the beginning of the conversation between Brutus and Casca:

"*Sennet*"
(which means not a fanfare but only a signal given by a horn or trumpet),
"*Exeunt Caesar and all his train but Casca. Casca:*
You pull'd me by the cloak; would you speak with me?"

down to

" . . . He fell down in the market-place, and foam'd at the mouth, and was speechless."

Definition of the word *mercantilism*; Jean-Claude Fage, beside Hubert Jourdan, who was wearing mourning, was rereading the second lesson of his *Physics Textbook*:
"The statics of solids, forces, experimental notion of force, measurement of a force, units, figure 17: standard kilogram, commentary: the weight in Paris of a cylinder of iridized platinum . . . , 18: marked weights, 19: divisionary weights . . . , 22: the chord BC represents the line of action of the force. . . . "
When Aunt Rose came back to the Rue du Pré-aux-Clercs apartment with the two younger children, Claude and François, whom she had taken to Monsieur Dumarnet, the nearest barber, she asked Uncle Henri what day he had invited you for dinner.
"I completely forgot to mention it to him."
"It doesn't matter. Remember tomorrow."
"No, I think Wednesday mornings he doesn't come to the lycée this

year; he used to, but this year he has every morning off except Tuesday."

"Tomorrow afternoon, then."

"If I run into him. No, it would be best to telephone him at his sister's."

He dialed the number, but the line was busy. He went back to reading the homework his seniors had handed in at three, dealing for the moment only with those who discussed the first of the three subjects: "Education in Rabelais and in Montaigne."

Alain Mouron had watched the end of the unloading in the Rue Servandoni with me. Once the spectacle was over, he had walked to the Rue du Canivet, where he had said goodbye to me, and then gone back to the Rue du Pré-aux-Clercs (the tall North African with the adhesive-tape mask, sitting on a bench on the Boulevard Saint-Germain, had got up when he passed and had followed him to the door of the building),

where, alone in the empty apartment, he didn't feel like getting to work before dinner (the Odyssey, Livy, the second preface to *Britannicus* and especially, for the afternoon, after gym, not geography, that was the other week, but math, three algebra problems and one geometry problem);

he set the table, turned on the gas under the soup and in the kitchen, near the stove, went on reading *Fiction* while waiting for his father,

"I should prefer, if possible, a woman who was older, more settled ... someone in whom I can have complete confidence. ..."

Uncle Henri dialed our number again. They sent Jacques to call you to the phone. You had already put on your coat to go and meet Micheline Pavin.

"Is that you, Jouret? For dinner? I'd like to very much, whenever you're free: tomorrow? Fine; it'll be a birthday celebration for me. Yes, I'll be thirty-five. You're older than I am, I think; oh, thirty-nine, on September fourteenth, yes, I remember, my nephews, our nephews mentioned it to me. Thanks. Goodbye!"

Wednesday, when Monsieur Bailly went home to the Rue Pierre-Leroux apartment with his two sons, his wife, who had just come in with Agnès, went to get a handkerchief in her room, then came into the study, closing the doors behind her.

"Someone's been going through my things."

"Probably the maid."

241

"She would have put things back."

"If it's one of the children, he'll get himself a scolding."

"The children were all at school."

"Then I haven't the faintest idea."

"That's it! You haven't the faintest idea!"

"What's the matter with you, Elizabeth?"

"What were you looking for? What do you want to get against me? And what if I started looking through your things like that too . . . "

Now that morning Monsieur Bailly's conscience was perfectly clear, he hadn't looked through his wife's things for several days. The key to the mahogany desk had remained in the lock since the day before and, in fact, he hadn't yet touched it, afraid of a trap. It was a mistake; he had had absolutely nothing to do with the little disorder that had occurred so mysteriously. It was probably Elizabeth herself who had taken something on her way out and forgot about it! But her indignation and her mistake proved her guilt and her fear! It would probably be easy to corner her, to convince her in a few days . . .

"You're not reasonable, Elizabeth."

"Listen, René, do you suppose I don't know everything?"

"I beg your pardon?"

"I don't know what's kept me from spitting in your face the last few days."

"I think you'd better calm down, Elizabeth, my dear; your pupils must have been a little unruly this morning. I think I'll take lunch out somewhere. When you come home tonight, we'll talk this all over more calmly. Have a good lunch."

That evening, Uncle Henri began correcting our Latin translations. Aunt Rose:

"It's his birthday, isn't it? How old is he now?"

"Thirty-five."

"That's right, I remember he's the same age I am—we're fifteen days apart."

"Are there any candles?"

"I think they're all used up, I'll send one of the children out for more."

"Have they finished their homework?"

"Tomorrow's Thursday."

"That doesn't matter. They must develop regular work habits. I'll go."

Monsieur Hubert, the dentist, had just extracted one of Alain

Mouron's molars; he was a talkative dentist; he discovered that his young patient was a student of his brother's, and your student as well. Alain, holding his jaw, went to get a haircut from Monsieur Dumarnet. Before going home again, he looked for a drugstore where he could buy some aspirin. Far down the boulevard, he noticed the figure of the tall North African approaching, hands in his pockets. Coming out of the drugstore, he met Uncle Henri with his package of candles and greeted him politely.

"What's his name?" my uncle wondered; "He's a good student, he sits in the first row; isn't he the one who wrote me that French composition about Saint-Cornély and the hotel, the one who's Monsieur Bailly's nephew?"

They walked upstairs together.

"Goodbye, Monsieur."

"Goodbye."

Uncle Henri looked at the notebook in which he kept his grades, he went to the kitchen to give Aunt Rose the candles.

"You know, that student I was telling you about, the one who spent his vacation at Saint-Cornély, is young Mouron, the one who lives on the third floor."

"He lives alone with his father, the concierge told me his mother's dead."

"Why don't we invite him here one of these days?"

"You're his teacher, he'll be intimidated."

"I know, it always makes things difficult. I had to go all the way to the Rue Saint-Sulpice. They only come in boxes of twenty, so I bought two; we can always use them."

"Oh, I'm going to need some candied cherries. It's Lucie's favorite. Tell her to come here for a minute."

On October 21, I met you again in the restaurant on the Rue des Saints-Pères where you had taken me to dinner on my fifteenth birthday. You ordered coffee and a cognac for me, offered me cigarettes, and I explained that I couldn't stay because I was supposed to go to the dentist. I told you about Alain Mouron, about Monsieur Bailly, about the classes of the day before.

Uncle Henri went to his barber.

Alain Mouron, alone, his hands in his pockets, was walking through the Jardin du Luxembourg and watching the men playing boules, waiting until it was time to go to Michel Daval's.

On October 25, Monsieur Bailly made his tenth-graders translate a passage from the *Jungle Book*; on the twenty-sixth, after having left us, he walked his two boys back to his house, but let them go up alone, took the métro at the Vaneau station and went to have lunch at Claire's.

That afternoon, Aunt Rose made a cup of tea for her husband, who had just brought Claude and François home and had begun reading some of our Greek translations.

As for the passage from the *Odyssey* for the next day, Bérard translated:

"And the divine Ulysses emerged from the thicket; his strong hand broke a leafy bough from the dense verdure, which he used as a veil for his virility . . . "

Alain Mouron had gone into Abbé Gollier's study, had sat down in a corner behind his cousin Michel, ignoring what the chaplain was saying about the Mass, had opened in his lap the complete Rabelais that he had borrowed, and was still reading, not understanding much but fascinated, the chapters at the end of the third book concerning the herb Pantagruelion,

then walked Michel Daval to the Rue Servandoni, returned the volume to Michel's mother and reached the Rue du Pré-aux-Clercs apartment just before seven.

"I got your note," Madame Davez said to him, "is that the young man who'll be coming back here? He looks very nice; I've made you a good dinner."

The next day, Charlemagne and his new Western Empire for the eighth grade.

In the classroom next door to yours, the sad reception Agamemnon had in store for his daughter,

"My lord, what is this unaccustomed haste . . . "

Alain Mouron, in front of me, was listening to you tell us about the rain: he wrote in his notebook from your dictation:

"The dry regions."

The afternoon of All Souls' Day, Monsieur Bailly went to the Rue de Jussieu to see Maître Henri Mouron, a first cousin of his mother's and a lawyer, to ask him how he should go about obtaining a divorce.

The following Monday, Jacques told me, he gave a three-quarters of an hour penalty to everyone in his tenth-grade class who had not handed in his homework; he got so angry over an error of pronunciation in the reading of a page of the *Jungle Book* that he had to stop talking for several minutes while huge drops of sweat ran down his face; there was a lot of reaction in the class.

On Tuesday, he ate lunch at home, which happened only rarely now, for it was his daughter Agnès' birthday; she was six; Elizabeth had made a splendid cake. Everyone looked pleased; if anyone had walked into the apartment, he would have seen the image of a happy and united family.

But Monsieur Bailly's moods were beginning to be talked about at the lycée.

He ran into Uncle Henri at four at the door of the elementary school and asked him if he happened to know a good lawyer who specialized in divorces. Uncle Henri, without asking any details, mentioned Maître Limours, Bertrand's father.

"Oh, that's right, I think Bertrand's studying Italian; you don't have him in your class."

"And how is poor Monsieur Bonnini?"

"He's back at the lycée, I saw him this afternoon."

Alain Mouron was only vaguely listening to Monsieur Hubert telling us about pairs of forces; he was making anagrams on his own name and writing them in the margin of his textbook: Omar Launino, Arnol Mainou, Minou Alanor . . . ; he had reached Marion Oula when the bell rang.

We went together to the Rue du Pré-aux-Clercs apartment; he made some tea; we were beginning to turn the pages of the Bailly Dictionary when he exclaimed:

"My God! I have a dentist's appointment at five-thirty!"

He went to look at the pad next to the telephone.

"Yes, it's today all right. I'm sorry, I have to go, there's nothing I can do. We'll do it separately. Oh, I'm late now. He always keeps you waiting though. We'll go down together."

Uncle Henri had just finished reading my composition on education in Rabelais and he was beginning Alain's.

In the eighth grade, the next day, the establishment of the Holy Roman Empire by the coronation of Otho the Great, the Normans in France, in Sicily and in England.

In the classroom next to ours, Arcas had just told the young princess that it was not to marry her to Achilles that her father was waiting for her at the altar, but to sacrifice her to the gods.

Alain Mouron, while listening to you, was looking in our textbook at a photograph of the Amazonian jungle, with creepers hanging down to a muddy river covered with leaves and bubbles.

On Monday, sitting down beside Michel Daval after drawing class, I took out of my briefcase the November issue of *Fiction*, with a red cover and enormous rats on a sphere on the horizon of a lunar landscape.

"Is it good?"

"Not bad."

"Here's *Galaxie*, don't keep it too long."

On the front cover: a man in a dentist's uniform screwing in the arm of a female robot, on the back: the same advertisement as in October, every Friday r*Ê*VEs, thirty francs.

Bernard de Loups wasn't able to tell you much about the equatorial climate.

"Eller, the subtropical climate . . . Estier, the desert climate . . . "

The Mediterranean climate.

In the seventh grade, the next day, after the questions about the Homeric period, the *Iliad*, the *Odyssey*, a lesson on the Greek city-state, the colonization of Ionia, of Sicily.

Uncle Henri collected the compositions of his seniors on the three subjects inspired by the *Lettres Persanes*.

Alain Mouron looked at the photograph in which he was standing between Michel Daval and me, in the second row, behind Bruno Verger and Joseph Abel sitting on the ground, in front of Denis Régnier and Jean-Claude Fage standing on chairs. Once the reaction provoked by this purchasing of the pictures had calmed down, he began writing again from your dictation:

"Galileo, dialogue on the two systems of the world (Copernican versus Ptolemaic, the earth turns around the sun), condemned by the Pope in 1632,

Kepler: orbits of the planets,

Napier: logarithms,

Harvey: circulation of the blood."

On December 7, you reminded us that the next day we would have a geography test, and on the following Tuesday a history test. The government of Louis XIV.

On December 13, results: first Hubert Jourdan, second Georges Tannier, third Alain Mouron, fourth André Knorr, fifth Rémy Orland, sixth Michel Daval, seventh Louis Pelletier; I came eighth. You had commented on the texts and we spent a long time deciphering your remarks in the margins, while you were starting to tell us about rivers, resigning yourself to spending at least two hours on this lesson, knowing perfectly well that those of us who were studying English or Italian had their tests the next hour and seeing that many of us, though trying to hide it, were busily reviewing their history for the next day.

On December 14, history test for the seventh grade too, "What do you know about Egypt?",

French test for the seniors: choose one:

"What are the reasons Racine says in his preface to *Iphigénie* that without the invention of the character of Eriphile he would never have dared write this tragedy?"

"Montesquieu makes Usbek, in the eighty-fifth Persian Letter, write: 'Since all religions contain precepts useful to society, it is good that they be zealously observed; now what is more capable of animating such zeal than their multiplicity?' What do you think of this statement?"

"Imagine a performance of *Antigone* in ancient Greece, and describe it in a letter to one of your friends."

Alain Mouron, bending over his desk, was telling about the discovery and conquest of America.

The winter went by, then the spring and the summer; in September I didn't go to Les Étangs; my parents had rented a house in Provence; I joined Michel Daval there. Your health kept you from making a long trip. You only spent a few days in Brittany, alone; Micheline Pavin had already gone back to work.

You had completely recovered by the time school began again; on Tuesday afternoon you taught your first history class to the eleventh-grade boys; my brother Jacques was in the third row, near the window, in the seat where Henri Fage used to sit, behind me, the year before.

"This year you have the Seventeenth and Eighteenth Centuries on your curriculum; in the tenth grade, you studied with me, or some other history teacher, the period from the French Revolution to the First World War . . ."

A few classrooms away, with Monsieur Devalot, our literature teacher, at the back of the room, near the window, beside Alain Mouron, behind Michel Daval, I was reading the death of Monseigneur, Dauphin of France.

The next Monday, yesterday according to the distorted—increasingly distorted—calendar of this account, he assigned us three subjects for compositions from the curriculum of the past year, to hand in the following Monday.

Portrait of the Princesse d'Harcourt:

" . . . because, she added, in gaming there is always some misunderstanding. . . . "

You questioned your eleventh-graders about the structure of the earth and its history, you spoke to them about its movements in space and the measurements of time.

Today (but already several days ago), in the seventh grade, where my cousin Claude Jouret is one of the students now, the landscape of Egypt and the great period of its ancient history.

Uncle Henri, who certainly would from now on be much better qualified than I to be designated by the first person in the continuation of this work in which I so greatly, so dangerously participated last year, and from which I have recoiled with a horror which will only gradually disappear, so that if you want me to read you, if you want me not to be repelled by the very first pages, you will have to put the phrases in another mouth besides mine, so that they will reach me and convince me, slowly and cunningly overthrow this whole rampart I have raised, which has been raised against you, against this whole enterprise, much better qualified than I since he has shown so much interest in it, since he has begun helping you with such solicitude,

is finishing the account of the Dauphin's death while Alain Mouron, beside me, is making an analysis of the long and magnificent sentence:

"The revocation of the Edict of Nantes, without the slightest pretext . . . "

down to, twenty-five lines later:

" . . . were forced to adore what they did not believe and actually receive the divine body of the holy of holies, while they remained convinced that they were eating only bread which they must still have abhorred."

⬛||||||||||||||||||||||||||||||||||| " . . . AS ALSO IN HIS Cabinet, all the living creatures that his Countrey or his Seas produced, were cast in gold; and the exquisite beauty of their Workes, in precious stones, in Feathers, in Cotton and in Painting: shew that they yeelded as little unto us in cunning and industry . . . ";

in the second row, to left of Robert Spencer, behind Gabriel Voss, Joseph Abel is drawing a tiny six-pointed star on his palm,

and his left-hand neighbor, Charles Baron, behind Claude Armelli, is emphasizing the shadows of the mines of Potosi and of the planter's house in the Antilles;

" . . . Why did not so glorious a conquest happen under *Alexander* or during the time of the ancient Greeks and Romans? or why befell not so great a change and alteration of Empires and people. . . . "

Last year.

That night, Monsieur Hubert awakened at two o'clock beside his wife.

"Aren't you asleep?"

"No, it hurts, it hurts terribly."

"It couldn't be . . . "

"No, of course not, not yet, it's still a month off, you know . . . "

"It's *supposed* to be a month off . . . "

"It's stopped now. Go back to sleep."

During the afternoon, André Knorr, still in bed, was reading *Tintin en Amérique*.

That night, getting into bed beside his wife, without speaking a word to her, Monsieur Bailly thought over his whole day's vain search, wondering if there wasn't some corner or hiding place he had forgotten. Of course there remained the two locked drawers of her mahogany desk; he would have to wait until she was up, search through her bag . . . She was reading students' papers.

The next evening, he didn't come home until very late, after having eaten dinner at Claire's and telling her about his search, about the locked drawers of the desk, about the key he hadn't been able to find. Several times he almost told her that he had searched through

249

his wife's handbag while she was washing her hands and that the key hadn't been there, but at the last moment he decided not to reveal that.

"She must keep it in her bag," Claire told him.

"I suppose that's the only place."

"The only place! Don't be silly! Look, there are ten thousand invisible hiding places for a woman in her own house, every jar in the kitchen . . ."

"Then you think she's hiding it from me?"

"How should I know? You shouldn't worry so much about those drawers. If you do get them open, you'll only find more food for this jealousy that's torturing you and frightening me a little too, I must admit."

"No, it would be a relief, a certitude, a weapon; it's for you I want to know, and for the children too."

"I don't need that kind of proof; as for your children, be reasonable . . ."

"You must understand, we could get a divorce . . ."

"I hate that woman, and I know one thing, that if you find letters in her mahogany desk, they will only be a proof for you, not for any court."

On Friday evening, before dinner, while he was correcting his seniors' translations, Monsieur Bailly noticed that the key to the desk drawers was in one of the keyholes; it was a little bronze key, it looked as though it had just been polished. From that moment on, it was impossible for him to go on with his work. A few minutes later, unable to bear it any longer, he stood up. His wife opened the door to say that the soup was on the table. He had a moment's dizziness when he realized that a second later she would have caught him with his hand on that key.

Saturday,

"*Inverness. A room in Macbeth's castle. Enter Lady Macbeth alone, with a letter. Lady Macbeth:*

They have met me in the day of success; and I have learn'd by the perfect'st report, they have more in them than mortal knowledge. When I burnt in desire to question them further, they made themselves air, into which they vanisht . . ."

On Monday, when his wife left her desk to begin preparing dinner, he noticed that she had again left the key in the keyhole of one of the drawers. He was correcting our homework; he didn't move.

On Tuesday night, the same maneuver, but on Wednesday, since this key had remained in the lock since the day before, since there had been a terrible scene before dinner, since he had controlled himself in order not to broach the subject with Claire, whom he had gone to see at once, of course, and who had consoled him, he took his handerchief in his hand, afraid of leaving some fingerprint, and opened the two drawers one after the other, cautiously; the first was empty, the second full of envelopes; he looked inside the first envelope, it was empty, in the second, it was empty; it wasn't even the envelope of a letter addressed to her; on it was written Monsieur René Bailly; he had thrown it away a few days before.

Elizabeth was coming up the stairs. He quickly closed the drawer and sat down again at his desk, picking up one of our compositions. Elizabeth glanced into the room and noticed that the key was no longer in the right-hand drawer, but in the one on the left.

On Thursday, the key had vanished again. The mahogany desk was covered with envelopes addressed to Madame Bailly, postmarked Orléans.

Matters remained at this point until Tuesday. Monsieur Bailly was coming home from the barbershop, the concierge stopped him to give him a letter addressed to his wife, postmarked Orléans, in an unfamiliar handwriting. One solution was to steam it open, according to a method often described in novels, and then to give it to her after he had sealed it again; or he could merely hand her the letter and see what her reaction was.

Finally he laid it on the mahogany desk. Elizabeth saw it as she came in, picked it up.

"Did you bring this up?"

"Yes."

She left the room smiling, using the letter as a fan.

The next day he went to show it to Claire, for he had found it in the morning on the mahogany desk, still sealed. She would probably know how to steam it open, which she did, saying:

"I'm doing what you tell me to do, but I'm sure you'll regret it."

"Open it, I beg you, I'm absolutely sure it's the man who's asking her to come back to him in Orléans over the All Saints' Day holiday;

I'm sure she's going to tell me about her Cousin Louise, that she's had a relapse . . . "

The envelope was empty.

"I'm going to find a lawyer, my uncle, Maître Mouron . . . "

"You couldn't tell him about this."

"You see what she's doing to separate us, you see the way she manages things so as to cover me with shame and with ridicule in your eyes."

"Stop spying on her this way, give up the idea of finding letters; give her her freedom and she'll let us alone."

"Just give me your permission to find out."

"Of course I do . . . Besides, you'd do it anyway."

"Don't you be nasty."

The following Tuesday, November 9, after tea, he went out with his daughter Agnès, whose birthday it was, and took her to visit Claire, who gave her candy and a doll.

"I want you to tell Mother that . . . "

"No, René, no. She'll tell her mother the truth, what can it matter now?"

"Elizabeth might throw the doll out the window."

"Don't worry . . . How silly you are! You'll tell your mother you went to visit her friend Claire, won't you Agnès?"

The next day, coming out of a barbershop on the Avenue Émile-Zola and waiting until it was time for his appointment with the dentist, Monsieur Viala, he went to visit Claire in order to tell her he had been to see Maître Limours.

"He was much more encouraging than my uncle . . . "

"Listen, I was wondering. Since your wife wants to settle things as much as we do, wouldn't a conversation . . . "

"Between the two of you?"

"Between the four of us."

"Which four?"

"What do you mean, which four—the man from Orléans—we have to find out just what his intentions are . . . "

"He was in Paris last week, I know that; but I know he left again."

"He'll be back."

"Of course, but when? And how can you find out ahead of time? And how could you reach him?"

252

"I'll have to settle that with Elizabeth."

"Elizabeth will never do it."

"I'm only asking your permission to try."

"I don't want you to see Elizabeth."

"Why not?"

"I don't understand you. How could you? You know she'd get the better of you."

"I know you think she's more intelligent than I am."

"Oh, Claire, how can you say such a thing, how can you even think it? Only she's cunning, she—she hates me now, her hatred has drowned her last scruples!"

"You exaggerate everything so! Yesterday, on her daughter's birthday, weren't you two on the point of forgiving each other for everything? I felt it. I'm trying to settle matters without too much damage. I'm only asking your permission to go and see her, because I have no confidence whatever in that lawyer of yours, that Limours, I'd rather make that clear now, if there were any hope, would your uncle . . . "

"You don't understand, it's the family; a divorce in the family scandalizes him, he began by lecturing me . . . Besides she'd never be willing to come here."

"I'd go to your apartment."

"She won't stand for that either."

"Then I'll ask her to meet me in a café or a restaurant; we'll have lunch together while you watch the children."

"She'll feel that we're at her mercy, she'll string us along . . . "

"The least we can do is try . . . "

"I know you'll try without my knowing it."

"That's not true, I'll tell you everything."

"You'll tell me everything, but you'll do it even if I tell you not to."

"If you forbid me to, I won't do it."

"I . . . Oh, it doesn't matter . . . Do whatever you want . . . But don't tell me anything; anyway I know there'll be nothing to tell, or more exactly, I know exactly what there'll be to tell, but at least you'll have done what you wanted, and I won't have forbidden you anything, you won't have any regrets; telephone her in a few minutes, while I'm at the dentist's, and I'll know by her expression when I get home . . . I have to go now."

The following Tuesday, after having handed back their compositions, Monsieur Bailly had his seniors begin the third part of *The Rime of the Ancient Mariner*.

> "There passed a weary time. Each throat
> Was parched, and glazed each eye . . . "

He was expecting the result of the lunch between his wife and his mistress that evening.

The following month, while proctoring his seniors' examination, he was rereading the letter he had just received from his lawyer, his uncle, Maître Henri Mouron, to whom he had returned; it was his wife who had asked for a divorce.

He is with his seniors (that was several weeks ago); he has my brother Denis as a student; he is giving an assignment for the following week, translate Keats's sonnet on his discovery of Chapman's translation of Homer:

> "Much have I travell'd in the realms of gold . . . "

The divorce has been granted, but he won't marry Claire.

III

i‖‖‖‖‖‖‖‖‖‖‖‖‖‖‖‖‖‖‖‖‖   " . . . WHEREAS CONTRARYWISE, we have made use of ignorance and inexperience, to drawe them more easily unto treason, fraude, luxurie, avarice and all manner of inhumanity and cruelty, by the example of our life and patterne of our customes."

On the other side of the wall in front of me, to Denis Régnier's left from your uncle's point of view or from mine, to his right from yours, Bernard de Loups is scratching his auburn hair.

"Who ever raised the service of marchandize and benefit of traffick to so high a rate?"

⸿⸿⸿⸿⸿⸿⸿⸿⸿⸿⸿ THE SECOND TUESDAY of the preceding school year, in the middle of the afternoon, Michel Daval, at the College Saint-Jérôme, translated, under the instruction of one of the Fathers, the first lines of the first book of the *Aeneid*.

I remember having questioned some girls for the baccalaureate orals in July, perhaps his sister Lucie.

We all left for Les Étangs except Gérard, who was camping with his Cub Scouts for the last time. I had to pick him up in Paris on August 3: I didn't want to leave him alone there, even for only a few hours, and he had to be cleaned up. Of course, Rose could have done better than I, who hardly manage to clean myself up properly, but it was better that she stay at Les Étangs on account of the younger children.

We celebrated Gérard's birthday the following Monday, he was thirteen; we had made a lot of jokes about the bad luck that this fatal number might hold in store for him, and he seemed to believe in it on account of some game that his scout leaders had made him play.

It was the next day, I think, that Michel Daval arrived at the Château de Beautreillis, two kilometers from Varçais, a town we used to go to during the summer for movies.

At the end of August the village fair was held; we took the children to ride on the merry-go-rounds, and they entered the bag race.

The following Monday, we prepared rooms for you and your brother Denis; Jacques was sick, your mother wrote me, and couldn't join you until a few days later on.

The next day, Michel Daval was on the train to Provence, sitting between his mother and his sister Lucie.

The following Sunday, while you had gone with Denis to see Baron Storck, owner of the woods, to ask his permission to build a cabin there, I was dawdling around the garden of Les Étangs with your parents, who had come down for the weekend, accompanying your brother Jacques who was finally over that stupid cough of his.

The next day, Michel Daval and his sister Lucie said goodbye, in the church square, to the Bonnini children who were taking the bus

258

for Cannes, where they would take the train to San Remo, spending the rest of their vacation there with their Italian grandparents,

then, with all the others, they crowded into the car one of the fathers had left for his son's use and went down to the beach.

They went to the beach every day, learned how to swim, sun-bathed. On Wednesday, since it was the birthday of one of the girls in the group, there was a big party at her villa, with drinks and dancing. That was the day Michel learned his first dance steps; before that he had always been the one who sat out and changed the records. He was quite startled by his own success. He was sweating, drank a lot; there was orangeade, but gin too; he drank, and the amount of alcohol in the mixture increased with each glass; suddenly feeling sick, he sneaked away, collapsed on a bed and fell asleep.

At Les Étangs, the autumn rains started, and the storms interrupted your labors in the woods. You had promised us on Monday that the cabin would be finished by the next day, and we had decided that we would have a picnic lunch there, weather permitting. Claude and Francis were asleep in their room; Rose was busy in the kitchen making sandwiches, and I was smoking my English tobacco and looking at the book about Italian painting you had given me.

The day of the picnic, Michel Daval went to the beach as usual, but the little band had already dispersed; he was walking alone among the red boulders, having abandoned his sister Lucie to one of her flirtations; he was surprised to find himself thinking about Paris, about the change that was going to take place in his life, now that he was going to leave the College Saint-Jérôme and enter the eleventh grade at the Lycée Taine, where he might have his Uncle René for his English teacher.

The last Sunday in September, you and your brothers and cousins, under the supervision of Rose and your mother, packed the trunks; the desk on which I usually read and worked had already been cleared of all its objects. Your father and I finished up the package of English tobacco; we left the house to walk around the village, went into the cool church that had been built by Saint Louis; your father looked through the scores on the harmonium.

The next day, Michel Daval and his sister packed the trunks under his mother's suspervision, then they went down to the beach for one last time.

Two days later, they were unpacking in the Rue Pierre-Leroux, putting away the contents in closets, saying: "Why not leave it all packed up, since we'll be moving as soon as Father has found a suitable apartment?"

On Saturday, great purchases of stationery: penwipers, notebooks, erasers, pencils . . . We ran into the three of you in a store, arguing over the advantages of the different kinds of lined paper; you stopped as soon as you saw us and asked our advice with the utmost courtesy, knowing that I would pay for whatever you bought.

On Sunday, Michel Daval, who was not a Scout and had his day free to prepare for his first classes at the lycée, covered the books he had bought the day before with blue paper, eagerly examining their illustrations. Three were left over from the year before: the Greek Grammar, the Latin Grammar, and the English Grammar; all the others were new:

Anthology of Greek Literature, with the Winged Victory of Samothrace as a frontispiece,

Anthology of Latin Literature, a view of the Forum,

Sixteenth Century French Authors, a bound book of the Sixteenth Century,

Seventeenth Century French Authors, a bound book of the Seventeenth Century,

Anthology of English Literature, the Canterbury Pilgrims, from a fifteenth century manuscript,

History for the Eleventh Grade, no frontispiece,

Geography for the Eleventh Grade, a fold-out frontispiece: annual averages of precipitation,

Physics, Chemistry, Mathematics.

On Thursday, the first day of freedom, Michel Daval went to the movie theater in the Rue de Sèvres with Alain Mouron; they saw a Western made mostly in the Colorado desert and a documentary about the château of the Loire.

I called on him the next day to read the beginning of the Épître à Lyon Jamet.

In the room next to yours, your Uncle Pierre, on the night that preceded his pact with you which you told me about one day when you were upset, was murmuring, as he turned over in bed, phrases from Marco Polo's Description of the World and from Montaigne's essay "On Coaches."

"So many goodly Cities ransacked and razed, so many nations destroyed and made desolate; so infinite millions of harmelesse people of all sexes, states and ages, massacred, ravaged and put to the sword; and the richest, the fairest and the best part of the world topsiturvied, ruined and defaced for the traffick of Pearles and Pepper: O mechanicall victories!"

On the other side of the wall in front of me, at the back of the classroom, next to Maurice Tangala, Jacques Estier, who plans to be an engineer, is reading in his *Physics Textbook*: various states of matter,
figures: 1) water is a liquid, 2) nitrogen peroxide, a red gas, fills the flask, 3) steel is elastic, lead is soft, glass is brittle . . .

"Never did ambition, greedy revenge, public wrongs or general enmities so moodily enrage and so passionately incense men against men, unto so horrible hostilities, bloody dissipation and miserable calamities."

▓▓▓▓▓▓▓▓▓▓▓▓▓▓▓▓▓▓▓▓▓ YOUR UNCLE PIERRE handed back to his eleventh-graders, including your brother Denis, the composition he had assigned them eight days before on Louis XV, Frederick the Great, the American Revolution.

A month later, he was giving oral examinations to the first-section baccalaureate candidates on the geography of France and her former colonies,

and to the second section, the following week, on the Great Powers: the United States, the USSR . . .

Since he needed to save money for his trip to Greece, he stayed in Paris through the entire month of July, eating lunch as usual in a neighborhood restaurant, cooking dinner for himself in your mother's kitchen while she was with you in Saint-Cornély; afternoons, long expeditions, either to museums or through the streets; the best thing to describe would certainly be his visit to the American wing of the Museum of Natural History and to the Musée Guimet and the Musée Cernuschi; I think that it was at the book counter of the latter that he first leafed through the edition of Marco Polo which he used.

On Monday, August 2, we spent the afternoon together; I had arrived that morning to be able to meet your cousin Gérard, who was due back from his camping the next day, and we spoke of your uncle's notion of writing a book about a class and about how such a thing could be done; it wasn't a new idea on his part, but it was becoming increasingly obsessive; I was sure that once school started he would make a stab at it.

The loneliness of Paris at this time of year was beginning to weigh on him, he made up his mind, before his trip, to spend a weekend with one of his former colleagues near Bourges. On Sunday, August 8, he was visiting the cathedral.

Alain Mouron had left the city for good some weeks earlier, and on Monday, while your Uncle Pierre was walking past the house where he used to live, Alain was taking the bus with his father from the village of Saint-Ferdinand to the sparkling sea.

The next day, at Saint-Florentin, Monsieur Bonnini called in a doctor from the coast, for his wife had a high fever once again.

262

On the twenty-fourth, your Uncle Pierre took the train for Marseilles,

and the following Monday, under a leaden sky, he was jolting in a dusty bus on the road from Athens to Delphi; I wonder if he wasn't really going there more or less to consult the oracle.

On the thirty-first, Alain Mouron arrived at Saint-Cornély, sent by his father who that morning had taken him, after a night on the train, from the Gare de Lyon to the Gare du Maine. They had stopped only long enough to eat a big breakfast; Alain had eaten lunch alone in the dining car. Monsieur Bailly was waiting for him on the platform.

The first Sunday in September, your Uncle Pierre went to the Piraeus to take the boat from Mykonos, for he was particularly eager to see Delos.

It was the next day that Madame Bailly received the telegram from Orléans asking her to come to the bedside of her cousin Louise as soon as possible. After lunch, she sent Alain to the station to find out not only what time trains stopped in Saint-Cornély on their way to Paris, which could have been found out at the hotel, but also the best way to change trains in Paris in order to leave for Orléans immediately afterwards.

When Alain returned, she and her husband were sitting on rattan chairs in the hotel living room; she decided it would be best to leave the next day at four-thirty in the afternoon.

"But it's René's birthday . . . "

"We'll celebrate at lunch, there'll be plenty of time."

"So you'll leave tomorrow?"

"Yes, I'll send a telegram."

"Just what's the matter with Louise?"

"I don't know exactly, René, I'm not a doctor. She wants me, that's all. It's a good thing Alain's with us."

"It is?"

"Alain, would you go to the post office to send this telegram for me?"

"They'll send it from the hotel."

"No, I want it to leave right away. Do you have enough money Alain? Here, take these five hundred francs and keep whatever's left."

The next day, Madame Bonnini was feeling much better, her husband was able to take her outdoors; they met the postman, who handed them a letter from Italy. Her husband's parents were expecting their grandchildren the evening of the thirteenth.

On Saturday, your Uncle Pierre accompanied Micheline Pavin on a last visit to the National Museum in Athens; it was their farewell to the city and to the landscape.

The next day was the fair in Saint-Cornély, Alain Mouron kept an eye on his cousins as they rode the merry-go-rounds; Monsieur Bailly had given him a thousand francs for the afternoon; he would have liked to try the shooting gallery, but Agnès wouldn't let go of his hand, and he kept having to chase after little René, who was constantly running away; luckily Georges was satisfied with his nougat.

Madame Bonnini continued to feel better; the doctor, however, had left the schoolteacher under no illusions, which is why the latter had asked his sister-in-law Geneviève to replace his daughter Isabelle, who was leaving for Cannes and Italy. His wife leaning on his arm, he watched Isabelle and her brother say goodbye to all their friends. Then the bus motor started up and they vanished in the dust.

On Wednesday, Madame Bonnini felt tired and preferred not to go out; she was surprised not to have had any letters from her children yet, though it was impossible, considering the mail service; luckily Geneviève was there, who advised her to take a walk, to distract her mind; he took the bus for Cannes.

On Sunday, after having eaten lunch with your parents, your Uncle Pierre went into his room, irritable and at a loss for what to do. It was raining. Micheline Pavin had told him she was going to visit her family for two weeks in the Morvan, and he hadn't even asked her the name of the village or town. He had her address in Paris, of course, and letters would be forwarded, but he actually had nothing to write her for the moment, save that he was eager to see her again. He tried to write, tore up his attempt, feeling silly; it would have been better to meet her unexpectedly in that village, for instance, where he might have spent the weekend, instead of loitering around Paris as he had done the day before; he would have come home in the evening in time to be at the lycée the next day to proctor the entrance examinations . . . He had to wait, he would see, the rain was beating against the glass; he picked up Marco Polo, which he hadn't opened since their return from Greece,

"Cipango is an island to the east . . ."

On the twentieth, in the hotel living room, Alain Mouron was reading the letter from his father:

"The furniture has arrived, I think you'll like your room; thanks to your Uncle René's recommendation, I've managed to register you in the lycée where he teaches, I think it will make things a lot easier for you; I'm sending him a letter by the same post, but you must thank him too. I've seen your Uncle Louis several times recently; his wife and children are in their house at Saint-Florentin and won't be back until the end of the month; it seems that Michel will be starting at the Lycée Taine this year too, he did very well on his exams last June; I hope you'll be in the same class. As you see, things look very promising. Kiss your Aunt Elizabeth for me . . . "

He doesn't know that Aunt Elizabeth is in Orléans, Alain thought, I'll discuss all that with him in Paris; it's too hard in a letter; he'll tell me what he thinks about it.

On the twenty-first, Monsieur Bonnini had taken first-class tickets because of his wife; she seemed happy, looked at the landscape. Had this stay in Provence done her any good? Wouldn't it have been better to stay another week, enjoying the sun until the end of his vacation? Why had that doctor been so pessimistic, and why had he urged him so vehemently to take advantage of this improvement to take his wife back to Paris?

Your Uncle Pierre was counting the days; he said to himself, on Saturday, in the café on the Boulevard Saint-Germain where he was drinking a beer and watching the crowd walk by:

"We got back to Paris on the evening of the fifteenth; she must have left for the Morvan on Thursday, she told me two weeks, so she should be back the thirtieth; but wasn't she supposed to go back to work on the first of October? And wouldn't she want to spend a few days in Paris before starting back to work?

In her place, he would come back on Monday the twenty-seventh, or even on Sunday.

Madame Bailly took the train from Paris to Saint-Cornély; she had come back from Orléans the day before and had spent the night alone in the Rue Pierre-Leroux. Monsieur Bailly had stayed at the hotel to be with the children, who were napping, and to write letters; he had sent Alain to meet his wife at the station.

"How did everything go?"

"Fine, nothing happened."

"And the weather?"

"It rains more every day."

"At least you won't have any regrets about leaving the seashore."

Monsieur Bonnini went to the Lycée Taine to ask the principal about his schedule this year.

"On the whole, the same as last, in any case the same classes, which means you won't have to change your curriculum; that's the main thing. There's that blank on Monday in the middle of the afternoon, I think I can shift your Saturday tenth-grade class there, but the schedules won't be set until the end of the week."

On Wednesday, another visit from the doctor, new prescriptions, a letter from Giovanni and Della, who would be coming back the following week; they had spent a day in Milan.

Your Uncle Pierre went to see the principal, who handed him, along with the list of his future students, his schedule, the same as the year before with one exception: the tenth-grade geography class on Wednesday morning had been shifted to Tuesday.

Alain Mouron put covers on all his books on Saturday, and looked through them,

Sixteenth Century French Authors,

a printing-house in the Sixteenth Century, Marot presents his epistle to the king, François I, surrounded by his court, receives a writer, page of a Psalter from Lyon, showing a psalm versified by Marot, Rabelais, Pantagruel holding a bottle . . .

On Sunday your Uncle Pierre ate lunch in the restaurant in the Rue des Saints-Pères with Micheline Pavin; in the afternoon, Madame Bonnini was able to get up.

All Thursday morning, your uncle waited for Micheline Pavin to call him, which she did at twelve-fifteen. She couldn't come for lunch, or dinner either; was she avoiding him? And the next day? For lunch, gladly, rather early, since he didn't have any morning classes; and why not have tea together this afternoon, around four-thirty? What? She had to work! You could tell he was a schoolteacher!

He went to lunch alone in the restaurant in the Rue des Canettes.

As soon as his wife began dozing Monsieur Bonnini went to his barber; when he returned she had awakened and got up. The concierge had given him a letter from their children saying they would be home the following day.

Your uncle had arranged to meet Micheline Pavin near her office, in a café off the Place de l'Opéra. She took him to a restaurant she knew.

"It's been a long time since you were at my place. Come to dinner tomorrow night. And what about that book you mentioned to me, when will you start on it?"

In his briefcase, *Modern History* for the tenth grade, *Geography of the Great Powers* for the seniors, *Medieval Europe* for the eighth grade.

"I'll be teaching my eleventh-graders that lesson on the discovery and conquest of America on Tuesday; I intend to read them passages from Marco Polo and maybe from Montaigne's essay "On Coaches", how do you think that will be?"

"Why the essay on coaches?"

"Oh, you don't know it, or else you've forgotten it. I'll bring it tomorrow. I have to go now."

Monsieur Bonnini assigned his seniors a mimeographed page of Svevo to translate; he discussed the beginning of Canto III of the *Inferno*.

On Sunday morning, your Uncle Pierre got up at nine and joined your family for breakfast; your mother was getting ready for High Mass.

"Isn't Pierre here?"

"He went to nine o'clock Mass at Saint-Hilaire, with his Scouts."

"Doesn't he have a birthday one of these days?"

"It's Tuesday."

"Tuesday?"

"Yes, he'll be fifteen."

"Is it all right if I take him out to dinner that night?"

"It'll be a great treat for him. He'll be so excited . . . "

The next day, his alarm clock rang at seven-thirty. He had no classes until afternoon, and was in no hurry to get up, but took from his night table the first of the books he had put there the night before in order to prepare his lessons,

History for the ninth grade, Chapter III, Europe exploits the world,

"Aztec art: the god Quetzalcoatl (Museum of Natural History, Paris), the form of a plumed serpent with a human head, basaltic lava; Inca art: anthropoid vase (Ethnographical museum, Goteborg), pottery, the form of a man crouching, the face strikingly realistic, Mayan art: Temple of the Warriors at Chichen-Itzá (Yucatán, Mexico),

the mines of Potosi,

the money-changer and his wife, by Quentin Matsys, 1466–1530 (Louvre, Paris), the man weighs a piece of gold, his wife watches, looking up from her book",

he closed the book, threw back his sheet, opened the window; he went to his bookcase and took out a work on Pre-Columbian art; he didn't begin shaving until nine o'clock.

During the night, you were trying not to think about the presents you would be given at lunch. You had to forget what you wanted in order to avoid disappointments. There was only one thing you were sure of, which was that your Uncle Pierre would take you out to a restaurant for dinner, which seemed to you an unexpected, almost inexplicable favor; he had never before invited any of you out with him. It wasn't your uncle himself who had told you, but your mother, who had advised you to get your work for this evening done ahead of time. Your brothers still didn't know anything about it. In the darkness of the bedroom, Denis was breathing regularly.

"Certaine Spaniardes coasting alongst the Sea in search of mines",

on the other side of the wall behind my students, in the third row, in front of Maurice Tangala, between Bernard de Loups and Bertrand Limours, Laurent Garrac crushes a tiny piece of chalk into a blob of blue ink

"Fortuned to land in a very fertile, pleasant and well peopled country, unto the inhabitants whereof they declared their intent, and shewed their accustomed perswasions" . . .

Last year.

Your uncle slept only a few hours that night; he kept thinking he heard Micheline Pavin's voice screaming. He got up and washed his face, he took an aspirin.

He awakened a second time; he thought he heard you shouting on the other side of the wall. He pressed his ear to the partition; nothing.

Europe in 1600, the Hapsburg dynasty, Philip II; Michel Daval, occasionally glancing at his *Chemistry Textbook*, water in its natural state, pure water, mixtures and pure bodies, composition of water, whispered in your ear:

"I don't know if I told you: my father went to the notary this afternoon to buy the apartment."

"And when are you moving?"

"Next week."

"Aren't you having it repainted?"

"No, it's already been done."

"I'll come and see you."

"Good."

A glance from your uncle made the two of you keep still, not a reproach, merely a reminder, as though from an orchestra leader, and you both leaned over your notebooks to write the third subtitle of the lesson: France.

And during the next afternoon, since there was no scout hike, Michel Daval was able to show Alain Mouron his new, still empty apartment in the Rue Servandoni.

On Thursday he had his penalty at the lycée, sitting beside Francis Hutter, who was wearing mourning. There was also a third member of your class, Paul Coutet, in another corner of the room. All three were waiting until four o'clock, when their imprisonment would be over.

Michel Daval hadn't wanted to bring his Greek dictionary, which is why he hadn't been able to take advantage of these hours of immobility to translate the lines of Homer we were supposed to work on together the next day; he counted, moreover, on asking for help from his cousin Alain and from you, who had been such a solicitous neighbor these last few days. He had brought with him only his *Sixteenth Century French Authors*; also, after having carefully read the end of how Gargantua was so disciplined by Ponocrates that he did not waste an Hour of the Day, glancing at some illustrations: a Sixteenth Century ship, lords and ladies, woman's costume, a religious colloquy, Louise Labé of Lyon . . . ,

taking advantage of the monitor's inadvertence, he slipped out of his briefcase the issue of *Galaxie* Hubert Jourdan had lent him and read Robert Sheckley's story: "Something for Nothing",

editorial comment:

"Sooner or later, you get the bill."

269

On Sunday, I took the children to the Museum of Natural History; we spent the longest time over the Japanese toys, but the Pre-Columbian feather textiles also pleased them, and the photographs of the bird men.

The next day, Michel Daval pressed his blotter on the written quiz he had just taken. He had no trouble with the inversion of temperature, but he had forgotten that the coldest point was in Siberia and had located it in Antarctica.

He handed in his paper to your Uncle Pierre, then, as the latter moved away, he bent down to take out of his briefcase the October issue of *Fiction* that Alain Mouron had returned to him the day before yesterday, and turned around to give it to Jean-Pierre Cormier behind him, to whom he had promised it that morning.

Illustrations of the day's chapter: variations in pressure according to altitude, convection currents, gradients, deviation of the winds under the influence of the earth's rotation . . . Boring!

Luckily for him, the following geography class was a little less austere, rain, photographs of clouds.

"What are you doing over the All Saints' Day holiday?"

"I'm going camping."

"Aren't you afraid of the cold?"

"Don't worry, I have a warm sleeping bag."

"Is Alain going with you?"

"No, it's just for the patrol leaders and the second-in-commands."

"He was at religious instruction last night, but you weren't—don't you ever come?"

You made him a sign to keep still. Your Uncle Pierre had given you a pleading glance. You both leaned over your notebooks to write from his dictation:

"Rain and the seasons."

On All Saints' Day, Rose stayed home because Gérard was in bed; I took the others for a walk. There had been some question of going to the cemetery, but Rose said she would put flowers on the graves the next day, that it would be better to visit the Jardin des Plantes, where we spent most of our time watching the birds. A fine rain began falling; we hurried into the métro.

On All Souls Day, Michel Daval went with his mother and sister to the Montparnasse cemetery; three graves, and in front of each one he recited ten prayers on his rosary; he carried the pots of chrysanthemums, one for each stone; wearing his raincoat, he walked under his mother's black umbrella or under his sister's white one.

On Sunday your aunt and I were alone for once; Gérard was with you at the scout meeting. We went to look at a little painting.

Taking advantage of the confusion created by the circulation of the photograph, you turned around toward Henri Fage who had tapped you on the shoulder to pass you the October issue of *Fiction*, which you handed to its owner, Michel Daval.

Fascinated by the illustrations of Wednesday's lesson: aerial view of the rain forests (Ubangi), acacia swamp near Nairobi (Kenya), vegetation of the plains south of Kalahari, the Dankali desert on the coast of the Red Sea, valley of the Ziz (southern Morocco), he asked you:

"Doesn't that make you want to go to Africa?"

On November 15, I was the one who stayed in bed, the third member of the household to catch the grippe, after Gérard and François, so that I couldn't teach your three morning classes, for which you had a substitute, nor the afternoon class with my seniors, upsetting my whole schedule, since the next day I had promised to hand back your compositions on this subject:

"What do you think of Rabelais' ideas on education; compare to-day's education with the kind he opposes and the kind he proposes",

which would be impossible even if I recovered, since I had as yet corrected only half of them, and there was no chance of my finishing this task in my present condition.

After having put the photograph of the class in his briefcase, Michel Daval wrote the second subtitle of the lesson:

"Readings."

On December 13 I reminded my seniors that they would have a test the next day, that it would last three hours, like the baccalaureate examination (I had arranged with my German and Spanish colleagues to shift their classes from four to five on Friday), so that they would be at the lycée until six, and that it would cover not only everything we had done since the beginning of the year, but also Voltaire, which we had only touched on, for by lingering over the *Lettres Persanes* I had fallen behind the schedule and in the second quarter we would have to go much faster,

I handed back their compositions,

"The day after the first performance of *Iphigénie*, a member of the

271

court writes to a friend, detained in the country to describe his impression",

"Portrait of the Duc de Saint-Simon",

"A Persian who has spent several years in Paris has made several friends there; back in his own country, he writes one of these to tell him about his trip and asks him to come and visit him in Persia."

Michel Daval, who had done well with the discovery and conquest of America, had trouble writing ten lines on the Thirty Years' War.

The year went by: the baccalaureate exams, the vacation that we spent at Les Etangs as usual. Your brothers came to join us, but you stayed in Provence with Michel Daval. You wrote me a letter on my birthday which reached me yesterday.

Back at the lycée, I found I had almost the same schedule; the first Tuesday, before discussing the Dispute between Ancients and Moderns, I assigned three subjects for compositions:

"Education in Rabelais and Montaigne",

"in his *Art Poétique*, Boileau states:

> *'There is no savage fiend or beast or blight*
> *That art cannot transform to please the sight.'*

Discuss this notion, making use of examples drawn from painting",

"Madame de Sévigné writes Madame de Grignan to tell her about the performance of a play by Racine."

On Monday, the death of Monseigneur the Dauphin,

" . . . all doors agape and everything in turmoil . . . "

Now (actually months ago), in the senior class, near the window, in the third row, just in front of you, Michel Daval went on:

"Such was the general abomination engendered by flattery and cruelty. From torture to abjuration, and from abjuration to communion . . . "

||||||||||||||||||||||||||||||| IN THE AUTUMN of 1953, your Uncle Pierre was already alternating, on Wednesday afternoons, between two and three:
one week, history for the ninth grade, the next week, history for the eighth grade;
and between three and four:
one week, history for the seventh grade, the next week, geography for the eleventh;
but unlike the year after, it was the tenth and the eleventh grades who came first, and consequently on the second Wednesday from three to four came the landscape of Egypt, the decipherment of its writing, the major divisions of its ancient history.

He was thirty-four on Tuesday. Your brother Denis, who was still only fifteen, was in his eleventh-grade class. The Thirty Years' War.

He was sixteen on November 10. European civilization in the middle of the Seventeenth Century,

El Greco: *The Burial of Count Orgaz*; Velásquez: *The Surrender of Breda*; *Las Meninas*; Zurbarán: *Saint Bonaventure Presiding over a Chapter of Minor Brothers* . . .

The year went by. On July 14, your Uncle Pierre spent the afternoon with us in Montmartre; there was the usual crowd.

Afterwards he remained in Paris, trying to save money for his trip to Greece, reading a good deal, particularly Balzac, who fascinated him and whom he knew much better than I did, listening to records at the house of one of his friends who left the following month for America.

Early in August, walking past a bookstore on the Boulevard Saint-Germain that specialized in geography, where he had already bought several atlases, he stopped and stared through the grille (it was a Monday and the shop was closed) for a long time at the cover of the *Description of the World*.

On Wednesday, in the Rue du Canivet apartment,

"Ye Emperors, Kings, Dukes, Marquises, Earls and Knights, and all other people desirous of knowing the diversities of the races of mankind, as well as the diversities of kingdoms, provinces and regions of all parts of the East, read through this book and ye will find in it the greatest and most marvelous usages and customs . . . "

After his trip to Bourges, he began arranging for his trip to Greece, making reservations on the boat that left Marseille on the evening of August 24, having his passport renewed at the prefecture of police, where he picked it up eight days later, after having bought in another bookstore, on his way, the *Guide Bleu* to Greece.

The day of his departure, you were back in Paris with your brothers, all three awed by his journey that seemed so mysterious, almost wondering if you would ever see him again, talking about it that afternoon while you were building a palace on the dining-room table in the Rue du Canivet, the Meccano-set towers soon turning into a maritime fortress with a drawbridge, like the ones you had seen in Brittany.

"Wouldn't you like to go away like that? Cross the sea?"

"I hear it's awfully hot there . . . "

"And what language do they talk?"

"Greek!"

"Like at school?"

"No, they talk modern Greek, it's not the same thing, Uncle Henri explained it to us, it's almost like Italian compared to Latin."

"Do you think Uncle Pierre knows Greek?"

"He must have studied ancient Greek in school, like us, but I don't know about modern Greek . . . "

"You can't use ancient Greek?"

"How should I know. Anyway, he's probably forgotten it all . . . "

"What'll he do then?"

"They speak French there, they speak French everywhere, it's the language of diplomacy."

"Is the sea in Greece the same as in Brittany?"

"No, it's a different one, I saw it at camp last year. You don't know what you're missing!"

He hadn't forgotten you; on the thirtieth, you received a postcard addressed to Messieurs Denis, Pierre and Jacques Eller, the bronze head of Poseidon found off Cape Sounion:

"I hope you can visit this part of the world soon. Have a good time at Les Étangs; best regards to your Uncle Henri. Affectionately, Uncle Pierre."

"Denis, which would you like best, going to Greece or to America?"

"It's so different."

The next day, your Uncle Pierre was returning from Delphi to Athens in the jolting bus.

On Sunday you asked if Jacques could join us at Les Étangs two days later. Since he didn't have any more fever, your parents let him accompany you to the Naval Museum, but half an hour later he began lagging behind; scared, you hurried back to the Rue du Canivet. He kept protesting:

"No, why didn't we stay there? I feel fine, really, I'm not tired at all."

Then he heaved a tremendous sigh, half closing his eyes.

Denis said:

"No nonsense now, if you want to come with us Tuesday; suppose you had fever tonight, Mother would never let you come with us."

At La Motte-Picquet station, we transferred to another line.

At the Hôtel de la Plage, Monsieur Bailly, after having watched Alain disappear with the telegram for Orléans, sat back in his rattan armchair, clasped his hands, tried to look his wife in the eyes.

"Listen, Elizabeth, wouldn't it be better if we discussed the situation a little?"

"You see, I was right to send Alain to the post office."

"You treat him like a servant, like a poor relation . . . "

"Is that what you wanted to talk to me about?"

"Not only that. Of course I'm wondering if your presence in Orléans is really indispensable . . . "

"It is indispensable, unfortunately for poor Louise; the terms of her telegram . . . "

"I was going to make you a proposition . . . "

"I'm listening."

"You know how disagreeable it is for me to stay alone with the children, I don't know what to do with them. Wouldn't it be better, as long as someone has to go to Orléans, wouldn't it be better if I went?"

"I wouldn't want to put such a burden on you."

"I'm glad to go, I think it would be better for everyone."

"My poor René! You can't really mean it! Louise has seen you maybe twice in her life; you don't know anyone there—what good could you do? It's sweet of you to have thought of such a thing, but really—forgive me, it's unthinkable. As for the children, your nephew Alain is very good at taking care of them. You'll see how right I was to have you invite him, you hesitated at first, but it's the least you can do to help your poor Cousin Henri while he's moving."

"Yes, Alain is very convenient."

"He's a very attractive boy, very intelligent and appealing, a little introverted, maybe; if you have him in your class next year . . . "

"Don't talk about school now."

"Besides, I won't be gone too long . . ."

"So you're leaving tomorrow?"

"Yes, tomorrow. Alain must be at the post office by now."

In the chalet rented for the summer, Madame Régnier,

"I know it's boring, darling, I don't understand a word in all those books myself, but it would be such a pity if you had to repeat the eleventh grade! All your friends would be seniors, and your father would make such fun of you! Come on, recite your lesson to me! Besides, it's raining today, you couldn't go out anyway."

On Wednesday, in Mykonos, the weather was normal for the region. The boat for the Piraeus was leaving the next night. In the hotel dining room, after his nap, your Uncle Pierre was waiting for Micheline Pavin to explore the island's interior with him. They would go back to Delos in the morning.

On Saturday, we went to meet your parents at the station, they were coming to spend the weekend with us and bring your brother Jacques, who was completely recovered now but still a little weak.

You told him about your plans to build a cabin in the woods; you would have to ask Baron Storck's permission, you would go to see him the next afternoon, when I had spoken to him about it after Mass.

"You know, on a vacation in the country, you have to have something interesting to do; so we'll build this cabin, and by the end of the month we could live in it most of the day, like the Sioux; they could come here from the house on visits, and it would be wonderful inside. The best thing would be to have it finished for Uncle Henri's birthday, you know, then we could have a real celebration. But between now and Tuesday, I don't think we can. It's a good thing you got here, we'll need you."

Monsieur Bailly, who had got rid of his children by sending them to the fair under Alain Mouron's supervision, finished his letter to Claire:

" . . . Of course Elizabeth hasn't come back yet; you see how she treats me, how she treats her children. I'm more and more pleased about having asked my nephew Alain Mouron to come, he's most helpful, such an intelligent boy, and so discreet. He lived in Bourges last year, but his father's moved to Paris—he's moving right now, in fact. I'll have to introduce Alain to you, I'm sure you'll like him."

On the way to the post office, he lingered for some time at the fair, observing his children and their cousin from a distance, keeping out of sight.

On Monday, Denis Régnier was climbing up the steep slope despite the rain, his hands in his raincoat pockets; he had long since left the path behind; occasionally he stopped to pick up a pebble, examined it, threw it away; he crossed a stream, climbed to the forest's edge; he caught sight of the glacier, decided to climb down, it was getting cold, his feet were wet, his mother was packing up; the next day they would leave for Paris, where he would have to take his promotion examination which he was sure to fail; he would have to wait for the results, then repeat the eleventh grade, not to mention hearing his father's sarcastic remarks.

On Tuesday, at six in the evening, your Uncle Pierre knocked at Micheline Pavin's door in the Hôtel Terminus. She put away her things and washed her face. They walked down the broad steps together to the old harbor, not saying a word. The breeze smelled of fish.

On Wednesday, Denis Régnier, after having lunch with his father in the Rue du Pré-aux-Clercs, went back to his mother's apartment in the Rue du Cardinal-Lemoine to prepare for his examination which would be given, as he had found out by going to the Lycée Taine and asking, on Monday and Tuesday of the following week.

On Thursday, your Uncle Pierre, leaving the Lycée Taine, stopped in the barbershop in the Rue Saint-Sulpice; he hadn't had his hair cut during his whole trip to Greece.

With your two brothers and my son Gérard, you finished the construction of the cabin on Sunday. You were proud of your handiwork, and it had to be admitted that you had done well. The roof wasn't finished yet, but there was a storm brewing and you had to run home along the paths that were full of puddles.

On Monday, in the living room of the Hôtel de la Plage, Monsieur Bailly was reading the letter from his first cousin, Henri Mouron.

"I can't tell you how grateful I am for all you've done for Alain. He writes me regularly, I imagine at your instigation, and I hear that he is getting along very well with your children; I hope he's able to be of some help to you, please don't hesitate to ask him if there's anything he can do. I've had a letter from the Lycée Taine, everything's in order there, he can enter the eleventh grade; I know that this is partly due to your recommendation. The moving is fortunately over; I hardly need to tell you how difficult it all is for a widower. I've managed to find a cleaning woman who can make breakfast for us and fix something for dinner as well; all we'll have to do is heat things up. For a man without a wife, these questions raise almost insoluble problems. Fortunately, Alain has been raised . . . "

Alain came in,

"Is that a letter from Father? He told me he was writing you. So it's all settled about the lycée! He was worried about it. I wanted to thank you for all you've done. I hope I'll have you for my English teacher."

"That's nice of you, Alain. You know, in spite of what your father thinks, I really had nothing to do with it. Last year, I had the class you'll be in this year, but from one year to the next, a teacher's schedule can be entirely changed . . . No one can tell if we'll be in the same class . . . And you'll have nothing to regret, you know, it's always more of a complication to know your students outside of school. I think it's time to get the children up. It's nice out, they should take advantage of the weather."

Denis Régnier struggled over his Latin translation, under your Uncle Pierre's supervision, the papers were collected at four and taken to the principal who gave your uncle those from the history and geography examination which were to be corrected for the committee meeting on Friday.

Before returning to the Rue du Canivet, he walked through empty Paris, thinking about Micheline Pavin, wondering if it wasn't time to change his life, to give up that little room he sublet from your parents and those dinners he ate with them almost every night.

There were no more than ten papers in each class, but there were papers for every class. This year, he had assigned the subjects himself:

seventh grade: what do you know about Egypt, cities,

eighth grade, Charlemagne, China,

ninth grade, the discovery of America, the Balkan countries,

tenth grade, Napoleon, the Mediterranean region,

eleventh grade, the American Revolution, the representation of the earth.

On the twenty-fifth, you went for the last time to look at your cabin in the Herrecourt woods. We wouldn't be leaving Les Étangs until Tuesday, but the next two days would be taken up by the turmoil of departure.

You had sent a formal invitation to Baron Storck the day before; you had taken a whole banquet down to the cabin, with tea in a thermos; the three of you were waiting while my children brought your guest of honor and we escorted your parents, who had arrived during the afternoon and were to leave on Monday, with Jacques. While Alain Mouron was coming back from the station with Elizabeth Bailly, your English teacher went up to his children's room.

"Well, what's this, you have to get dressed! What will Mother say if she finds you like this?"

"We were waiting for her to help us, or else Alain."

"You can do it by yourselves, I know you can! And Georges or René can help Agnès."

"Alain told us not to put on our clothes before he came up."

"He went to get Mother at the station; hurry up, now!"

"We picked these flowers for her this morning, but they're wilted now, we should have put them in water, Alain . . . "

"Alain didn't think of it, Alain hasn't had time. You should have shown them to me when you came in, I would have told you . . . "

"We asked Alain, and he said it wasn't worth bothering about . . . "

"What do you mean, not worth bothering about?"

"You know, showing them to you, but he was wrong, because then he would have put them in water."

"Wasn't worth bothering about! All right now, come here, let me lace up that shoe for you, you big baby! Now the other one. Your turn, Georges. Oh, dear, it broke. Here, I'll fix that. Alain spoils you, that's the trouble, you don't give him a minute's peace, he does everything you ask and now you can't do one thing for yourselves; in Paris, you'll have to get along by yourselves, it isn't so hard, really! Now, Agnès, we have to comb your hair; all right, that will do. Where are those flowers? Oh. No, we'll have to throw them away, there's nothing else to do, it's too bad. You boys have your handkerchiefs?"

Denis Régnier went to find out the results of the promotion examinations. He had failed. He would have to tell his mother, tell his father, with whom he was to have lunch the next day, start the eleventh grade over again . . .

And your Uncle Pierre, after having taken the letter he had just written Micheline Pavin to the post office in the Rue de Rennes, finished the *Description of the World*:

" . . . for, as we have said in the first chapter of this book, there has never been any man, neither Christian nor Sarracen nor Tartar nor

279

Pagan, who has ever visited such vast regions of the world as has done Messer Marco, son of Messer Nicolo Polo, noble and great citizen of the city of Venice."

On Tuesday, at six o'clock, he took the métro at the Mabillon stop to go to Micheline's room on the Rue Linné, a fifth-floor walk-up, with a narrow bed, flowers in the window, photographs on the wall, a kitchenette, everything well arranged and very clean.

"Are you looking for something bigger?"

"It's all right for now."

"Can I help you? I'm not much good at cooking; I've made several attempts . . . "

"I hate men who are good cooks. But if you don't mind going down and up the stairs, you could do me a big favor by getting some bread."

"Gladly, just tell me where."

"Turn right as you leave the building, there's a bakery at the corner. Bring one loaf. I have everything else I need; don't expect a banquet, of course! Oh, if you happen to see any grapefruit, I know you like them . . . I have cheese, cold meat, sardines, oh! a bottle of wine too, I'll give you a market bag, otherwise you won't be able to manage it all; I'm sorry to use you as an errand boy, but you know, necessity is the mother . . . I must admit I had vaguely intended to ask you tonight, only I didn't realize we'd be spending the whole afternoon together. Oh, the wine's a little farther down the street, on the other side, and you'll find the grapefruits to the left as you leave the building, there's a little grocer who has all kinds of things, if he doesn't have any that means there are none. Here, I'll make a list and draw you a little map."

He went down with his market bag, night was falling, the street lights were on; he didn't find any grapefruit, but he bought a tart at a pastry shop and a bag of Kalamata olives from the grocer.

When he climbed back up the stairs, he found the table set on an extremely pretty embroidered cloth.

On Wednesday, Denis Régnier spent his afternoon sorting out the stamps his father had given him the day before, saying as he did so:

"Here, this will console you."

Your uncle was leafing through his history textbooks, ninth grade: Christopher Columbus taking leave of Ferdinand and

Isabella, a galleon, the Battle of Marignan, Charles VIII, Pope Julius II by Raphael, Aztec art: the god Quetzalcoatl . . .

tenth grade: interior of a nobleman's house under Louis XVI, wealthy merchants at table, shopkeepers, the peasant's burdens, a riot in the Faubourg Saint-Antoine . . .

the geography textbooks the next day, last illustrations in the seventh-grade textbook:

. . . first discovery of America by the Normans or Vikings, legendary monsters illustrating the Book of Wonders by Marco Polo, the great maritime discoveries: first voyage of Christopher Columbus, Magellan's expedition, voyage of Vasco da Gama.

On Friday, the three of you stood in line at a bookstore where, on Saturday, Monsieur Bailly stood in line with his two boys; and on Sunday Denis Régnier helped his sister Sylvie make covers for the tenth-grade textbooks she had bought. He had had to buy new physics, chemistry and mathematics textbooks.

At four, your Uncle Pierre and Micheline Pavin went to a movie theater on the Champs-Élysées. When they came out,

"Shall we have dinner together?"

"I have to telephone my sister."

"I don't want to keep you from preparing your classes for tomorrow."

"Oh, you know, the first day . . . And besides, I have the morning to myself."

The next evening, after having refreshed his memory about the Earth in the universe, the topography of Africa and the presentation of France, your Uncle Pierre ate dinner with your family; but although you had been very talkative at lunch, you didn't open your mouth in his presence. Of course, on the first day of school, your new experiences had tired you out somewhat, but above all, from that day on your Uncle Pierre had once again become a schoolteacher, someone with whom you had to watch what you said.

He was used to this change, but this year he sensed it more deeply; he felt more lonely than ever back in his room, he couldn't get down to his work immediately, and yet he had to prepare three lessons for the next afternoon, all three first classes—in other words, it was essential that they be successful if he wanted to establish a healthy relationship with his students, a true teaching relationship. He went out to drink a beer in a café on the Boulevard Saint-Germain.

281

Back in the Rue du Canivet at ten, the history textbook for his seventh-graders . . .

On Tuesday, after dinner, Europe quarrels over Italy, our prehistory, the world after 1848.

Around ten, in order to prepare his lesson on the discovery and conquest of America, he picked up his Montaigne to reread the essay "On Coaches", looking for a passage he intended to use.

On Wednesday, since he had no lessons to prepare for the next day, he went out looking for a movie. None of the programs on the Boulevard Saint-Michel looked interesting; he felt dirty; he decided he would ask your mother's permission to take a bath the next morning; he walked to the Panthéon, walked around it, came back along the Boulevard Saint-Germain, bought a pack of cigarettes and drank a glass of beer.

Coming in at ten-thirty, he pressed his ear against the door on the landing; the radio was still on, your parents hadn't gone to bed. He rang, your mother answered, her knitting in her hands; she shouted to your father:

"It's Pierre."

"I didn't mean to bother you, I just wanted to know if I could use your tub tomorrow morning?"

"Why didn't you ask before? The boys will be in there all morning, unless you come very early. Can you wait until Friday? Do you have a class Friday morning?"

"No."

"That would be better, then."

"Thanks. See you tomorrow."

He went to bed, continuing the essay "On Coaches."

On Thursday, Denis Régnier carefully sorted out the stamps his father had just given him in a big envelope. He asked his mother for some money, and he went downstairs to a stationery shop on the Boulevard Saint-Germain to buy a notebook for duplicates bigger than the one he had used last year.

After having drawn a diagram of our degrees of relationship, your Uncle Pierre took another sheet of paper on which he wrote:

"Teachers:

1) Pierre Vernier: history and geography;
2) Henri Jouret: French, Latin, Greek;
3) René Bailly: English;
4) Antoine Bonnini: Italian;

5) Hubert (first name?): physics and chemistry;
(both more or less related to Denis Régnier, who is repeating);
6) du Marnet or Dumarnet (first name?), new this year: mathematics;
7) Alfred Hutter: German (relationship with the student Francis Hutter?), new this year, was at Nancy last year;
8) Tavera (first name?): Spanish;
9) drawing (his name?);
10) gym (his name?);
11) Should Abbé Gollier be included on the list? Isn't there a Protestant minister more or less attached to the institution?"
Montaigne:

" . . . Our world hath of late discovered another . . . "

On Friday morning, since you had gone to the stadium at Croix-de-Berny with your classmates under Monsieur Moret's supervision, you didn't come home for lunch until quite late, and your brothers left for the lycée ahead of you.

Since you thought you would have a little free time, you hadn't looked at the *Épître à Lyon Jamet*; hoping you could glance at it while one of your classmates was struggling through Homer, you congratulated yourself on not having made the same mistake you made last year—sitting in the first row.

Denis Régnier had studied this text with me last year; I was watching him out of the corner of my eye during Michel Daval's recitation; how bored he was already! What a shame he hadn't passed the promotion exam! He wasn't listening, turning the pages of his book instead, reading another passage; I didn't have the heart to interrupt him; I saw under his textbook a big notebook that he was showing to the boy next to him, Bernard de Loups; but Bernard made him a sign that I was watching.

What are the Middle Ages? Then, back in the Rue du Canivet, for the next day, presentation of Europe, the Renaissance and the Reformation, the flow of ideas in the middle of the Nineteenth Century; progress in the sciences, religious disputes, transformations in the arts.

On Saturday, at eight, he rang at Micheline Pavin's door. This time the table was set; everything was ready. He leaned out the window:

283

"Nice view over the rooftops."

"It's all yours, you can come whenever you like."

"I'd like to come every night."

"Every night!"

"Don't worry, I won't come without letting you know first, I won't get in your way. I know you're very busy, you have a lot of friends, relatives too probably, you have to see a lot of people . . . "

"I have a few friends, almost all my relatives live outside of Paris, and the ones that are here I only visit once a year, on New Year's Day; I don't see many people and you'd never bother me."

"You know, the thing is, I'm tired of eating with my sister and her three boys every night—they're all three my students this year. I've explained this situation to the principal, but there was no way of doing anything about it, because of schedule requirements, apparently. It's a big disadvantage but it might be useful for one thing, for my project—they could give me a lot of information . . . Of course I don't have to eat dinner with them to get this information, but I hear them talking about their day to their family then, or at least I used to hear them, for all week they've been rather silent and suspicious, suspicious about me; I'll have to find a way to put a stop to that . . . All this, of course, depending on how I get on with the work: I want to get started, and at the same time I'm afraid to, it's all laziness, of course . . . Well, tonight I'm lucky enough to have dinner somewhere else without having to go to a restaurant; you know, I eat lunch in a restaurant every day; I don't make many changes. I like having settled habits, and at the same time I have a kind of terror of coming back to the same place every day . . . You see, I'm telling you everything. You must forgive me, I'm so touched by . . . "

"Come here as much as you like, but won't it affect this work you're about to begin?"

"What do you mean?"

"You won't have time to work on it, you'll get back to the Rue du Canivet too late."

"It will have to go very slowly anyway."

"I hope it won't be too slow; I'd be disappointed; I'm very interested in it, you know, I've been thinking about it a lot lately . . . "

"I know. I want to start soon, but there's something stopping me, a kind of exhaustion in advance, but . . . "

"But I feel you're going to start it anyway, and I'll do all I can to help you; I'll adopt you, so to speak, you'll come and take dinner with me here whichever days you want; but that's enough talk about future dinners, I'd feel better if you'd eat some of this one."

"I chatter so much . . . "

"Only once in a while."

"It's you who make me talk, it's seeing you . . . "

"Not always, I'm beginning to get to know you, I'm sure that between now and the end of the evening you'll fall into one of your meditations."

Which is what happened. Around ten, after a long silence, she said to him:

"I know what you're thinking."

"You do?"

"You're thinking about your eleventh-graders, about how you're going to represent them. You see that you can't get away from it. But you probably haven't found the way in yet, the way to begin."

"I have found the way to begin."

"Tell me about it."

"You see, it's a little hard to explain; it's all still very obscure in my own mind, but I can tell you this much: if I begin (I still don't know if I'm going to begin; the more I talk about it with you, the more I feel obliged to, somehow, but I don't know, really, I don't know, it depends on . . .), anyway, if I begin, it will be Tuesday night, and if I haven't begun by Tuesday night, I don't think I'll ever begin; I'm so afraid of seeming ridiculous to you; yes, Tuesday night, I'll begin with that class I want to teach about the discovery and the conquest of America, and I . . . Yes, what intrigues me, you see, what made me decide on that day is that it's my nephew's birthday, the one who's in that class, and so it's an occasion for me . . . It's too complicated; I'll tell you later how it goes, if it goes at all; but you see, I must teach the class well, it has to affect the students as an exceptional hour, and that's why I've done so much outside reading. I'll read them some passages from Marco Polo and also some pages from that essay of Montaigne's I told you about yesterday. I brought it in my briefcase because you said you didn't know it, and I'd like to read it to you, if it wouldn't be too boring for you, before I read it to my students; it's such an extraordinary passage. I've brought the *Description of the World*, too, the book I was reading in Greece, but that'll be for another time. You see, it's a kind of occupational disease, I can't help myself . . . Why are you laughing like that?"

"It's just that it was so easy for me to make you start talking again!

I'm beginning to know how to play you like an instrument; if I press the right key . . . No, read me your Montaigne, I love being read to."

"Here, this is where it begins. I have to make some cuts for the students, otherwise it would be too long . . . "

"But I'm not an ordinary student, am I? I'm entitled to the whole text. Let's hear how you read."

"Here we are: 'Our world hath of late discovered another (and who can warrant us whether it be the last of his brethren . . .).' "

On Sunday, during the detective film in the Champs-Élysées movie theater, when there were revolver shots, she clenched one hand around her other wrist, and he felt like putting his arm around her. He watched her, ignoring the film; she, on the other hand, was absorbed by it and paid no attention to him. He was wondering how far he dared go, what she expected.

Suddenly she looked at him with a smile; he was so unaware of what was happening on the screen just then that he wondered what her smile could be for; he was almost crying from hesitation and uncertainty; he was beginning to feel hungry. He leaned toward her, his knee touched hers for a moment, then he withdrew.

They came out into the rainy night. They ran toward the métro, he took her hand to help her, she stumbled on the sidewalk, he put his arm around her waist. Then he took her arm and his fingers squeezed tighter; she said nothing. They went to her apartment.

"Of course there's something to eat!"

He climbed the stairs with his heart pounding. He didn't say a word once he was inside. He looked at her; he ate with a smile; she wasn't surprised at his silence.

"If I tell you to kiss me, would that help you?"

He took her hands in his, opened them, looked at the palms as though they surprised him, kissed them both, and raised his head, almost trembling, then calm, smiling, pressed them to his face and let them continue their caress by themselves, until they met behind his neck. He put his hands on her shoulders, then grasped her head, brought it toward his own and then suddenly, as though changing his mind, kissed her chastely on the cheek. He let his arms fall to his sides; he looked into her eyes for a long moment; she couldn't mistake the ardor of that look; she was waiting.

"Tell me."

"What?"

"What you told me before . . . "

"What do you mean?"

"That order you gave me."

"Yes?"

"Was it serious?"

"Yes, quite serious. You asked me to give you an order, and I took you seriously."

"Do you still order me?"

"I repeat it as strongly as I can. I don't know what you're afraid of, and I can't even tell you that you're wrong to be afraid of it, but there's no other way out."

"I have the feeling the doors of a prison are about to close behind me."

"But you're already in prison, dear schoolmaster; now you're taking advantage of a crack in the wall to escape. You'll get out by the skin of your teeth."

She had spoken in a very low voice, almost without moving her lips.

She pulled him against her, kissed him fiercely.

He offered no resistance, feeling only a tremendous exhaustion. He murmured:

"It's a good thing you're with me."

They walked over to the window together.

"What were we talking about?"

"I don't remember."

"It's raining."

"Yes, it's raining."

"I'd like to come back tomorrow."

"Come back tomorrow."

"I'll be waiting for you at that café on the Avenue de l'Opéra. You come out at seven, don't you?"

"It's more likely to be between seven-thirty and eight."

"I'll be waiting for you at eight, I'll bring you the Marco Polo. I must go now."

On Monday,

" . . . in this city, Kubla Khan built a vast palace of marble. . . . "

He walked home that night. He had a class the next morning at nine, but he couldn't decide to go to bed; he walked around the Place

287

Saint-Sulpice, he sat down on one of the benches: the Bonaparte was already closed, the police were in their commissariat.

I had already been in bed an hour; Rose was lying beside me, neither of us was asleep; she was pressed against me, caressing my chest; the children were quiet. On the floor above, a door slammed, I heard footsteps in the room over ours, the sound of running water.

At around three, I awakened; Rose wasn't beside me any more, the little lamp near the door was lit, François was crying; I pulled on my bathrobe to see what it was; he was crying in his sleep: "I don't want to go to school."

Rose was smoothing his hair. She went for a glass of water. Claude turned his head on his pillow. She pulled up his covers. François went back to sleep. I walked to the kitchen for a glass of wine.

" . . . That they were quiet and well-meaning men, coming from farre-countries, being sent from the King of Castille, the greatest Prince of the habitable Earth",

on the other side of the wall, at the back of the classroom, Georges Tannier, next to Frédéric Wolf, behind Gilbert Zola, is sharpening a red pencil with his pocket knife,

" . . . unto whom the Pope, representing God on earth, had given the principality of all the *Indies. . . .* "

Four o'clock in the morning, by the chimes of Saint-Sulpice. To-morrow, what was there to do for tomorrow, it was no longer for to-morrow but for this morning, since it was after four, class was going to start again, in how long? In five hours; you were hoping to get back to sleep soon, otherwise you would be sluggish all morning, your at-tention would wander, you had actually prepared nothing for this morning, all this morning with me, luckily you had had tea with me, I wouldn't be nasty enough to call on you, I had asked you if you had finished your work, but only with a smile, you were hoping it had been just a joke; how could you have finished the preparation of the Greek I had assigned you only this morning, you meant the morning before, Homer, *dicunt Homerum caecum fuisse,* they say Homer was blind, *caecum?* Oh yes, Homer, no one even knows if he existed, what had I already told you about Homer? You were hoping that Michel Daval . . . Above all, you were hoping he would have brought you the issue of that magazine . . . Ulysses has reached the shore, he is afraid of the morning cold; when did the morning cold come? He's afraid of wolves, there were no wolves in this room; on the other side of the wall, there was Uncle Pierre and his wolf eyes and you wanted to fall asleep now, the cold of the dawn coming, like in camp when you woke up and found the tent, the ropes, the stakes covered with frost, all the grass, all the dead leaves etched with white, the sunbeams yellow through the tree trunks . . . ;

five o'clock; but for Livy you wouldn't have the same excuse (which excuse? oh, yes), and I certainly would have an excuse to call on you since it was the day before yesterday that I had assigned you the passage in Livy for the day after next, no for this morning, since it was the day before yesterday, Monday, it was Wednesday already, Hannibal crossing the Alps, he had only one eye, or was that his father, you weren't sure, Livy bored you so much, why did it have to be Livy, those long sentences, it must bore me too, but I didn't care, I read it off as if it was French; this morning, that is, yesterday morning, it had been Virgil, now that was different, that was why you had prepared Virgil Monday night and why you had completely forgotten Livy;

as for Racine, the preface to *Britannicus*, you had even less excuse, since it was a week ago I had assigned it; you had started to look at it, but you hadn't read it, you hadn't felt up to it, you were falling asleep; luckily the afternoon began with an hour of gym, not that you liked gym so much, especially when it was in the lycée courtyard, but at least once it was over you didn't talk about it any more, it didn't overflow like all these other lessons you had to learn afterwards and recite, these others that you had to prepare, that dragged their assignments after them;

and then geography, what had Uncle Pierre been talking about last Monday? Hours, that was it, hours, seasons, years, time zones, the date line, but with him you didn't have to worry, yes, you didn't have to worry, he wouldn't ask you, knowing what time you had gone to bed, what time he had made you go to bed, because it was on his account, mostly on his account that I hadn't been able to prepare this morning's classes and especially . . .

But he didn't know, he wouldn't know, that you weren't sleeping, that you wouldn't have slept, that you had heard the clock strike every hour or almost every hour; five-thirty, it would be light soon; was there frost in Paris? Maybe not at this time of year; and if you hadn't managed to fall asleep by six, you'd go and open the shutters . . .

But he might think that by lunchtime . . . No, he wouldn't risk it, he had looked so attentive when he talked to you, he had been so serious, as if he really needed you, he was going to be nice to you, you knew that, he was going to be good to you from now on, that was it, you knew that . . . you never knew, you could never count on what a teacher said, but your Uncle Pierre wasn't only a teacher, he was your uncle too, I was your uncle too . . . there was no way out, they couldn't help it, in the back of their minds they always wanted to make you sweat . . .

Six already! It still didn't seem to be daylight; but hadn't Uncle Pierre explained to you on Monday something about six in the morning and the autumn equinox, that the sun around the end of September rose at six in the morning and that this was true for the whole earth? But he had also mentioned some kind of delay, about an hour more or less, you didn't remember any more, the time it used to be summer had become the time for all year round.

He had put a lot of emphasis on the fact that you had to be a good student, that it was indispensable if you really wanted to help him, that it was the only way to camouflage the work you'd be doing for him and that it was particularly important for you to be a good student in his class, until you had started to wonder if this whole business wasn't a schoolteacher's trick, a way of getting you to work harder, to do better, a kind of promotion campaign for the parents and the principal and the inspectors, the authorities, a trick to make you learn your lessons better, a decoy, maybe because last year you didn't do well enough, Denis and you, you had taken advantage of the situation a little, the fact that he was your uncle, and that may have annoyed him, maybe his colleagues had pointed it out to him, or your parents; unlikely, highly unlikely;

and he had made it very clear you were not to mention it to your parents, and above all not to mention it to your brothers; and you were the only one he had invited to dinner; maybe he would invite Denis for his birthday too, next month, but he had started with you;

and he had told you not to mention it to me, and that was why you had decided he must be telling you the truth, he really needed you, really needed you to work because of that, of being able to count on you;

and it was settled, you would learn his lessons, besides, he knew how to make things interesting and it was too bad he didn't read things to you more often, things like he read yesterday, those descriptions of China or about the conquest of America; you had almost wanted to

290

ask him for those two books, but they were probably in old French with s's all over the place, and you already had a hard enough time now with that bastard Rabelais; maybe later on;

only if he needed you so much, he wouldn't make things hard for you and so he wouldn't call on you this afternoon, he'd keep it for the next week, for instance; to make things easy for him, if you wanted him to do you a favor like that, you'd look tired.

Wasn't it dawn now? You could see the slits in the shutters, and it looked like it was going to be a nice day; there might have been frost on the roofs, it seemed colder; wouldn't it be better to wait until six-thirty to get up? But maybe by then the frost would have melted already. The sun was rising in the east; where was the east in relation to Saint-Sulpice? Weren't churches always built facing east? Who told you that? Where had you seen that? Then the back of the towers would get the sun on them.

You stood up, you opened the window, you pushed the shutters, they creaked. Your father had just come out of his room, he opened the door.

What's the matter, Pierre? You're up early today. Is it dinner with your uncle that did it? If you got up to work, that's a good sign. But I think you might just as well go back to bed and sleep until eight. Why don't you close those shutters and go back to bed?"

Denis sat up in bed, making a face.

"What? What time is it? Oh, Pierre!"

It wasn't dark in the room any more, but it was quiet again. You fell asleep at once.

On the other side of the wall, your Uncle Pierre, who had also got up when he heard the noise, who had pressed his ear to the wall, but the murmurs of conversation were too faint to reach him, opened his shutters, they creaked and he saw the first gleams of daylight gild the backs of the towers of Saint-Sulpice.

He went back to bed but didn't fall asleep again, watching the sky from his bed until seven-thirty.

He took a sheet of paper and the various lists of textbooks for each of the classes at the lycée; the first thing was to get hold of all the textbooks his students used, and as soon as possible; he would have to buy them this morning;

Sixteenth Century French Authors, Seventeenth Century French Authors and why not Eighteenth and Nineteenth Century French Authors so he could follow my senior-year course as well,

291

Anthology of Latin Literature, Latin Grammar, Anthology of Greek Literature, Greek Grammar,

Anthology of English Literature and the *English Grammar* Bailly used,

that was already a good ten volumes, enough for a first trip. For a second, eleventh-grade and senior *Physics* and *Chemistry Texts,* Italian, German, Spanish; it would take his whole morning, that was certain, and there would scarcely be time to prepare his own afternoon classes, what were they anyway?

Schedule: from two to three, history for the ninth grade or the eighth grade, this week, for the eighth grade:

textbook: second lesson: continuation of the Roman Empire, Justinian . . . ;

fine;

from three to four, history for the seventh grade, or geography for the eleventh grade, this week, for the eleventh grade, more serious:

textbooks: third lesson: representation of the earth: longitude and latitude, projections, scale of a map, representation of relief;

fine;

he would ask them about the measurement of time, the hours, seasons, years; it would be amusing to call on you, but you'd probably be tired;

from four to five, history for the seniors, thorniest:

triumph of materialism: the new economic factors, capitalism in full swing, the beginning of urban civilization;

of course all this would have to be looked into closely, but he could still rely on his experience as a teacher.

He was in his pajamas, it was cold; he got up, washed, shaved, dressed; he went to your parents' dining room for his coffee at eight. Denis came in first, then Jacques. Your mother went to call you for the second time, you came in still half-asleep; your uncle asked you if you had slept well, if you felt in good form.

"We came back late last night."

You couldn't say anything but yes. He looked at you with a kind of affection that reassured you about this afternoon's class.

"Don't sleep too much during your Uncle Henri's classes, he'll hold it against me."

Denis laughed stupidly; Jacques was starting to laugh too, but he stopped when he saw the look on your Uncle Pierre's face. Both of them started buttering their toast very intently. Pierre Vernier left the room without a word; he went back to his room for his briefcase in order to buy a set of your textbooks at some big bookstore.

He took his breakfast with you regularly only on Tuesday morning, because he had to be at the lycée at nine that day, like you, and eating at your house saved him time, but on the other days of the week he usually preferred to take coffee and a croissant in one of the cafés on the Place Saint-Sulpice, and he decided on Thursday that this was certainly the best thing to do.

He had awakened at seven-thirty with a terrible headache, had stayed in bed until nine, glancing at the October number of *Fiction*.

Coming back up to his room, he went to say good morning to your mother; you were in your pajamas, waiting for Denis to get out of the tub; you could hear him splashing around. Your Uncle Pierre would be coming in for a bath the next day.

According to the schedule he had made for himself the day before, Thursday morning was supposed to be spent studying the textbooks his colleagues used. He began with *Sixteenth Century French Authors*.

After his bath, your mother insisted on serving him some breakfast and asked if he would come to dinner.

"Yes, of course, gladly."

He went back to his room to prepare his afternoon classes, constitutional monarchy, the regional aspects of the United States, Mohammed and the Arab conquest.

Not for years had he prepared his classes so carefully, with the exception of the class the Tuesday before; he would have liked to check everything, review everything.

On Saturday, before lunch, the authoritarian empire of Napoleon III (he would have to repair the bad impression last Wednesday's class had made on the seniors), Europe in 1600, the relation of land and sea in Europe.

He took his lunch in the Rue des Canettes, his coffee on the Boulevard Saint-Germain.

In the afternoon, Monsieur Bonnini discussed with his seniors the beginning of the fifth canto of the *Inferno*, the entrance into the second circle where the carnal sinners are punished.

On Sunday morning, according to his schedule, exploration of your textbooks,

Anthology of Greek Literature,

ochre cover, title printed in reddish-orange,
frontispiece: the winged victory of Samothrace, marble, in the Louvre,
1) epic period (Tenth to Seventh Centuries B.C.),
plate: Athens, the acropolis from the Zappeion,
(the Zappeion, that park, his trip, Micheline Pavin whom he was going to meet in a little while on the Boulevard Saint-Germain, with whom he would be having lunch in the Rue des Saints-Pères, the cool gardens of the Zappeion that he had first seen alone, then with her),
2) the epic, Homer, the Odyssey, Book Five, résumé of the preceding chapters:
"By order of the gods, Calypso permitted Ulysses to leave the island where she was delaying him by her magic arts; but Poseidon roused a violent storm in which the hero would have died without Athena's assistance",
caption:
"Ulysses, rescued, approaches the coast of Phaeacia",
text:
"Autar Athènaiè, kourè Dios, alla noèsèn . . . ",
note:
"alla noèsèn: had other thoughts" than those of Poseidon, who continues rousing the waves:
(kourè Dios, Dios genitive of Zeus, autar must be an enclitic particle, something like as or then),
translation:
"Then Athena" (probably), "daughter of Zeus, had other thoughts";
but by the second line, he had to give up; he didn't have a dictionary, but he knew that a dictionary would not be enough, he would also need a translation; the Victor Bérard translation in the Guillaume Budé series had a good reputation, he had read some of it once; he probably wouldn't be able to find a better one; before leaving, he jotted on a sheet of paper these two necessary purchases: Bailly Dictionary, Bérard Odyssey. He would get them tomorrow morning; but tomorrow was a Monday, the bookstores would probably be closed, and on Tuesday morning he had his classes, which would postpone buying them until Wednesday, if he didn't want to encroach on the late afternoon hours set aside for writing, and he mustn't encroach . . .

He was already late; Micheline Pavin was waiting for him at the Royal-Saint-Germain.

"There you are! How are you? How's your work?"

"What about yours?"

"I've started."

"We haven't seen each other for ages."

"It's only a few days."

"I've got used to seeing you, I missed you."

"Yes, it's been ages, so many things have already happened to me since Monday."

"Tell me about them."

"Shall we eat lunch in the Rue des Saint-Pères?"

"If you like."

After lunch, Monsieur Bonnini, his children and his sister-in-law Geneviève went to the hospital to see his wife; she was wide awake. At three o'clock a nurse came to tell them she had to rest.

"In a few days you'll be able to come home again."

"Yes, in a few days. I'll see you tomorrow."

They walked home without a word; they went up to their apartment, and everyone picked up a book, though no one was able to read. They stayed in their chairs for a long time without moving.

"You should go out," Monsieur Bonnini said to his children.

"So should you," Geneviève answered.

"She really looked better today."

On Monday morning, your Uncle Pierre went to find his dictionary and his translation.

Greek, without which a man may be ashamed to call himself a scholar, that's what you were learning, but it flowed over you, Greek, like raindrops over a leaf; to write this book, he would have to study Greek again; that would allow him to help you . . .

All the bookstores were closed, as he had expected; he couldn't have the books until Wednesday; and it would undoubtedly be the same thing for Latin; he would have to get a dictionary and translations.

He didn't go back to the Rue du Canivet until around eleven. Hastily,

the translation of European society,

climate, temperature,

the French Revolution: fall of the monarchy, Girondist convention, Revolutionary government, Revolutionary victories.

Tuesday morning, his alarm clock went off at eight. He leaped out of bed, went to take his breakfast with you; he had to be at the lycée at nine to tell his seventh-graders about the earth's movement around the sun,

illustrations:

"Like this top, the earth spins on its own inclined axis at the same time that it describes an ellipse around the sun,

according to the length of the shadow at noon, is this region far from or close to the pole?,

how can you tell that in this landscape the sun is at its zenith?",

before moving a few classrooms down to the eighth grade and the inhabitants of Africa.

Wednesday morning he went back to the bookstore, this time successfully. He returned to the Rue du Canivet with a Bailly Dictionary under his left arm and the three volumes of the Odyssey, text and translation, in his briefcase.

The passage we were dealing with began at line 382 of Book V; obviously the best thing would be to read the whole book in order to understand them precisely. They were in smaller type than the rest, the lines set closer together; a note at the bottom of the page explained this anomaly:

"The apparition of Athena, lines 382–387, is not only superfluous and recounted in spurious lines, but it makes line 388 incomprehensible",

line 388:

"For two days and two nights, on the swollen waves . . . ",

but in the textbook you and I were using, there was nothing to indicate that this line was incomprehensible, and was it actually? Which side to take?

Bérard translated:

"But Pallas Athena"

(why Pallas, where had he found this word?)

"had then conceived her plan"

(oh yes, he had added Pallas because of his detestable habit of making lines of blank verse; your uncle remembered that this defect had

once made this translation intolerable to him and that he had sworn
never to look at it again):

> "Arresting the winds, this daughter of Zeus
> Commanded them all, subsiding, to give over;
> Then she summoned the steady Boreas
> In order that the strong Phaeacian oarsmen
> Her divine Ulysses might approach, fleeing
> Fate and shipwreck . . . "

Here the small print and the close-set lines stopped; the translation of the following lines was printed normally. There was not
much time; there were the afternoon's implacable lessons to prepare:
the great European monarchies, Charles V, François I, Henry VIII,

the great empires of the Near East (luckily, this week, that
wasn't for the eleventh-graders; from the point of view of the book, it
was therefore somewhat less important, but that was still no reason
for . . .): Sumerians, Assyrians, Chaldeans, Hittites, Lydians and
Persians,

the achievement of national unity: Cavour, Bismark;

and there was no question of encroaching on the time for next
Wednesday's lunch, since it was his birthday and your mother had insisted that he come and celebrate it with you, blowing out the thirty-
five candles.

He went on with his work on the Odyssey the next morning; he
knew that we had already finished Book V and had reached line 84
of Book VI. He tried to catch up with us, but of course at the end of
the second page he had to give up checking the words in the dictionary and the forms in the grammar, deciding that he would come
back to these passages later in order to examine them with the attention they required, and since the time was passing, since he had
arranged to meet you at two in the restaurant in the Rue des Saints-
Pères, and since it was one already, he confined himself to skimming
the Bérard translation up to line 84 of Book VI:

" . . . Then Nausicaa got into her cart. Her mother gave her, in its
golden flask, some smooth oil to rub upon her skin after bathing,
for herself and her waiting-women . . . "

In order to imagine what our Greek classes were like, the two
mornings of work he had set aside each week to study what his col-

leagues were teaching would be quite inadequate; he would have to devote a good number of his evenings to it as well. As for the other subjects . . .

Back in the Rue du Cardinal-Lemoine with his two children, Monsieur Bonnini was unable to answer his sister-in-law's questions. It was his son who said:

"She was sleeping, we didn't want to wake her; she's not doing well."

Hutter, Wolf and Tannier absent; your uncle reminded your class that there would be a written geography quiz the following Monday on all you had covered so far, asked Jacques Estier to discuss the exploitation of America and the slave trade, asked Jean-Claude Fage to discuss the commercial companies, asked Henri Fage to discuss the corporations.

England at the beginning of the Eighteenth Century, the Puritan revolution, Cromwell's dictatorship.

On Sunday, Alain Mouron went for a hike with the Chamois to the Verrières woods.

Hastily the Renaissance
(da Vinci: project for a battle chariot . . .),
atmospheric circulation
(. . . different stages in the development of a cyclone . . .),
Bonaparte's rise
(. . . Napoléon I as emperor, detail of a painting by Girodet-Trioson),
lunch in the Rue des Canettes.

During the afternoon, Monsieur Bonnini gave his tenth-graders an hour of written work; he knew it was only a question of days for his wife.

The principal interrupted agriculture in Africa. It was the eighth grade's turn to be photographed; the tenth grade's turn came only during the afternoon, so your uncle was able to talk undisturbed about the French watershed; then, since the restaurant in the Rue des Canettes was closed, he went to eat lunch in the Rue Mabillon.

He stopped at a candy store to buy mint drops for your brother Jacques, who was in bed with another cough; he went upstairs to give them to him and replace the three textbooks in his briefcase by three for the afternoon classes.

On Wednesday, he put into his bookcase the Gaffiot Dictionary,

the two volumes of the *Aeneid* (text and translation) in the Guillaume Budé series and the third *Decade* of Livy in the Garnier series;
   lunch in the Rue des Canettes
   during the afternoon, Monsieur Bonnini and his two children were obliged to leave the room where his wife's body was lying.
   On Sunday, your Uncle Pierre was in bed with the grippe that was so prevalent and that had attacked him so virulently on acount of his state of fatigue and tension.
   On All Saints' Day, Alain Mouron, who had gone to lunch with his father at the Davals', in the Rue Servandoni
   (other members of the family were there too; it was a kind of housewarming, but the Baillys were not there, and they were often referred to in the conversation),
   in his cousin's room, beginning to work on a Meccano construction,
   "How boring that stuff is about René and Elizabeth!"
   "What do you think about it all? You were with them in Brittany during the whole month of September."
   "That's funny, Pierre Eller asked me the same question."
   "What do you think of Pierre Eller?"
   "He's very nice, very conscientious."
   "Sure he is, but don't you think he's a little curious?"
   "Curious?"
   "You know, nosy."
   He's curious because he's interested in you, in me, in all of us, in Uncle René . . . "
   "I can't help wondering if it isn't something to do with his uncles; you know, when you have two uncles in the same year, a history-and-geography teacher and a French-Latin-Greek teacher, it has to have some effect on you."
   "Did you ever think of telling what he says to you to Uncle René?"
   "No, of course not, but his two uncles are nearer relations to him than Uncle René is to me."
   "You sure are suspicious!"
   "I come from a Jesuit school."
   "You have a warped character. Pierre Eller's a good guy; we do our homework together and he's a lot more help to me than you are."
   "The three of us could work together."
   "Sure. Pierre would like that."

"That's what I mean, I know he would."

"What are you talking about? Why should he want to spy on us, if that's what you're trying to suggest, why should he tattle on us? Spying would be much more to his advantage in the other direction, if he spied on his uncles; besides, he isn't like that, he's a Scout, he's even the head of his patrol, he's out on a hike right now, in this weather . . ."

"He's a Scout, he's a patrol leader, but he doesn't go to religious instruction."

"So what, neither do I. The sermons of the troop chaplain are enough; I never thought you were so narrow-minded. It must be your Jesuit background."

"Narrow-minded, listen, I'm not as narrow-minded as you are! Besides, if it bothers you so much that I go to Abbé Gollier's classes, you can relax, I won't be going there any more."

"Why? Did he give you a hard time?"

"Suspicious, right away! No, that's not it. I just think it's a waste of time."

"Then you won't have any religious instruction at all! At least I have the chaplain's sermon, like Pierre Eller."

"Don't worry about me, I have my Fathers."

"Oh, you do whatever you want, I'm not going to . . . But as far as Pierre Eller's concerned, I don't . . ."

"All right, he's a good guy, but there's something funny all the same, I'm watching out for him."

"But you're together a lot."

"Sure, we're friends."

"Well, then?"

"We'll see."

On All Souls' Day, your Uncle Pierre went out to lunch with Micheline Pavin, still vacillating.

During the afternoon, Monsieur Bonnini went back to the Boulevard Montparnasse, where he had already been that morning with his children and his sister-in-law; he needed to be alone in the rain, among the mournful, rain-washed crowd.

The written quiz set for October 30 and which the grippe had prevented: the discovery and conquest of America, Philip II, Cromwell,

absent: Michel Daval, Denis Régnier,

Louis XIII, Richelieu, the colonies.

In this game your troop was playing based on the conquest of

America, Alain Mouron belonged to the Cortez side; he would have preferred to be on Montezuma's side.

Monsieur Bonnini stopped talking, began to cry in front of his tenth-graders.

Industrial resources and transportation in Africa

(forests opened up by the exploitation of diamond mines in Ubangi . . .),

the sea and the coasts of France

(a low coast north of Boulogne . . .);

in the Rue du Canivet, your Uncle Pierre left his three textbooks for the morning classes and took those for the afternoon;

lunch in the Rue Mabillon.

Monsieur Bonnini, who had no class on Wednesday, was alone in the apartment in the Rue du Cardinal-Lemoine; his sister-in-law had left during the morning, his two children were at the Sorbonne, where classes had started.

On Sunday, your Uncle Pierre said to Micheline Pavin:

"I've managed to arrange the whole first part of my work by using family connections, but it isn't possible to use such a method for all the students that are left; I'm going slower and slower because of the effort demanded by the subjects my colleagues teach; few teachers, believe me, would be capable of going through the eleventh grade again; I wonder if from now on I'm not going to focus everything on my nephew Pierre, without telling him, of course."

The Mediterranean climate; Alain Mouron was daydreaming over the illustrations:

fallow land in the Languedoc, mulberries, olive trees, cypresses in Provence.

On Tuesday, for the seniors, the evening prayer in *Purgatorio*.

The following Tuesday, written quiz in history:

Richelieu, Mazarin, science at the beginning of the Seventeenth Century,

absent: Gabriel Voss, Claude Armelli,

Versailles.

Monday,

absent: Henri Buret, Paul Coutet, Octave de Joigny,

there would be a test the day after tomorrow,

Rémy Orland questioned on erosion, Louis Pelletier on faults in strata, Denis Régnier on alluvial deposits,

destruction of mountains by frost, wind, water, landslide

(the Grépon needle on the plateau of Mont Blanc . . .);
Tuesday,
The revocation of the Edict of Nantes.

Alain Mouron was thinking about his neighbor, the Protestant Francis Hutter,

dragoon raids, drawing from 1686,

"Under the threat of a musket (an invincible reason) held by a dragoon wearing a saber (a penetrating reason), the heretic, kneeling on the ground, signs his conversion on the drum (evangelical appeal). . . . "

The following Sunday, to Micheline Pavin, who had a little grippe,

"I'm making my nephew tell everything now; he doesn't know about it; but I'll have to stop for a while because of the tests I must correct, the teachers' conferences, everything that comes at the end of this quarter. Do you think it's going to snow?"

Fluvial erosion; Alain Mouron, who was third in geography, couldn't help thinking about the English test the next hour, about the history test the next day, regretting the fact that he had sat in the first row, reviewing the chapter headings:

the end of the Middle Ages, the Renaissance and the Reformation, the discovery and conquest of America, Europe in 1600 . . .

For the seniors, the Italian test.

Then the new year came, during which everything was upset, during which your Uncle Pierre got so sick that he was forced to give up his classes in the third quarter, during which his relations with you and your family deteriorated so badly that he had to give up his room in the Rue du Canivet and take refuge with us, in the maid's room we had on the top floor. During the month of August he was at the hospital again, and Micheline Pavin decided to stay in Paris to be able to take care of him.

He left the hospital early in September; Micheline Pavin served as his nurse until the day she went back to work. We were at Les Étangs; we had asked him to join us there, but he decided to go to Saint-Cornély alone; for months he had abandoned this work, now he had a burning desire to get back to it, to start everything over, and he was hoping that by being where you had spent the month of August in 1954, where Alain Mouron and René Bailly had spent the month of September, he could reconstruct this whole passage of your life, of the lives which he needed for his exploration and his edifice; he left on the sixth from the Gare du Maine.

On the twelfth, after several days of complete rest, he took a long walk along the seashore, he had gone to another village for lunch, he was feeling terribly lonely when a storm came up and there was a cloudburst, he went into the doorway of a chapel to keep from getting soaked, he was afraid of a relapse; if only Micheline Pavin had been with him, if only . . .

He fell asleep. He awakened murmuring:

"I know I won't make it."

"Yes you will," said the curé to whose room they had carried him, "I don't know what you mean, but just try . . ."

"I can see you don't know what I mean . . ."

"Explain it to me."

"It's too complicated, but I'm going to try to go on all the same."

"Do you feel better? Can you walk?"

"Of course I can. I don't know what came over me!"

"The sky has cleared now, look how beautiful it is outside."

Alain Mouron was in Savoie with his father.

Your uncle took the train back to Paris the twenty-seventh; he had neither finals nor entrance examinations to correct this year.

School started again on October 3.

Name, date of birth, former school, parents' profession, address, seat occupied in the classroom on the sheet in front of him,

the baccalaureate examination the following year,

what is general geography, the dimensions and the shape of the globe, the atmosphere, oceans and continents, terrestrial and oceanic relief, the structure of the interior of the globe, the geological epochs . . .

The following Sunday, to Micheline Pavin:

"I've gone back to it, you'll see, it'll all begin again, this time I've really got off to a good start."

▓▓▓▓▓▓▓▓▓▓▓▓▓▓▓▓▓▓▓▓ IN SEPTEMBER 1954, the Huberts left their Savoie village rather early, because the baby was expected at the end of November, and they wanted to be back in Paris in time.

They had already stayed quite late, according to the doctor Madame Hubert had gone to see because there had been a tiny warning: but there was nothing to worry about from now on, everything was developing normally.

The twentieth was Michel Daval's birthday, his fourteenth; he had begged his mother to invite everyone, he was particularly eager because most of his friends were older than he was. Everyone was to come for dinner, and so the afternoon was spent preparing sandwiches. The two Bonnini children, unfortunately, were not the only ones to have left; there would certainly be a smaller crowd than at that girl's party the week before.

The next day, Monsieur Hubert was at the Lycée Taine to proctor the promotion examinations.

On the twenty-sixth, Michel Daval and his sister escorted several friends who were going back to Paris to the bus; they themselves would be leaving in two days; they were almost the only tourists, or rather vacationists, left in the village.

The next day Monsieur Hubert, after the last decisions on the promotion examinations, came in and found his wife lying down, knitting a little sweater.

"We should take advantage of our last free week; eight days from now I'll be in school, most likely with my seniors, I'm taking the senior class this year, Monsieur Le Gagneur has retired, so I'll have more work."

Consequently, every afternoon of this week except Tuesday, of course, they visited the museums, starting with the Louvre on Wednesday.

After having left the Lycée Taine where you had gone with your brothers to pick up the lists of your textbooks for the year, you looked through the one your brother Denis had used last year which you could still use:

The *Anthology of Greek Literature*, the *Sixteenth Century French Authors* . . .

On Saturday, Michel Daval lined up in a bookstore with his mother and sister to buy the last books he still needed:
the *Anthology of Latin Literature,* the *General Geography.*
On Sunday, Monsieur Hubert, sitting beside his young wife who was lying down, her belly mountainous under the quilt (it was rather cool that day), was studying the *Physics Textbook* for his seniors. On the mantelpiece, a photograph of his first wife, in front of which the second was careful to keep a fresh bouquet of flowers.
In the Saint-Hilaire troop headquarters, the leader encouraged you all to work hard at school; the new chaplain came in.
On Tuesday, after dinner, Homer:

"Woe unto me," Bérard translates, "when Zeus against all hope . . . "

(you were picking your way through the pages of the dictionary, seeing the text not as a continuity, but as a succession of words, each of which required an exhausting effort),
Livy:
Hannibal ab Druentia . . . :
Hannibal: Hannibal,
Druentia (?),
dictionary: "*Druentia, Druentiae,* masculine: river of the Narbonnaise: (today the Durance), Livy (XXI, 31, 9)",
so, *ab Druentia*: from the Durance . . .
On Wednesday, since it was the day before a free day, you stayed with your brothers in the dining room, listening to a play on the radio. Your parents were talking in low tones.
"Pierre was quite nervous tonight."
"Did you notice his shirt collar?"
"He should pay more attention to his clothes."
"How can I tell him? I already take care of his laundry, but I can't stand over him while he dresses in the morning . . . "
"The best solution for him, of course, would be if he . . . "
"Yes, that Micheline is an appealing girl."
"We'll have to ask him to bring her some evening, so we can have a more-or-less official introduction, then we can tell the children about it . . . "
"Boys, don't you have any work to do tonight?"
"We're listening!"
"Tomorrow's Thursday."
"And you don't want to get ahead for Friday?"

"It's only the first week . . . "

"Yes, Father, the first week there's not so much . . . "

"Besides, I don't have any classes Friday morning; the whole class goes to the stadium with the gym teacher."

"I go Saturday."

"Which stadium?"

"La Croix-de-Berny."

"We go there too."

"What about you, Jacques?"

"I went this morning."

"Which stadium?"

"La Croix-de-Berny."

"Are you through?"

"What?"

"Don't say 'what' like that."

"Oh . . . "

"I thought you wanted to listen to the play."

"We do . . . "

"Then keep still. And what time's that play over? Denis, you have the paper."

"It's over at five to ten."

"Well, you can stay till the end, but I want you in bed as soon as it's over!"

Thursday afternoon, Monsieur Hubert left his wife asleep to meet an old school friend who had just arrived in Paris; they went to a café in the Place de la Sorbonne.

We were both visiting cousins; I was in the living room with the grownups, you with your brothers, my children and my other nieces and nephews, you were playing parcheesi around the dining-room table.

It was almost time for tea; we asked you to stop the game; we had to lay the cloth, arrange the cups. You walked one after the other in front of the grownups.

"How he's grown!"

"What grade is he in now?"

"Already!"

"Almost time for finals . . . "

"And what do you want to do afterwards? Any ideas yet?"

"He has plenty of time."

"It goes so fast!"

"I remember his baptism."

"It was just after we were married."

"You were enormous, you could scarcely drag yourself to the church."

"Which do you like best, literature or science?"

"Except for his Meccano set . . . "

"He'll be an engineer . . . "

On Friday, Monsieur Hubert had his first laboratory session with his seniors; anticipating his lessons, he made them verify the law of falling bodies with General Morin's machine.

You went back to the Rue du Canivet where you had your tea alone, ahead of your brothers who came home only an hour later, and you took advantage of Denis' absence to look through his drawer and examine his new textbooks, particularly his *Eighteenth and Nineteenth Century French Authors*.

On Saturday night, while Denis was doing his assignment for Monsieur Bailly too;

"Banquo:
What, can the devil speak true? . . . "

monopolizing the dictionary, you had to wait to do yours:

"Brutus:
What means this shouting? . . . "

looking through your textbook

(Doctor Faustus, from a painting by Jean-Paul Laurens; a 1631 woodcut of Faustus and Mephistopheles, after Marlowe's *Faustus*; the room where Shakespeare was born);

"You be through soon?"

"Yes, just a minute; don't you have something else to do?"

(portrait of Shakespeare; portrait of Caesar; the death of Caesar, after the painting by Rochegrosse; Hamlet and Ophelia, from a drawing by Dante Gabriel Rossetti);

"What are you translating, *Hamlet*?"

"No, *Macbeth*."

"What's it about?"

"It takes place in Scotland. There are witches in it."

"Is it hard?"

"Of course it's hard. Shakespeare's always hard."

(a performance of *Hamlet* in Berlin in 1780; the witches in *Macbeth*, after a painting by H. Fuseli; Lady Macbeth, after a painting by Kaulbach);

"What did you translate last year?"

"*Julius Caesar* . . . "

"You too?"

"Everyone does."

"Is it hard?"

"Much less hard; let me do my work, if you want me to give you the dictionary"

(title page of Shakespeare's *Sonnets*, 1609; Ben Jonson, after the portrait by Gerard Honthorst . . .)

"There I'm through."

"Can't you help me?"

"What do you mean, help you?"

"If you could tell me . . . "

"Caesar gets himself killed by Brutus, who was his adopted son. Those Romans . . . "

"No, I need more details."

"I've forgotten it, you think I don't have anything else to worry about . . . ?"

"But if you translated it last year, there must be parts you remember."

"Let me look at it a minute."

"*Act One, Scene One, Rome, a street.*"

"You understand what that means? All right, go on."

"*Flavius and Marullus rebuke Roman artisans for rejoicing in Caesar's triumph over Pompey* . . . "

"What an accent, poor Pierre! How do you expect me to understand you?"

"Let me hear you read it!"

"*Flavius and Marullus* . . . "

"Who are they?"

"I don't know, two minor characters . . . "

"Don't you know anything about them?"

"It doesn't matter, it isn't even in the play, it's just a stage direction, let's go on."

"Still you have to be able to read it to understand what comes after . . . "

Flavius and Marullus rebuke; you have to know what rebuke means . . . "

"Don't you know?"

"I've forgotten; you'll see, next year, how much you forget. Oh here it is—reprimand. Flavius and Marullus reprimand Roman artisans because they're rejoicing over Caesar's victory over Pompey; you see, that's not hard . . . "

"Yes, but that's only the résumé, wait till you get to the speeches . . . "

"When we get to the speeches, you figure it out by yourself, you have to do some work . . . Caesar's victory over Pompey, that's because he's afraid, I mean everyone's afraid Caesar's going to wipe out the Roman Republic; you understand?"

"More or less, go on . . . "

"Listen, if you didn't understand that, I can't help you; all right, I'm going on: *Scene Two, a public place, the festival of the Lupercalia is being celebrated* . . . "

"What's the *Lupercalia*?"

"The *Lupercalia*? You've heard of the *Lupercalia*, haven't you?"

"No."

"It's a festival."

"Yes, I got that, but what kind of festival?"

"It's hard to explain; what do you need to know details like that for?"

"In other words, you don't have the vaguest idea. Well, I want to know."

"All it'll say in the English dictionary is *Lupercalia*."

"Well, I'm going to look it up in the French dictionary."

"You'll be at it until midnight if you start like this."

"*Lupercalia*: annual festival celebrated on February fifteenth in Rome in honor of the god Lupercus (surname of the god Faunus): the Lupercalia were licentious festivals. What does that mean, licentious?"

"You see, a lot of good that did you! And you don't know what licentious means? Well, you can look that one up too. Listen, I'll translate down to the end of the italics, and after that you go on by yourself . . . "

"Wait a minute! Here it is: *licentious*: excessive, immoderate: *licentious* behavior; contrary to decency: *licentious* verses."

309

"So they're celebrating the Lupercalia, an indecent festival; the multitude salutes Caesar with acclamation. *Flourish:* that means a fanfare; and *shout:* that means cheers; now Brutus speaks, you go on by yourself."

Once Denis left the room, you went to get the Latin dictionary.

"*Luperca:* name of an ancient Roman divinity, perhaps the she-wolf . . .

Lupercal: grotto under the Palatine Hill, consecrated to Pan by Evander, where according to legend the she-wolf nourished Romulus and Remus . . .

Lupercalia: Roman festivals in honor of Lupercus or Pan . . . "

If you dared, you would ask Monsieur Bailly or me for details about the Lupercalia.

You wouldn't dare; you went back to the English text:

"*Brutus:*
What means this shouting? . . . "

In your bed, on Sunday night, while Denis was working at his desk, the events of the day, the game, the speeches, the return,

the classes the next day: Ulysses swims, he's at the mouth of a river, he calls for help, Poseidon, Hannibal crossing the Alps, Clément Marot, Rabelais, lunch, drawing, geography, celebration of the feast of Lupercalia, Brutus speaks to Cassius and Cassius tells him that Caesar was swimming and about to drown, and that he shouted to him:

"Help me, Cassius, or I sink! . . . "

and this man, Cassius said, this man is now become a god . . .

Finish copying the most remarkable day of your vacation, then since your mother had whispered to you that because of your birthday you wouldn't have much time, if for instance your uncle invited you out,

"Before or after dinner?"

"I don't know. He'll tell you himself; he'll be here for lunch."

"If it's before, I'll have time to work."

"No, you won't have time."

"Then it's for after, we'll go to the movies!"

"I don't know a thing about it."

"Will he really?"

You tried to continue your reading of Homer beyond line 473:

"Of wild beasts I become the food and prey ... ",

but you were already so bogged down . . .

You scarcely had time to prepare the rest of *Julius Caesar* (Monsieur Bailly was not one of the family).

Tomorrow you would be fifteen; tomorrow you would have money, like Denis, and from now on you would have an allowance every month, like Denis.

During the night, Alain Mouron started dreaming: he was swimming off the beach at Saint-Cornély; the sea was full of dead leaves that were sticking to him; Michel Daval was on the shore and he shouted to him:

"Help me, Michel, or I sink";

then the waves grew thicker; he realized that he had a chamois pelt, the hands, feet and body of a boy, but all covered with brown hair and extremely hard nails, and he knew that he no longer had a boy's face, but a chamois' muzzle with two little horns; the shore was very steep, but he didn't have the slightest difficulty climbing up the rocks; there were grottoes here and there, he heard tigers roaring, bisons lowing, and the trees were shaken by the enormous squirrels running through them, with teeth gleaming like chisels.

He was very surpised not to meet Michel Daval; he was tired, but he was afraid of all these wild beasts, and he was looking for a safe hiding place; in the hollow of a valley he found a big pile of dead leaves and tunneled into it; inside, he found a little dry room with a table and books; above this table the moonlight came in through an oval window with a pane of glass against which dead leaves were pasted. Someone knocked at this pane; it was the postman, it was Michel Daval with a postman's cap, he was bringing a letter; Alain made him a sign to come in, but he didn't hear, he didn't even recognize Alain, he kept knocking, knocking, he held up the letter; Alain didn't know what to do, he didn't know where the door was any more; in despair Michel tore open the envelope, unfolded the letter and pasted it against the wet pane, then he ran away, it was just in time, the bisons and the tigers were beginning to chase him, he had to hurry up and read, the lines of writing were already starting

311

to run, some passages were hidden by the dead leaves; it was a letter from his father:

MY DEAR ALAIN,
I'm not sure I understand why you wanted to become a chamois, it would have been better for you to have turned yourself into a tiger or a bison, even a squirrel; the chamois have difficulty swimming, especially during storms, and at night, when they sleep, they are in danger of being eaten up; I hope you've found a good pile of dead leaves to settle in and that you can join me soon in Paris. Don't forget that to become a true chamois you must learn Greek, without which a man may be ashamed to call himself a scholar. . . . "

A tremendous gust of wind carried off the pane of glass along with the letter, Alain tried to catch it.

" . . . So bloody a butchery, as upon savage beasts; and so universal as fire or sword could ever attain unto",

at the back of the classroom, in the corner, next to Georges Tannier, Frédéric Wolf is carving his name,

"having purposely preserved no more than so many miserable bond-slaves, as they deemed might suffice for the digging, working and service of their mines."

I awakened around four, and I couldn't fall back to sleep, thinking about the two of you, you and your Uncle Pierre, wondering what had occurred at that dinner you had told me about, if your uncle had started writing that book he had mentioned to us, if his invitation to you had been inspired by this project.

After having eaten dinner late and alone in an expensive little restaurant near the Champs-Élysées, your Uncle Pierre telephoned from a café to that neighbor of Micheline's whose number she had given him in case . . . ; she was out.

He walked back to Saint-Germain-des-Prés; it was a mild evening and the sidewalk cafés were full. He called back at eleven-thirty; the neighbor was there, but Micheline hadn't come in yet.

At midnight, he wondered if it was too late to call, if she would

312

be annoyed with him for disturbing her, and for disturbing her neighbor in the middle of the night for the third time. He hesitated for a long time, smoking cigarettes, drinking beers, reading "The Game of Silence" in *Fiction*, furious with himself and with her, for it would have been better to spend the evening on his book instead of wasting the time so stupidly . . .

At twelve-thirty, unable to stand it any longer, he went to the telephone booth of the café to call her one last time, stumbling on the way.

"Hello?"

"I'm sorry to disturb you again, I wanted to know if Mademoiselle Pavin has come in."

"As a matter of fact, I think I heard her."

"Could I speak to her."

"She must be in bed by now."

"I'm terribly sorry, I hope I haven't got you up, I must apologize, but I was worried, I was supposed to see her . . . "

"That's all right, I don't mind, I'll go knock at her door, but could you tell me who's calling . . . "

"Pierre Vernier."

"Who?"

"Pierre Vernier, just tell her the schoolteacher . . . "

"Hold on."

"I don't know how to thank you, I'll just take a moment . . . "

There was no one on the other end.

"Hello?"

"It's Pierre Venier."

"I thought it was you, Pierre, but what's the matter?"

"Have you been home long?"

"Not long, I came in at midnight, I was just getting into bed . . . "

"Oh, I'm terribly sorry, I've tried to call you several times tonight . . . "

"Is something wrong, Pierre?"

"No, no, everything's fine, please don't be angry with me for disturbing you at this hour."

"Of course not, it's all right. Have you begun working on your book?"

"Yes, I've begun."

"Did you teach your class on the discovery of America?"

"Yes, yes I did."

"Did you read them the passages from Marco Polo and Montaigne?"

"Yes."

"Were they interested?"

"I think so."

"Did you have dinner with your nephew?"

"Yes."

"And did you tell him about it?"

"As much as I . . . "

"And what did he think?"

"He was delighted, delighted with dinner, with the movies, with this new game . . . "

"Then everything worked out according to your plans, you ought to be pleased."

"Yes."

"Then what is it, Pierre, tell me, you must have something to tell me if you called at this hour of the night. You aren't calling from your sister's?"

"Oh, no. I'm in a café, I've been hanging around all evening, ever since we were supposed to meet."

"Meet—tonight?"

"Didn't you tell me last Monday . . . "

"Look, Pierre, what's got into you? I told you last Monday that I had to have dinner with my boss tonight, but that it wasn't absolutely definite. That was when you suggested meeting me in the café on the Champs-Élysées if the dinner fell through, in which case I would have called you at your sister's . . . But your mind's so deep in Marco Polo, Cathay, Mexico . . . "

"Yes, I'm sorry, I remember now, you told me you'd call . . . "

"If I hadn't had this dinner, I would have asked you to call me later, tomorrow at my office, for instance, if I hadn't reached you today so we could make a date . . . "

"Because I, you see, there were so many things happening these last two days . . . I wanted to talk to you so badly, I felt that if I took any longer I couldn't go on, couldn't go on in the same way; I mixed up what you told me; I'll have to be careful from now on, and I'll have to be careful in my classes too, I must explain it to you, but not to-night, of course, it's too late, it would take too long, and besides it

314

wouldn't be possible on the telephone, particularly this telephone since . . . I'm sorry, please tell your neigh . . . "

"Well, when will we be seeing each other?"

"We could have lunch together Sunday."

"Or dinner before?"

"No, not before, I'd better . . . I have to clear things up first, I have to get off to a good start, you know; I've already wasted this evening so stupidly; afterwards, it won't matter any more, because I'll be on the right track, it will go on of its own accord, but from now . . . "

"All right, Sunday, we'll spend the day together Sunday."

"We'll have lunch together . . . "

"Will you ask your nephew?"

"For lunch? Oh, he can't . . . "

"Then after lunch, I'm curious to see your new secret agent . . . "

"I'll try . . . "

"Go to sleep now; I'm half dead myself. All right, be good now and go to bed."

"Please forgive me."

"Of course, good night, see you Sunday."

She hung up and your uncle realized, as he hung up too, that he would have to call her back the next day because they hadn't arranged either the time or the place of their next meeting.

He went home to the Rue du Canivet, staggering as he walked; crossing the Place Saint-Sulpice he bumped into a bench and fell down; he pulled himself to his feet with difficulty; a policeman came over, gave him a hard look, decided he was harmless, turned around and walked back to his station, and your uncle said to himself:

"If Micheline saw me, if Pierre saw me, if my students, if my colleagues saw me . . . "

When your brother Denis left the bathroom, you filled the tub again and stretched lazily in the water, making your toes stick out until they were reflected on the gently shifting surface, then you heard the handle of the locked door turn; it was Jacques.

"Hey, when'll you be through soaking yourself in there?"

"Wait a while, I need time to get clean."

That evening, your uncle's head was still too heavy to get back to his work after dinner; he went out for a walk, passing through the Rue du Pré-aux-Clercs, carefully examining the outside of my building, then read *Fiction* in bed, unable to fall asleep:

"Behind the bars, the naked man was fast asleep; in the next cage, a bear was rolling on its back and with its eyes half closed was watching the rising sun; not far away a jackal . . . "

Friday morning, in the gym, Monsieur Moret was waiting for your class, shouting at the late-comers:

"Line up so I can count you off, columns of five, all right there, line up, that makes twenty-eight, there are supposed to be thirty-one of you, three missing. It's already nine-fifteen, we have to catch the train at nine-thirty, I'll call the roll when we get to the stadium. Break ranks! Now no noise and no rough stuff on the way to the Gare du Luxembourg; everyone buys a round trip ticket for La Croix-de-Berny."

The grass in the stadium was shiny with dew; there were patches of mud in places; the sky was gray; you took off your coats and jackets; some of you put on shorts and gym shoes; but not you; during roll call it began to drizzle.

That evening, your uncle wrote almost without stopping until eleven.

On Saturday, after lunch, you put in your briefcase, along with your *Anthology of English Literature*, your *History* and *Chemistry Textbooks* and the issue of *Fiction* Michel Daval had asked you to give back to him this morning.

Henri IV and the Edict of Nantes; Denis Régnier, whose neighbor was absent, was examining Rémy Orland's stamp notebook.

The rise of Napoléon III, the rebuilding of Paris.

At five, your uncle went to telephone from a café.

"Micheline Pavin?"

"Yes."

"Pierre Vernier."

"What's new?"

"Have you forgiven me for my Wednesday-night call?"

"There was nothing to forgive . . . "

"Your neighbor . . . "

"He's very understanding."

"Have you forgiven me for not having called you since?"

"Don't be silly. We're seeing each other tomorrow, aren't we?"

"Of course, but we had forgotten to say where and when. I was in such a state . . . "

"Have you been drinking a lot since . . . ?"

"Oh no, I've been good; Thursday night I was a little tired, I went to sleep right away; but yesterday I made up for it."

"Drinking?"

"No, working!"

"I think that's better."

"I don't drink very often, you know . . . "

"I get drunk too, and it's certainly much worse for a woman. You'll find me quite indulgent, but not very encouraging."

"How about one o'clock at the Royal-Saint-Germain? Afterwards we could go to the restaurant in the Rue des Saints-Pères for lunch; I'll tell my nephew Pierre to meet us there around four. We'll have something to drink, but not too much; you'll supervise."

"We'll supervise each other, that's the best way; at one, you said?"

"Yes, one o'clock, I can't get there before, I'll explain, I've made myself a schedule so I can keep everything going, and Sunday morning's reserved for studying my colleagues' textbooks, I've bought them all, or just about . . . "

"All right, explain later; tomorrow at one, at the Royal, I'll be there."

After lunch on Sunday, your brothers were discussing which film they were going to; they expected to take you with them and didn't believe you when you told them the programs of the neighborhood theaters didn't interest you; you tried to make your work into an excuse, your English translation for the next day, your Latin translation for Tuesday, and they were almost scandalized by your remarks:

"No, you're kidding! You think I don't have more work than you do? If you don't want to come with us, just say so! If you want to go with someone else, we won't stop you, will we, Jacques?"

"Of course not!"

"Well, have you decided?" your father asked, just finishing his coffee.

"Yes, we're going to the Bonaparte, Jacques and me, but Pierre doesn't want to come."

"Too bad for him."

"Listen, Pierre," your mother said, "you're not going to stay in the house all day reading one of your stupid magazines?"

"I won't stay here all day."

"I thought you weren't coming on account of your work."

317

"Pierre, you'll work a lot better if you get out a little, and in weather like this . . . "

"I'll work when they do, but I have an appointment with a friend."

"That's different, someone from school."

"Yes."

"He lives around here?"

"In Saint-Germain-des-Prés."

"But why didn't you say so in the first place?"

"Because your questions make me sick! I don't have to go to the movies if I don't want to!"

"Don't get so mad, Pierre, what's the matter with you?"

"Listen if it's being patrol leader that's making you so touchy, you better give it up!"

"All right, Denis, you shut up. God, how can anyone be so dumb!"

"Boys, are you through bickering? What time does the movie go on?"

"At two."

"All right, get going! And what time's your appointment with your friend?"

"At four."

"Four exactly?"

"Yes, he told me not to be late."

"Well why don't you see most of the movie with your brothers?"

"I hate leaving before the end."

"You certainly are edgy today—why don't you go to your room and try and find something intelligent to do!"

Denis Régnier put in his duplicate notebook the stamps from Lebanon his father had just given him.

Your uncle congratulated you when he saw you come into the restaurant:

"It's good to be prompt."

You didn't dare look at Micheline Pavin, who asked you all kinds of questions. Your uncle was smiling. He asked you what you'd like to do: have tea, go to the movies?

"Oh, there's a movie at the Bonaparte I'd like to see."

"What's it called?"

"Treasure of the Sierra Madre. An American movie."

"What time does it start?"

"I think at four-thirty."

"It won't be over before seven. Your parents will be worried about you, won't they? When did you tell them you'd be back?"

"I didn't."

"And your work—is it all done?"

"Oh, Pierre, it's Sunday, it's a vacation for you, for him, and for me too; forget you're a schoolteacher for once."

"His teacher!"

"Forget it!"

"It's just that I don't want . . . "

"I know, I know, but let him decide; he's old enough to know; you've made him your collaborator, you owe him that much confidence . . . "

"Are you sure it's a good movie?"

"I don't know if you'll like it, but I will, I've heard a lot about it."

"From whom?"

"Classmates."

"All right, you're dying to see it, so don't worry about us. Let's go!"

He drew you close to him and murmured in your ear:

"Don't tell your brothers!"

"Can't tell them I saw *The Treasure of the Sierra Madre*?"

"Oh, if you want to! But don't tell them it was with us."

"And not my parents either?"

"No, better not; it's a secret between us, you understand, between the three of us."

"All right. Don't worry. I said I was going to see a school friend."

So that the next day you were lucky not to be called on, for you hadn't opened your Greek book to prepare:

"*Thou art asleep, Nausicaa . . . *"

nor the Latin book to prepare Livy.

After dinner, the temple of Luxor, the Sphinx, the Pyramids at Giza . . . ,

the mines of Potosi, the planter's house in the Antilles, the plan of the Saint-Germain market,

making maple sugar, Arvida, the aluminum city deep in the Province of Québec.

When I came into the class, you were already sitting at your desk, your *Anthology of Greek Literature* open in front of you, page 21. Before explaining Homer's text starting:

319

"But Aurora, mounting upon her throne . . . ",

I assigned you your first Greek translation of the year, a passage from Plutarch's life of Caesar. During Nausicaa's request to her father, Alcinous:

"Dear father, won't you let me have the high-wheeled cart? I'd like to take our washing down . . . ",

you reread your Latin translation that you had done the night before with Alain Mouron:

"The pillage of Sicily, by Verrès:
I come now to this man's passion, as he himself calls it, his disease and his madness, as his friends call it, his plundering, as the Sicilians call it . . . "*,

to correct some mistakes in spelling before handing it in to me the next hour, during which I questioned you about Virgil's lines beginning:

"Quam tu urbem, soror, hanc cernes . . . "
(What city, my sister, will you see this one become).

That night, at Micheline Pavin's:
"What a day! You can't imagine how tired six hours of class can make you."
"Is your work coming along?"
"Since Sunday? How could it? Yesterday morning I prepared my afternoon classes; I spent all evening preparing today's; coming home this afternoon I had just time enough to introduce three new characters, and then my nephew came; he had a lot to tell me."
"And your colleagues' textbooks, are you learning your lessons properly?"
"Oh, that's not coming along well at all—I haven't done a thing since Sunday, of course, that was to be expected; but according to the schedule I've made for myself, I'm afraid I was terribly optimistic on that score; I've just glanced at the *Sixteenth Century French Authors* and the *Anthology of Greek Literature*, only what they're reading right now: Rabelais, Homer; I'll have to get at it seriously later on."
"You won't be able to read anything else?"

"Not for a while, no; I won't read anything except what the students have in their hands; that is, their textbooks and the magazines they lend each other; last week I read a science-fiction magazine I saw them passing around the class."

"But since you're having the teachers in it too, you'll have to do all their reading too."

"Yes, the textbooks they use in the other class first; I'll do it gradually, it's a tremendous amount . . . "

"And what they're reading outside of class too—for relaxation or for their work, a thesis, an article, or for . . . "

"In most cases I'll have to make it up, to imagine reading for them, and that will come in its place . . . "

"And the newspapers, have you thought about the newspapers?"

"For the moment, I'm dealing with only the most urgent things, and I have to hold myself down at the start; you see, things keep getting in the way, for instance, tomorrow I won't be able to keep to my schedule because I have to go to the dentist first, then because it's my birthday, I don't know if I told you, but tomorrow I'll be thirty-five and I think they've been thirty-five years badly spent, I think it's time, high time I did something about it; well, tomorrow I have to have lunch at my sister's with my nephews; we set great store by such traditions in the Rue du Canivet, I'll have to blow out the thirty-five candles, and tomorrow night my colleague Jouret, the French-Latin-Greek teacher, invited me to dinner so nicely I couldn't refuse; that's Pierre Eller's other uncle: there may be candles to blow out there too, because of the children, you know, they enjoy it; I must introduce you to him, he'll be pleased to meet you; you see that I'm well provided with family."

"So tomorrow you'll be thirty-five and you won't have a minute for me to offer you thirty-five little flames to blow out?"

"We'll see each other Friday."

"Yes, but that'll be a little late. Still, I'll try to give you a celebration too."

"And . . . "

"What?"

"I . . . No . . . "

"Well, my birthday's next month; I'll be twenty-eight and I'm beginning to feel that mine have been years pretty badly spent too . . . "

"What day of the month?"

"The seventeenth."

"It's a Wednesday. I'll put it down."

"You must be dying of hunger. We'll eat right away."

While Henri Buret and then his neighbor Robert Spencer were translating the rest of Hannibal crossing the Alps for me, on the other side of the classroom you were asking Michel Daval if he had finished his math homework.

"Sure, it was easy!"

"Then you're lucky."

"Was there something you didn't get?"

"Oh, no, I got it all, only . . . "

I rapped the ruler on my desk and looked at you both.

"Go on, Spencer."

You put away your homework, but you took it out again during the next hour, while we were reading the second preface to *Britannicus*:

"Of all my tragedies this is the one of which I can say that I labored the most upon it . . . "

because you hadn't completed the operation: $-39 + 65 - 26$ over -13, having kept it for the end and forgotten it when you went to bed. So you scribbled on the narrow margins of your edition of the tragedy: $-39 + 65 = 24$, $24 - 26 = -2$, -2 over $-13 =$

(minus divided by minus gives plus, $2/13$, plus $2/13$, no need to put the plus sign, so)

$2/13$.

You copied this out onto your math homework, slipped it under your notebook and then quickly reread everything we had just finished discussing.

Gabriel Voss, with an odd Northern accent:

"Britannicus' age was so well known that it was not possible for me to represent him as other than a young prince of great valor, strong feelings and frankness, the ordinary qualities of a young man. He was fifteen . . . "

Fifteen . . . , strong feelings . . .

"Daval, when will you be fifteen?"

"I was fourteen in September."

You began thinking about Micheline Pavin.

The thirty-five candles for your Uncle Pierre, the evening at our house; I asked him if he had started that work we had discussed; he described Micheline Pavin to me, and I told him how pleased I would be if he would bring her to meet us. We agreed on the following Tuesday.

The next day, after dinner, you told your parents that you had to go see one of your classmates before going to the dentist, and you went to the restaurant in the Rue des Saints-Pères where your Uncle Pierre was expecting you.

Denis Régnier, instead of pasting into his album the stamps he had acquired during the week, was detaching from the pages certain stamps he used to value the most, in order to put them into his duplicate notebook.

The written sheets, on your Uncle Pierre's desk, already formed a considerable pile.

The USSR, nature and man,

glacial landscape in the Caucasus, sports festival in Red Square, Cromwell,

you were thinking about the chemistry lesson that was coming next, about the one from last week on which you might be questioned:

atomic theory, molecular hypothesis . . . ,

Oliver Cromwell by Walker (National Gallery, London), in armor, holding a staff . . .

On Sunday, Monsieur Bailly told Claire about the key.

On Monday, after lunch, you reviewed your geography:

climate, temperature, isotherms, influence of altitude,

. . . accumulation of air in the tropics, the wind, pressure zones . . .

Hubert Jourdan was asking Jean-Claude Fage to pass Denis Régnier, by the intermediary of Rémy Orland, a scrap of paper on which he had written:

"If you've finished Galaxie, would you please give it back",

and on which Denis Régnier answered:

"Not finished yet, I'll give it back to you tomorrow afternoon or the day after",

before sending it back to him through Jean-Pierre Cormier.

"Cassius:
But soft, I pray you. What, did Caesar swound?
Casca:

He fell down in the market place, and foamed at mouth, and was speechless . . . "

then, instead of going straight back to the Rue du Canivet, you accompanied Denis Régnier to the Rue du Cardinal-Lemoine, you asked him about his parents, his sister, his stamps, his vacation, and you didn't get home for lunch until almost one, which earned you some sarcastic remarks from your brothers and a brief scolding from your father.

Your Uncle Pierre called for Micheline Pavin as she left her office; they came to dinner at our house. Your Aunt Rose asked Micheline:

"Do you know Pierre's family?"

"I met his sister once, and his nephew Pierre, but never his brother-in-law or his other two nephews."

"You will, you will, no need to rush things . . . "

"And your work?"

"It's coming along, I already have a huge pile of manuscript, but I'm going slower and slower because there are so many things I have to learn . . . "

"Here are our children, Mademoiselle: Gérard, the oldest, who's in the ninth grade and is one of Pierre's pupils too, Lucie, who's in the eighth, and the two youngsters, Claude and François, in sixth and fourth grades . . . "

After making sure the issue of Galaxie reached Hubert Jourdan, Denis Régnier

(the seasonal distribution of precipitation . . .)

began looking at the illustrations of the last chapters of your textbook, the ones he had not been able to study because of his illness last year:

a symbol of the new European organization, the train car EUROP, the new Franco-Italian border at the Col du Petit-Saint-Bernard, the Italo-Swiss border near Lugano, the Spanish border at Hendaye, a frontier marker near Basel . . .

From three to four on Thursday, your uncle worked on his project in order to make up, he said, for the hour lost at the dentist's the day before.

On the thirty-first, in the rainy woods, with the other patrol leaders and the seconds-in-command from the Saint-Hilaire troop . . .

On All Saints' Day, Monsieur Bailly took his children to the Montparnasse cemetery.

On All Souls' Day, Denis Régnier went with his mother and his sister to the Père-Lachaise cemetery.

On Wednesday your uncle, recovered, went back to the lycée, the maritime peoples: Cretans, Phoenicians, early Greeks . . .

And you, also recovered, went back to school the following Saturday, and you had to take the written history quiz like the rest, since it had already been announced for the preceding Saturday and hadn't been given then on account of your uncle's grippe:

the discovery of America, Philip II, Cromwell,

lesson on Louis XIII: Marie de Médicis and her foster sister, Léonora Galigaï, the fowler Albert de Luynes, the murder of Concini, his wife, Léonora, burned as a witch . . .

and on Richelieu: the proscription of duels, the siege of La Rochelle, Samuel Champlain in Canada, sugar cane in the Antilles, the slave trade, the spice trade . . .

On Sunday, the whole Bailly family went to visit the Davals' new apartment.

On Monday, Denis Régnier, in bed since the Saturday before, grippe again, got up for lunch but had to go back to bed because of a rise in temperature.

"Caesar, to the soothsayer:
The ides of March are come.
Soothsayer:
Aye, Caesar, but not gone . . . ";

it was Hubert Jourdan whom you accompanied to his métro stop, then, passing a newspaper kiosk, you bought the November issue of Fiction.

Your Uncle Pierre went to call for Micheline Pavin outside her office and brought her to your apartment for dinner; it was more or less her official introduction to the family.

Denis Regnier, still in bed, found great solace in the notion that he had just missed an hour of gym and that he was at this moment avoiding an hour of geography.

On Thursday, your uncle continued, in Sixteenth Century French Authors, with the study and annotation of the selections we had discussed:

"How Gargantua was so disciplined by Ponocrates that he did not waste an Hour of the Day, The Rules according to which the Thélèmites lived, Why the Plant is called Pantagruelion, and something about its marvellous properties. . . . "

On Sunday, in the Meudon woods with your patrol . . .

On Monday, Monsieur Bailly unfairly kept your brother Jacques after school.

On Tuesday Denis Régnier returned to school;

painting in the Seventeenth Century: two descents from the cross, an anatomy lesson, Jesus curing the sick (the famous hundred-florin piece), the Wyck mill, the witch, the smoker, the lacemaker . . .

On Wednesday, after having asked questions about the *Iliad* and the *Odyssey*,

the Greek city-state, Greek colonization, Ionia, Sicily . . .

And the following Tuesday, Gabriel Voss on Mazarin, Frédéric Wolf on the Fronde, Gilbert Zola on the Peace of the Pyrénées,

absent: André Knorr, François Nathan, Bruno Verger,

lesson: Europe in 1660.

And the following Tuesday, the thirtieth, after the written quiz:

Richelieu, Mazarin, science in the early Seventeenth Century,

while he was beginning to tell you about Versailles, you decided:

"it's impossible, my classmates are beginning to be suspicious of me, but I can't give him away, I have to go on helping him",

and you made another private vow of loyalty;

and the following Monday,

streams, floods,

you were thinking about Micheline Pavin, you were drawing clumsy women's bodies in the margins of your textbook, and you wanted to ask him:

"But why aren't you engaged? Don't you want to marry her?"

On Tuesday, Monsieur Bailly told his seniors:

"Next week there will be a test",

and he made them translate several stanzas of the last part of *The Rime of the Ancient Mariner*,

Coleridge's marginal gloss:

"And ever anon throughout his future life an agony constraineth him to travel from land to land",

the line:

"I pass like night, from land to land";

and on Wednesday, your uncle gave you three subjects on your geography test:
the measurement of time, the representation of the earth, the Mediterranean climate;
on Sunday with your patrol in the Saint-Cloud woods . . . ; and on Wednesday the fifteenth, your uncle made his seventh-graders take their history test:
Egypt, the Greek religion, the wars of the Medes and the Persians; on Tuesday the twenty-first, he handed back your tests: Alain Mouron was first, André Knorr second, Hubert Jourdan third, Georges Tannier fourth, Michel Daval fifth, and you were only twelfth.

In January, he had lost weight, his face had grown pale, his shoulders were hunched and his eyes had a dark and painful gleam in them; he avoided looking at you.

The roll call in an extraordinarily weary voice; it was very cold; five absentees: Alain Mouron and Francis Hutter, so that the first bench near the window was empty; Michel Daval, so that you were alone on your bench, Denis Régnier and Philippe Guillaume, so that it made a kind of void around him and around you.

Very slowly he questioned the boys at the other end of the classroom, near the wall of the corridor, Frédéric Wolf, Georges Tannier, Gilbert Zola, then, very slowly, very softly, as if he had grown several years older over the Christmas vacation, he told you about the last years of Louis XIV, about the great winter . . .

On Wednesday, September 14, 1955, your Uncle Pierre, in bed, was thinking about the letter he had just received from me. Yes, no doubt, it would be best to adopt this solution, staying at his sister's was no longer feasible on account of you, on account of that terrible conversation that had taken place between the two of you, about which his parents had not been able to obtain any explanations from you or from him. He stood up, went to his desk and wrote me:

DEAR HENRI JOURET,
I was deeply touched by your letter, I had intended to leave this apartment in any case; I have taken no meals here for several months, since January, in fact. It is above all the consideration of my nephew Pierre that forces me to take this

step; I have led him into too dangerous an adventure, and he has had to reject me in order to maintain his normal relationships with his classmates and with his brothers. That is natural, that is my fault, that changes nothing, it is for him that I have done everything, it is all for him, you know that, no doubt there was no way of avoiding this for him; at least let him benefit by it, let me conclude what I have undertaken; let this break, this rupture which he has suffered, not be in vain, for I think I shall die of it . . .

I can confide this only to you: something collapsed that day, and since then I have been sinking, every day; I am sinking, I have the feeling I spread devastation about me, and yet sometimes how much hope too . . .

I admit that I don't know where to turn next; the obsession which still pursues me has kept me from concluding my search for a new apartment; if that room you mention in the Rue du Pré-aux-Clercs is free and if it is no trouble to you, I shall accept it with great pleasure. You will have brought me more comfort than you can believe.

I come to you like a beggar.

I believe I remember that today is your birthday, I wish you a good year, and many long and happy years to come.

My warm regards to Rose and to all the children.

Yours,
PIERRE VERNIER

A week later, he was writing to Micheline Pavin:

How much I miss you! From the start, I have asked you to forgive me, and you must go on forgiving me; I have the impression we are on opposite banks of a river that is widening, that has grown monstrously wider already; but thanks to the kindness of my colleague Jouret, the question of my lodging in Paris this winter is settled at last. I can now go on with everything, like last year, save with regard to Pierre, of course; I shall have to avoid walking in the neighborhood of the Place Saint-Sulpice, except at night, in secret; it will take more than a year for him to recover from this wound, this thunderbolt that has fallen on him, and for him to accept me again. For a long time I supposed that it was less serious, that things would be all right, and then . . .

This stay at Saint-Cornély will have done me good. Micheline, I would have liked to offer you a work, to offer you a work and a life, to offer myself to you as a husband, as you expected me to do, as you have continued to expect with a patience that confounds me, but I can no longer offer myself to you now, save as an invalid . . .

When shall I be through with it, Micheline, when will this tremendous obstacle be surmounted, this murderous obstacle, this work covered with blood?

I must go on, I know that is right, there is no other way save to go on, forgive me.

I am coming back to Paris in a few days, and I shall telephone you at your office as soon as I can.

You returned to Paris the following week, in the same compartment with the Davals.

The day school began, with Monsieur Devalot: Greek (Homer, the Iliad, Latin (Virgil, Aeneid, Book IX), French (Saint-Simon).

Your Uncle Pierre was back with his eleventh-graders, including your brother Jacques.

On Sunday, you stayed in the Rue du Canivet, in the room that had been your Uncle Pierre's the year before and which you had now moved into because, since that obscure business which everyone preferred not to discuss with you, you had become quite nervous and obviously needed peace and quiet.

You were thinking about your classmates in the Saint-Hilaire troop, about the boy who had been appointed leader of the Bison Patrol, Alain Mouron; you had resigned at the end of last winter; no one had understood your decision except for your Uncle Pierre, Micheline Pavin and I, but it had been irrevocable.

On Wednesday, October 12, your Uncle Pierre, while he was with his seventh-graders, questioning them about the Stone Age and the Bronze Age, while he told them about Egypt, its landscape, its ancient writing and its decipherment by Champollion, the major divisions of its history down to the Persian conquest, observing especially my son Claude,

was thinking that today was your sixteenth birthday, that he had not been invited to the birthday lunch, that if he had ever thought of inviting you out to dinner, you would have refused with your last breath, wondering how to heal this wound, to soothe this bitter pain, to bridge this abyss that had opened between you, this abyss of hatred and shock.

And the following Tuesday, he found himself facing your brother Jacques for his history lesson, your brother Jacques who had remained outside the whole affair and whom he questioned about Henri IV after having asked two of his classmates what they knew about Ivan the Terrible, Suleiman the Magnificent and Philip II, before telling them about Europe's exploitation of the world, the pirates and the buccaneers, the slave trade, the dangerous prosperity of Spain, the birth of international law and the development of corporations.

On the second Tuesday of November, the written quiz on the discovery and conquest of America,

the lesson of Louis XIII and Richelieu,

the reading of the page from Théophraste Renaudot's *Gazette* reproduced in the textbook:

"The Kynge of Persia with fifteen thousand horse . . . "

Your Uncle Pierre will not write any more. Your Uncle Pierre is no longer in the room I rented him on the top floor in the Rue du Pré-aux-Clercs. Your Uncle Pierre is in the hospital, and Micheline Pavin has left her job to be with him. I am writing; I am taking up where he left off; I shall shore up this ruin a little.

████████████████████ FRANCIS HUTTER, in a Basque village several kilometers from the one where Alfred Hutter was staying.

Francis Hutter reached Paris on September 27, with his brother Jean-Louis, who was to enter the ninth grade, his sister Adèle who would be starting the sixth, while he, of course, would be repeating his eleventh-grade courses, for he had missed too much the year before on account of his pneumonia.

On the twenty-ninth, he went to the Lycée Taine to ask for the list of textbooks.

On Saturday, October 2, Madame Bonnini made a noticeable recovery; my Italian colleague said to his sister-in-law:

"I think she'll be able to get up tomorrow."

On Sunday, Francis Hutter made covers for his textbooks.

On Thursday, he was looking for a barber, whom he found in the Rue Frémicourt; he came home to prepare for his next day's afternoon classes:

Greek with me:

(according to Bérard) "If I continue to swim along the coast, hoping to find a bay and a sloping beach, I fear the gale may catch me again and carry me out to the deep sea full of fishes . . . ",

French with me:

"Whereat this lyonne, stronger than a sus[1]
note 1) sus: boar,
saw thereon that the rat knew not . . . ",

and German with that distant uncle whom he had discovered the preceding Wednesday and whom he had no desire to know better.

It was Francis Hutter whom I called on to read the end of the epistle the next day:

" . . . When Messer Rat begins to gnaw
This heavy cord . . . ",

before telling your class, since the hands of my watch and those of the clock on the wall indicated that the bell was about to ring that the following Monday we would begin to talk about Rabelais and would read the passage:

"Of the Mourning Gargantua made for the Death of his Wife Badebec."

On Saturday after dinner,

"End of the Chronicles of Pantagruel, King of the Dipsodes, drawn in their natural colors, with his terrible deeds and exploits, composed by the late Master Alcofribas, abstractor of the quintessence,"

the dizain by Master Hugues Salel to the author of this book:

"If for combining profit with delight . . . ",

the author's prologue:

"Most illustrious and most valorous champions . . . ",

of the origin and antiquity of the great Pantagruel:

"It will be no idle or unprofitable matter, seeing that we have leisure. . . . "

On Sunday after dinner,

Livy, the passage on Hannibal crossing the Alps.

And on Monday night, when I went to bed, your Aunt Rose:

"Is your nephew Pierre all right?"

"I think he'll be all right."

During the night, Monsieur Bailly awakened in a sweat; he turned on his bedlamp; his wife was snoring in her sleep; he leaned on his elbow; he was thinking:

if I took her neck in my hands, if I shook her, if I forced her to tell me everything she did in Orléans . . . patience, patience, there must be a way of freeing myself of this presence, don't rush things, try the legal means . . .

He turned out his lamp; he was thinking:

when she awakens in a sweat, thinks of her lover and sees me snoring in the bed beside her, when she leans on her elbow and has to control herself in order not to take me by the throat and scream all kinds of insults at me . . .

"Tomorrow we have geography, I shall question you on the movements of the earth in space and on the measurement of time",

in front of Georges Tannier, behind Bruno Verger, Gilbert Zola is putting his textbook away in his briefcase,

332

"and we shall talk about the representation of the earth" . . .
at dawn on Wednesday the thirteenth, Alain Mouron fell back to
sleep, and the snatches of the previous day's lessons mingled with
premonitions of those that were to take place in a few hours and that
he had prepared:

"There rises from the waters a cold breeze with the dawn . . . Divine Ulysses scraped armfuls of leaves over his body . . . Like a
smouldering brand someone has hidden under black ashes, in order
to keep the seed of fire . . .
Anna, I confess it to you, this man is the only one who has aroused
my senses . . . the pale shades of Erebus and the darkness there . . .
Here, not by open war, but by her wiles, her deception and her
snares . . .
The divine Hannibal scraped armfuls of leaves over his body. Anna,
my sister, I fear lest warm and relaxed I may yield to the sweetness of
sleep . . . In the sight of this bed, what delight . . .
I see the brigands, the executioners, the adventurers, the highway-
men of nowadays more learned than the learned doctors and preachers
of my time . . . Anna, my sister, of beasts I become the food and the
prey . . . I have always regarded him as a monster. But he is here a
nascent monster. He hasn't yet set fire to Rome . . . I sense within myself the traces of the fire with which I burned . . . In the remote coun-
tryside, one hides the brand beneath the ashes, an olive tree, the
leaves strewed the ground; all the birds of the air, all the trees, shrubs
and bushes of the forest, all the sorts of herbs and flowers that grow
upon the ground, all the various metals that are hid within the bowels
of the earth, together with all the diversity of precious stones that are
to be seen in the Orient and Southern parts of the world—let none
of them be unknown to you, Cathay, Mexico, the kilogram of iridized
platinum. Yet may the earth open and engulf me in its abyss . . . What
a night of painful agony! Hold in suspicion the abuses of the world.
Set not thy heart upon vanity. There are those who have sided with
Nero against me . . .
Athena shed sleep upon his eyes that he might quickly rest from
his weariness after sore tribulation . . . "

That evening at ten, when your brother Denis went to bed, you
were reading *Fiction* in bed. You finished "The Game of Silence":
" . . . Lili realized that in a moment she would be able to speak";

you began the next story: "Wolves Don't Cry", editorial comment:
"The werewolf is a familiar creature of traditional fantastic para-phernalia; so familiar, in fact, that its use is now a shibboleth of the genre . . ."

(shibboleth, what did shibboleth mean? Dictionary? No, this wasn't homework, this was something you were reading for your own enjoyment: Rabelais, Homer, Livy, Virgil, Shakespeare—that was enough!),

"Behind the bars, the naked man was fast sleep . . ."
On Thursday night, armed with the Bailly Dictionary, in your room,

"Now, while the stalwart hero lay in his thicket, heavy with sleep, Athena made her way . . .",

with the Larousse:

"This done, Gargantua was eager to put himself at Ponocrates' disposal in the matter of his studies . . .",

in bed,

" . . . and the last emotion he felt about his adventure was an in-finite pity for his poor little boy who, some fine night, under the silvery light of the moon, would begin walking on all fours and see his body sprouting fur . . . then would lope away to prowl through the darkness . . . searching for what? He would never know . . . "

On Friday night, since Michel Daval had asked you during the afternoon to give him back the issue of *Fiction* the next day, you quickly read through:
"Mrs. Hinck", by Miriam Allen de Ford,
"One Fine Sunday in Spring", by Jacques Sternberg
"Enemy of the Fire", by Robert Abernathy,
letters from our readers,
advertisement: a new work of topical interest: *Was Louis XVII Guillotined?*
How *Sub Rosa*, a clandestine film, was made,
You are What you Know . . . exciting illustrated free booklet No. 1428 by request from the French Cultural Institute . . . (enclose two stamps to cover cost of mailing),
bibliography: novels: *Heaven's Convicts*, the *Forgotten World*,

334

Through the Ages, Robot Territory; miscellaneous: Parapsychology (*Haunted Houses, Ghosts, Radioesthesia, Telepathy, Knowledge of the Future*), the *Psychology of Myth, Ghosts I Have Known,*

The next issue of *Fiction*, Number 12, will appear during the first week in November . . . "

Monsieur Hubert left his wife at home to come to the Lycée Taine to show you how to gauge dynamometers.

And the next day, walking with her on the swan island in the Bois du Boulogne, he was telling her how much he enjoyed his senior class, how they renewed his sense of professional dedication.

Livy:

"Indeed almost the whole way was steep, narrow and uncertain, so that one could scarcely manage to keep from falling, so that those who stumbled even a little could not keep their footing and fell one upon the other, and so that the beasts of burden fell upon the men."

I reminded you that your Cicero translation was due the next day: the pillage of Sicily by Verrès, that you were to prepare lines 31 to 49 of Book IV of the *Aeneid*:

"*Anna refert* . . . "

(Anna answers: O thou whom thy sister loves more than light . . .),

and that next Wednesday we would be reading the rest of the passage on Hannibal crossing the Alps.

The bell rang; most of you had already put away your Latin textbooks and taken out your *Sixteenth Century French Authors*.

After dinner, you carefully copied the Latin translation you had just finished with Alain Mouron,

Homer:

" . . . Startled and amazed at her dream, Nausicaa went straight through the palace to tell it to her parents . . . ",

Virgil:

" . . . Will all your youth be consumed in the mourning of widowhood? . . . ",

Shakespeare:

" . . . Yon Cassius has a lean and hungry look.
He thinks too much. Such men are dangerous . . . "

Europe in 1600, *cuius regio, eius religio,* Elizabeth, Ivan the Terrible, Suleiman the Magnificent, Philip II, Rudolf II who, melancholic and half mad, shuts himself up with his alchemists in his palace in Prague, Henri IV, the Edict of Nantes,

forces, dynamometer, standard kilogram, vector.

I called on you to read the passage:

"Hinc Getulae urbes . . . "

(you are surrounded on one side by the warlike tribe of the Gaetuli, by the Numidians, matchless horsemen, and by unfriendly Syrtis) . . .

At the bell, only thirteen of you stayed in your seats to wait for Monsieur Bailly, whom I passed coming up the stairs.

After dinner, math homework, Racine:

" . . . He has not yet killed his mother, his wife, his tutors, but he has within him the seeds of all these crimes; he is beginning to desire to shake off his yoke. He hides his hate under false caresses. In a word, he is here a nascent monster . . . "

Denis leaned over your shoulder:

"Say, isn't tomorrow Uncle Pierre's birthday: Mother wants to know if we've done anything?"

"Done anything?"

"Jacques and I haven't, but you're his pet . . . "

"Are we celebrating tomorrow night?"

"No, he's coming to lunch?"

"Lunch? Why didn't he tell me?"

"Does he tell you everything?"

"But I don't have time to do anything now . . . "

"Because you were hanging around his room just now?"

"What business is it of yours?"

"You probably had a lot of secrets to tell each other . . . "

"Jealous?"

"Imbecile! Can't you see he's using you?"

"Sure, you're just running errands for his girl friend, what's her name?"

"You don't know what you're talking about."

"And he's not so tough on you in class, is he, he lets you know what days he's going to call on you . . . "

"What an evil mind you have. Nosy! You're saying all that because you're nosy and jealous, but you might as well not bother, you'll never find out a thing."

"I'll find out what I want to know!"

"Oh, sure."

"Bet you!"

"There's nothing to find out. He's my uncle, after all! I can talk to him whenever I want—why should that bother you so much?"

"Well, tomorrow your uncle's thirty-five; by the way, I better remind you he's my uncle too."

"Listen, it's your birthday pretty soon, isn't it?"

"November tenth."

"And you'll be . . . "

"Seventeen."

"And then he'll ask you out to dinner too."

"How do you know?"

"I know."

"Because you'll ask him to, because you want him to, and he can't refuse you anything. What devotion!"

"Because I'll tell him you're dying to go, that's all!"

"Dying to go! What are you talking about? Dying to go . . . What do I care about eating in a restaurant with him just so he can talk to me about my schoolwork?"

"About your schoolwork or something else."

"Something else?"

"No, no, about your schoolwork. I won't say a word to him."

"Of course, if he asks me . . . "

"Yes, what then?"

"I can't refuse, I have no reason to refuse . . . "

"But maybe you won't have much to talk about . . . "

"Unless he's spying on me . . . "

"Listen, if he comes to lunch, if there's a birthday cake, we'll leave the table just in time to get to the lycée . . . "

"Probably."

"Then I have to get done with my math tonight."

"For tomorrow afternoon? Yes, you better."

"Then help me."

"You mean you can't do it by yourself?"

"It'll go much faster, there's one easy problem I can do tomorrow morning during Latin, because I was just called on; I've done the geometry, but I still have these two algebra things . . . "

"Why don't you ask your uncle?"

"Dope!"

"All right, show it to me! You always put on such an act with your secrets; now you're smoking cigarettes too, don't bother lying, I saw you, besides I don't care, you're old enough, but you still come to me when you need something . . . "

"Simplify the expressions: $3(a+b-c) - 2(a-b+c) + 5(a-b-c)$ and . . . "

"Wait a minute, let me think. You know, I have a lot of other things to do."

Bruno Verger or Gabriel Voss:

" . . . of great valor, strong feeling and frankness, the ordinary qualities of a young man. He was fifteen years of age, and it was said that he was very intelligent, whether this was the truth or whether his misfortunes made this appear to be true without his having been able to give such evidences . . . "

That evening, in the Rue du Canivet, your Uncle Pierre's chair was empty. Since you had neither class nor scout meeting the next day, you went to the Bonaparte with Jacques and Denis; Denis met one of his classmates and his sister in the lobby. He seemed to know her very well. He sat between her and you. When it was dark, he took her hand; after a while he kissed her; he saw you looking at him; he whispered in your ear: "Listen, if you tell Uncle Pierre about this I'm going to make trouble for you."

"Don't worry, but if you see me going to his room, don't say anything about it to Mother or Father. All right?"

"All right."

Sitting beside his wife, who was taking a nap, Monsieur Hubert was correcting his seniors' homework.

On Friday:

" . . . after which Gargantua with his tutor briefly reviewed in the manner of the Pythagoreans all that he had read, seen, learnt, done and heard in the course of the whole day . . . "

On Sunday, Michel Daval, in the Rue Servandoni, shifted the

furniture in his new room then drew a cross section of an interplanetary rocket.

On Monday, Monsieur Hubert handed back to his seniors their
homework and talked to them about the theory of kinetic energy and
the principle of the rocket.

At noon on Tuesday, I called for the two youngsters at their elementary school; they told me they had been photographed.

That evening you spent quite a long time with your Uncle Pierre,
then you went to the Rue du Pré-aux-Clercs where Alain Mouron was
waiting for you. On the Boulevard Saint-Germain, the tall North
African with the mask of adhesive tape was sitting on a bench; he
watched you pass, stared after you with his wolf's face. Madame Davez
had set the table.

"My father won't be here before eight. We could start on the
Homer . . . "

"Let's forget about Homer. You were called on recently, and so
was I . . . "

"You don't think it's worth it?"

"I didn't say that . . . "

"It's true that Monsieur Jouret's your uncle . . . "

"No, that would make me do it; for instance, I don't think that
Monsieur Bailly shows any special indulgence for you . . . "

"I've already started on it, to get ahead . . . "

"Oh, if you've done it already, that's a different story, hand me a
sheet of paper."

"I've only done the first few lines."

"That's better than nothing; I'll copy the words."

"He has heard girls' voices, he wants to see them, that's the place;
so saying, the Divine Ulysses emerged from the thicket, he broke off
a bough of leaves from the dense foliage with his strong arm, so that
he might conceal himself; then I don't understand the next part at all,
mèdéa photos, you see—mèdéa can mean thoughts or sexual organs,
photos can mean light or man; is it to hide his thoughts? And what
about péri chroï? chroï means skin."

"There's no note?"

"No. The dictionary says: the male sexual organs, hence: urine . . . "

"Oh, I see . . . Look, he's naked, so to show himself to the girls, you
see?" . . .

"I hope I don't get called on."

"Embarrassed?"

"I wouldn't be able to say it."

"Don't worry, Uncle Henri will go through it fast, very fast . . . "

"That's where I stopped."

"You only did the first few lines . . . Too bad, but it's better than nothing."

"Say, what do you think of Monsieur Bailly?"

"Monsieur Bailly, why?"

"I'm going to tell you something, but don't mention it to anyone . . . "

On Wednesday Monsieur Hubert told his seniors about periodic motion, torsion and springs.

On Thursday, you were reading the issue of *Galaxie* that belonged to Hubert Jourdan.

On All Saints' Day, after having talked about you, Michel Daval and Alain Mouron came back into the dining room in the Rue Servandoni to take their tea.

On All Souls' Day, Monsieur Hubert stayed with his wife to correct his seniors' homework.

On Wednesday, in bed, you were reading a story by Richard Wilson called "Tell Me Whom You Haunt", in the issue of *Galaxie*, in italics:

"How can you tell whom you're dealing with in a mysterious world? You might get caught in your own trap. . . . "

You had asked Alain Mouron to come to your house for tea after school: it was the first time he had come to the Rue du Canivet.

As your mother was walking down the hall, you asked her if you could invite him to dinner soon.

On Sunday, Michel Daval had recovered; the whole Bailly family was there; Michel made some cars with his Meccano set for his young cousins, but they kept wanting to help and dropped the screws and bolts which rolled into the cracks between the floorboards.

On Monday, Monsieur Hubert talked to his seniors about the mutual transformations of heat and work.

On Tuesday, before lunch, I thought up composition subjects for my seniors. We were up to the *Lettres Persanes*.

That evening, in the Rue du Canivet, with Alain Mouron, the *Odyssey*:

"When he returned, sitting at a distance upon the beach, he was shining with comeliness and grace . . . "

You had decided to invite him to dinner some evening when your Uncle Pierre wasn't there.

On Wednesday, before questioning his seniors on the various forms of energy, Monsieur Hubert informed them that he was the father of a son.

The next day, patrol meeting.

On Wednesday the seventeenth, you weren't able to hand in your math homework because your Uncle Pierre had unexpectedly asked you to lunch to celebrate Micheline Pavin's birthday. Monsieur du Marnet kept you after school the next day.

And on Tuesday the twenty-third, while your Uncle Pierre was talking to you about the siege of Vienna by the Turks and about the King of Poland, John Sobieski, you turned around to Henri Fage and asked him to pass the November issue of *Fiction*, which Jean-Pierre Cormier had just given back to you, to Hubert Jourdan, speaking in such a loud voice that all your classmates turned to look at you.

There was a moment of complete silence; you could hear me talking on the other side of the wall; glances passed from you to your uncle and from your uncle to you; gradually, a kind of titter broke out.

"Eller, what's the matter with you?"

You stood up.

"But it was . . . "

"Not another word. Four hours on Thursday!"

He was pale. There was another long silence; your classmates all bent over their notebooks. You felt terribly upset; you had a patrol meeting the next day. Luckily, since you were the only one in the class being kept on, he could secretly suspend this penalty.

On December 8, during the geography test, Michel Daval whispered in your ear:

"I guessed right: I thought I knew which questions he would ask."

"Lucky you."

"Don't kid me; I bet you knew them."

"No I didn't! Just because he's my uncle . . . Monsieur Bailly's your uncle and . . . "

"He's not just your uncle,"

"What do you mean?"

"Why else would he let us talk like this . . . "

"Let me alone, I want to do my work . . . "

341

A lean and hungry look, a wolf's gaze that burned with anxiety when he turned toward you, deeper and deeper, as if he had a mask, a false skin,

a different look, but it was like the face of that North African who had called to you in the twilight,

"Little boy, come here, little boy",

and you had hurried on, filled with a kind of fury and fear, and you caught yourself thinking of your Uncle Pierre then,

and if you pulled off that adhesive tape, what would you find? Wolf fur.

The representation of the earth, the meridians, the parallels, the Mercator projection . . .

On the fifteenth, during the math test:

"How's it going?"

"How's yours?"

"I'm not much good at math, you know."

"Neither am I."

"And this time it isn't an uncle."

"What do you mean?"

"Nothing."

"Then shut up."

"You're the one who's talking."

"Monsieur Jouret's my uncle . . . "

"I'm not talking about Jouret."

"I was with him on vacation."

"Shut up."

"But what do you have against me?"

"I don't have anything against you except that you're too nosy."

"I'm not looking at what you're doing, don't worry about that."

"I don't care what you look at, it's that you'll tell everything."

"To whom? not to du Marnet. . . . "

"Shut up, he's looking at us."

"You're the one who's talking."

"I hear your uncle's pretty nosy too, your history-and-geo uncle; I heard mine talking about it."

"When?"

"Shut up and let me work; he's coming closer."

On December 21, after the results of the history test were announced:

"You see, I'm only twelfth, you're fifth, and yet I swear I worked."

"I worked too, so what?"

"That's not what I mean. Can't you see he's not prejudiced in my favor, in geo I was only eighth, I was twelfth in history . . . "

"Don't be silly, if he put you first it would have been a little too obvious . . . "

"Why don't you read my test!"

"I don't need to; I bet he even gave you a grade less than you deserved because he was being cautious, because he knows we all can tell there's something funny going on between you two . . . "

"You're crazy!"

"Shut up, he's looking at us."

"I don't know what's the matter with you."

"Listen."

"Not so loud."

"Don't look at me!"

"Not so loud!"

"You hear me?"

"All right, hurry up!"

"If he catches us, he'll have to punish us worse than the others because he's been too easy up to now."

"If that's all you have to say . . . "

"No, that's not all, Francis Hutter told me what he heard Monsieur Hutter say to my Uncle Bailly . . . "

"Is that it? Watch out, wait a minute . . . All right, go on!"

"And they were talking about him, about your uncle . . . "

"Shut up; write it on a piece of paper . . . "

"So you can give it to him afterwards . . . "

"Dope! Shut up, he's looking at us."

"He'll keep us both after school if you don't watch out."

"Wait till he's looking somewhere else."

"Swear it."

"Shut up."

"All right for you."

"Swear what?"

"That you won't show it to him."

"Let me alone."

"You see . . . "

"Let me alone."

"Spy!"

"I won't show him anything."

"Write it down."

"What?"

"Take a piece of paper."

"Watch out."

"Write: 'I swear.' "

"There."

"What can you swear by?"

"He's watching us."

"Write: 'I swear on my scout's honor.' "

"Shut up."

"You don't want to?"

"Let me alone!"

"You're afraid to?"

"He's watching us."

"He won't say a word, you see, he's not saying a word, you know he won't say a word."

"The others are watching."

"You won't find out anything, I won't tell you anything."

"Shut up."

"Too bad for you."

"I wrote it down."

"Not to tell what's on this paper to Monsieur Vernier, to my uncle, Monsieur Vernier."

"There."

"And sign it. All right."

You saw him write on that paper:

Monsieur Hutter:

"I hear our colleague Vernier is still going on with his little narrative."

Monsieur Bailly:

"Has he interrogated you yet?"

Monsieur Hutter:

"And I have the impression he's using his nephew Eller as an informer."

Michel Daval folded the sheet of paper twice and put it into his briefcase.

Your breathing grew hoarse; your lips began to protrude; you felt that your teeth were growing longer, that your whole body was sprouting hair, not bison hair but wolf fur.

And after the Christmas vacation, when you turned around toward Henri Fage to pass him another science-fiction magazine, your Uncle Pierre, in a terrible, unrecognizable voice:

"Eller! Will you sit still? Don't start that again! This time you'll stay in four hours, and don't come sniveling to me about a scout meeting this time!"

You sat up, you stared at him with burning eyes, you screamed, and you didn't even recognize your own voice:

"No, I won't do it for you any more!"

You walked out of the classroom, you slammed the door behind you. Tears ran down your uncle's face. He pounded his fist on the desk and he said:

"We'll see to it that this unfortunate incident is punished. Let's go on: write in your notebooks: the religious difficulties . . . "

Your open book and your open notebook were still on your desk; your open briefcase was still under your chair; your coat was still hanging beside the others, next to the door. It was snowing; you stayed in the corridor, motionless, breathing hard. You heard your uncle's voice through the partition, and mine a few yards away.

The year went by. School began again. In French, you began with Saint-Simon, and on Wednesday Monsieur Devalot told you about the life of Racine.

On Sunday, I was saying to your father, who had come to see me without your knowing it:

"I think it will be all right now. I've questioned Pierre's teachers, it's still a little early to be sure; of course I informed his history and geography teacher about last winter's incident. As for Pierre Vernier, he seems pleased with his new quarters. He's probably up there now with Micheline Pavin, whom you must have met."

On Wednesday the twelfth, you were sixteen. While Michel Daval in front of you, was reading the preface to Iphigénie:

"There is no subject more celebrated in poetry than the sacrifice of Iphigenia . . . ",

you were saying to your neighbor Alain Mouron:

"You know, today's my sixteenth birthday, and my parents asked me if they could invite Monsieur Vernier, the geo teacher from last year who's my uncle, but I said no."

345

The following Tuesday, it was you who were reading:

"The inhabitants of Paris are curious to the point of extravagance . . . "

After school, Michel Daval:

"Here, I found this in my things; I don't need it any more."

He gave you a piece of paper folded twice, which you recognized and crumpled up in your fist.

And since Monsieur Devalot went much faster with you than I did with my seniors the year before, on Tuesday, November 8, you heard one of your new classmates read this passage from Voltaire's *Essai sur les Moeurs*:

"Of all the nations of the East, Japan does not deserve the least attention from a philosopher. We should have recognized the nation in the Thirteenth Century in the narrative of the celebrated Marc Paul. This Venetian had traveled over land to China, and having long served under one of the sons of Genghis Khan, he had one of the first conceptions of those islands we call Japan and which he names Zipangri. . . . "

You took out of your pocket a ball of paper which you flattened out; it was uniformly covered with ink; slowly you tore it into tiny fragments which you put in an empty matchbox and carried around with you for a long time before showing it to me and telling me the story.

Your Uncle Pierre will not write any more. How long will it be before you read the ruin of his book? You go into his hospital room; Micheline Pavin is sitting beside him; he opens his eyes, he recognizes you, you tell him that I'm on my way. You don't know that the book is for you and that he is dying because of it, and yet you have forgiven him. You put beside his head, as though it were an offering, the matchbox full of tiny pieces of inky paper.

Now the bell is ringing. Your Uncle Pierre puts into his briefcase his notebook, the *Description of the World* by Marco Polo, the *Essais* of Montaigne. You all get up, take your coats. As your uncle goes out the door, Bertrand Limours steps back to let him pass.

During the night, Monsieur Bailly awakened; he looked at his watch, it was four in the morning. A voice was murmuring in his head:

"If I were absolutely sure you haven't told that to any other woman since your wedding";

what did "that" mean? What had he said? What hadn't he said? What wasn't he sure of not having said?

Not only is there no question of my finishing your uncle's book, of completing the project which he had undertaken and which crushed him, but no longer even any question of continuing it; it is a ruin; in the construction of this tower from which one was supposed to see America, something was generated that must have made it explode; he couldn't erect more than a few pieces of the walls, and then that conflagration occurred which not only suspended all labor, but undermined the very ground upon which the walls were being raised, and that is why all that is left for me to do, confronting this fragment of a consciousness and of a future music, is to shore it up a little, so that the passer-by may suffer from it, so that the things around it, so that this state of incompletion, of ruin, may become unendurable to him, for in these twisted beams, in this dilapidated scaffolding, the sun changes the rust to gold, and the wind . . .

When I went to bed Wednesday night, I said to your Aunt Rose: "Pierre Vernier must have have started on his project; I wonder what will come of it."

Thursday night: How Gargantua was taught Latin by a Sophist, How Gargantua was put under other Pedagogues, How Gargantua was sent to Paris . . .

Friday evening, your Aunt Rose:

"You know, that book you were talking about with Pierre Vernier . . ."

347

"Yes . . . "

"It's about the class you both teach?"

"Yes."

"About the real class?"

"Of course."

"The one Pierre's in?"

"Eleventh grade."

"And about your colleagues too?"

"That comes into it."

"And what are they going to think?"

"They must know nothing about it . . . "

"And how could he know . . . "

"You'll have to ask him."

"Isn't it a little dangerous?"

"It's certainly an adventure."

"I'm a little afraid for Pierre."

"He's taking a risk. We'll see."

"I meant your nephew."

The Edict of Nantes, the assassination of Henri IV. The bell. Francis Hutter hurriedly looked at the résumé of the preceding lesson in his *Chemistry Textbook*:

"Water in its natural state contains substances in solution . . . "

On Sunday, Francis went to the swimming pool with his younger brother Jean-Louis.

On Monday night,

" . . . which depopulated a quarter of a kingdom, which ruined its commerce, which weakened it in every member, which delivered it for so long to the public and avowed pillage of the dragoons, which authorized the torments and the tortures by which they actually murdered so many innocents of either sex by the thousands . . . "

On Tuesday evening, the correction of my seniors' compositions on education in Rabelais and in Montaigne, then I reread *Britannicus*:

"Yet even as Nero abandons himself to sleep . . . "

On Wednesday evening, your uncle came to dinner; he was thirty-five; all my children congratulated him; he was good with children, he was good with all of you until . . .

While he was kept in after school, while his fellow prisoner Michel Daval was absorbed in *Galaxie*:

" . . . They handed us samples of ordinary objects, pieces of jade covered with strange and beautiful carvings . . . , bars of radioactive metal . . . ",

advertisement for *Detective*: "Each Saturday, stories, adventures, jury trials, sports, the magazine of the world's secrets",

Francis Hutter was reading *Fiction*:

" . . . Where was his meat? Where was his bone? How could he sharpen his fangs on such food as this? What were they trying to do, make his teeth fall out? . . . "

His head was heavy; he wondered if he had fever.

He didn't come back to class until Monday. When the bell rang at the end of geography, (the foehn, the mistral), he waved goodbye and went to put on his coat. Like everyone who was taking German and Spanish, his school day was over.

Tuesday night, the *Odyssey*:

"Thus naked, Ulysses walked toward these curly-headed girls; need impelled him . . . ",

the second act of *Iphigénie*:

"Nor shall we urge them, Doris, let us leave . . . "

at the line:

"Is Calchas not preparing votive sacrifice?",

Your Aunt Rose came in and interrupted me:

"Would you go out and get some wine? I completely forgot."

"Wine? We're out of wine?"

"We still have some, but I want something better, to go with the lamb."

"We're having lamb?"

"It's a party, why not?"

"A party?"

"For Pierre Vernier and his girl friend—tonight. Haven't you heard? they've already set the date!"

"Oh my God, that's right! Is it really settled?"

"Apparently. You should have seen his face when he was telling me."
"I'm eager to see her."

Snowfall, five months in Siberia, sixty days in Iceland, five in Brittany; the bell; Francis Hutter squeezed against his desk to let Alain Mouron by; like you, like everyone who was taking English or Italian, Alain was leaving the classroom; then, heaving a sigh, Francis put away the geography textbook and took out the German textbook.

On All Saints' Day, Francis Hutter tried to play Beethoven's twelfth sonata.

On November 8 he got sick again.

After having read your composition on Rabelais' ideas on education, I read Alain Mouron's, then Michel Daval's, Denis Régnier's (Francis Hutter hadn't been able to hand his in), in the order in which your Uncle Pierre was interested in you. He had asked me to let him read them, just those, and I intended to bring them to him the next day so that he could give them back to me on Friday.

That is how things were taking shape; and then, on Tuesday, January 11, 1955, after having read to my seniors (I was far behind schedule) Voltaire's text on Japan:

" . . . but his contemporaries, though they credited the most absurd fables, did not believe the truths that Marc Paul declared to them. His manuscript long remained in obscurity; it fell into the hands of Christopher Columbus and was of no little service in confirming him in his hopes of finding a new world that might connect East and West . . . ",

since I left a little ahead of your Uncle Pierre, I found you in the corridor, and seeing what a state you were in, I asked you to come and see me at home, in the Rue du Pré-aux-Clercs, after your physics class, without mentioning it to him.

On the following October 12, I began discussing with my new senior class a new play by Racine, making them, as always, read the preface first:

" . . . this murder committed in the temple . . . This scene, which is a kind of episode, naturally calls for music . . . Add to this, that such a prophecy greatly serves to augment the emotion in the play, by the consternation and the divers movements into which it throws the chorus and the chief actors."

The following Tuesday, the passage of Saint-Simon on the revocation of the Edict of Nantes:

"... which finally, crowning horror with horror, filled with perjurers and hypocrites every corner of the realm, which echoed to the screams of agony of these unfortunate victims of error, while others were sacrificing their conscience to their wealth and comfort, purchasing the one as the other by feigned abjurations ... ",

but I went much faster with Montesquieu, and we were able to begin Voltaire on November 8.

Your uncle Pierre will not write any more; I am the one who will tell you that this text is for you, and it is Micheline Pavin to whom I shall entrust it. You are both bending over his bed. His eyes are open, but it is you he is looking at, he pays no attention to me. I greet him; he murmurs:

"Who's that?"

PIERRE ALBERT-BIROT, *Grabinoulor.*
YUZ ALESHKOVSKY, *Kangaroo.*
FELIPE ALFAU, *Chromos.*
　Locos.
　Sentimental Songs.
IVAN ÂNGELO, *The Celebration.*
　The Tower of Glass.
DAVID ANTIN, *Talking.*
DJUNA BARNES, *Ladies Almanack.*
　Ryder.
JOHN BARTH, *LETTERS.*
　Sabbatical.
SVETISLAV BASARA, *Chinese Letter.*
ANDREI BITOV, *Pushkin House.*
LOUIS PAUL BOON, *Chapel Road.*
ROGER BOYLAN, *Killoyle.*
IGNÁCIO DE LOYOLA BRANDÃO, *Zero.*
CHRISTINE BROOKE-ROSE, *Amalgamemnon.*
BRIGID BROPHY, *In Transit.*
MEREDITH BROSNAN, *Mr. Dynamite.*
GERALD L. BRUNS,
　Modern Poetry and the Idea of Language.
GABRIELLE BURTON, *Heartbreak Hotel.*
MICHEL BUTOR, *Degrees.*
　Mobile.
　Portrait of the Artist as a Young Ape.
G. CABRERA INFANTE, *Three Trapped Tigers.*
JULIETA CAMPOS, *The Fear of Losing Eurydice.*
ANNE CARSON, *Eros the Bittersweet.*
CAMILO JOSÉ CELA, *The Family of Pascual Duarte.*
　The Hive.
LOUIS-FERDINAND CÉLINE, *Castle to Castle.*
　London Bridge.
　North.
　Rigadoon.
HUGO CHARTERIS, *The Tide Is Right.*
JEROME CHARYN, *The Tar Baby.*
MARC CHOLODENKO, *Mordechai Schamz.*
EMILY HOLMES COLEMAN, *The Shutter of Snow.*
ROBERT COOVER, *A Night at the Movies.*
STANLEY CRAWFORD, *Some Instructions to My Wife.*
ROBERT CREELEY, *Collected Prose.*
RENÉ CREVEL, *Putting My Foot in It.*
RALPH CUSACK, *Cadenza.*
SUSAN DAITCH, *L.C.*
　Storytown.
NIGEL DENNIS, *Cards of Identity.*
PETER DIMOCK,
　A Short Rhetoric for Leaving the Family.
ARIEL DORFMAN, *Konfidenz.*
COLEMAN DOWELL, *The Houses of Children.*
　Island People.
　Too Much Flesh and Jabez.
RIKKI DUCORNET, *The Complete Butcher's Tales.*
　The Fountains of Neptune.
　The Jade Cabinet.
　Phosphor in Dreamland.
　The Stain.
WILLIAM EASTLAKE, *The Bamboo Bed.*
　Castle Keep.
　Lyric of the Circle Heart.
JEAN ECHENOZ, *Chopin's Move.*
STANLEY ELKIN, *A Bad Man.*
　Boswell: A Modern Comedy.
　Criers and Kibitzers, Kibitzers and Criers.
　The Dick Gibson Show.
　The Franchiser.
　George Mills.

　The Living End.
　The MacGuffin.
　The Magic Kingdom.
　Mrs. Ted Bliss.
　The Rabbi of Lud.
　Van Gogh's Room at Arles.
ANNIE ERNAUX, *Cleaned Out.*
LAUREN FAIRBANKS, *Muzzle Thyself.*
　Sister Carrie.
LESLIE A. FIEDLER,
　Love and Death in the American Novel.
FORD MADOX FORD, *The March of Literature.*
CARLOS FUENTES, *Terra Nostra.*
　Where the Air Is Clear.
JANICE GALLOWAY, *Foreign Parts.*
　The Trick Is to Keep Breathing.
WILLIAM H. GASS, *The Tunnel.*
　Willie Masters' Lonesome Wife.
ETIENNE GILSON, *The Arts of the Beautiful.*
　Forms and Substances in the Arts.
C. S. GISCOMBE, *Giscome Road.*
　Here.
DOUGLAS GLOVER, *Bad News of the Heart.*
KAREN ELIZABETH GORDON, *The Red Shoes.*
GEORGI GOSPODINOV, *Natural Novel.*
PATRICK GRAINVILLE, *The Cave of Heaven.*
HENRY GREEN, *Blindness.*
　Concluding.
　Doting.
　Nothing.
JIŘÍ GRUŠA, *The Questionnaire.*
JOHN HAWKES, *Whistlejacket.*
AIDAN HIGGINS, *A Bestiary.*
　Flotsam and Jetsam.
　Langrishe, Go Down.
ALDOUS HUXLEY, *Antic Hay.*
　Crome Yellow.
　Point Counter Point.
　Those Barren Leaves.
　Time Must Have a Stop.
MIKHAIL IOSSEL AND JEFF PARKER, EDS., *Amerika:*
　Contemporary Russians View the United States.
GERT JONKE, *Geometric Regional Novel.*
JACQUES JOUET, *Mountain R.*
HUGH KENNER, *Flaubert, Joyce and Beckett:*
　The Stoic Comedians.
DANILO KIŠ, *Garden, Ashes.*
　A Tomb for Boris Davidovich.
TADEUSZ KONWICKI, *A Minor Apocalypse.*
　The Polish Complex.
ELAINE KRAF, *The Princess of 72nd Street.*
JIM KRUSOE, *Iceland.*
EWA KURYLUK, *Century 21.*
VIOLETTE LEDUC, *La Bâtarde.*
DEBORAH LEVY, *Billy and Girl.*
　Pillow Talk in Europe and Other Places.
JOSÉ LEZAMA LIMA, *Paradiso.*
OSMAN LINS, *Avalovara.*
　The Queen of the Prisons of Greece.
ALF MAC LOCHLAINN, *The Corpus in the Library.*
　Out of Focus.
RON LOEWINSOHN, *Magnetic Field(s).*
D. KEITH MANO, *Take Five.*
BEN MARCUS, *The Age of Wire and String.*
WALLACE MARKFIELD, *Teitlebaum's Window.*
　To an Early Grave.
DAVID MARKSON, *Reader's Block.*
　Springer's Progress.
　Wittgenstein's Mistress.

CAROLE MASO, *AVA*.

LADISLAV MATEJKA AND KRYSTYNA POMORSKA, EDS.,
*Readings in Russian Poetics: Formalist and
Structuralist Views*.

HARRY MATHEWS,
The Case of the Persevering Maltese: Collected Essays.
Cigarettes.
The Conversions.
The Human Country: New and Collected Stories.
The Journalist.
Singular Pleasures.
The Sinking of the Odradek Stadium.
Tlooth.
20 Lines a Day.

ROBERT L. MCLAUGHLIN, ED.,
*Innovations: An Anthology of Modern &
Contemporary Fiction*.

STEVEN MILLHAUSER, *The Barnum Museum*.
In the Penny Arcade.

RALPH J. MILLS, JR., *Essays on Poetry*.

OLIVE MOORE, *Spleen*.

NICHOLAS MOSLEY, *Accident*.
Assassins.
Catastrophe Practice.
Children of Darkness and Light.
The Hesperides Tree.
Hopeful Monsters.
Imago Bird.
Impossible Object.
Inventing God.
Judith.
Natalie Natalia.
Serpent.
The Uses of Slime Mould: Essays of Four Decades.

WARREN F. MOTTE, JR.,
Fables of the Novel: French Fiction since 1990.
Oulipo: A Primer of Potential Literature.

YVES NAVARRE, *Our Share of Time*.

DOROTHY NELSON, *Tar and Feathers*.

WILFRIDO D. NOLLEDO, *But for the Lovers*.

FLANN O'BRIEN, *At Swim-Two-Birds*.
At War.
The Best of Myles.
The Dalkey Archive.
Further Cuttings.
The Hard Life.
The Poor Mouth.
The Third Policeman.

CLAUDE OLLIER, *The Mise-en-Scène*.

FERNANDO DEL PASO, *Palinuro of Mexico*.

ROBERT PINGET, *The Inquisitory*.
Mahu or The Material.

RAYMOND QUENEAU, *The Last Days*.
Odile.
Pierrot Mon Ami.
Saint Glinglin.

ANN QUIN, *Berg*.
Passages.
Three.
Tripticks.

ISHMAEL REED, *The Free-Lance Pallbearers*.
The Last Days of Louisiana Red.
Reckless Eyeballing.
The Terrible Threes.
The Terrible Twos.
Yellow Back Radio Broke-Down.

JULIÁN RÍOS, *Larva: A Midsummer Night's Babel*.
Poundemonium.

AUGUSTO ROA BASTOS, *I the Supreme*.

JACQUES ROUBAUD, *The Great Fire of London*.
Hortense in Exile.
Hortense Is Abducted.
The Plurality of Worlds of Lewis.
The Princess Hoppy.
Some Thing Black.

LEON S. ROUDIEZ, *French Fiction Revisited*.

VEDRANA RUDAN, *Night*.

LUIS RAFAEL SÁNCHEZ, *Macho Camacho's Beat*.

SEVERO SARDUY, *Cobra & Maitreya*.

NATHALIE SARRAUTE, *Do You Hear Them?*
Martereau.

ARNO SCHMIDT, *Collected Stories*.
Nobodaddy's Children.

CHRISTINE SCHUTT, *Nightwork*.

GAIL SCOTT, *My Paris*.

JUNE AKERS SEESE,
Is This What Other Women Feel Too?
What Waiting Really Means.

AURELIE SHEEHAN, *Jack Kerouac Is Pregnant*.

VIKTOR SHKLOVSKY,
A Sentimental Journey: Memoirs 1917-1922.
Theory of Prose.
Third Factory.
Zoo, or Letters Not about Love.

JOSEF ŠKVORECKÝ,
The Engineer of Human Souls.

CLAUDE SIMON, *The Invitation*.

GILBERT SORRENTINO, *Aberration of Starlight*.
Blue Pastoral.
Crystal Vision.
Imaginative Qualities of Actual Things.
Mulligan Stew.
Pack of Lies.
The Sky Changes.
Something Said.
Splendide-Hôtel.
Steelwork.
Under the Shadow.

W. M. SPACKMAN, *The Complete Fiction*.

GERTRUDE STEIN, *Lucy Church Amiably*.
The Making of Americans.
A Novel of Thank You.

PIOTR SZEWC, *Annihilation*.

STEFAN THEMERSON, *Tom Harris*.

JEAN-PHILIPPE TOUSSAINT, *Television*.

ESTHER TUSQUETS, *Stranded*.

DUBRAVKA UGRESIC, *Thank You for Not Reading*.

LUISA VALENZUELA, *He Who Searches*.

BORIS VIAN, *Heartsnatcher*.

PAUL WEST, *Words for a Deaf Daughter & Gala*.

CURTIS WHITE, *America's Magic Mountain*.
The Idea of Home.
Memories of My Father Watching TV.
*Monstrous Possibility: An Invitation to Literary
Politics*.
Requiem.

DIANE WILLIAMS, *Excitability: Selected Stories*.
Romancer Erector.

DOUGLAS WOOLF, *Wall to Wall*.
Ya! & John-Juan.

PHILIP WYLIE, *Generation of Vipers*.

MARGUERITE YOUNG, *Angel in the Forest*.
Miss MacIntosh, My Darling.

REYOUNG, *Unbabbling*.

LOUIS ZUKOFSKY, *Collected Fiction*.

SCOTT ZWIREN, *God Head*.

FOR A FULL LIST OF PUBLICATIONS, VISIT:
www.dalkeyarchive.com